Readers love the Gods of War series by XENIA MELZER

Casto

"I fell in love with Xenia Melzer's writing and I can't wait to see where this story goes."

—Diminishing Thoughts

Love and the Stubborn

"...*Love and the Stubborn* was mesmerizing."

—Prism Book Alliance

Ummana

"...I am in love and so eager for the next book. Kudos to Ms. Melzer for this FABULOUS series."

—Love Bytes

By Xenia Melzer

ARTHROPODA
Arthropoda

GODS OF WAR
Casto
Love and the Stubborn
Ummana
Braving the Storm

Published by DSP Publications
www.dsppublications.com

ARTHROPODA

XENIA MELZER

DSP PUBLICATIONS

Published by

DSP PUBLICATIONS

5032 Capital Circle SW, Suite 2, PMB# 279, Tallahassee, FL 32305-7886 USA
www.dsppublications.com

Arthropoda
© 2021 Xenia Melzer

Cover Art
© 2021 L.C. Chase
http://www.lcchase.com
Cover content is for illustrative purposes only and any person depicted on the cover is a model.

Trade Paperback ISBN: 978-1-64405-903-6
Digital ISBN: 978-1-64405-902-9
Trade Paperback published March 2021
v. 1.0

For all the people who are trying to save the bees.

Acknowledgments

ARTHROPODA IS my first dip into the mystery/detective genre, and I have to thank my husband Michael and my sister for encouraging me to give it a try. I also have to thank my editors, Gus, Anastasia, and Brian for being so invested in my story and for trying really hard to make it shine. Without them, it would have been a lot shorter and not nearly as polished and good as it is now.

ARTHROPODA

XENIA MELZER

CHAPTER 1
THE NEW BOY IN TOWN

GEORGE DONOVAN maneuvered his shiny new Escalade into the parking lot of the Charleston Police Department on Lockwood Drive. His appointment with Amanda Norris, the chief—his new boss as of today—had been postponed till lunch. This was good, since it allowed him to find a parking space. The officer who had called him about the change of time had warned him about the lack of parking, and for a moment, George had even contemplated walking there since his apartment in West Ashley wasn't that far from the station and he would get a better feel for the city that way. After poking his nose outside into the hot, humid air, he decided meeting his new boss without sweat stains under his armpits took precedence over acquainting himself with his new home. Not that George planned on being in Charleston for longer than two or three years. The city was merely a steppingstone on his way to the top, and when the opening for a homicide detective here had popped up, he had decided it was time to quit Narcotics and applied for the job. Luckily for him, there had only been ten other applicants, none of them with a resume to rival his own, which meant the job had landed in his lap without too much effort from his side. If everything went according to plan, he would use his time here to get intimate with the proceedings of yet another police station and how they handled capital crimes so he could start looking for openings as a police lieutenant. The city of Charleston was definitely not the worst place to be, it even ranked among the top ten cities to live in the US, whatever that was supposed to mean, and the surrounding area promised great opportunities for outdoor sports, which he was a big fan of. He couldn't wait to go hiking and kayaking, as soon as he got used to the climate, which was very different from his hometown in Boston.

Once he had found a suitable parking space—unfortunately not in the shade—he got out of his car, locked it, and went to the main entrance of the Charleston PD. A young man at the front desk handed him a visitor's pass, even though he was scheduled to get his official ID after his meeting with the chief. Amanda Norris's office was on the second floor, at the far end of an impressive bull pen, where the hectic noises of at least twenty people working were accentuated by the rustling of cellophane and the telltale screeching of plastic spoons dragging over takeout boxes. The smell was a mixture of stale sweat, lemon detergent that was probably used to keep the old linoleum floor in a semblance of cleanliness, though it was a lost battle, different kinds of food, coffee that was strong enough to make even the most hardened criminals beg for mercy, and a cacophony of colognes and perfumes that could kill one's sense of smell faster than any aniseed bomb. In short, it smelled familiar, if a bit exotic.

George ignored the curious looks on his way to the office, where bold white letters announced "Amanda Norris, Chief of Police," and knocked. He was immediately asked inside, and a short glance at the glass walls confirmed his suspicions that this was privacy glass—the people inside the office could see what was going on outside, but not the other way around. Amanda Norris got up from her chair and shook his hand in greeting. She was a tall woman, around six feet to George's own six three, with a generous build that gave her an appearance of being motherly when she was anything but—as George's discreet investigations had shown. Amanda was as career-driven as he himself, and she hadn't gotten the position of chief by being nice. She was forty-three, African American, mother to a fourteen-year-old son, and married to an artist who was still waiting for his big break. At least there was always somebody home for the child.

"Detective Donovan, it's a pleasure to meet you. I'm so glad you could accommodate the change in time. I'm afraid I was swamped this morning."

"No problem, Chief. It's not like I have signed another contract." George made his voice sound light, the tone he had learned to adopt in small talk from a young age. It didn't fail to work on Amanda Norris, who smiled broadly at him before gesturing at the comfortable-looking chair in front of her desk.

"Please, Detective, have a seat. I'm afraid we have a lot to talk about."

George furrowed his brows. He had anticipated something minor, like lack of a signature somewhere or that his badge wasn't ready yet. The way the chief's tone had changed told him it was more serious. She sat down in her own leather chair, steepled her fingers on the desk, and cut right to the chase. "There's no way of easing you into this. Your assigned partner, Michelle Stevenson, called me this morning to tell me she has to take a leave of absence, starting now, because of a family emergency. I don't know when she will be back, which means you're technically without a partner at the moment."

George thought about this. Now he certainly understood why his meeting with the chief this morning had been postponed. What worried him, though, was the way she had phrased the second part of her announcement. "What do you mean 'technically'? I'd say I either have a partner or I don't."

A brief smile flitted over Amanda's face. "I knew you were a smart one. Now, I'm pretty sure you already know that I'm rather new to this position."

George nodded. "You started six months ago."

"Exactly. And until last month, the former chief, Harry Renard, was still here to help me with the transition." Her gaze went to the glass walls and the bustling outside. "I was very grateful for his help, but we didn't see eye to eye about one thing. Or rather, one person."

George lifted a brow. He knew the chief wanted something from him, and he was more interested in what she was going to offer in exchange than in what she was going to ask of him. From the way she was dancing around the subject, he already had an idea that it had something to do with personnel.

"You see that guy over there, in the left corner, next to the printer?"

George turned in his seat to look in the indicated direction. A man was standing there, staring at the printer as if he was waiting for a miracle. From this angle, George had a good look at his profile, and he was close enough to pick up details. Like the way the man's hair was a bit too long to be considered professional, or how he wore jeans a bit too big and a bit too shabby for the precinct, or that his shirt was a washed-out white with a slight hint of red, suggesting he didn't sort his laundry before putting it in the washing machine, or how his skin was nicely tanned but seemed ashen nevertheless. All in all, the man looked more like somebody who should sit in an interrogation room about to be questioned regarding his habits of substance abuse than be out wearing the badge he had currently clipped to a frayed leather belt that surely had seen better days, even if it was a long time ago.

"Yes, ma'am. I see him. Doesn't look like he belongs here." George usually didn't make a habit of talking people down without getting to know them first, especially not in front of superiors, because such things could easily come back to bite you in the ass. In this case, though, he already knew Amanda had a problem with this guy, and he figured feeding into that would get him brownie points.

The quick expression of disgust on her face told him he had played his cards right. "No, he doesn't. That's Andrew Hayes. The detective with the highest crime-solving rate in the entire city, if not the state."

Her sour tone made George a bit wary. "If he's that good, I don't understand the problem. I mean, having a detective like him should thrill you."

Amanda sighed. "Normally it would. Don't get me wrong, his performance makes the whole precinct look damn good."

"But—"

"But that's just it. How can he be so good? He works alone, apparently always has, and he breaks cases nobody else can. He even solves cold cases sometimes, when he runs out of recent ones."

George was getting impatient. He knew the chief wanted something from him, and now he knew it had to do with Andrew Hayes. "Again, I fail to see the problem."

Amanda massaged her temples. "I'm telling you all this, hell, I'm only talking to you about this because you're the new guy and this is my one chance to have Andrew Hayes discreetly watched without making it look as if I don't trust my best detective. I don't want IA all over this place, especially should it turn out my gut feeling was way off the mark."

"I gather your gut feelings are usually spot on?"

Amanda shot him a glare that told him to tread more carefully. Yes, she needed him, but no, she wasn't desperate.

"They are. And my gut tells me there's something wrong with Andrew Hayes. I want you to watch him for me, to see if there's something fishy going on. I don't wish to jeopardize this entire precinct because of the actions of one man. If he's clean, fine, I'll follow Chief Renard's shining example and just let him be, but before I can do that, I need to know if he's legit."

"Which is where I come into play. What a happy coincidence that Michelle is gone."

"Believe it or not, that's indeed a coincidence. But I'd be a fool to let such a chance slip through my fingers. I'm not asking you to get into his personal business; I just want you to be his partner and see up close how he works, how he handles evidence, if he follows protocol. That's all. And in a few months, when you have solved a crime or two, we can see about either getting you another partner or even letting you do solo work as well."

"Sounds fair. Now what's in it for me?"

Amanda leaned back in her chair. "I did some digging about you as well, Detective Donovan, and I see a man who wishes to reach certain heights. If you do this for me, you'll have my full backing once you wish to move on to greener pastures."

George held Amanda's gaze. What she was propositioning wasn't exactly legal, but it wasn't illegal either. She was asking him to watch a fellow detective who might become a problem for the precinct. If anything came of his little side investigation, he would even get some credit. And if it turned out to be nothing—then IA wouldn't be the wiser and Amanda still owed him a favor. It was win-win all around. He held his hand out to her.

"Deal."

She shook his hand. "Deal."

They both looked through the glass wall at Andrew Hayes, who was still standing in front of the printer, waiting for only God knew what.

Amanda rose from her chair. "I'd better get him. He won't like this."

CHAPTER 2
PINNED LIKE A BUG

"DETECTIVE HAYES? Could you please come to my office?" Chief Norris's voice grated on Andrew "Andi" Hayes's nerves, but since the insufferable woman was his new boss, he had to play nice. The new chief reminded him of a botfly maggot that was trying to burrow into his skin. Why couldn't she leave him alone like Chief Renard had done? He was doing the precinct a service, and everybody knew it, which was the reason his colleagues mostly left him to his own devices and accommodated him when needed. But no, Chief Norris had to be all suspicious of his success rate, which he *had* to achieve through some sort of trickery. Of course she was right, but that wasn't the point. He just wished Norris would leave him alone, because the "trick" he used wasn't illegal or anything like that.

When he had been a small boy, Andi had thought his *geschenk*, as his mother called it—Andi himself now thought of it more as a curse—was absolutely cool and put him on a level with Spider-Man. Once he started elementary school, he had quickly found out his *geschenk* was nothing but trouble. By the time he had reached high school, he was an introverted loner who didn't even attempt to appear well-adjusted anymore. Being able to establish a link with every insect on the planet did that to a boy. Andi's world was never silent. Even now, at thirty-two, when he had finally mastered the art of tuning all foreign impressions out, there was still a never-ending background of soft noises, strange smells, and odd vibrations swamping him with mostly useless information.

The first awkward stirrings of a butterfly whose wings had just dried after leaving the cocoon, the dry rasping of mandibles chewing through wood, a dragging sound of chitin forcing its way through a narrow gap in the wall, the overwhelming scent of the trash cans behind the building roasting in the sun, a feast for flies and their maggots, the indistinct taste of rain on the air, the tantalizing odors of human sweat, like a beacon for mosquitoes and fleas, the chirping and trilling and clicking accompanying the life of arthropods. And he was privy to it all, could feel it, hear it, sense it, without ever getting a break, without ever being able to make it stop, without ever daring to share it with anybody.

Insects were the largest class of animals on the planet, and they were literally everywhere. If his colleagues knew how many beetles, spiders, ticks, flies, ants, termites, and other creepy crawlers were living in the precinct, they would never set foot in it again. They wouldn't be able to return to their homes either, because there they were as well. No matter where a person went, insects were already there. Which meant Andi had no place to hide.

When it came to police work, his connection with the world of arthropods was helpful, to put it mildly. It was the reason he could solve cases other detectives would never touch or had been forced to give up on, because his informants were omnipresent. Even years later, they could still help him, especially if a crime had happened close to insects with a hive mentality, like bees, ants, or termites. Scientists would be baffled at how much information these animals could store—and how long they could store it.

That he was able to help others with this curse of his was the only reason Andi got out of bed some days and the force that had driven him to law enforcement in the first place. The risk of exposure was greater in his line of work, since most people who joined the force were not known for being unobtrusive or inattentive, but Andi had found out early in life that being an ass kept people at bay and helped explain away some of his stranger quirks and habits, of which he had quite a lot.

Being constantly assaulted by myriad impressions was taking its toll on his mental health and made him antisocial at best, downright rude at worst, the upside being that it helped him keep others at bay. Meditating helped his state of mind, and he had developed strategies to deal with the worst excesses of his condition, but there were still days he wanted nothing more than to climb on a rocket and fly to the moon, because burying himself in the ground would only make matters worse.

And now Chief Norris had it out for him again. On his short trip to her office, Andi wondered briefly what she had come up with this time, but when he entered the room, he immediately knew. It didn't take a genius to deduce that the stranger getting up from one of the chairs in front of Norris's desk was a detective as well. Even though Andi didn't interact a lot with his colleagues, he wasn't deaf and always on top of office gossip out of necessity. When you had a secret to keep, knowledge about the goings-on in the precinct was pure self-defense. It was also amazing how a few well-placed rumors, spoken into the right ears, could completely derail unwanted attention. This system had its limits, though, and Andi feared he would now have to face the music in the form of a distrusting chief. Why, oh why did Chief Renard have to grow old and leave the precinct? And which vindictive god had sent Andi somebody like Chief Norris, who clearly valued her career above everything and everybody else?

He knew there was a new guy supposed to start today, as Michelle's partner, but she'd had to leave due to a family emergency, and here they were, in the chief's office. It wasn't a hard guess where this would lead, and Andi racked his brain to figure out how to wiggle out of this one. If there was one thing he didn't need, it was a partner. Even if said partner wasn't too bad-looking in a gray suit that was too well-fitted to have been cheap. The man seemed like a blueprint for the perfect detective, if such an elusive creature even existed.

"Detective Andrew Hayes, this is Detective George Donovan. He's the new transfer from Boston, where he worked in Narcotics, and is here to see how our Capital Crime Unit works. He was supposed to be Detective Stevenson's partner, but as you probably already know, she's no longer here. Since you don't have a partner either, I want you to team up with Detective Donovan until he knows his way around the precinct and the city."

Andi stared at Donovan. The man was taller than him, with a skin tone that hinted at a mixed Caucasian/African American heritage. He was bulky, but not so much that he had problems moving gracefully, as Andi could see when Donovan politely stepped aside to make room for him to take the other chair. He was also dressed impeccably, which made the contrast to Andi's own rough exterior even more glaring. Not that Andi cared about how people saw him or the way they looked themselves. When they were forced on him as his new partner, though, he did take an interest, and so far, Detective George Donovan failed to impress Andi.

"You know I don't do partners." The words came out gruffer than he had intended, but it was Norris's own fault. He hated being ganged up on.

The chief's eyes narrowed in warning, which didn't really faze Andi. The woman was tough, but she had nothing on his German grandmother, who could slice a person with a well-placed look. His grandmother—or *Oma*, as she had insisted on being called—was also the one he had to thank for his *geschenk*, and without her teaching him how to handle it, he probably would be dead already, though this was not important at the moment. He had to get out of a partnership he neither needed nor wanted.

"As I said, it's only temporary, two months tops, until I know for sure how long Detective Stevenson is going to be gone. Then I can find a new partner for Detective Donovan and you can go back to your reclusive ways."

Andi stared at her intently. He knew she was suspecting something, like Chief Renard had. Only the old chief had been more direct about his suspicions.

"The way you solve your cases, is it illegal?"

"No, Chief. Definitely not."

"Can you promise me that? There won't be anything to come back and bite us in the ass?"

"Not only can I promise, I can swear. It's perfectly safe."

"Fine. Do your job."

And that had been it. Renard had done a quick survey of the pros and cons to letting Andi have things his way and had decided the praise he got for his spotless statistics was worth being kept in the dark about Andi's methods. Apparently Chief Norris didn't share Renard's pragmatic approach.

He knew he could dig in his heels and create quite the ruckus, but that would be tedious and only serve to feed her suspicions even more. If working with Donovan meant she would leave him alone in the future, he could put up with the man for some time. Maybe. Probably, if he remembered to use his rusted social skills. It wasn't as if Donovan would be able to find anything out. Not if Andi didn't want him to. If there was one thing Andi had learned over the years, it was how to keep his secret, well, secret. It came at the cost of being seen as an antisocial grump, which at the same time freed him of expending precious energy into social connections he couldn't afford to have for fear of being found out. All his energy went into keeping the images the arthropods threw at him at bay, filtering out only those he needed for his cases. Technically, a partner would force him to redirect some of his attention, but since the goal was to lose the man as quickly as possible, Andi didn't see a need to change his ways, apart from perhaps the most basic forms of politeness, which he was almost sure he could manage. And if the man went back to Chief Norris to complain? Then Andi could tell her it wasn't his problem if the new guy couldn't deal with his special brand of people skills.

"Fine. Two months. After that, I'm solo again. And no more attempts to partner me up." He put enough of a growl into his words to show her he meant business. Her eyes widened in surprise for a moment; she had probably expected more of a fight.

"Two months. And watch the attitude."

It was kind of lame. They both knew she would think twice about doing anything that could tarnish the reputation of her star investigator. As long as she didn't have anything to pin on him, his position was quite safe, and he could get away with a lot. Though it didn't pay to overdo it. He didn't want the chief to be his enemy. He just wanted her to leave him alone.

"Is that all?"

"Yes. Please show Detective Donovan around. He can take the desk next to yours. I will inform tech to set him up. He also still needs his badge and weapon. Please help him with that."

Andi nodded and rose from his chair. "Let's go. See you, Chief."

Donovan said his own goodbye, and they left the office. Every pair of eyes in the bull pen was directed at them. Andi knew people were wondering if the chief had finally managed to saddle him with a partner. They would find out soon enough.

CHAPTER 3
SETTING UP FOR DISAPPOINTMENT

GEORGE FOLLOWED his new partner out of the chief's office and wondered if his involvement had been a good idea. While Andrew Hayes wasn't openly hostile toward him—yet—he didn't seem like a man who just rolled on his back and played dead. As much as this whole thing was only temporary in his eyes, he still had to be able to rely on Hayes to have his back. Homicide was a tough department, and detectives never met people at their best. Having a partner who didn't like or even detested you could be a death warrant, so his main priority had to be making nice with his new partner.

"Hi, Andrew, can I call you Andrew? I'm George. Sorry about all that."

Hayes turned around very slowly, his expression completely closed off. George was usually good at reading people, and it annoyed him that he couldn't get a read on his new partner. It made him vulnerable in a way he rarely experienced. Usually he was the one in the control of a partnership, or any social interaction, come to think of it. He always knew how to handle people, how to coax and win and manipulate them to his advantage. Somehow, he got the impression Andi Hayes would not only see through any attempt to manipulate him but also take it very negatively. With no point he could attack, George was reduced to simply observing his reluctant partner.

This close, he could see Hayes's eyes were a muddy mixture of blue and green he probably shouldn't have found so intriguing. He could also feel another kind of interest stirring in his groin, which didn't help the situation at all. George hated labels with a passion, and if pressed to define his sexual orientation, he could say without a doubt that he was an equal opportunity fucker. Which wasn't the point here. He had to get on Hayes's good side, not check him out as a potential adventure between the sheets. He was supposed to be his partner, not a hookup from a bar.

"People call me Andi. And it's fine. You heard her; we only have to rough it for two months. After that, I'm free and you can get a decent partner you don't have to babysit."

Andi turned back and proceeded toward a door George hadn't seen when he had first come to the precinct. He hurried to keep up with his reluctant new partner, while at the same time, he tried to make sense of what Andi had just said. It almost sounded as if he knew what Chief Norris had asked of George, which was impossible. He was being paranoid. Starting a new job and being immediately tasked with spying on the new partner could do that to a man. They entered another hallway, where Andi stopped in front of a double door.

"Here are the showers and locker rooms. You should get a key with your badge and all the other stuff you're gonna need."

Well, that wasn't a complete dismissal. It wasn't a glowing declaration of perfect partnership either, but at this point, George would take whatever Andi offered. So he followed his new partner through the precinct, acquainted himself with the break room and its nondrinkable coffee, the gym that also housed a sparring ring, and several other detectives and officers who all had problems hiding their surprise at seeing Andi with a partner. George kept up the well-meaning small talk while he tried to read people's reaction to Andi. It was obvious that he wasn't close to any of his colleagues, though he seemed to get along better with the officers than with his fellow detectives. Given his success rate, George wasn't surprised. Envy was the same everywhere.

After two hours of walking and talking to people that weren't Andi, George finally got his badge and keys, as well as his clearance for the entire building. Since it was already nearing five o'clock and it didn't look as if a hot new case would land in their lap this day, George and Andi left. With every other new partner, George would have asked if they should have a beer together, but the determined way in which Andi went straight for his car, a beat-up white sedan, told him the man wouldn't be receptive to the idea. Sighing, George went to his own car and drove home, trying to make sense of his new partner and the situation he found himself in.

THE NEXT morning saw George getting his PC set up on a desk next to Andi's, behind a portable room divider that created the illusion of privacy. Their desks were the only ones shielded in this manner, and George could see how people thought Andi was a lone wolf. The man wasn't sociable in the least and seemed to be happiest when his colleagues ignored him. George's tentative attempts at starting a conversation had all been shot down with monosyllabic answers and in one case even a grunt. If something didn't change soon, he would probably never find out anything about Andi. George decided to give it one last try this morning before he gave up for the day.

"Hey, Andi, I was thinking about going to the Starbucks at the corner to get some decent coffee. Do you want some?"

Andi looked at him as if he had offered to bring him a cup of arsenic topped with rusty nails. "I don't do coffee. The caffeine makes me all twitchy."

"Sorry. I didn't know. Anything else you want?" At least there had been a kernel of freely given information. No coffee for the loner. Although George wasn't sure if this intel would ever be of any use—despite indicating that Andi was indeed kind of strange. Most cops lived on coffee, and if there were a possibility to get it intravenously, he was sure the country's entire police force would run around with permanent access to an artery.

"A plain bagel." The words cut through George's musings. He hadn't really expected an answer, not after his faux pas with the coffee, but Andi seemed to be getting into a sociable mood. What was it his father always said? Strike the iron while hot.

"A plain bagel it is. Be back in five."

Andi didn't bother to respond. Instead, he stared at his computer screen as if it had suddenly told him the secret to life. George headed for the door, intent on getting a decent cup of coffee. Perhaps then his brain would come up with an idea how to crack Andi.

"Don't try too hard." The female voice made George stop dead in his tracks. A woman in her late forties, if George had to guess, was approaching him from the side, a friendly smile on her face.

"Hi, I'm Rose, Rose Carter. I've been working reception forever, and I do know Andi."

"Hi, Rose. I'm George Donovan. As you seemingly already know, I'm Andi's new partner. If you have any insights as to how I can get to know him better, I'm willing to not only listen but also pay handsomely. The man is as closed off as an oyster with a precious pearl."

The light banter paired with a flirtatious tone came easily to George and payed off almost immediately. A slight blush colored Rose's light cheeks while she subconsciously patted the immaculate brown bob that framed her face till chin level.

"I don't know about payment, but I can give you some advice, out of the goodness of my heart."

"At this point, I'll take anything I can get."

A perfectly shaped eyebrow came up. "It's only your second day. And yesterday hardly counts since you came in after noon."

The bush drums apparently worked perfectly in the precinct. "And I've been running against a brick wall ever since. I have to admit, I'm getting desperate. At least he told me he doesn't drink coffee. That was the most personable thing I got out of him."

Rose watched him long enough to make George squirm a bit. He wanted to get along with the people on the force, because it never paid to be an asshole. At least not in the long run and with the career aspirations he had. When Rose finally spoke, her tone was softer, almost pondering, as if she wasn't entirely sure how much she should tell him but wanted to help him regardless. For his first—or second—day, that wasn't too bad.

"Andi started out as a beat officer here and worked his way up to detective in the shortest time possible. You may have already heard how spotless his statistics are. In that regard, he's the best partner you could have hoped for. Unfortunately, he's always been a loner. I think most people simply annoy him. He's not malicious, though. He just wants to be left to his own devices."

George sighed. He had already assumed as much. "I get it. But for the next few months, we're stuck with each other. Is there anything I can do to make him at least tolerate me?"

"Do you ride, George?"

"No. What has that to do with Andi? Does he like horses? Should I start riding?" At this point, no idea seemed too ridiculous.

Rose shook her head. "No and no. I do ride, though, and sometimes a horse can be wary of humans for various reasons. Do you know how you get their attention and—ultimately—their trust?"

George looked at her blankly. His experiences with horses were limited to watching *Lord of the Rings*.

"You very pointedly ignore them while being in their vicinity. It makes them curious, and eventually they gain the courage to approach on their own because you appear nonthreatening."

"Do you want to tell me Andi had bad experiences with other people?"

"Nobody knows. What I do know is you won't crack his armor by doing direct attacks. That'll only make him retreat further into his shell and detest you for being a pain in the ass. Pardon my language. Giving him space while at the same time being there could be the key."

"You don't know if it works? Then why are you telling me this?" George was beginning to think this whole conversation was fruitless.

"No, I don't know if it works. He sometimes talks to me because I bribe him with baked goods now and then, which is also a way to a horse's heart, by the way. I wouldn't say we're friends, because I don't think Andi understands the concept, but he does communicate with me more than with anybody else in the precinct. You're already at a disadvantage because you were forced on him. Don't make it worse by wanting too much too fast. Give him room to breathe and he might surprise you."

"And if not?" George had a sinking feeling.

"Then you'd get exactly as far as you would have by keeping your current strategy." She patted his hand. "It's up to you, of course. I wouldn't dare meddle in your affairs."

She turned and walked back to where she had come from, leaving George with more questions than answers, which seemed to be his natural state as of yesterday. He squared his shoulders. He was a Donovan. Donovans never backed down when there was a challenge. He would crack Andrew Hayes if it was the last thing he did.

CHAPTER 4
A FEAST FOR ANTS

ANDI WATCHED Rose intercepting George on his way out. She talked to him intently, probably filling the poor man in on all of Andi's misgivings. If it weren't for her delicious cakes, Andi wouldn't talk to that nosy busybody at all, but who was he to pass up cake? Especially since his cooking skills were next to nonexistent. After Rose had imparted her wisdom to George, the man left the precinct, which gave Andi a few much-needed moments of utter peace. His other colleagues knew better than to disturb him, especially not when he was trying to write a report. Chief Norris had put him on a cold case, no doubt to test him and at the same time keep him from working recent cases. Unfortunately for her and the poor young man, finding him had been a matter of minutes. Two hours if he counted the time it had taken to dig up his bones.

The young man had gone missing some fifteen years ago. His conservative white parents had reported him two days later, but the police hadn't been able to find any trace of him. Back then there had been no reason to suspect the grieving parents, and so the case had gone cold within a few weeks. It took Andi one visit to the house in Harleston Village to know the corpse was under the floorboards in the cellar. The ant colony living in the wood under the porch still remembered the tantalizing smell of the feast just outside its reach. They had only gotten some skin and blood with a few crumbs of brain from the place in the garden where his own father had killed him for dating a black girl. Finding an excuse to search the cellar had been the biggest obstacle, but once Andi had convinced the judge to let him do a sweep of the house due to new studies regarding the psychology of killers and the most likely suspects in abduction cases, it had been easy to get a cadaver dog down into the basement. That the father had been stupid enough to bury the murder weapon with his son, including all the lovely DNA traces on it, had only served to close the case that much faster. Now all Andi had to do was make the report look convincing enough to not raise Chief Norris or IA's suspicions. *I had a hunch* worked only on a restricted number of cases, and only when there actually was any evidence that could have triggered a hunch. Going straight to the basement in the house of the parents of a missing person and then finding a corpse was way out of the range of hunches and deep in *we need hard evidence* territory. It was almost cynical. Writing the reports about his successfully closed cases was most of the time a lot more tedious and hard than solving the crime. Andi stared blankly at his computer screen. His *oma* would say that such was life, and tough shit if you couldn't deal with it, while his gran would go and make him hot chocolate with lots of little marshmallows in it. Sometimes Andi wondered how two so vastly different women could have produced offspring that fell in love with each other and ultimately produced him.

A soft thud next to his mouse caused him to look up. It was his new partner, who was back from the Starbucks. "Your bagel."

"Thank you. What do I owe you?" Andi reached for his wallet in the back pocket of his ratty jeans. George furrowed his brows.

"It's fine. We're partners. Next time, you pay." With that, he sat down at his own desk, placed his extra-large cup of coffee next to his computer, and started clicking away as if he already had something worth his attention on it. The ringing of his phone spared Andi from reacting to this strange behavior. Then again, who was he to judge other people?

"Detective Hayes."

"A corpse has been found at the Extra Space storage unit on St. James Avenue in the Goose Creek area."

"I'm on my way." Andi ended the call and got up, realizing that he now had a partner who was looking at him expectantly. "We have a body."

George nodded, grabbed his cup and his car keys and got up. "Where are we headed?"

"Goose Creek area."

"Should I drive?"

Andi hesitated. Since he was always on his own, he usually drove himself, even though he hated it. It required a huge amount of concentration to block out all the impressions he got from the insects in the air and on the ground to drive safely. Suddenly seeing the street from high above through the kaleidoscope sight of a dragonfly while still driving was a sure method to produce a crash and one of the many reasons Andi didn't bother getting a new car or having the dents in his sedan repaired. It wasn't worth the time and money.

With George, he wouldn't have to face this particular problem today.

"Thank you. That would be great."

George seemed surprised at his answer but didn't comment. They went to the parking lot, where George's Escalade gleamed in the sun. It was a very new car, the typical factory smell still lingering inside. Andi almost felt bad sitting down on the passenger seat with his shabby clothes. They weren't dirty or anything, just old, because he hated shopping with a passion, but he felt out of place in this pristine car, next to his partner, who again wore a suit despite the heat. If George had similar thoughts, he didn't voice them, for which Andi was grateful. He told his partner to drive in the general direction of Goose Creek while he tried to ignore all the information he was getting from the insects nearby.

The breeze was just right to float in the air, watching the huge blobs move about jerkily like in an old black-and-white movie, the new spread of soil in the huge flower pots along the road was woefully devoid of anything nourishing like dead leaves or bits of roots, and there was an invisible barrier in the air where a shopkeeper had just cleaned his window, much to the chagrin of the fly that was trying to get into the darker space to lay her eggs.

It was all like a constant thrumming in the back of his head, one he couldn't turn off. His *oma* had told him he would be grateful for it once his own senses started to deteriorate—at the end of her life, she had been blind, but still able to "see" through the eyes of the insects—but at the moment, it was simply overwhelming. The human brain couldn't even properly deal with the five senses the human body possessed. How was it supposed to process the information coming from creatures who experienced their world through pheromones, different colors of the color spectrum, vibrations, or even sonic? Not at all, that was how. Even though Andi had learned to interpret the signals he was getting, he was still confused most of the time, so reducing the influx to a low hum was the best he could do.

Fortunately, George had to concentrate on traffic, thus sparing them both any awkward conversation. It only took them twenty minutes to reach St. James Ave., where the Extra Space storage unit was located. The yellow police tape as well as the blue flashing lights guided them the last few yards. George found a parking spot close to the building, and when they got out, they were greeted by a young beat officer who looked fresh out of the academy.

"Detective Hayes?" The woman looked at him questioningly. Andi extended his hand.

"That's me. This is Detective Donovan, my partner. You called this one in?"

"Yes. I'm Officer Mayfair. We got a call about forty minutes ago from a man named Christopher Palmer, who informed us about a body on the premises. He's the janitor and was supposed to do some repairs on two of the units today." Officer Mayfair gestured to an elderly man with a potbelly and thin graying hair, who was sitting with a blanket around his shoulders on the passenger side of the patrol car Officer Mayfair must have come in.

"Thank you. What exactly do we have?"

"Female, looks underage, African American, deep head wound. That's all I could see without moving her."

Andi nodded. "Very good. Please show us the place."

Officer Mayfair led them along the building to the back, where weeds were growing through the asphalt, reclaiming the ground. They were trampled, and a few feet before the next corner, Andi saw the corpse. He approached slowly, trying to take everything in, already relying on what his little friends could tell him as well. In situations like these, he was grateful for the additional input.

Two blobs had come out of the building, only one had left, the other was now a feast to be consumed, the first tendrils of the scent of decay already spreading around the premises, crawling over the trampled grass and rapidly heating asphalt like fog in the early morning, enticing more and more tiny scavengers to come closer long before the warm-blooded ones even knew there was food to find.

Andi was by now so familiar with the pheromones of death they no longer threw him off guard like in the beginning. The eager buzzing of the flies and the hurried scuttling of the ants also informed him of the other two bodies inside the building. The scavenger insects were almost going crazy from all the food they were getting.

"We need to go inside the building. Now. Can you ask the janitor for the keys?"

Officer Mayfair looked startled. "But... I already checked the locks. They weren't tampered with. And the janitor said it all looked normal. Nothing out of the ordinary."

"We would have to take a look inside no matter what. I just want to do it now."

Something in his tone must have told the woman how serious he was. She hastened back to get the keys while Andi stared at the girl on the ground. She was on her belly, so he couldn't get a good look at her face. Her clothes were flimsy, too thin even for this time of year, and he could spot bruises on her naked thighs. Whatever had happened here, it wasn't pretty, and it wasn't just this girl. Sometimes Andi hated his job from the bottom of his heart.

"Poor thing. Do you have some hunch, or why do you want to check the building already?"

George's voice was low, almost soothing, as if he didn't want to spook Andi.

"Let's just say I got a feeling. Could be nothing. But I doubt it. Young girl, dressed like this, in a quiet area? That's trouble." He didn't elaborate further, keeping things purposely vague, and George seemed to get the hint. With one last look at the girl, he started back toward the main entrance, where Officer Mayfair was hopefully waiting with the keys.

CHAPTER 5
HOW DID HE KNOW?

GEORGE WATCHED Andi closely while Officer Mayfair fumbled with the lock to the storage unit. The man was calm, which could be expected of a seasoned officer, and also resigned, as if he already knew what they would be finding, which in turn made George edgy. Even though they had been at the crime scene for only a short time, he had taken a very close look, and nothing had hinted at the girl having been in the building or even having a connection to it. So why was Andi so adamant about going inside when the crime scene was so obviously in the open?

Officer Mayfair finally managed to wrestle the lock into submission. The gate to the building opened with an ominous creak, making it obvious why the janitor had to come to do repairs. Inside there was a long hall with storage units on each side. Andi found the switch for the light, and for a moment the hall looked like an underground rave until the halogen lamps finally settled, shedding their cold glow on the units, which were all secured with heavy padlocks. Nothing seemed out of the ordinary, and yet Andi walked down the hall with determined strides, making it clear he knew where he was going. After about fifty feet, the hallway made a curve. George felt a strange tingling in his stomach, one that had saved him countless times already. He knew something was wrong, that Andi had been dead on. They rounded the corner, Andi in the lead. George almost ran into him when his partner suddenly stopped dead in his tracks. A storage unit to their right had caught Andi's interest. It was closed, like the rest, and George wondered what had Andi so riveted until he realized it himself. There was a black stripe leading from a crack in the wall to the gate, vanishing beneath it. Upon closer inspection, the stripe was moving. Ants. George approached the gate and pressed his ear on the thin aluminum. The buzzing of flies had his heart sinking. While working in Narcotics, he had stumbled upon a few corpses. To him, the worst was not the smell or the often-gruesome sight. It was the steady hum of flies that turned his stomach. For some reason, the image of those small black bodies all over a dead person made the hair on his nape stand up.

He turned to Andi. "Can we just open it, or do we need a warrant?" If this were a narcotics case, they wouldn't be allowed to open the unit just because they suspected something. The flies, though, should be probable cause in a homicide case, or so he thought.

Andi shrugged. "I don't know about you, but I think I just heard somebody calling for help. It was very faint… I could be mistaken."

George hesitated only a second. "I think I heard it as well. We should take a look. Just to be on the safe side."

Somehow this conspiratorial exchange gave him the feeling of being closer to Andi. It was probably because the man had kept him at arm's length so far, even though it was only their second day together, and he was simply glad to finally get that partner feeling he liked so much about his line of work.

They both bent down to inspect the lock on the gate. It was new, with several scratches, as if somebody had been in a hurry to insert the key.

"Do you happen to have a bolt cutter around here?" George looked at Officer Mayfair.

"I'm so sorry, but I don't. I could see if the janitor has something, though." She blushed, seemingly thinking a good officer should always have such a tool with them.

"That would be good. Thank you."

The officer rushed off, which gave George the privacy to talk to Andi. "How did you know?"

Andi's expression immediately closed off, shutting George out like he had done the day before and this morning. "I told you, it was just a hunch."

George furrowed his brows. He wasn't sure if he should press the matter. Andi had moved way too purposefully for just a hunch. On the other hand, what did he hope to prove at this stage of the investigation? He was pretty sure Andi hadn't known about the first body, not before they got the call. Something at the crime scene must have tipped him off, perhaps even something George could have seen had he known what to look for or had he been more alert. If anything, he could probably learn a lot from Andi.

"I'm sorry. I didn't mean to pry. I mean, I did see my fair share of bodies while I was in narcotics, but focusing on the dead person and not the drugs is still kind of new to me."

Andi stared at him intently, the dark circles under his eyes making his head look a bit like a skull. "It's okay."

That was the best he was going to get, and George knew it. The return of Officer Mayfair prevented any further awkwardness. George took the bolt cutter she had brought and opened the lock. Andi pulled the gate up, and what they saw in the pale light filtering into the unit from the hall made George curse. Two more bodies, young girls, one African American, the other Caucasian, lay on the naked concrete, their eyes still open, staring blindly at the ceiling. The ant street parted in front of the bodies, distributing the workers evenly between the two girls, while the flies buzzed around them, busy with fly things.

Carefully, George stepped into the unit, led by the light of Officer Mayfair's flashlight. It wouldn't do any good to destroy evidence by being too rash. He heard rustling and knew Andi was directly behind him, though he didn't seem too interested in the bodies. *As if he already knew all about them!* The treacherous thought raced through George's head before he could stop it. He mentally shook himself. How should Andi have known? They had come here together, and Andi had had no chance to do any investigating by himself.

Again, there was the rave-flickering before the unit was bathed in cold light, baring the poor girls in all detail. As far as corpses went, they didn't look too bad. Since there weren't any maggots crawling around yet and the smell was still bearable, they couldn't have been dead for more than forty-eight hours. Whoever had killed them had strangled them, so no blood or other fluids were staining the concrete floor. If it weren't for the dark bruises around their necks and the purple spots of postmortem lividity forming around their naked shoulders where they touched the ground, a casual observer may have even thought they were just sleeping. If people slept with their eyes open. On cold concrete. George shuddered. No matter how often he saw death, no matter how used to the depths of human depravity he got, he would probably never get accustomed to the cold senselessness of a life forcibly taken, no matter the reasons. To him, it showed one of the ugliest sides of humankind, one he wished didn't exist. These girls were young, too young to be dead. Too young for the one outside to be wearing clothes so skimpy they barely covered her, too young for the two in here to be naked. And to be strangled. It was a cruel way to die. Cruel and drawn-out and so unnecessary.

"And we have a winner." Andi's voice pried George from his contemplation of the fragility of human life. He turned around to see his partner lifting up a battered crowbar with latex-covered fingers. The paint on the thing was chipping, and the naked steel underneath was rusty and—bloody. "I'd say we've found our murder weapon for victim number one."

George could only stare at Andi. While he had been busy doing nothing but overthinking every little thing, his partner had found important evidence that could very well help them find the culprit.

"That's great. Let me get a bag for that. Hopefully, there are fingerprints on this one."

Andi simply nodded, watching the crowbar as if it held all the answers to this case. With some luck, it would at least provide them with a solid lead. They bagged the tool and kept looking around, waiting for the coroner to arrive. Once the three bodies were photographed from every possible angle, their liver temperature taken, and then put in body bags to be driven to the precinct, CSI descended on the scene. The two men and one woman were taking the storage unit and the place where they had found the first girl apart, dusting for fingerprints, collecting cigarette stubs, miniscule bits of dust that, according to them, were out of place, and some of the flies still buzzing around. George imagined the bluebottles sounded kind of angry for being denied their meal, but who was he to understand those creepy flying undertakers? While George did his best not to get in the way of the CSI team, at the same time trying to form some working theories on what had happened, Andi was just standing near the entrance to the storage unit, his eyes distant, as if he were listening to something only he could hear. George had to admit it was kind of odd—just like everything Andi had done since they'd arrived at the crime scene. He knew intellectually that every detective went about his work differently and they all had some unique ways to process the information they gathered or were given, but with everything the chief had told him about his new partner, George couldn't help but wonder what exactly Andi was doing.

After CSI was done, they went back to the precinct, Andi being tight-lipped the entire drive, no doubt focused on the case. At least that was what George forced himself to believe. As prickly as Andi had been to him since the moment they were partnered, he didn't want to think the worst of a man he had known for less than forty-eight hours. He also had some thinking of his own about the case to do, which wasn't pleasant at all.

George didn't like where his own speculations where leading him, so he could relate to Andi's silence. Three young girls, none of them older than twenty, one in clothes usually found on professional sex workers, the other two naked, brutally murdered in a storage facility that—according to the shocked janitor—didn't see much action in a good week, let alone during the night, led to one obvious conclusion. Sex trafficking. If they were lucky, using the term in the loosest way possible, it was only a small-scale organization, perhaps even just one pimp. If they weren't and these girls had been the victims of some large group, the case would jump state borders in no time flat. Though that wouldn't be too bad in George's opinion. Because then the Feds would get involved, and their resources were far greater than those of two city detectives. Unlike many of his colleagues, George didn't guard his cases like a jealous lover. His attitude was that whatever or whoever got the bad guys behind bars deserved a shot. As for the credit, George knew how to phrase his reports to get maximum recognition for his accomplishments.

He pulled into the precinct's parking lot, and they both got out. They headed back to their desks, where George decided to brave another attempt at getting a few words out of his partner. Rose's advice still resonated in his head, but this was about the case. They had to work together and exchange ideas if they wanted to solve it.

"So, how do you usually proceed at this point? Back in Boston, we had a whiteboard where we wrote down everything we had. I liked that very much, but if you do things differently, I'm happy to give it a try."

The look he got could have frozen hell over. "I don't have a whiteboard."

Andi made it sound as if that explained everything. George decided to ignore Andi's obvious lack of enthusiasm. "I'm sure we can find one. Their natural habitat is the conference room, where they catch dust and are written on with pens unsuitable for their sensitive surface."

Was that a twitch of lips? Did Andi actually find this amusing? George felt stupidly elated. "If I remember right, there's a conference room down the hall. Let me see if I can catch us our very own whiteboard."

That got him an actual smile. A quick one, granted, but a smile nevertheless. George hurried to the conference room, and lo and behold, a whiteboard was sitting there, even with the right kind of pens in a case next to it. He shoved the pens into the right pocket of his suit, opened the brakes on the whiteboard, and navigated it toward their working space. Almost all eyes were on him, making him a tiny bit uncomfortable. He parked the whiteboard on the wall opposite his and Andi's desks so they both could see it clearly. Andi was watching him with a hint of disbelief in his eyes. "You really did it. I thought you were joking."

George winked at him. "Surprise, partner."

For a moment, he thought he had overdone it, but then another smile flitted across Andi's features, making him look almost friendly. The amiable expression vanished quickly, though.

"Since we have the whiteboard now, we might as well use it."

George nodded and got a black pen from the case. In the middle of the board, he wrote: *three Jane Does. One bludgeoned, two strangled. Time of death—*

He looked at Andi. "We don't have that yet."

"If I had to bet, I'd say they were killed roughly at the same time. The one outside likely tried to get away. Judging from the absence of maggots, two days, tops."

He sounded so sure, not at all speculative. As if they had the facts from the lab already. George decided not to dig deeper. He already knew Andi didn't like to have his methods questioned, and unless George had proof Andi was doing something shady, he would not rock the boat and make the man retreat into himself even more. For this reason, he dutifully wrote down: *time of death—roughly at the same time. Murder weapon—crowbar.*

"The bruises around the necks of the other two victims looked like handprints to me. We have to wait for the coroner's report on that."

So there were things Andi didn't know. George felt better. "What else do we have?"

Andi leaned back in his chair, staring at the ceiling. He was obviously thinking hard. "One of them tried to flee. If it was before or after the other two were killed, we don't know." He sighed. "And I think it's safe to assume we're dealing with sex trafficking here."

"I'm afraid you're right. I usually don't like jumping to conclusions, but if it walks like a duck and quacks like a duck…."

"Then it probably tastes good with blue kraut and potato dumplings."

George knew he must have looked pretty clueless, because Andi rolled his eyes. "That's how duck is traditionally eaten in Bavaria, with blue kraut and potato dumplings."

"Oh. Now I get it. Have you been to Bavaria?"

Andi's expression became guarded again, as if he was weighing the pros and cons of divulging a particular piece of information. "My mother is German. Her entire family lives in a small village in the Bavarian Alps. It's all very traditional there. I've been a few times when I was younger. Not recently, though."

That was more than George had hoped for. And he was quick to reveal something personal about himself as well, to keep up the illusion of quid pro quo. "My father is Irish. I haven't been to Ireland yet, but I want to go one day. Must be nice to connect with part of one's heritage."

Andi muttered something unintelligible under his breath, and George was sure it wasn't in favor of connecting with anything. He smiled. "Back to the case. Sex trafficking?" He wrote the words in red into the upper right corner, complete with a question mark, since they weren't a hundred percent sure.

"Yes. Sex trafficking." Andi sounded resigned.

Chapter 6
The Non-Peace of Conferring with Bugs

THEY TOSSED all kinds of ideas into the air, none of them feasible until they got the report from the coroner. Andi was very careful not to suggest too many things he knew would turn out to be true later. George was a suspicious SOB and already on his case after they found the bodies of the two other girls. But there had been no helping it. Not going into the storage unit would have meant a delay in finding the corpses, which would have hindered their investigation. As things were now, they could work focused on the real direction of the case, even though it was—at the moment—still under the pretense of being a suspicion. Andi knew, though. The ants and flies had told him. Not in terms humans used, but they had witnessed the deaths of the girls, first the one outside, then the other two, when the man with them had panicked. Their fine senses had also picked up on the drugs in the girls' systems and the stench of the man who killed them, a mixture of booze and cocaine the ants didn't like.

Screaming, shoving, heavy footsteps disturbing the ground, sending shock waves into the nest, causing some of the older tunnels to cave in in some places, the hurried scuttling of thousands of legs relocating the precious brood, the eggs, while others made sure the queen's chamber was still intact, still solid. Another scream, experienced by the ants as a disturbance in the air, a thud of something with weight going down, then silence, cursing, a rapid series of swirls in the air, retreating footsteps, the vibrations in the ground gradually fading, leaving peace again. Peace and a meal, still smelling of life, still warm, yet missing the pulsing of something that could fight back.

Later came footsteps again, choking wafts of acid and fermented sugar and sweat and blood, followed closely by the much fainter impression of even more death, even more food for the colony.

If he were still working alone, Andi would already be following that particular lead, checking out the usual haunts in Charleston where alcohol, girls, and drugs went together like Kaiserschmarrn and applesauce, to keep the Bavarian food analogies. With George in the picture, he had to wait for solid proof from the lab before he could go out hunting, a delay he hoped wouldn't cost them the chance to catch their suspect. It all depended on how nervous the murderer was. If he thought himself safe, he probably wouldn't try to go into hiding. So far, the murders hadn't made the news, and Andi hoped it would stay that way for at least a few more days. Anything that bought them time.

A glance at his watch told him it was almost six, high time to leave the precinct and get home to let the events of the day sink in. Time to meditate and calm his inner turmoil, which didn't just stem from seeing the murder through the eyes of a nest of ants and countless bottle flies this time. Having a partner was grating on Andi's nerves, even though George was obviously trying to put him at ease. The danger of slipping up and revealing something that could potentially not only cost him his job but also land him in a mental institution was an additional source of stress Andi didn't need in his life. Perhaps he should have thought his decision to let Chief Norris have her way through more, but it was too late now. If things kept developing at this rate, he would have to resort to alcohol to dull his senses, never a good idea, because the temptation of snuggling into the sweet oblivion offered by beer and schnapps got more irresistible every time he had to call on it for help.

Meditation it was. And a long round of yoga. Just to get his body on different ideas.

"I think I'm calling it quits for today. See you tomorrow. Perhaps the lab will have something for us by then."

For a moment it looked as if George wanted to protest or, worse, invite him for a beer or something equally tiring, but then the man shut his mouth again and waved. "Fine with me. See you tomorrow."

The relief of not having to fend off a polite invitation must have shown on his face, because George looked as if he had bitten into a fresh lemon. Before the situation could get any more awkward, Andi hurried out, glad to be finally free.

The eight-minute drive to his home in Stiles Point on St. James Island was so familiar, he barely had to concentrate because he already knew all the impressions the insects were forcing on him.

The sweet, cloying scent of the lantanas and butterfly weeds and tickseeds just starting to bloom, the crumbly quality of the soil in the flower beds of the bigger houses compared to the hardness of the underground stretching into the pavement, the flies caught in spiderwebs, the juicy leaves feasted on by caterpillars, the rotting wood of an old porch....

Of course, there was always something slightly new, but usually never so bad it threw him off-balance. Funnily enough, most insects liked their routines and things to stay the way they were—made it easier to keep up with food sources and safe places to hide.

Insects didn't have the same kind of awareness other animals, especially mammals, had; their lives were so much shorter and knowledge more fluid. Every species "saw" the world in a different way, and it was the combination of impressions from different kinds of insects that helped Andi find his culprits.

The man who had killed the girls was an undesirable bag of rotten blood to the ants, the kind that was a dime a dozen in certain areas of the city, and with their sensory information alone, Andi would never be able to find the man. But combined with the knowledge of the flies—a dark blob of a man, smelling sweetly of decay; the ticks—not their favorite kind of meal, but worth going for; the moths—nothing of interest, just pheromones that did nothing for them; and a whole bunch of others, like silverfish and roaches, he was able to picture the man quite clearly, and when he saw him, he would immediately recognize him, even though his own eyes worked in a completely different way. Thanks to his *oma*, he had learned to translate the language of the insects into images his human brain could understand. Unfortunately, explaining this to George or the chief or any authority wasn't a viable option.

Andi pulled into the driveway to his one-hundred-and-fifty-year-old plantation-style house, a gift from his American gran, who had made it her mission in life to make things as easy as possible for Andi so he didn't have to deal with such mundane things as housing or finances on top of his *geschenk*. That he had inherited the beautiful two-story house with the bright white front porch, the wraparound veranda, and the huge garden, not to mention the interior complete with various valuable antiques, had only served to broaden the rift between him and his father that had started to show once it became apparent what he had inherited from his mother's side. His parents' divorce when he was ten had been a brutal hit on Andi's already fragile mind. The constant blame coming from his father, directed equally at him for being an abomination and his mother for passing on her flawed genes, had destroyed something inside Andi. Now he found it hard to trust anybody, and the meaning of kindness was lost to him.

His mother had never blamed him for anything, though she did look at him with a sad expression in her eyes when she thought he wasn't seeing it. After the divorce, they had visited her relatives in Bavaria for almost a year. The good thing was his *oma* had used the time to teach him how to live with the *geschenk*.

After they had returned to the States, his gran had taken them in, and the moment Andi hit eighteen, his mother had booked a flight back to Bavaria. They sometimes phoned or even skyped, usually around Christmas, but they didn't really have anything to talk about. His father called more regularly, every three months, usually when he was drunk, to remind Andi how he had no right to the gorgeous house he was living in. After a call from his dad, the constant assault from the insects always seemed tame in comparison.

He parked his car in the double garage his gran had built when he and his mother had moved in with her. The empty left bay was a daily reminder that the one person who had truly loved and cared for him was gone. Gran had died six years ago, and it still hurt Andi to think about it. Her bedroom on the first floor remained untouched, in an attempt to preserve the illusion of her spirit still being there. Andi knew it would be healthier to repurpose the room, give it a new meaning so he could move on. He also knew it wouldn't happen anytime soon, most probably never. If things got too bad, if the temptation of drowning his stress and sorrow at the bottom of a bottle became too great, Gran's room was his fortress, the last defense line against the slide into self-destruction.

Sometimes Andi considered going to a shrink, to have somebody to talk to who was bound by law not to spill the beans about him. The question was, could a psychologist show him any new ways of dealing with his problems? He was already using every possible coping mechanism he could read about, and still the temptation was overwhelming sometimes. No, it was better to just keep going, hoping for the best and knowing, deep inside, that for him a happily ever after wasn't in the cards.

Andi entered the house, already tuned into the bustling of all the insects living in his home and garden. His *geschenk* had an automatic range of about half a mile. He could go farther if he really needed to, though he hadn't done it for quite some time. It was extremely draining, something he only contemplated when all else failed. Besides, there could be up to two thousand different kinds of arthropods in one square mile, and having all of them practically screaming at him was not on his list of enjoyable things to do regularly. Today everything was fine. The ants, roaches, and silverfish were satisfied with the weather, the atmospheric pressure, and the available food. The wild bees were buzzing away on the spring flowers in full bloom, and the creatures of the soil, worms, centipedes, the larvae of June bugs and others, showed him how wonderfully soft and rich the soil in his garden was.

The only disturbances were the cadaver of a mouse that was already being taken care of by the ants, and a huge mound of dog poo where his garden met the sidewalk. The flies were not unhappy about it, but dog poo was just nasty in Andi's opinion. With a sigh, he got a plastic bag, went outside again, and found the offending remains.

After the crap had been disposed of, Andi washed his hands twice—knowing what was in dog poo had him contemplating using hand sanitizer as well, even though he hadn't come into direct contact with the stinking mass—and then he made himself a sandwich. After the day he had had, something more substantial would have been good, but the mere idea of cooking required more energy than Andi had to spare at the moment.

Once the sandwich was gone, he changed into his yoga pants, forgoing a shirt, before he returned to his favorite spot in the garden—a cozy gazebo with a wrought-iron fence where he did his yoga routines when it was warm enough. He rolled out his mat, stepped onto it, and started with a salutation to the sun to warm himself up. The sun still had a lot of power despite it being evening, and the warmth helped his muscles get smooth more quickly. The more he concentrated on his flows, on the correct positioning of his limbs, the harmonization with his breathing, the fainter the thrum of pictures, colors, scents, and vibrations whirling through his consciousness became. After an hour of vigorous training he was dripping sweat, his mind in a rare state of peace and calm.

When he was exhausted enough to fall asleep as soon as he was showered, Andi went back into the house. He let the warm water relax his body further, drowning out the soft rustling that was trying to return to his mind with the hard beat of the shower. Sleep came swiftly, and Andi shoved all worries about the case and George from his mind.

CHAPTER 7
A NAME TO THE FACE

GEORGE WAS running a bit late because he had underestimated the morning crowd in the Starbucks. He really should have anticipated a rush, but for some reason he had thought it wouldn't be as slow going as in the early afternoon the other day. Some days his detective skills took a little time to wake up. Since Andi didn't drink coffee, he ordered herbal tea and a plain bagel for him and a black coffee and two chocolate chip muffins for himself. George was usually more careful with what he ate, being of the firm belief that his body was a temple he needed to treat reverently. The events of the previous day had him indulging, though. He was still gnawing on the fact that Andi seemed to have known there were two more victims, and even though he tried to tell himself countless times to give it a rest, to wait for more clues, he couldn't stop replaying the expressions on Andi's face—especially when George had confronted him about his "hunch." Something was indeed wrong with Andi; he could practically smell it. What it was, though, he couldn't imagine. The man didn't strike him as crooked. Unsociable and prickly like a hedgehog with a sore nose, definitely, but cops who were crooked needed to be amenable in some way. George just couldn't see Andi being approached by anybody for anything. Hell, the man made buying coffee an impossible task. So what was Andi hiding from him? And was it something bad? No matter what Chief Norris thought, if Chief Renard had not only tolerated but also protected Andi, it couldn't be a horrible secret. George hoped he would find out something soon. He didn't like scrutinizing his partner while working a huge case with the potential to make some big waves.

Laden with his gifts, George entered the precinct, finding Andi already at his desk. The man looked a bit better than the day before; the circles under his eyes were a little less pronounced, and his scowl was—for a very brief, precious moment—replaced by the ghost of a smile. It seemed he was making some leeway with his difficult partner.

"Good morning, Andi. I brought you tea and a plain bagel." He offered Andi the bag and the cup. His partner gave him a funny look but took the gift without mentioning that last time Andi had offered to pay. Perhaps he had forgotten, and George surely wouldn't remind him when they were finally getting a little closer to each other.

"Thank you. I appreciate it." That was politer than George could have hoped for. He sat down at his own desk, taking a sip from his coffee.

"Do we have any news from the lab yet?"

Andi attacked his keyboard. "The coroner's report isn't done yet, but we seem to have a hit on the victim from outside. We got a match with missing persons. Her name is Lilly Cordon, age sixteen. She's from Spartanburg and was assumed kidnapped on her way home from school almost a year ago. They never found a trace of her and had no leads on who could have been responsible. The pictures of the other two are still running through the system; so far no matches."

George put his muffin aside, went to the whiteboard, and put Lilly's name on top of the Jane Doe writing. "Is there a report about her disappearance?"

"I already pulled it from the system. It's not very telling, though. The precinct up there was swamped with a huge drug case when she vanished, and there weren't that many leads to begin with. They put it on cold cases after only a couple of months. I'm sure the fact that she's black and her parents are poor had nothing to do with it." Frustration laced Andi's voice, giving George another small glimpse into the mind of his partner. He obviously had a strong sense of justice, something else that spoke against him being crooked.

"Do you think it would help if we talked to the detective responsible for her case?"

Andi shrugged. "Depends. We'd have to make sure he doesn't feel cornered or accused, though I think it would be more informative if we talked to the parents. Since we have to inform them of their daughter's death, we could kill two birds with one stone, so to speak. Also, I don't want them to hear it from the officers who weren't able to find her."

George shuddered. Telling somebody a loved one had died was high on his list of things he hated to do. During his time in narcotics, it had happened only a few times, but he was always rattled afterward.

"Should we go today?"

Andi sighed. "It's a four-hour drive. Perhaps we'll have to stay overnight."

"I can drive. And I don't have a problem driving late at night either, should things really take longer than anticipated." George loved driving. It gave him a chance to let his mind wander.

Andi checked his watch. "It's quarter past eight. With some luck, we're there at noon. Should give us plenty of time to talk to the detective and the parents. Perhaps we can even have a look at where she was supposedly taken."

"Then we shouldn't waste any time. Can you call the detective from the car?"

Andi grabbed a pen and wrote a number down on a yellow Post-it. "Of course."

A familiar rush went through George when he grabbed his car keys, the bag with the muffins, and his coffee. The hunt was one of the things he really liked about his job.

As soon as they were in the car, Andi dialed the number from the Post-it. When he heard the ringtone, he realized Andi had put the call on speaker, which George found oddly polite, considering how rough their start had been.

"Detective Harris speaking."

"Detective Harris, this is Detective Donovan and Detective Hayes from the Charleston PD. We're calling concerning the case of Lilly Cordon. She went missing roughly a year ago, and I'm afraid we found her body yesterday. We're on our way to Spartanburg at the moment and wanted to ask if you had time to meet with us."

"That's unfortunate. To be honest, when I worked on the case, I was convinced she'd been murdered. Given the area she was from, it wouldn't have been a surprise."

From the corner of his eye, George saw Andi gritting his teeth. Detective Harris wasn't impolite, just indifferent as all fuck. His attitude rubbed George the wrong way as well.

"Well, she died only three days ago. We had a look at the report in the system, and since there weren't any leads, we thought we could talk to you. Perhaps there's something you remember that didn't make it into the reports?"

The silence at the other end of the line lasted a second too long. If it was because Detective Harris felt insulted or because Andi had hit a little too close to home was impossible to tell.

"I'm not sure if I understand you right, Detective Hayes, but every little detail I found about the case is in the report." Harris sounded stiff.

"And we don't doubt that, Detective. We know very well how difficult missing persons cases can be. But we also know that sometimes people remember something weeks or months later. We were hoping this was the case here." Andi was working his jaw muscles, trying his best to remain calm. George admired his restraint. He wasn't so sure he would have kept it together like that.

"Well, I can't keep you from coming, but I can assure you the report holds everything I know."

"Thank you, Detective Harris. I think we'll spare us all the trouble. And don't bother calling Lilly's parents. We're going to tell them in person." With that, Andi ended the call. "So much for not aggravating him." He sighed.

"It wasn't your fault, Andi. He's a prick with zero interest in the case or what happened to Lilly. He didn't even ask how she died. That tells us everything we need to know."

"I know. It still annoys me. Fucking idiot." Andi stared at his cup with the tea.

"See it like this. We save time by not talking to him, which frees us to talk to the parents in depth and to take a look at where she was taken."

Andi mumbled something unintelligible and took out his bagel. "Do you want your muffins?"

"Thank you." George took the first muffin and ate it with gusto. Andi reverted back into silence, but it wasn't as loaded as it had been the day before, or so George told himself.

CHAPTER 8
THE MEMORY OF BUGS

THEY ARRIVED in Spartanburg at exactly noon. After a short stop at a drive-thru, they made their way through the town to Church Street, where Lilly's parents lived in a dilapidated bungalow standing in a yard full of junk. It was a bit of a gamble to arrive there unannounced, but in this kind of area, they were fairly sure at least one of them would be at home. Plus, the only thing worse than telling somebody a loved one had been murdered face-to-face was doing so over the phone, and not just because one could miss vital clues from their reaction. Unemployment and poverty were high in this area, and it showed in the trash on the street, the graffiti on the walls, the houses in various stages of decay. The people who lived here were the forgotten ones, the ones who had lost the race, and sadly, most of them were black.

George parked his car as far up the driveway as possible, which was sensible. If they wanted to drive home in it, they needed to keep an eye on it. Andi reached for the door handle on the passenger side.

"Do you want to give them the news, or should I?"

George hesitated. "It's probably better if I tell them. At least my skin color should calm them somewhat. If they think I'm the one in charge, they're more likely to cooperate."

"You're right. I don't like it, but you're right. They don't know me, and all they're going to see is another white asshole like Detective Harris telling them their beloved girl is dead." He opened the door. "Let's go."

As it turned out, Michael and Chloe Cordon were both at home. He had just returned from his shift in a factory, and she was getting ready to start hers in a diner. The way Michael's face closed off the second George and Andi showed their badges made Andi's heart constrict. This small reaction told him everything that was wrong with their current system. George even had to ask if they could come in. Finally, after a long minute of absolute, laden silence, Michael stepped aside to let them inside the house.

The interior looked a bit better than what the outside suggested. Everything was clean, and the furniture looked worn but well-kept. Pictures of a girl from an infant on hung on the walls and stood in frames on the coffee table and a huge wooden dresser at the far end of the small living room. Lilly was still deeply loved. Andi's heart broke when he thought about the pain George and he would soon lay at their feet. Chloe sat down next to her husband with her eyes full of sadness, as if she already knew why they were there. She couldn't be older than forty yet looked almost a hundred when she reached for Michael's hand.

George cleared his throat. "Thank you, Mr. and Mrs. Cordon, for inviting us in. We're very sorry to tell you that we found your daughter Lilly yesterday. She was murdered in Charleston."

Chloe gasped and hid her head on Michael's shoulder. The husband just stared at nothing for a moment. He, too, was surely under forty. His broad hands and muscled body spoke of a life of hard labor. The expression in his eyes, though, made him look like a vulnerable little boy.

"How—I mean, how long had she been dead?" His voice was barely above a whisper, and Chloe started sobbing. He pulled her into his side, trying to give comfort when he so obviously had none for himself.

"She died about three days ago. I'm so sorry about your loss, Mr. and Mrs. Cordon. And if it weren't for the lives we could save, we would leave you to mourn in peace."

Chloe looked up. Her eyes were tearstained. "What do you mean?"

George glanced at Andi for a moment, silently asking how much he should reveal. Andi simply nodded imperceptibly, deciding to trust George's instinct on this. Also, it wouldn't look good if he started taking over the conversation at this point. Andi was pretty sure the only reason they were sitting in the Cordon's living room at the moment was because of George being African American. He hated the fact that the Cordons wouldn't trust him because of the bad experiences they'd had with other white cops. For the first time since George had been assigned to him, Andi was glad about having a partner. Had he worked alone, this would have been a lot more difficult. And not just because the Cordons wouldn't have talked to him. It took most of Andi's mental capacity to shield himself from the onslaught of images he was getting from the arthropods in the area. With many of the yards being unattended, not to mention all the empty or badly cleaned houses, the number of insects was higher than usual. He had already picked up on five bodies in the vicinity, three of them at least two years old, the other two still fresh, a feast for the scavenging insects. And he couldn't do anything about them. They were all buried, either in yards or in cellars, and he would have a hard time explaining how he knew about them in the first place. Five souls who would probably never see justice because people's minds were so limited. If he could be open about his *geschenk*, things would be so much better—or so he hoped. It was this fantasy of a different reality that kept him sane in situations like these.

"We can't reveal too much at this point of the investigation, but it seems Lilly's abduction wasn't random. We're doing everything in our power to get to the bottom of it all and to get everybody who had anything to do with it behind bars."

"Then you should probably start with that sleazy detective who couldn't be bothered to take our girl's disappearance seriously. That Harris guy." Michael Cordon was angry, and rightfully so.

George held up his hands in a placating gesture. "I can assure you, we're very much aware of Detective Harris's attitude. And because he's so incredibly unhelpful, we'd appreciate it very much if you could tell us everything you remember about the day Lilly vanished." George paused. "I know it's hard. If you need a moment…."

Michael shook his head. "No, it's fine. We can grieve later."

Chloe looked up from her husband's shoulder. "Are you sure it's Lilly? I mean, it's been a year…." An insane hope blossomed in her eyes.

George looked at Andi for help. With a sigh, Andi took out his phone and pulled up the picture of Lilly Cordon the coroner had sent him before she had started working on her. It was a ritual between them. Evangeline Melcort always sent him the pictures of the victims, and Andi kept them on his phone until their case was closed. Some of those pictures had been with him for some time now, because regardless of how good he was, there were cases even he couldn't crack. He turned his phone and showed the picture to the Cordons.

"I'm so sorry, Mr. and Mrs. Cordon."

As Chloe Cordon stared at the picture with huge eyes, the glimmer of hope that had sparked there for a moment winked out. She didn't say anything, just buried her face in her husband's shoulder again. Michael Cordon tensed, his whole stance becoming rigid, determined.

"What do you want to know?"

"Can you just walk us through the day of her disappearance? What happened and when? Did you notice anything strange before or after Lilly vanished?"

Michael Cordon pressed his lips into a thin line. "Lilly was such a wonderful girl. She was very good at school and working hard to get a scholarship for Oakbruck Preparatory School, a fancy private high school where her teachers wanted to send her because her grades were so good. She never hung out with the bad kids. In fact, she only had one close friend, Tricia, but she moved away about two months before Lilly was taken. Getting into Oakbruck was Lilly's big dream. She wanted to become a doctor, study at the Medical School of South Carolina. The day she vanished, both Chloe and I had double shifts, so we only came home at ten in the evening. When Lilly wasn't there, we first thought she might have gone to get some groceries, but she didn't answer her calls. When she wasn't home in the morning, we called the police. Detective Harris informed us that we could file a missing person report once she was gone twenty-four hours. Before that, he said his hands were tied. He wasn't even interested in what we told him, that she would never just leave or not answer her phone.

"So we started searching on our own. We walked the entire way she took to the bus stop, and then we even followed the route the bus takes every day. We didn't find anything until we went back in the direction of our house. About halfway between the bus stop and the house, I tried calling her again, more out of desperation than real hope. That's how we found her cell. We heard her ringtone and followed the sound into a small park with a few trees. It's so tiny, it doesn't even have a name. Junkies meet their dealers there." Michael Cordon scowled. "Her cell was battered, the casing chipped. I knew not to touch it and called Detective Harris. He took it with him for evidence but informed us later there weren't any fingerprints except for Lilly's own."

Andi shared a look with George. There had been no mention in the report about a cell phone.

"That's very good, Mr. Cordon. Now do you remember if Lilly said anything about being followed or feeling threatened by anybody?"

Michael Cordon shook his head. He had his wife cradled close to his side, as if to protect her or to draw strength from her, Andi didn't know which.

"No. Nothing like that. She was so busy studying, she spent most of her time either in the library of her school or here in her room."

George nodded. "Can you give us directions to where you found her cell?"

"That's easy. You turn right at our driveway and just follow the street until you see an old factory to your right. On the left, you'll find the park. It's not fenced in, just some trees with a few small trails leading through."

"Thank you, Mr. Cordon. My partner and I will take a look. And of course we will keep you informed about the progress of the case."

Michael Cordon stroked his wife's upper arm. "When do we get our baby girl back so we can bury her?" His voice broke at the end of the sentence.

Andi could see George struggling to keep up a professional front. "As soon as the coroner's done with her, I will see to it that she's transported to Spartanburg."

"Thank you, Detective Donovan. Detective Hayes. We need to be alone now."

It was a comparatively polite dismissal compared to the chilly welcome they had gotten.

"Do you want to walk?" George didn't sound happy about leaving his new car alone. Andi could relate.

"How about you drive there and I walk? It's not far, and we would get two different perspectives. We meet at the park and explore it together."

George's relief was a tangible presence in the air. "A great idea. See you there." He opened his car and entered the driver's seat. When the motor started, Andi walked toward the end of the driveway, already opening his senses in search for information that was over a year old. He still maintained enough control to be able to walk along the littered sidewalk, but the avalanche of impressions was overwhelming.

Blood and corpses and flesh and drugs and acid and death and decay, great feasts already transported to the nests or filled with eggs to nourish the brood.

It was all in abundance everywhere around him, almost all of it caused by human sins. Finding the clues that were relevant to their case was close to impossible. Insects had no clear concept of time, and most of them didn't even live long enough to span more than a few months.

When he wanted to know something about crimes that happened a long time ago, he needed to rely on social insects like wasps, ants, termites, and bees, with bees and termites being the most reliable sources while the "memories" of wasps and ants were a bit more sketchy and harder to interpret. Andi didn't know the reason for it and had no way of finding out why some things just were a certain way. There was always the "dead space," as Andi called it, indicating winter, where the life of social insects was almost completely halted, which helped a little in determining how much time had passed, but wasn't accurate enough to truly rely on. To make matters worse, he only knew what Lilly "looked like" dead in the minds of ants, flies, and worms. It was hard to tell if he would be able to recognize her living shape in the collective memory of the thousands of little witnesses who saw every crime.

The arthropods in this area were doing well for themselves. The decaying houses were homes to termites, ants, spiders, roaches, and countless other creepers who needed damp and dark spaces to flourish. They also provided precious intel, though not the kind Andi was looking for. There were at least a hundred offenders—dealers, bandits, pimps, murderers—running around this place. And catching them would be easy, should the authorities know about the *geschenk* and recognize it. But they didn't, and so the scum of society went unpunished to commit their crimes another day.

The way to the small park wasn't long, just like Michael Cordon had explained. It couldn't be called a forest, didn't even come close, was just a loose collection of surprisingly healthy trees—then again, given the vast amount of human tissue they were getting on a sickeningly regular basis, it was probably surprising they hadn't grown even more. George was already there; he had parked his car practically on the sidewalk, no doubt to be able to keep an eye on it.

"I haven't seen anything out of the ordinary." George made a vague gesture with his left hand.

"Me neither. It looks like every poor city area in the States. Let's see if we can find something under the trees." They both knew it was highly unlikely after over a year.

"I can definitely see why her kidnappers chose this part of the way, though. I mean, most of the houses are empty anyway, but the trees offer sight protection from this side. It's the most convenient spot for abducting somebody."

Andi listened to George's soothing voice. It became his anchor as he opened his senses even wider in the hopes of finding a glimpse of Lilly Cordon. Luckily for him, there was an ant's nest, as well as a nest of wild bees, close by. Ants and bees saw the world very differently, and combining the information coming from them gave Andi a picture close to 3D. Of course, there were blank spots with things neither ants nor bees either perceived or deemed interesting, and then there was the dead space of winter, which in this case was actually helpful, since Andi knew that there had only been one since Lilly had vanished. Like a blind man in a house full of cobwebs, Andi fumbled along the memories of both nests, carefully adding impressions from other insects where he could see them aligning until he found the day Lilly had been abducted. It had been sunny and warm, perfect weather for insects. Lilly's living shape only vaguely resembled that of her dead body; he mostly recognized her from a sweetness to her scent that was quite distinct and hadn't been diminished by the drugs and death. If pressed to explain where that scent originated from, Andi wouldn't have known. All he knew was that ants liked the scent of some people more than that of others, and Lilly seemed to have an especially alluring aroma, which fit with what he had gotten from the insects on her corpse. There had been two men whose general shape resembled the one of the murderer. They were likely somehow linked, if only through the drugs they were taking, which came from the same source.

Apparently, Lilly had fought the men. The ants remembered carrying some of that sweet blood into their nest, and the bees recalled a sharpness to the air Andi had learned to associate with physical resistance.

There wasn't much else related to the case. Andi started erecting his mental shields again. He had been exposed for longer than he had anticipated, and he felt like somebody had hit him on the head with a hammer. At least now he had confirmation of the place of abduction, even though he didn't know yet what to make of that knowledge. With a tired gesture, he wiped his face, wishing that for once his world could be completely quiet, if only for a few minutes. Shielding himself from the hum of the insects meant George's voice was quickly turning from an anchor to a nuisance, and it took all of Andi's remaining self-control to stay civil.

"Andi? Everything all right? You seemed out of it for a moment."

"I was just thinking. Trying to picture what could have happened. Too bad Detective Harris did such an abysmal job."

George furrowed his brows, no doubt picking up on some of the things Andi wasn't saying out loud. "You think he doctored the report?"

Andi raised a brow. "You don't?"

"Fine, I do. Should we talk to IA?"

Andi shook his head. "Too soon. All we have is the word of grieving parents against a member of the force. If he's not a complete moron, which I doubt, he destroyed the cell the first moment he was alone. We could ask our IT guys to try and find traces of Lilly online, which will perhaps give us clues about who could have possibly taken her, though I doubt it. This whole scenario reeks of organized crime, and I don't think they used a decoy to lure her in, especially if she was more of a loner, like her parents said. No, these people just take whoever they want, and I hate to say it, but in an area like this, it was their bad luck that her parents realized it so soon and even went to the police."

George huffed with a pained expression. "I know. Still, letting Harris off the hook feels wrong. He's dirty; I can feel it in my gut."

"We won't let him off the hook. We're just giving him some room. Perhaps he'll make a mistake and we can catch him even sooner. But our main focus has to be Lilly and the other two girls. If we manage to get one of the big bosses, perhaps even the mastermind, then we can unravel the entire net."

"So no surprise visit at Harris's precinct?"

"No." Andi glanced at his watch. "It's past five. I thought we might be faster sweeping the place of Lilly's abduction, but I prefer being thorough over doing a hasty job, even though we didn't find anything revealing. If we start driving now, we can be back at our precinct at nine."

George seemed to hesitate for a moment. His mouth opened as if he wanted to say something, then closed again. Finally he said: "Let's get something to eat for the drive. You look like you could use it."

Against better knowledge, Andi felt a tingle of warmth in his stomach. His partner was looking out for him. That was new and unfamiliar and kind of nice.

"Yeah, I do feel a bit famished."

CHAPTER 9
GAINING PERSPECTIVE

GEORGE THREW a discreet glance in Andi's direction when he had to stop at a red light. His partner looked exhausted; the dark rings under his eyes had become so deep within the last hour that George was seriously worried about Andi's health. Their little trip to Spartanburg had been more successful than George had hoped. Aside from the fact that something fishy was going on with Detective Harris, as the vanished cell phone proved, Andi seemed pretty sure Lilly had indeed been taken close to that park, and he appeared to be convinced that her kidnappers and her murderer were somehow linked, even though he had downplayed the conclusions he had drawn from the abduction site. George's own gut instinct was leading him in a similar direction, though he wasn't as sure as his partner.

Against his will, George was impressed by Andi's confidence. It also made him wary. As far as he could tell, Andi had just stood next to one of the trees, staring into nothing for over ten minutes. After that, he seemed to have adopted their trafficking theory as a hard fact.

George had to admit every sliver of evidence they had found—and to be honest, there wasn't much of it—so far pointed in that direction, but he didn't like dismissing all other possibilities simply because of his partner's lively imagination. If he was completely honest with himself, dismissing what he *wanted* the evidence to show, then they didn't have enough to really formulate a theory just yet. Though on the other hand that was what detectives did—playing with what-ifs until some of it solidified into a concrete lead. To not repeat the mistake of not paying close enough attention like George was convinced he had done at the murder scene, he had been extra vigilant in the park. The countless needles strewn everywhere had told him he was definitely at a crime scene, but nothing he had found had even remotely hinted at it also being a kidnapping site. Andi, on the other hand, seemed to be absolutely sure. It mystified and unnerved George, as well as the fact that Andi was looking worse with every passing minute. He had stopped giving answers to even the simplest questions about an hour ago. His eyes were closed most of the time, yet George was sure he wasn't sleeping. It weirded him out, and he seriously considered driving straight to the next hospital. The only thing keeping him from doing exactly that was the fact that they were already at the outskirts of Charleston. Another thirty minutes and they would be at the precinct. Perhaps Rose would be there to shed some light on Andi's condition. His partner didn't seem worried, though that could also be because he was completely out of it.

George breathed a sigh of relief when he finally pulled into the parking lot of the precinct. "We're here," he informed Andi, who grunted something in response. It was almost painful to watch how slowly Andi was straightening in the passenger seat, before he turned the handle on the door.

"See you tomorrow. Thank you for driving."

"Are you sure I shouldn't drive you home? You could be coming down with something."

"I'm fine." Andi sounded as if he wasn't sure whether he should be annoyed by George's care or happy about it. "I just need some rest. And I feel better having my car at home. Nice of you to offer, though." With that, Andi left the car. George followed his slim figure with his gaze until Andi reached his own car. When he was behind the steering wheel, George put the Escalade into reverse and left the parking lot.

At home, he ordered pizza and took an extra-long shower to wash off the grime of the day. His thoughts were constantly circling around Andi and their case, spinning faster and faster until George decided he either needed to go on a long run—which was probably not advisable at midnight—or to talk to somebody who could put things into perspective.

He dialed Daniel's number. His brother was with the MP as a staff sergeant and currently on vacation, otherwise George would have never dared to call him at such a late hour. Daniel picked up after only three rings, indicating he had still been awake, which spared George the guilt of waking him up.

"Hello, little brother. What can I do for you at this late hour?" Daniel sounded as cheerful as always. Unlike their older brother, Griffin, who would have used the sentence as a general dig against not only the late hour but also by implication on George's general habits, Daniel just meant it as a friendly greeting.

"Hi, Daniel. I could use somebody to talk to. If you're not busy."

The snort coming through the phone made George pull it away from his ear. "George, you know as well as I do that if I were busy, I wouldn't be answering my phone at this late hour. You actually just made my evening a lot more interesting, or so I hope."

For a moment, George closed his eyes, contemplating the wisdom of calling Daniel, of all people. Sadly, his brother was the only one he *could* call about a situation as complicated as this one.

"Your hopes will be fulfilled. Though you have to promise me not to tell anybody about it. It's not exactly classified information, but…."

"I get it. Trust your big brother, George. Have I ever let you down?"

"Do you want me to answer that?"

Daniel's laughter caused George to remove the cell from his ear once again. "Point taken. Now spill. What has your panties in a knot?"

"You know I just started as a homicide detective in Charleston."

"What? Already? I thought it was still a few weeks…. Man, I got my dates mixed up again. Sorry."

"No problem. I don't keep track of where you're stationed either. Anyway, I had an appointment with the chief three days ago, and she told me my intended partner had to leave for a family emergency and that she would pair me up with another detective who usually works alone."

"Ooh. Let me guess, he's a grumpy old idiot who's mean to you. Shall I come and kick his ass?"

"No!" George hurried to derail his brother from this train of thought because he knew he was only half joking. "Andi is about my age. Though he *is* grumpy. Anyway, Chief Norris told me she wants me to keep an eye on him and his methods, unofficially, of course. If I do so, she'll help me with the next step in my career."

"And you agreed, didn't you?" Daniel sounded a bit disappointed, which hit George harder than he had expected. His older brother's approval was important to him.

"Of course I did. It sounded like a no-brainer. This guy's crime-solving statistics are what freshmen see in their wet dreams after their first classes on criminology! They're so good, it's almost unreal. The chief is just wary of him because she doesn't know how he's doing it.

I thought I'd watch him a bit, realize he's just that good, and have her indebted to me."

"And then something happened."

"What makes you think so?"

"Because *A*, you wouldn't be calling otherwise, and *B*, it's enough to freak you out, as I can hear in the tone of your voice." Daniel sounded almost bored. "Oh, and *C*, I *know* you, George."

George huffed for a moment. "Fine. Something has happened. I mean, I didn't expect him to be super happy about our partnership, considering he's apparently always worked alone, but he took it better than I feared. Then we were called to this body. The crime scene was outside a storage unit, and everything looked like either a drug deal gone south or some kind of spat between lovers or hooker and john. I was already running possible scenarios through my head when Andi gets this absent expression and declares we have to take a look inside the storage unit. He was real insistent too. So we go in there, me and the officer who reported the body both thinking Andi is slightly bonkers, and what do we find? Two more bodies in one of the units. I mean, how did he know that? And he definitely *knew*. No guessing on his part as far as I could see. I would have never suspected anything like that. I mean, I would have surely come back at some point to take a look around, but nothing indicated that anybody had been inside the building."

"Did you ask him?"

"Of course I did. He clammed up faster than I could say the word 'hunch.' Claimed he'd had a 'feeling.'"

"Well, his feeling was right. Or is there any possibility he could have known about the bodies beforehand? Even killed them himself?"

"If he did know about the first one, he should get an Oscar for his acting skills. He was surprised and annoyed about the call, and when he saw the first body, there was absolutely no indication of recognition. Nobody is that good."

"His hunch paid off. You know some people are gifted in that department. Their instincts are way better than their ordinary senses. When he's truly in tune with them, I don't see why he couldn't have had a hunch like that."

George wiped his face with his left hand. "That's not all. One of the leads brought us to Spartanburg today. We inspected a possible crime site, and it was practically the same, sans the bodies. He stared into nothing for some time and then declared our most likely scenario to be valid. And he's so convinced I'm tempted to go with it."

"So do it. Aside from the fact that it's absolutely wrong to spy on your brand-new partner without probable cause, you might learn a thing or two from him. If he really is gifted, you can become a better detective just by watching him work. Don't get me wrong, you're good at what you're doing, but you're also very much the son of our mother, just like Griffin and me. We tend to cling to the facts, leaving no room for—other options."

Daniel was right. They had inherited their mother's rigid belief in facts. Feelings and hunches were for dreamers and underachievers. The Donovans followed cold hard facts, no matter the cost. Aside from the lack of the aforementioned facts, George had another problem as well. "And if there's indeed something wrong with him?" Even though he'd only known Andi for three days, George didn't *want* anything to be wrong, no matter how irrational that feeling was.

"Then you learn something else from him and you get that favor from your chief. Win-win." Daniel was being pragmatic now for his sake.

"I guess you're right. It just feels wrong, spying on him, I mean. And I think he has some kind of condition. He looked like shit when we drove home today, as if the whole trip had exhausted him, but he's fit. No body fat as far as I can tell."

Daniel made a hooting sound. "And you know that because—"

"Because I've got eyes, dummy. He's my partner. Temporary partner, but my partner."

"You're such a stickler for rules. Boring." Daniel laughed. "The way I see it, you need to man up and start trying to be a real partner. Forget about the temporary thing. Forget about spying on him. Try to get closer, to learn how he ticks. He's probably just freakishly good at combining small clues to form a bigger picture. You know, kind of like a hawk who does all that incredibly complicated math in his head when chasing a dove, without even noticing it."

Comparing Andi to a hawk was not something George would have ever contemplated. A rabid raccoon perhaps, or an old growly badger on its evening round. That was more like it, though he didn't know how good a badger's dove-hunting mathematical skills were. Probably nonexistent. What did badgers eat anyway?

Even though the discussion with Daniel had been kind of anticlimactic, George did feel better. Daniel was right. He had to forget about all the baggage that came with this partnership and concentrate on the important stuff—finding the killer of the three girls.

"Thank you, Danny This really helped."

"It was my pleasure, little bro. You know you can always call me."

"Yeah, I do. Good night."

"Night."

George ended the call. He stared at his cell for a few minutes before he went to the bathroom to get ready for the night.

THE NEXT morning, he got up half an hour earlier than the day before to avoid the rush at the Starbucks. After he had gotten Andi's tea and bagel, as well as some coffee for himself (no muffins this time, he had to stop slouching off), he drove to the precinct. When George approached their desks, he spied Andi, who looked almost worse than the day before, as if he hadn't slept a wink.

"You look like shit," George said in greeting before he could contemplate the wisdom of being so blatant with his very recent partner. Andi lifted his head, brows furrowed. His mouth opened, no doubt to give a harsh answer, but George beat him to it. "Here, your tea and a bagel."

Andi's mouth closed. He still looked kind of annoyed, which didn't stop him from taking George's offerings. It seemed the grumpy god could be placated with food. He had to remember that. Hadn't Rose said something about winning horses over with treats? If this was the way to Andi's heart, George would walk it without hesitation.

"The coroner called. We can come down now," Andi announced after chewing and swallowing a piece of his bagel. "And the report from forensics has come in. I haven't looked at it yet. What do you want to do first?"

George didn't have to think. "The report can wait. It's rude to keep a lady waiting." Truth be told, he'd only met Evangeline Melcort briefly when she had bagged the three bodies two days ago, so he didn't actually know how ladylike she was. To be fair, she looked more like a professional shot putter than a coroner, with long wavy black hair and tribal tattoos on her face that told of her Samoan heritage. Evangeline was a stunning, if intimidating, woman.

Andi got up. "Let's go."

They went downstairs into the basement. George wondered briefly why so many pathology departments were underground. Almost as if people wanted the dead to feel at home already. Theoretically he knew it was mainly for practical reasons, such as accessibility and climate control, but his overactive imagination had no problems coming up with totally different explanations. George wasn't too proud to admit that the pathology department weirded him out. If Andi had similar problems, he didn't show it. His stride was determined, even though at closer inspection he looked even worse than George had initially assumed. The need to take care of his obviously stressed partner rode George hard, especially after the talk with his brother Daniel, and it was only the knowledge that Andi wouldn't appreciate his concerns that kept him from reaching out and touching him.

They arrived at the heavy metal door leading into pathology itself. It swung open as if they had been expected. Evangeline invited them in with a grim smile on her full lips. She, too, looked as if she had missed more than a night's sleep.

"Come in. I have news for you, none of it good," she said instead of a formal greeting.

Andi followed her with furrowed brows. "How bad is it?"

George strode in after the two with the distinct impression they'd had this exact conversation too many times before.

"Bad enough to have me reconsidering how much I value my integrity." Evangeline sounded grim. "Mind you, I've only done Lilly Cordon so far, because she was the one we could ID. The other two are next on my list, and I just wish I was already done."

She entered the room where the bodies were kept and stopped in front of a metal drawer that was pulled out all the way. A blindingly white sheet obscured the body underneath, and George felt even more like an intruder in this cold, sterile world where the dead had to give up the last of their secrets. Evangeline took the sheet off Lilly's body with a quick, practiced movement, and George had to remind himself there was nothing left of Lilly in this sack of rotting meat and bones, or otherwise the incision in her skin, the ugly black stitches, and the bruises all over her body would have made him puke.

"Before we start, let me just say, if you manage to get your hands on the sons of bitches who are responsible, I wouldn't mind having a private chat with them. Here, in the morgue, after hours, when nobody can hear their screams."

Andi lifted his hands in a placating gesture. "You know me, Evangeline. If there's a chance to make it happen, I'd do it for you."

The ghost of a smile crossed Evangeline's lips. "You're always such a charmer, Andi. The perfect gentleman."

George did a double-take. Andi a charmer? A gentleman? Granted, he wasn't as grumpy with Evangeline as with everybody else, though he had assumed it was professional courtesy. Pissing off such a vital well of information as the coroner was one of the single most stupid things a detective could do. And yet these two seemed to share a connection George still hoped to establish with Andi sometime soon. Because he didn't want to disrupt whatever flow was going on between them, George kept his mouth shut and tried to appear alert.

"As you can see, she was beaten brutally, and not just once. I found trauma easily a year old, which also fits the time of her abduction. At one point, three of her ribs were broken. She must have been one hell of a fighter. Tough girl." Evangeline gestured to various bruises on Lilly's body, an almost proud smile on her face. "I hope you got some of them real good." She cleared her throat. "Cause of death, as you probably already assumed, was a couple of hits to the head with a blunt object, namely the crowbar you found with the other two victims. The first hit came from behind and at an odd angle, which suggests her pursuer aimed for her while running. It didn't stop her, though. She kept on running, or rather stumbling. The second blow killed her. It came from the side, and it's obvious the murderer went for the temple. It was still sloppy. He didn't hit where a professional would have to end her quickly, which could mean the man was either in a panic or is an amateur or both."

She held up her hand when Andi opened his mouth. "Before you ask, yes, I'm almost a hundred percent sure the murderer is male. He was definitely taller than her five six by at least seven to eight inches, and while there are women that big—" She gestured at her own stature of easily six three. "—the strength and brutality of the blows suggest a male attacker."

Andi stared at Lilly's body, his brows drawn together in concentration. "There's more?"

It was as much a question as it was a statement. Evangeline's face contorted into an angry mask. "Yes. I found traces of sexual activity and proof of rape. Multiple times." She hesitated, and the rage in her dark eyes burned holes in George's mind. "If you can't get me some time alone with them, perhaps you could shoot off their balls? Totally accidentally, of course."

"Of course." Andi did something George would have never thought possible. He briefly touched Evangeline's hand, as if he wanted to soothe her. It was a surprising gesture from a man who appeared so closed off most of the time. "We'll do what we can. I promise."

"I know. Just get them. I've already sent the blood tests up. She had traces of cocaine and benzodiazepines in her blood. And you can bet your ass she didn't take those voluntarily."

"Thank you, Evangeline. Call us when you find something on the other two victims."

"Will do."

Apparently this was their cue to leave. George followed Andi to the door. When he cast a last glance back, he saw Evangeline dragging the sheet back over Lilly's body with a soft, sad smile on her face. Her lips were moving, but George couldn't understand what she was saying.

"She's either telling her what a brave girl she'd been or saying some prayers to help her passage into the next world." As if he had read his thoughts, Andi offered this explanation while holding the door for him.

"That's—nice of her, I guess. Most coroners I've met were a lot more jaded."

"Not Evangeline, no. She has kept her compassion." The admiration in Andi's voice told George how much his partner respected Evangeline. It was good to know, because so far, he'd gotten the impression Andi didn't have a high opinion of most people.

"So next is the report?"

"You got it." Andi sounded a bit frustrated. "Let's hope there's something interesting in it."

They went back to their desks and pulled up the report on their PCs. George's was apparently a bit slower than Andi's, because before he could open the file, Andi let out an aggressive "Yes!"

George looked around his screen to his partner. "I gather there's something good?"

"You can bet your ass on it. They got a partial fingerprint and were able to link it to one Ronald Wallace. He's twenty-five, a small-time dealer for all kinds of drugs, though mainly cocaine, as well as a pimp. Charming young man, I have to say."

"Aren't they always?" George came over to look at Andi's screen. The man in the mug shot had a haunted expression in his big, expressive eyes. Had he not been the suspect in a triple murder, George might have even called him attractive. Knowing what he had been convicted for and what he was suspected of having done erased all notions of acknowledgment George might have had. All he could see now were the blackness of his soul and the ugly stain of his deeds. "He lives in Sangaree, Marion Road."

"One of the less desirable parts in this city." Andi got up. "Let's see if Mr. Wallace is home."

With the heat of the hunt awakening in his veins, George grabbed his keys.

CHAPTER 10
THE BUGS DON'T ERR

ANDI STARED at the old house. In his line of work, he was used to seeing the darker sides of not only people but also the city, but this case was quickly becoming one of the most gruesome he'd ever had. The ants living in the house, as well as the mosquitoes in the garden, had already confirmed Ronald Wallace was indeed their murderer.

Blood tainted by drugs, the taste despicable but unique like a fingerprint, giving the only blob from the storage unit to walk away that night a distinct shape made of scent and color and the feel of his blood, all twirled into something no human eye—or brain, for that matter— would ever recognize as human, but then again, being human was a point of perception, nothing else, really, just matter taking on a certain shape for different kinds of senses. Sometimes Andi wondered if his dislike for humanity stemmed—at least in part—from the way he was able to see his fellow crowns of creation.

Deep down in his gut, Andi also knew that this case didn't end with Ronald Wallace. He would be convicted for killing the girls, thus giving their families and friends some kind of closure—should they ever be able to identify the two Jane Does—but this was only the beginning. Ronald Wallace was not the kind of man who could drive into another city, abduct a girl in broad daylight, and have the very white police cover his tracks. Somebody else was pulling the strings, and Andi was determined to get the bastard.

"Shall we?" He looked at George, who seemed to be having some grim thoughts of his own.

"You know this isn't over should he be our murderer, don't you?"

Andi almost smiled. Chief Norris might have forced George on him, and the man's presence might be a nuisance most of the time, but he was a good cop, a good man. If he had to endure a partner, George Donovan was one of the better choices.

"I know. This is bigger than Ronald Wallace. I hope he's going to be the thread that helps us unravel the entire fabric."

"Such a way with words. You think he's going to cooperate?" An evil gleam appeared in George's eyes, one Andi was sure he was mirroring.

"He won't have a choice."

They left the car and walked up the narrow path to the front porch. A car without wheels stood in the thigh-high grass to their right, a palace for woodlice, mosquitoes, and countless beetles. Andi had to concentrate to keep the images all the arthropods were pushing on him out of his mind.

The scratching of hundreds of tiny chitinous legs on rusting steel, mandibles chewing through fresh green, the soft plop of tiny eggs being opened from the inside as larvae entered this world that was, in truth, theirs, miniscule kings and queens of an environment shaped by the blobs but ruled by them.

He shook his head. Their murderer was here; nothing else was of interest at the moment.

And apparently their murderer was trying to make a run for it. Andi caught the distinct vibration signature termites used to "see" their surroundings. The ones living under the back porch of the house were sensing heavy pounding approaching them. Andi didn't take the time to think; he simply darted around the house, drawing his gun while jumping over old tires and what looked suspiciously like a bathtub.

"Andi! What are you doing?" George's voice followed him around the house.

"He's trying to escape through the back door!"

"Fuck!"

Andi heard—and sensed—George bolting after him, the steady thumping of his footsteps strangely reassuring after Andi had worked so long without a partner. Ronald Wallace was already on the lawn, scrambling to get to the half-rotten fence dividing this property from the neighbor. Andi put on some more speed, felt his legs working overtime, his heart pumping his blood through his veins. When he gave chase, all his protective barriers went down because of the adrenaline flooding his system. So he had the dubious joy of seeing himself through the insects around him, a highly attractive bag of blood to some, a nuisance to others. He also saw Ronald and George, the former a less desirable source of nourishment than Andi himself, the latter a prize to be taken. If he weren't chasing after a killer, he might have found it amusing.

Ronald had almost reached the fence, and Andi tensed his muscles, bent his knees, and jumped forward. He crashed into Ronald's back, taking him down like the worthless piece of shit he was.

"Ronald Wallace, you're under arrest. You have the right to remain silent. Anything you say can and will be used against you in a court of law. You have the right to an attorney. If you can't afford an attorney, one will be provided for you." While reading Ronald his Miranda rights, Andi pulled out his handcuffs. George was there, his gun pointed at Ronald's head.

"Hey, man, what the fuck? I didn't do nothing!"

"Yeah, and Santa Claus is just an evil vampire," George huffed. Andi looked up at him, raising a brow in question.

"Just a story I've read. More plausible than I care to admit."

"You have to lend me that book. Sounds interesting."

George looked a little flustered. "I'm not sure I still have it. It was on my kindle."

"Stop talking about fucking books! You come to my home without a warrant and throw me down in my own backyard! What right do you have?" Ronald sounded so righteously indignant Andi had to suppress a chuckle. George didn't feel so generous and started laughing.

"We are the police, Einstein. When we find evidence of wrongdoing, we have the right to question the suspect, even if it's an upstanding citizen like yourself." Andi found he liked George's sarcasm. It was like a breath of fresh air around this foul-smelling excuse of a human being. He straightened and pulled Ronald to his feet.

"We're going to have a nice long chat at the precinct. Now move it."

They walked Ronald back to George's car, put him in the back seat with the security net up, and drove back to hopefully get some answers.

INTERROGATION ROOM number three was the smallest, and even though the air ventilation worked overtime, the sour stink of Ronald Wallace had already permeated the entire room. Andi felt slightly sick every time he had to draw a breath. Talking was even worse because of the revolting taste it left on his tongue. In addition to obviously not being a great fan of things like soap, water, and a toothbrush, Ronald was also sweating bullets. He had been nervous from the beginning, which had become worse when George had shot down his attempts at playing the black membership card with a few choice words, and then escalated when they had shown him pictures of the three girls and the crowbar. The man was guilty as sin and dumb as a field of lard. Unfortunately, the two brain cells he had to rub together had made him lawyer up immediately. Now they were sitting here waiting for the lawyer, and Andi seriously contemplated the wisdom of staying in the room with Ronald as part of their intimidation tactic. They should have left him to simmer in his own stinking sweat, but now it was too late to change tactics.

A beeping sound from the speaker in the left corner told Andi Ronald's attorney had arrived. Together with George he left the room, taking a deep breath as soon as the door had closed behind them. It said a lot that even the stale air in the first floor seemed sweet in comparison to the interrogation room. Andi relaxed even more when he saw who had come to counsel Ronald. Lewis Brackenport was a whip-thin man in his early fifties who had worked with Andi several times. Lewis knew the people Andi brought in were always guilty.

"What do we have today, Andi?" Lewis looked resigned. Working as a defense attorney was taking its toll on the man, and Andi secretly wondered how much longer Lewis would keep on doing the ungrateful work of public defender, though these were thoughts for another day. Now they had a murderer to crack.

"Lewis, this is my partner, George Donovan. George, this is Lewis Brackenport, a public defender with whom I've worked before."

George and Lewis shook hands, and Andi went on. "Ronald Wallace's fingerprints were found on the murder weapon for a girl named Lilly Cordon. We have two more bodies we found close to her, and once Evangeline is done examining them, I'm convinced she'll confirm he killed these two as well. Especially since the murder weapon for the first girl was found with the other two."

Lewis furrowed his brows. "What do you need from him?"

"What makes you think I need something from him?" Andi grinned, signaling Lewis how dead on he was.

"Because you have that gleam in your eyes. I've worked with you often enough to know how you look when you're done with a case and how you do when there's more."

"If I've become that transparent, I guess I need to switch attorneys."

Lewis snorted. "You can't, thanks to our beautiful system, and you don't want to, because deep down in that cranky heart of yours, you love me."

"Idiot." Andi only muttered because Lewis was right. Aside from Evangeline and perhaps Rose, Lewis was somebody he could tolerate, mostly because he didn't see him that often and respected his moral integrity and work ethic.

"What do you want me to tell him? Are you willing to offer him a deal in exchange for information?"

Andi scowled. He hated making deals with murderers, but they needed information. According to what the insects had picked up at the storage unit, there had only been Ronald and the girls. They had nothing to work with. Sacrificing his deep-rooted sense of justice for the greater good of hopefully cracking a human trafficking ring was a small price to pay.

"Tell him we can see to it that the death penalty is off the table. Nothing else."

Lewis nodded. "I'm going to convince him that's the best he's going to get. Give me ten."

Andi went to open the door for Lewis. "Take a deep breath before you go in there and try to ration the oxygen you get. It's not pretty in there."

"Thanks for the warning, Detective."

CHAPTER 11
A NEW LEAD

GEORGE STOOD next to Andi as they watched Lewis talking to Ronald Wallace through the one-way mirror. The public defender had surprised George. He seemed to be on good terms with Andi, which made him automatically interesting for George. Apparently the two had already worked together, and the ease with which Lewis had accepted the evidence presented by Andi told him the attorney trusted Andi's work. It could of course always be that he was simply lazy, though George doubted it. The man practically screamed integrity, which made him the second person in a position of authority who trusted Andi's judgment. Third if he wanted to count Evangeline. She may not be one of the decision-makers in the precinct, but the position of coroner asked for a level head. George had a growing feeling Chief Norris might be barking up the wrong tree with Andi. His musings were interrupted by Lewis, who very pointedly stared at the mirror.

Andi turned toward the door. "It's on."

They entered the interrogation room, the air in it even thicker than it had been before. George made a mental note to complain about the lack of ventilation and to never use that room again. He sat down next to Andi, facing Ronald Wallace and Lewis Brackenport. Lewis was all business now, his face the serious and impenetrable mask George knew from his mother and oldest brother. It was the kind of face that had made him confess his sins as a child faster than he'd been able to commit them.

"Mr. Wallace here has, after carefully weighing his options, decided to cooperate with the police regarding this case. He's going to answer all questions to the full extent of his knowledge."

The empty gaze entering Ronald's eyes upon these words made George's heart sink. They were off to a wonderful start. Andi cleared his throat.

"Mr. Wallace, you admit to being at the storage unit with Lilly Cordon and the other two girls?"

Ronald fidgeted, glanced at Lewis, who nodded, then back to Andi. "Yeah. They were supposed to go to Columbia."

"I assume not voluntarily?" There was a hint of steel in Andi's voice, and George tensed inwardly, keeping a close eye on his partner. They needed answers, and they wouldn't get them if Andi punched the man.

Ronald seemed to sense the danger he was in, because he answered the question quickly and even provided some information on his own.

"No, not voluntarily. I don't know who they belonged to. I was just hired to watch over them at the storage unit. It was supposed to be an easy job, quick money."

Andi's knuckles went white when he grabbed the edge of his chair. George shifted his weight, signaling to his partner he was there for him.

"What went wrong?"

Ronald shrugged. "One of them tried to run. Was damn fast too. She made it outside, and all I had was that crowbar. Conked her hard. I didn't mean to kill her, but she wouldn't stop running and... I had to hit her again and then she was dead, and I panicked a bit. I went back to the other two, and they went hysterical when they saw the blood on the crowbar. I slapped one and started choking the other, trying to make her shut up, but I guess I was a bit out of it. And suddenly they were dead too. I wiped the crowbar down and left it with them. I figured if nobody found the murder weapon, I'd be safe. Then I closed the storage unit and left."

George furrowed his brows. It sounded plausible, not a murder done in cold blood, rather one out of panic, which was corroborated by their evidence.

"What did your contact say? I mean, you fucked up the job and all."

"I called him. He said it wasn't so bad since they weren't top notch merchandise anymore. Already getting too old, he said."

George had a hard time keeping the disgust for this human vermin from showing on his face. Given how Andi's molars were visibly grinding together, he was experiencing similar problems. Sucking in a quick lungful of air, Andi went on.

"He wasn't angry at all?"

"Well, he wasn't happy with me, but this was the first time I fucked up, so I guess he let it slide."

"The first time?" The hint of steel was back in Andi's voice. "How often have you 'looked after' girls like these?"

Ronald hesitated, and George was sure he would stop talking now, realizing how deep of trouble he had found himself in. When he opened his mouth again, George was afraid what would come out of it.

"Maybe every two months since summer last year? I don't know. I was approached by this Vance guy, at a party where I had two of my girls working. He said I was the perfect guy for the job and the pay was great."

"This Vance, does he have a surname?" Andi sounded as if he was holding on to the last shreds of self-control.

Ronald just shrugged. "That's his surname. His first name's Taylor."

"Do you know where he lives?"

"No. Never asked. We weren't friends. Just work partners. No weekend barbecues with him." The way Ronald was talking about shuttling young girls across the state as work, as if forcing them against their will was no different from changing the tires on a car, made George seriously regret their offer of taking the death penalty off the table. Not that they actually had the power to do so, something Ronald didn't seem to know, since this was something the DA had to decide. But both Andi and Lewis had seemed sure the DA would agree to the offer, which meant they had a good working relationship with him or her as well. Another hint that Andi's work was solid and Chief Norris was off the mark. George returned his focus to their perp, hardly able to contain his disgust. The worst thing was that if he confronted Ronald about his attitude, the asshole wouldn't even understand why George had a problem. It was sick. Andi seemed to have come to a similar conclusion, because George could hear the disdain clearly in his tone.

"Do you know anybody except this Taylor Vance, or was he your only contact when it came to the human trafficking?"

"I only ever worked with him. He called a few days in advance whenever he needed me. I'd drive to the storage unit, meet him there, take on the cargo, keep them in the unit for a few hours until they were picked up, then go home. Three days later, my money always arrived in an envelope, usually delivered by some young boy. All done."

Andi nodded. "Thank you for your cooperation, Mr. Wallace. If we have further questions, we'll drop by. Mr. Brackenport, a word?"

Lewis got up from his seat next to Ronald, unable to hide a relieved expression. "Of course, Detective Hayes. After you."

They exited the interrogation room, finally able to breathe freely again. Andi turned to Lewis and shook his hand. "Thank you, Lewis. It was a pleasure to work with you, as always."

Lewis grinned. "The pleasure's all mine, Andi. I just hope you find the big players in this one. Because as much as it galls me, while putting Ronald Wallace behind bars will make the streets a bit safer, especially for young girls, he's obviously not the mastermind here. Whatever is going on has already become a routine operation, and he's the most insignificant pawn in this."

"Don't worry, Lewis, we will find the king." Andi had a determined glint in his eyes. "Whoever it is, they won't be getting away with it."

Lewis dipped his head in acknowledgment. "And I'm going to talk to the DA, explaining to Bill Waters why he has to refrain from asking for the death penalty for Ronald Wallace."

Andi's hand came up in a lazy but serious salute. "Thank you, Lewis. You're the best."

Lewis sighed. "I know. And thanks to you I'm getting quite good at golfing." He turned to George. "Bye, Detective Donovan. It was a pleasure working with you."

"Goodbye, Mr. Brackenport. It was nice meeting you."

With a wave, Lewis went for the elevator, picking up his phone even before he reached the doors. George waited until Lewis was on his way down. "What was that about golfing?"

Andi huffed. "Our DA, Bill Waters, he's a golf fanatic. Spends more time there than in the courtroom. If you want something from him, it's best to approach him on the course, because he's a grumpy old bastard when he has to work but approachable when he's got a club in his hands. Lewis and I, we've done this before. With Bill Waters, it's easier to apologize than to explain, especially when part of the apology is telling him about a success. He's not going to be over the moon that he can't ask for the death penalty here, but he's smart enough to appreciate the chance of getting even bigger fish to fry. Speaking of which, what do you think about our case?"

For some reason George felt almost giddy about being asked his opinion. So far, Andi had worked the case almost as if George hadn't been there, finding all the clues and doing his silent lone wolf thing. Why

Andi suddenly decided to open up, at least in relation to the case, was a mystery George didn't want to find the answers to. They were acting like real partners, which was all that mattered.

"I think Lewis is right. Ronald hardly has the brains to run a large-scale operation. And I think we—and he—were lucky to get to him before the people from that organization. Even if the girls weren't 'top notch' anymore, not losing them should have been about principle. Now the question is how big is that organization, have they crossed state borders yet, and how do we get the guys at the top? If Taylor Vance turns out to be a dead end, we're stuck, I'm afraid."

"You're right. Let's just hope we can find him—if he really exists and Ronald wasn't lying to us. Though I doubt it. He didn't strike me as somebody who's very good at getting creative, and Lewis has surely told him that lying would put the death penalty back on the table immediately. Now if Taylor Vance has been doing this for some time, there's a chance we have him in the system. If not, there are other options. I have some reliable—informants."

The way Andi said informants had George wonder if this was Andi's secret—somebody who had an in with the criminal underbelly of Charleston and helped Andi for whatever reason.

"Sounds good." George glanced at his watch. Arresting and then questioning Ronald Wallace had taken most of the day. "It's already five thirty. How about I run Vance's name through the database? If I find anything, we can go there first thing tomorrow."

Andi tilted his head. "Yeah, let's do that. I wanted to check with Evangeline, see if she has come up with anything else." He turned in the direction of the staircase. "See you tomorrow!"

George lifted his hand. "See you tomorrow!"

It almost felt as if they'd been partners for some time and not three days. George waited till two officers came to transport Ronald Wallace back to his cell. Then he went to his PC and ran Vance's name through their database. After the search engine started working, George decided it was time to get some coffee. On his way to the common room, Chief Norris came out of her office.

"Detective Donovan, do you have a moment?"

George sighed inwardly but put a smile on his face. "Of course, Chief. What can I do for you?"

"In my office." She went back through her office door, not looking back to see if he was following.

"Please close the door, Detective."

Chief Norris was already sitting behind her desk, motioning for him to take a seat as well once he had closed the door. George sat down, waiting for the chief to start talking. It didn't take a genius to guess why she called him, but he didn't want to make it too easy on her. Not after his talk with his brother.

"I gather your case is going well, Detective?"

"I'm not sure about going well. We've found the murderer of the three girls, yes, but there's something more going on, and at this point we have more questions than answers."

Chief Norris nodded. She steepled her fingers on her desk, narrowing her eyes at him. "You found the murderer within two days? That's fast."

George understood the implication. He shrugged. "We had a partial fingerprint on the murder weapon, and the perp isn't the sharpest tool in the shed. He thought we wouldn't find the weapon, and he stayed in his own home instead of going underground after the deed. The moment Lewis Brackenport explained to him how close to death row he was, he started singing like a gospel choir. Which is how we know there's more going on."

"So you were just lucky?"

George thought about his answer for a moment. They *had* been lucky in finding the other two girls plus the murder weapon for Lilly Cordon immediately, which was thanks to Andi's hunch. If they hadn't found them, Ronald Wallace would have either gotten away or—more likely—been killed by the people who employed him. The murder case itself had unraveled unusually fast, but it was the first tangle in a net they still didn't know the size of. And even though he was still suspicious of Andi's intuition, he'd already started seeing it the way his brother Daniel had suggested—as a gift Andi was using to help bring justice to the victims of crimes and their families. The question was should he let Chief Norris in on his thoughts or keep his cards close to his chest for a little longer? He finally decided to tell her his honest opinion. There was nothing to be gained by playing it safe.

"I guess we were. It was lucky Ronald Wallace hadn't ghosted or been murdered. The rest was good, solid police work. As far as I've seen it, Andi Hayes is an incredibly talented detective. You should be glad to have him in your precinct. He's an asset, not a liability."

Chief Norris narrowed her eyes at him. "You can say this after three days?"

"Yes. And quite confidently. We were thrown into a triple murder, which left Andi little room to be sneaky around me. I've seen him interact with both Evangeline Melcort and Lewis Brackenport, and both of them have a deep respect for him. As did your predecessor. I know you're worried about the precinct's reputation and ultimately your own, but to be honest, I think it would be beneficial for you to just let Andi do his thing and revel in the credit the whole precinct gets for his work."

The chief mused over his words for a few moments. "Are you sure there's nothing fishy going on?"

"As sure as I can be after only three days. I think he's just insanely talented. Add to that his stubbornness, and it's no wonder he cracks so many cases."

"I'm listening. What you say fits what I've heard about Detective Hayes so far. Most people have a thing or two to say about his cranky personality, but nobody ever doubted his proficiency at doing the job." She sighed deeply. "Since you're partnered with him, I'd like you to keep an eye on him until this case is closed. Just to be absolutely sure. Needless to say, if anything suspicious comes up, I want to be informed immediately. You can leave now."

George wasn't too happy about being dismissed like an errand boy, but he knew all about power games, and at the moment, Chief Norris was trying to come to terms with a truth she hadn't wanted—or even expected—to hear. It was obvious that, despite her stellar career, she still had to learn a thing or two about self-control and maintaining a poker face. Two things George had learned from his parents, especially his mother, at a young age. Never let anybody, especially a potential enemy, get a read on your emotions. A stoic expression was key in the shark-infested waters of politics and society. So he got up and left the office. A quick check of his PC showed the search engine was still combing through the system to find Taylor Vance. George's heart sank. If it took this long, it usually meant there was nothing to be found. He took the time to broaden the search to all accessible databases; then he gathered his things to go home for the night, leaving the computer to do the work for him.

CHAPTER 12
LIKE A COCKROACH

ANDI STUMBLED into the precinct, barely able to walk straight. He'd had one hell of a night due to a massive termite swarm in the area where he lived. He didn't have any termites in his own house, but several of his neighbors had healthy colonies either in their homes or on their properties. Conditions for swarming had been perfect the last few days, and he had felt it building up. Yesterday the alates had finally taken flight, resulting in a battering of images and impressions. It was never just one colony that swarmed, but all the colonies in a certain area, which made it even harder to bear. Even though the swarming itself had taken place during the day, sparing Andi the feeling of flying into a thousand different directions at once, the residue of the day's excitement still lingered everywhere. Predatory insects who had taken their fill. The digging of newlywed couples in their search for the perfect spot for their new nest. The strange emptiness of the established colonies that had just lost a junk of their populace. It was all intensified, way more than usual, and not even two hours of meditation had helped.

Andi refused to take a sleeping pill, since they made him woozy. He also didn't want to be helpless in his own home in case anything happened. Being slightly paranoid in addition to his *geschenk* certainly made his life even more complicated than it already was.

When he reached his desk, after trying very hard not to acknowledge how everybody jumped out of his way with a panicked expression, he found a cup of herbal tea and a plain bagel in front of his keyboard. George was sitting behind his own desk, drinking coffee and eating what looked like a salmon sandwich. In the morning. Andi tried his best not to hurl.

"Good morning, Andi. Rough night?"

Andi opened his mouth to give a sharp retort and thought better of it. George had done nothing—yet—to deserve getting his head chewed off, and he had brought tea. Andi decided to give him an honest answer.

"Like you wouldn't believe. My neighbors were a bit—lively. I feel like I didn't get any sleep."

The look of surprise on George's face told Andi he hadn't expected an answer, not to mention a nice one. Andi shrugged. "Did the computer find anything on Taylor Vance?"

The grin lighting up George's face told Andi they had a hit. If only he'd had the mental capacity to truly appreciate it. Andi had been afraid Taylor Vance would be a dead end for them, so actually having found him or at least a trace leading to him was a reason to celebrate. Some part of him knew that, while the rest of his body, together with any thoughts more complicated than setting one foot in front of the other and safely placing his ass on the seat of his chair, felt like it was covered in slowly drying resin—sticky, restricting, suffocating. And Andi was the mosquito arthropologists would be finding trapped in amber in about two million years from now.

"When I left yesterday, I extended the search to all databases, just to be on the safe side. And we have a lead. Taylor Vance isn't in the system as a processed criminal, but I found his name in connection to a car accident six months ago. There's only the picture on his driver's license, and that's blurry as all hell, though the address is promising. He lives in Sangaree, just like Ronald Wallace, on General Davis Drive. The house is in the name of one Ichabod Vance, presumably Taylor's father."

Andi grabbed his tea and bagel. "What are we waiting for?"

George grinned, slipped into his jacket, and took his keys. They made it to Sangaree in less than fifteen minutes. It took them a few moments to figure out which house belonged to Taylor Vance, since they all looked neglected. When they approached, Andi could feel the house was empty. No humans inside, as the countless ticks, bedbugs, and mosquitoes attested. His shoulders slumped. This was so far their only solid lead. If it led them to a dead end after he'd felt this small sliver of hope....

Andi hesitated. Their chances were already slim. It couldn't hurt to at least open himself up a bit and check their immediate surroundings. After the night he had, it was a risk—his defenses were still low—but what if he did find something they would otherwise miss? There were still a few steps to the front porch, and since he knew there was no danger inside except for the mold, he purposely dipped into the minds of the arthropods in a half-mile radius. The avalanche of impressions promised a massive headache later on, but what mattered was the presence of a person he picked up in the house to the left of Taylor Vance's home.

Sweat that carried an abundance of pheromones, turning the person into some kind of psychedelic color cluster amidst the information about vibrations on the ground, quality of soil, currents on the air, and the state of the rotting wood in most of the houses.

This one was definitely abandoned, the windows nailed shut with planks, the door hanging slightly ajar because the hinges were so rusted. Why somebody would go to the trouble of barring the windows and then leaving the door open would have puzzled Andi if he hadn't gathered from the termites living in the walls that there was an intruder. Somebody who didn't belong. Just like dogs or cats, social insects knew the people who lived in the homes they occupied. They could identify them by the pheromones they emitted. The person currently lurking in the living room was a stranger, not welcome at all. The real owner hadn't been there for at least two "dead spaces" and probably would never return, which was of no interest to the termites. All they knew was that the person inside at the moment didn't belong.

Andi knew it was a long shot, a wild speculation. The man could be anybody from a squatter to a junkie who was hiding from God knew what. But even if it wasn't their suspect, perhaps the person had seen or heard something that could help them. Andi decided to risk it and drew his weapon. George arched an eyebrow at him when he veered off to the left. There was no time for explanations, so he just awkwardly jerked his head in what would have been a more impressive gesture if he weren't already feeling the beginnings of a migraine. At the moment, the adrenaline kept the pain at bay, which would change the moment he came down from this particular high. Right now, though, he was on the hunt and nothing could stop him. He sensed George falling in line behind him, his weapon undoubtedly drawn.

The termites in the house sensed his approach and got restless, not happy about another intruder into their peaceful home. Since the insects were so upset, they broadcasted everything going on inside as if through loudspeakers. The man had become aware of their presence and wanted to flee. Unlike Ronald Wallace, he didn't go for the back door but opted to jump out of a window instead. The rotten planks barring the empty frame gave easily, as if they had waited for this chance to return to the soil. He rolled through the weeds and came to his feet in a fluid motion that didn't quite fit with a junkie or some homeless guy.

Andi put on an extra burst of speed, raising his weapon. "Freeze! Police!"

The man whirled around in the direction where once upon a time a fence had divided this property from the next one. Now there was only the distinct thickening of the grass one usually got along the perimeter of fenced-in property, where the lawnmower could somehow never reach. It was surprising that even after years of negligence, this line was still discernible.

The suspect didn't even come close to it. Out of nowhere, George appeared on his right flank, threw himself forward, and caught the man around the waist, bringing them both down with a heavy thump. The man struggled beneath George, getting in some good hits against George's ribs and even one to his temple, all the while screeching like a madman. "That's police brutality, that's what it is! Let go of me!"

George took the abuse with a stoic face and then simply grabbed the man, a Caucasian, presumably in his late thirties and about five eight, and turned him on his stomach. While he slapped some cuffs on him, he read him his Miranda rights.

"Fuck you, you fuckers! You have no right! I want a lawyer, now!"

Andi sighed. The good news was, the way the man was behaving he was definitely hiding something. If it had anything to do with their case, they would know as soon as they had his identity confirmed. He looked different from the man on the driver's license, but not different enough to convince Andi he wasn't their guy. And wouldn't that be lucky?

"Chill, man. We just wanted to ask you a few questions. But you decided to make a run for it, which makes my deeply suspicious cop mind wonder what you're hiding. Plus," Andi gave the man a smile full of teeth, "you resisted your arrest and assaulted an officer of the law. That's something the CPD takes *very* seriously, considering all the things going on at the moment. Now, why don't you show your goodwill and tell us your name? Since I assume you're an upstanding citizen and all of this"—he made a sweeping gesture with his hand, not bothering to hide his sarcasm—"is just one big misunderstanding on our side."

A glare full of hatred was all Andi got and all he had expected. The man's mouth opened and shut a few times, but he was definitely smarter than Ronald Wallace—he remained silent. Fucking damn. Andi shared a glance with George before they hauled the man to his feet. One of his front teeth was broken, and he smelled like mold and old dust. He had no doubt camped out in the abandoned house for some time.

As soon as they were back at the precinct, they processed the guy, confirmed with a facial recognition program and his fingerprints that he was indeed Taylor Vance, and let him make his call. While they waited for Vance's lawyer to arrive, George motioned Andi into the empty room next to interrogation room four.

From the tension George was radiating, Andi knew what was coming, so he waited patiently for his partner to phrase his questions. This was the exact reason Andi didn't do partners. Had he been alone, he would have just told everybody he had heard or seen something in the other house. Unfortunately, that kind of explanation wouldn't fly because George had been there with him and knew damn well how devoid of suspicious sounds the area had been and how impossible it had been to see anything from the front yard of Vance's house.

George walked back and forth with his hands linked at his back. Suddenly he stopped in front of Andi with a strange expression in his eyes Andi couldn't quite decipher. There was anger, as he expected, but also worry, a certain resignation, and perhaps even a tiny hint of— admiration?

"Listen, man, this is totally weird. You know what I'm going to ask, and I know you're going to lie about it, for whatever reasons. So I'm not going to ask how you knew. Just like I'm not going to ask again how you knew about the dead girls inside the building. I'm almost sure I don't want to know. Just tell me one thing—is what you're doing in any way, shape, or form illegal?"

Andi was genuinely surprised. He had expected something entirely different from George: a rant, threats, accusations, the end of their short partnership. Not this strange mixture of openness and—was that hope? Andi wasn't sure. And since George had just proven how different from most of their colleagues he was, Andi decided to let him in, if only just a bit.

"I swear to you on everything that's holy, nothing of what I do is illegal." Most probably because nobody *knew* what he could do, but that was details. Nothing of importance. "I know how it looks, I know you've got many questions, and you're right. I would lie to you and you don't want to hear the truth anyway. So—can you trust me on this?"

It was blunt as far as confessions went, very much in the same tone in which George had started this conversation. Andi couldn't keep the hint of aggression out of his voice; he was simply too tired in combination with adrenaline pumping through his system from the chase. In this state, it was a miracle he hadn't bitten George's head off.

George dragged his hands over his face. "We've been partners for less than a week and you... we...." He sighed. "I talked with my brother about you. He thinks I should roll with whatever 'instinct' you have. See it as a way to learn something. And even though you're a grumpy asshole most of the time, you're also a good cop. I'm tempted to take his advice. It just feels strange, having talked to you about it, knowing about this silent truce, wondering what your secret is. I'm not sure how this is going to play out." The look in his eyes was almost pleading, as if he wanted Andi to help him solve this—admittedly crazy—puzzle.

Andi sighed, felt the aggressiveness slowly subsiding into mere exhaustion. This whole partner thing had been a bad idea from the start.

"You're right. It's strange. I had a few partners before, now and then, never for long. None of them ever picked up on things the way you did in just three days. I usually managed to get rid of them before they got too suspicious. Perks of being a grumpy asshole. People tend to focus on the bad and ignore the strange."

"Lucky me. I had myself almost convinced it was some kind of eerie instinct when you found those two other girls. But today? I was extra vigilant because we were going after a potential human trafficker. There was absolutely nothing hinting at our guy being in the building next door."

"If it helps, I didn't know it was him. I just knew there was someone in there. Could as well have been a junkie."

George looked at him intently. "And you knew nobody was in the house we were approaching." It was a statement. "Believe it or not, I can live with that."

George sounded almost convincing. Almost. There would be more questions coming, now that he knew Andi was indeed hiding something. It was only natural for a cop. But for the moment, things had calmed down, or so Andi chose to believe.

He somehow managed to tug the corners of his mouth up. This situation was completely new to him as well. He'd had the last partner at the beginning of his career as a detective, and that partnership had lasted only until Detective Amber Lowey had successfully convinced the chief back then that Andi was impossible to work with. As a beat officer, he'd of course had partners, but his field of responsibilities during that time had made it easy for him to mostly hide his strangeness. He'd never been a social butterfly.

All of a sudden, he felt the urge to keep the fragile closeness he had established with George. Tentatively he held his hand out.

"Partners?"

George hesitated just long enough for Andi to feel insecurity creeping in. Then he grabbed Andi's hand.

"Partners."

They shook on it.

"How do we proceed? I can hardly ignore your strange hunches."

Andi thought about it. "You don't have to. I mean, you know I have a way of finding things out; you just don't know what it is. I know you know, so I don't have to waste time finding ridiculous excuses for my findings. In fact, now *you* can help me find those excuses for the reports." It was a rather weak attempt at a joke. There hadn't been a need for him to keep his social skills polished because everybody kept their distance from him, just as he liked it.

George grinned nevertheless. "You think I'm going to get creative for you? What's in it for me?"

"An immaculate solve rate that will help you propel your career." Andi was half-serious. He was pretty sure Charleston was just a stepstone for George. The man had *ambitious* written all over him.

"Deal. I could use that."

Andi winked at him. "Wonderful. Let's see if Vance's lawyer has showed. We need the information he can give us."

George nodded, serious all of a sudden. "I want to get those fuckers. All of them."

"You and me both."

They left the room, and for the first time Andi felt a sliver of the connection partners on the force were supposed to have. It was rather nice.

CHAPTER 13
SMALL RATS

As IT turned out, Vance's lawyer was delayed. They used the time until she showed to talk to the tech guys about the cell they had found on Vance. Cracking his phone had been a bit of a hassle, but now the information on it was flickering over a huge screen, making George wish he could go down to the interrogation room and punch Taylor Vance to death. He didn't know what repulsed him more—the pictures of countless victims, all of them painfully young, or the cold manner Vance talked about them. To him and the people he was connected with, the victims were just merchandise, nothing of worth or importance apart from their ability to make the traffickers money. George glanced at Andi. His jaw muscles were so tense, George was afraid he would break the bone if he didn't relax them soon.

"How long will it take to go through everything?" Andi looked at Shireen, the queen of the tech geeks in the precinct. She shrugged, causing the countless pendants hanging from her neck to jingle.

"A few days, probably. The good news is, your perp is an idiot. He kept everything he did on his cell. Hell, he even put his meetings with Ronald Wallace and others on his personal timetable. It may take some time to run them all through the database, but I can guarantee you we're going to find some more pimps like that Wallace guy."

"And the bad news?" George kept his gaze on the screen where Vance's calendar was now displayed.

"The bad news is his superiors aren't half as dumb as him. All those other numbers are for prepaid cells. Old models as well, which makes them even harder to track. Not that it would do any good."

"You're saying?" Andi lifted a brow.

Shireen made a frustrated gesture with her tablet. "So far we've found enough incriminating stuff to screw that Vance guy into the next millennium, but we've got zero, zip, nada on the organization he's been working for. And the clock is ticking. If they don't know he's been taken into custody yet, they're going to find out soon. And then they'll be gone."

"So we need him to cooperate." George didn't like that. Unlike Ronald Wallace, Vance had called a private lawyer, meaning he probably wasn't as easily intimidated as Ronald. Plus, even though they could link him to Wallace, they couldn't place him at the storage unit. They didn't have much to work with. Depending on how good his lawyer was, Vance might even opt to say nothing at all. The mere thought made George angry. The pictures of all the girls and boys he had been trafficking were something to build on, though. Sadly enough, human trafficking didn't weigh as heavily as murder, but it was leverage. Beggars couldn't be choosers.

"Do you have anything else we could use to our advantage?" George intended to go into that interrogation as well prepared as possible.

Shireen started tapping away on her tablet. "There's this conversation with a dude saved under 'Trigon'—stupid but fitting, if you ask me—which could be something. It's in code, and I'm almost sure it's about a shipment. I haven't cracked it yet, though. Could take me a bit to get all the details."

"If you haven't cracked it yet, how do you know it's about a shipment?" George looked at her incredulously.

"First of all, I said almost sure. Not totally. Second, I've been doing this for a while, and they didn't go to the trouble of coding the numbers. There's a lot I can gain from numbers alone. Like this line." She magnified a block of three numbers on the screen. "That's tomorrow's date. And this one—" She drew their attention to the next block. "—is the time. One hundred. I bet my Ankh protection amulet he's not planning to visit Mommy dearest an hour after midnight." Shireen beat a staccato rhythm on the side of her tablet. "The million-dollar question is who is he meeting and where?"

"You can't find out?" Andi's voice sounded pleading.

Shireen pursed her lips. "I'm going to try. Run cross-references, check where he's been the last few weeks to get a pattern, but with just these random letters, I can't guarantee I'm going to find anything within the less than thirty hours we have. Sorry."

Andi shook his head. "It's fine, Shireen. Just do your thing and we'll try and do ours." He turned to George. "Shall we?"

George nodded. They waved at Shireen, who was already busy with her tablet again, the rest of the world forgotten to her. When they stepped into the corridor leading back to the interrogation room, George stopped Andi with a hand to his shoulder. "How are we going to play this, Andi? I've seen my share of interrogations, and this one won't be pretty. Technically, Vance has us by the balls. And given how smug he's been since we booked him, he knows it."

Andi closed his eyes for a moment, which made the black circles seem even more prominent. George also noticed how Andi's cheekbones protruded from his face like scythes, making him look like death warmed over. All of a sudden cracking their suspect was no longer number one on George's priority list. "Hey, man, are you okay? You look even worse than you did this morning."

Andi dragged his hand over his face. "Just tired. As I said, it was one hell of a night."

"You should call the cops on your neighbors."

Andi smiled weakly. "Would you come to my rescue?"

"Maybe." George winked at him. "If it means I don't have to watch you drag your tired ass through the day… I might be tempted."

"Thank you so much. You're a real ray of sunshine, aren't you?" Andi punched his shoulder, though without much heat. "As for how we play this—I don't know. Let's just roll with it."

"You sure that's wise?"

"Probably not. But we know nothing about this fucker. He's not as dumb as Wallace, though that's not a feat. He sure knows to lawyer up, which is a problem, as you well know."

"This one not under your spell?" George dug his elbow into Andi's ribs.

"No, unfortunately not. I know her, though. Alice Springton. Ambitious, sharp, and quick-witted. Never underestimate her, and never ever talk to her outside the interrogation room. She's like a shark and smells weakness ten miles downwind."

"Let me guess, you had a run-in with her already?"

Andi snorted. "She tried to dismiss some of the evidence I had gathered for one of my cases. Claimed I hadn't gotten it legally. She lost."

"Have you?"

Andi raised a brow, feigning ignorance. "Have I what?"

"Gotten it illegally?"

"I already told you, nothing about the way I solve my cases is illegal. Case in point, the lawsuit she—or rather her client—lost. She couldn't prove a damn thing." Andi sounded smug. George decided to let the subject drop and focus on their current problem.

"So I let you do the talking, and if I pick up on anything, I weigh in?"

"If you want. We can do it the other way around as well."

That surprised George. While he was pretty sure by now that Andi was the least alpha male of all the detectives he'd ever met, he hadn't expected him to give up the reins so easily.

"You wouldn't mind?"

"Why should I? You're not a rookie. Chief Norris wouldn't have chosen you for this job if your credits weren't valid. And as you said, you've seen your share of interrogations at narcotics." He hesitated a moment. "Plus it's no secret I hate people. If having a partner means I don't have to lead on interrogations anymore, thus limiting my interactions with people who breathe and therefore annoy me, I'm all for keeping you."

George wasn't entirely sure whether this was supposed to be a joke. Andi's serious tone suggested he meant every word. And wasn't that flattering—in a way?

"You're just using me!"

"Yes. Finally you've caught on. First-class detective here." Andi grinned. This time, his response was definitely a joke. George laughed. His grumpy partner could be quite funny.

"Fine. I'll take the lead on this one. Let's try to somehow crack this bastard."

"That's the spirit."

They walked along the corridor side by side, the feeling of having established a connection with his elusive partner like a drug on George's mind.

ALICE SPRINGTON certainly looked like a predator. Her black hair was done up in an immaculate chignon, her sharp, slanted eyes were emphasized by a hint of kohl, and her lips accentuated with a killer red. She wore a pencil skirt that ended midthigh, but instead of being sexy, it only made her look more dangerous. She could probably kill somebody with her stilettos, if her looks didn't do the trick.

"Detective Hayes. I see they still let you work. What an unpleasant surprise."

"Mrs. Springton, still a sore loser, I see. Not that I'm surprised." Andi nodded at her, then gestured at George. "This is my partner, Detective Donovan. He's going to lead this interrogation."

Alice Springton fixed her gaze on George. "So they've given you a watchdog?" Something in her voice told George not to react to this taunt. Andi certainly didn't.

"Hello, Mrs. Springton. Since you're finally here, we can start with the interrogation of your client, Taylor Vance." George couldn't keep the little jab at her being late back. Her face scrunched up in distaste.

"Not my fault. You had no right taking my client into custody. He wasn't doing anything illegal."

"Yeah, I didn't do anything!" Vance piped up, which earned him a sharp glare from Springton. He immediately shut his mouth. George winced inwardly. Great. Vance was on her leash.

"That remains to be seen. We came to your house to talk to you about a certain Ronald Wallace, who gave us your address. Do you know a man of that name?"

"He doesn't. Next question." Alice sat ramrod straight, exuding confidence. If it hadn't been for a quick glance in Andi's direction, George would have bought her tough lawyer act. She definitely knew something was wrong with her client, and she was afraid of what Andi might conjure up. George felt a surge of adrenaline. They could nail this.

"Why weren't you in your own house but squatting in the neighboring property? Which, by the way, is a crime."

Alice opened her mouth, then hesitated. She looked at Vance, who took this as permission to speak. "I was afraid somebody would come to get me, so I hid next door."

"Who would come to get you? You try to make us believe you're a model citizen, and model citizens don't have a reason to be afraid in their own homes."

George watched as a bead of sweat formed on Vance's brow. Making the man nervous was almost too easy.

"In an area like the one where Mr. Vance lives, being worried about one's safety is normal. Not that many police there," Alice Springton chimed in, casting another glance at Andi. Interesting. George couldn't be sure if Andi had picked up on it, though. He seemed kind of absentminded.

"Fine. So you don't know anybody by the name Ronald Wallace, you were squatting in the house next to your own because you were worried about your safety in general, and it had nothing to do with the human trafficking you're obviously involved in."

George let that sentence sink in for a moment. Alice's eyes narrowed.

"This is the first I'm hearing about such serious allegations. I was told this was about an unlawful arrest."

Vance squirmed in his seat.

"Oh no, Mrs. Springton. Your client must have been sparing with the information he's given you. You see, Mr. Wallace, the man Mr. Vance supposedly doesn't know, has already admitted to 'looking after' young women and men who were part of shipments Mr. Vance here had organized several times. That's how we found him. And guess what? His cell shows quite a few meetings with Mr. Wallace and some others who we're in the process of checking. I don't think you or your client are going to like what we'll find. Not to mention all those other interesting appointments your client has saved in his cell...." George spread his hands in a noncommittal gesture. "All I'm saying, Mr. Vance, is things would look a lot better for you if you started talking to us *before* our techs are done tearing your cell apart."

Alice Springton looked as if she had just fallen face-first into an entire basket of lemons. "Is that true, Taylor?" George thought he detected a hiss in her voice. She certainly looked like a rattlesnake about to strike. Being on the other side of the table, far away from the unfortunate Taylor Vance, was a blessing George appreciated.

Vance held up his hands. "Hey, chill, Alice. That's why I called you. You can make it all go away, can't you? They have nothing, not really. Otherwise they wouldn't question me." Taylor Vance sounded so smug, George wanted to introduce him to his fist. As it turned out, he didn't have to. Alice rose from her chair, emanating fury from every pore of her being.

"You're a fucking idiot, Taylor. I came here because our grandfathers were friends, but I'm not going to help you if you're caught up in something as despicable as human trafficking. Even I have standards. If you're involved like the detectives think, my advice is to work with them and give them everything you know. That way you may be able to shave a few years off your sentence."

"What? Alice, I told you, they don't have any proof! Just the word of a murderer!"

"And how would you know about the murder? We haven't mentioned it yet." Andi's voice was like silk on a sword. "And before you start looking for excuses, it wasn't in the media either. We've kept a lid on it."

Alice Springton pierced Andi with her gaze. "You have proof? Like in that other case?"

Andi simply nodded. She turned back to her unlucky client. "Come clean, Taylor. And work with the attorney they assign to you. I'm done with you. Never call me again, understood? You make me sick!" She grabbed her slim leather briefcase. "Detective Donovan, Detective Hayes, have a nice day."

With that, she went for the door, her stilettos clicking ominously on the linoleum floor. George waited till the door closed behind her before he turned his full attention back to Vance. "It seems to me you've been dropped like a hot potato, Mr. Vance. Do you want us to call a public defender for you now, or do you want to make it easier for all of us, especially yourself, by helping us out?"

For a brief moment, George was afraid Vance would be stubborn about the whole thing. His jaw worked furiously, as if he were chewing some hardened bubble gum.

"If you decide to answer our questions, I'll see to it that you get methadone in prison so you don't have to go cold turkey." Andi had barely raised his voice, and yet what he'd said made both George and Vance whip their heads in his direction. George bit his lip to not question Andi in front of their suspect. Vance did it for him. "How do you know?" He started rubbing his arms in what George was sure was a subconscious gesture.

Andi shrugged. "There are signs. I'm just good at reading them."

Vance's shoulders slumped. "Fine," he finally said. "What do you want to know?"

CHAPTER 14
MESSENGER FLEAS

ANDI WAS sprawled on a patch of grass between two brushes opposite the place where Vance's latest shipment was supposed to arrive. Next to him was George in a similar get-up to his own: black cargo pants, black long-sleeved shirt, Kevlar vest, and a balaclava. They had their guns at the ready and were connected to the SWAT team via in-ear speakers. Andi was doing his best to focus on their case while all around him the insects of the night were bombarding him with less than useful information.

The night was nice, just the right amount of hot to go flying, and there were all those bloodbags, though covered up and hard to get to, little light here where to gather, the occasional swish and shadow when bats thinned the cloud of winged arthropods, never enough, though, they were many, looking for a partner to mate, laying eggs, fluttering toward the streetlight way down, yes, come here, the fat spider caught another unsuspecting moth in her web, quickly injecting venom, wrapping it in fine silk, what a nice night indeed, good hunting, the thrumming of cars in the distance, always there, a familiar rumbling felt through legs and membranes and wings, pheromones luring the males, hunting, feeding, mating, all in a frenzy, all the time....

"Estimated arrival in five minutes. No visual yet." The voice of the SWAT leader sounded slightly distorted through the speaker in his ear and was accompanied by strange whirling noises and a feeling as if he were caught in a bass drum during a metal concert, which was how some of the bugs experienced the voice and the static. Next to him George fidgeted a bit in an attempt to get more comfortable. Since Vance's interrogation the day before, where the human rat had finally given them all the information they wanted, George hadn't so much as hinted at how Andi had known about Vance's addiction. He had to give it to Vance; the man was hiding it well. Unfortunately for him, his sweat didn't lie, and the tick he had in the back of his left knee—probably from when he went through the weeds to get to the abandoned house—had attested to him being a regular user. It was information Andi had gladly used. If he hadn't had that little talk with George before and established their truce, he would have thought twice about bringing it up, because how should he explain that he detected an addiction a former narcotics detective didn't spot? But as it was, he could make use of his talent without worrying too much about plausibility. And unless he told George his secret—which he didn't plan to—the man had no way of figuring it out.

"We have movement." There was a certain tension in the SWAT leader's voice now. Andi felt it too. They were about to intercept possible human trafficking.

A black van came around the corner and stopped next to the empty walkway. The headlights went out.

"Hold it." Again SWAT. "They're waiting for the other guy."

A rumbling sound told Andi the second party was arriving. This van was dark blue and didn't sound too good. The second van stopped opposite the first, but unlike the first, the headlights stayed on. There was a sequence of signals, after which the headlights of the first van came to life. It answered with a different sequence before both vehicles turned dark again.

"Hold. Let them get out."

The doors to both passenger sides opened, and two men stepped out. It was too dark to see them clearly because three of the four streetlights in the area were broken. Andi tightened his hold on his gun. Any moment now.

"We strike in three, two, one…. Go!" The SWAT team erupted from their hideouts in the ditches and behind the crumbling houses on the other side of the street. Andi and George jumped up as well, their weapons trained on the two men outside the vehicles who seemed to have frozen in shock. Two SWAT members went for each driver, dragging them out of their seats and onto the asphalt. Nobody was too careful about hurting them, seeing what their cargo probably was.

Andi exchanged a short glance with George and cocked his head in the direction of the dark blue van. He was getting vibes from some fleas telling him this was the van with the victims inside. George followed without hesitation. The trust he was showing in Andi's "instincts" evoked a strange warm feeling in his chest. As peaceful as working alone was, it was nice to have somebody have your back.

When he reached the van, he took a moment to listen. He heard faint scratching noises and whimpers. While reaching for the handle of the back door, Andi spoke loudly and, as he very much hoped, reassuringly.

"Everything's fine. This is the police. I'm going to open the door now. Please remain calm."

He heard a clicking sound behind him, no doubt George getting his gun ready. Even though Andi was almost a hundred percent sure the people inside the van were victims, one could never be too careful. The door opened easily, and Andi briefly wondered why it wasn't locked. When he looked inside, he knew.

As far as he could tell in the dim light, there were three girls and one boy chained inside the van. Their ages were hard to guess, but Andi thought somewhere between fifteen and eighteen. A wooden rail ran from back to front on both sides, roughly at head-height above the seats. The victims were chained to the rails with handcuffs, while their feet were secured with rope through loops on the floor. None of the four wore much. Their eyes were riveted on Andi, full of fear and a deep distrust that no doubt came from their time in captivity. Andi put away his gun before raising his hands to show he meant no harm.

"Hello, my name is Andi Hayes. I'm a detective with the Charleston PD, and this is my partner, Detective Donovan. We're here to get you out. Please bear with us for a moment while we try to find the keys."

The three girls just stared at him as if they couldn't believe he was really there. It was the boy who talked. "The keys are in that box over there." He motioned toward a small wooden box screwed to the wall behind the driver's seat. Andi went there, lifted the latch, and opened it. There were two sets of keys. He took them all and dangled them in front of the boy. "Which ones?"

The boy cocked his head to the side. "The right set. Try the third in the row, the one with the strange bit key."

Andi obliged. He was aware of George getting out a knife and starting to work on the ropes binding the feet of the girl to their right. At the entrance of the van, the SWAT leader appeared.

"Everything good?"

"Yeah. Thank you, Adam. We're getting the victims out of their bindings. Is the ambulance here already?"

"On their way. Five minutes tops." The SWAT leader—Adam Forard—stepped back again. He had worked with Andi before, and they trusted each other. Andi tried the key the boy had suggested and was happy to be rewarded with the telltale click of a lock opening. The boy lowered his arms, his movements a bit awkward. Andi furrowed his brows.

"How long have you been like this?"

The boy shrugged. "I'm not sure. Where are we? We started in Columbia, though I don't know how long ago that was."

"Columbia? You've been like this for over two hours?" George looked up from where he was cutting through another set of ropes. The boy shrugged again.

"Probably longer. They took a break at some point, to eat something."

"Let me guess, you didn't get anything." Andi didn't have to ask, not really. Yet he did, because the brutality of what these young people had experienced was just too cruel to be simply accepted.

The boy laughed, an ugly, disillusioned sound not fitting for a face so young. Then again, his eyes, as well as those of the girls, showed an age and a wariness of the world Andi would expect in people a lot older than himself. "If they give us too much food, we might get fat and too strong to be handled. No, food has to be earned through good behavior and excellent services." He spat on the floor. At least his spirit seemed unbroken. Or perhaps it was just courage born of despair. Andi couldn't tell, and he hoped these young people would get a decent second chance in life. They more than deserved it.

"What's your name?" He looked at all the victims, the boy last.

"I'm Greg Smith. They tried their best to make us forget our names, but I held on to it." Stubborn pride shone through his words.

Andi nodded. "Very well done. Don't let them take any more from you than they already have."

"I'm Rose Everton, and this is my sister, Mia. We haven't been with those men for long," one of the girls said. Tears started streaming down her face. "They just took us when we walked home from school." She was shaking. Andi saw George leaning toward the girl, reaching out in a slow, controlled movement as not to spook her.

"Shh, it's fine, Rose. You're free now. The nightmare is over." Rose allowed George to stroke her arm while her apparently younger sister— Andi felt his blood boiling when he estimated her age to be around fourteen—snuggled into her side. He turned toward the third girl, who seemed to be the same age as Greg.

"I'm Kathy Sacks. I didn't forget either." Her voice wobbled, but she didn't cry. Andi smiled at her.

"Very good, Kathy. I'm proud of you."

The sound of sirens coming closer had Andi taking a look outside. "The ambulance is here. How do you feel about leaving this van? Or would you rather stay in here to get looked after? It's entirely your choice. Whatever makes you feel safest."

Greg shot to his feet so fast, he almost stumbled over. George had cut his ropes last, and Greg kicked them aside when he went for the door. Kathy followed immediately, while Rose and Mia stayed with George.

Andi exchanged a look with his partner. "I'll go with Greg and Kathy."

"I'll stay with Rose and Mia. Send the paramedics in, please."

"Of course."

Andi followed Greg and Kathy outside, where Adam Forard was already gently directing them toward the first of the two ambulances parked behind the blue van. On their way they passed the last of the four men SWAT had taken into custody. He was on his knees, hands zip-tied behind his back, with a SWAT member guarding him. Greg moved so fast, none of them had time to react. He kicked the guy in the balls with all his might, causing the criminal to topple over with an anguished scream. Adam hurried to pull Greg away from the man, though not before Greg got the chance for a second kick, which the boy dished out with a broad smile on his lips. Kathy watched with gleeful satisfaction written all over her face.

"Serves you right," Andi spat when he passed the groaning man. The SWAT man winked.

After a thorough check, the paramedics declared all four victims outwardly more or less hale, apart from the bruises and being underfed. There was a short discussion with Adam, and then Andi and George agreed to have Rose, Mia, Kathy, and Greg taken to the hospital for a round of intense testing and to monitor them for the night. Once the ambulances had taken off with one SWAT member as guard in each of them, Andi and George went back to the vans. CSI had arrived by then, scrutinizing the vehicles closely. Andi knew from a few fleas who had recently taken residence on Mia that the children had been in contact with a man who didn't smell appealing because of anemia before they were sent to Charleston. Since the four drivers all were quite healthy apart from the drugs in their system, which were the same as Taylor Vance and Ronald Wallace had used, Andi could safely assume this man was somebody else, hopefully not just a customer but a part of the organization.

Until they could follow any leads, though, they had a group of human traffickers to interrogate. Andi and George left the CSI team to their work, said goodbye to Adam, who was getting ready to drive back to the precinct as well, and went to George's car. Once they were inside, George started the engine.

"That went well." It was a neutral comment.

Andi nodded, leaning his head on the passenger seat. He was bone-tired, and their night wasn't even close to an end.

"Yeah, it did. I was afraid the spot Vance gave us would be a bust. That they somehow got wind of him being arrested and changed it. So glad it turned out golden."

George threw him a quick glance before he concentrated on the street again. "You didn't know if he was telling the truth?"

Andi groaned inwardly. He couldn't hold it against George that he tried to get more information. And he was trying to be polite about it, so Andi decided to work with him.

"No, I didn't. I'm not a lie detector per se. Only when it comes to certain facts."

"Like if somebody is a user."

"Yep."

George hummed. "You know, I think I could get used to working with you. You certainly make the job look easier than it truly is."

"I'm so glad you approve of my weirdness." Andi knew he sounded sarcastic, but it was too late in the night to try and rein it in.

George just shrugged. "You're not weird as such. I've seen worse, believe me. The more time I spend with you, the more curious I become and the less suspicious I get. I don't know if that's good, though."

"Believe me, it is. Makes it easier for both of us. Just keep trusting me and everything will be fine." Andi tried to sound dismissive to not show how George's growing interest in him as a person was affecting him.

"I'm usually not a trusting man, Andi. But just to see how this goes, I think I'll take a chance with you."

"You do know curiosity killed the cat, don't you?"

"Yeah. I'm no cat but a cop, and I do have a capable partner to have my back." George grinned broadly.

"You're a fool. Luckily for you, I kind of tolerate you more than anybody else I know."

Andi made sure to keep his tone light. George simply laughed.

"Lucky me."

CHAPTER 15
PARTS OF A PUZZLE

THE INTERROGATION of the four traffickers was a bust. It was six in the morning, and after two hours of fruitless questioning, George wanted nothing more than go to bed. As it turned out, the four men weren't part of the human trafficking ring but, just like Ronald Wallace, outside contractors who got their information via burner phones from an unknown person. Whoever was behind this was so careful it bordered on paranoia, which made it impossible for George and Andi to get useful information. The whole setup had apparently been going for two years and had started with an ad on the darknet. Shireen was trying to find out who had posted the ad, which took time George and Andi didn't have. So far, each person involved in the trafficking had led them to the next one in a short amount of time, which had been in their favor. Like stitches on a sweater, one after the other had given. Now they seemed to have reached a knot, and if they couldn't untangle it in time, their investigation would be halted. Although they had caught the murderer of Lilly Cordon and the other two girls and had even saved four other innocent young people, George didn't want to think about how many more they had missed and would never know of because their bodies were rotting away in some unmarked grave somewhere.

From his desk, George stared at their whiteboard, where a huge red question mark now marked the mysterious head of the trafficking ring. So far, all the lines connecting to it had turned from green—promising lead, to black—dead end. Behind him there was rustling and soft cursing. Andi looked even worse than the day before, the dark circles now accentuated by a red tinge to his eyes. His movements had an almost robotic quality, as if he were operating on his last shreds of energy.

"Should I get us some breakfast?" George reached for his wallet.

Andi stared at him as if he hadn't understood the meaning of his words. "Breakfast?"

"Yeah, you know, something hot and liquid to wake us up again and something solid with sugar to refuel. Lots of sugar in your case. You look like you want to audition for a part in *The Walking Dead*. And not as one of the living persons. No offense."

Andi stared at him some more. "Why would I want to audition for anything?"

"Okay, buddy, that's it. We're getting breakfast." George took his keys, reached for Andi's arm, and dragged him from his chair. "We won't be able to catch some sleep before we talk to the four victims. I just hope they're up to it."

"Greg seemed to be quite capable. Kathy too. Rose and Mia, I'm not so sure about. We'll have to see."

"Wow, man, that was actually a coherent contribution to the topic at hand. I don't dare imagine what you'll be capable of once I've fed you." George glanced at Andi to see if his attempts at joking had even been registered. A faint smile on Andi's lips confirmed the man wasn't dead yet.

"As soon as my blood sugar is up again, I'm getting back at you."

"Promises, promises."

They left the precinct and drove to the Starbucks, where George was by now greeted with his first name. As it had been the last few days, the same barista nodded at him from behind the counter. "Good morning, George. You're early today. The usual?"

"Good morning, Chrissy. The usual beverages, but we need some real food today. Something with an extra sugar punch. Any recommendations?"

The young woman with the neon green hair looked them over. She didn't seem impressed. "I'd say two chocolate chip muffins, two croissants, and our special rye sandwiches with smoked salmon and farmer cheese to provide some real sustenance."

A gagging sound made George turn to his partner. Andi was shaking his head vigorously. "Yes to the sugar, no to the salmon. Not in the morning."

"Would you like something else? Perhaps a plain bagel? You know, Chrissy is right. You need something with actual nutritional value."

"A bagel sounds good." Andi shuddered. "I think I'll go and secure us a table."

George looked around in the almost empty place. Andi really was running on his last reserves.

"Tough night?" Chrissy was placing plates with the muffins and the croissants in front of him. The sweet and buttery smell woke at least a dozen of George's brain cells.

"Very. And it's not over yet." He sighed.

"You're taking good care of him. Like a partner should."

For a moment George wondered how Chrissy knew he was a cop. He hadn't hinted at it yet, and he certainly didn't look like one, or so he liked to believe. Then it hit him.

Chrissy thought Andi was his romantic partner. How she came to that conclusion was beyond him as well, but he was too tired to correct her. If people deduced from seeing him and Andi together that they were an item, it could only mean something in their partnership was going well. Or it was way too early to be up, and he was operating in some kind of twilight zone where reality was just a figment of his imagination. He decided it was time to get some of that sugar into his system. Grabbing the plates with the croissants, he went over to where Andi had found them a table next to the window but in the back where they could keep an eye on the entire room. Even half-asleep, Andi's cop brain remembered the basics. George put the plates down. He opened his mouth to make a comment on how Andi could help with carrying their breakfast, but one look into Andi's absent gaze confirmed he was definitely the fitter one. Forcing Andi to get up and do something as complicated as carrying a plate or a hot beverage might even be considered torture. So he went back and forth three more times to get the rest of their breakfast before sitting down next to his partner. Andi hadn't touched any of the food, though George wasn't sure if he was being polite—which was unlikely given his reputation but not impossible since George had gotten to know him—or simply too tired to do much more than stare at it. As soon as George was seated, he pushed the plate with the bagel in Andi's direction. "Eat."

Andi looked at the bagel, then up at George. "If the victims can't tell us something solid, we're back to square one."

So Andi hadn't shut down. He'd been mulling over the same problem George had. "Yeah. I'm afraid so. It's a pity those guys we busted tonight were just contractors." George bit into his rye and salmon sandwich.

"Whoever is running this organization is beyond careful. All the jobs with potential exposure to the police seem to be given to people who aren't part of it. Even Vance was just a pawn, and he was responsible for organizing the transports." Andi ripped his bagel in two.

"I hate to admit it, but it's pretty clever. We've taken out the basic level and have no way of reaching the next. What works in our favor is that it makes them slow to react. If Wallace had been part of a traditional organization, he would have probably died the same night as Lilly and the other two girls."

"True. It could also be losses like this are part of the calculation. I know a lot of cops who would take Ronald Wallace and close the case because the murderer was found." Andi took a bite from his bagel, a mixture of fury and sadness in his eyes. George could relate. In times where the police force was rattled by several scandals and public opinion was taking a nosedive, many detectives opted for quick results. George couldn't even blame them. The pressure was there; they all felt it. The fact that Chief Norris wanted him to investigate Andi before contacting IA was a prime example as well. Under normal—or rather ideal—circumstances, IA would've already been all over Andi's cases. But his shining statistics reassured the public, which was the most important thing, and also kept his former chief from interfering. Andi's way of solving cases might be clean, but the methods of many of their fellow detectives were anything but. It was a difficult field to navigate, the criminals no longer their only enemies.

"We won't do that." George made it a statement.

"No, we won't. But it's going to be tough. If the victims can't provide us with any new leads, we're stuck. I doubt Evangeline's going to find much from the other two dead girls." He sighed. "If they had family, we can at least give them some peace."

Frustrated, they both stared at their plates. The rye sandwich and the bagel were gone. George had finished his croissant and was getting ready for the final sugar infusion from the muffin. Andi was clinging to his tea.

"We might have to wait until another case like this one pops up." The mere thought made George angry.

"We could also check if there were incidents like it here in Charleston and in the nearby cities during the last two years. Though I don't want to kick up too much dust yet."

"Detective Harris."

"Yes, Detective Harris. He's probably just another paid pawn, but if not, we can't afford to alarm him unduly. He could very well become crucial to the investigation." Andi picked a chocolate chip out of his muffin.

"I agree with you. We keep it on the down-low for the time being. Who knows, perhaps we'll get something solid from the victims."

"Here's to hope." Andi raised his tea.

TWO HOURS and three cups of coffee later, George entered the room where Greg and Kathy were staying in the hospital. Rose and Mia hadn't been very helpful; they were both terrified and—according to the doctors—pumped full of drugs, most of them tranquilizers. No wonder the girls remembered next to nothing. George only hoped they would have more luck with Greg and Kathy. The two were older and had perhaps seen or heard something they shouldn't have. They were both sitting in their beds, watching a rerun of *Two and a Half Men*.

"Good show. I think Charlie Sheen is a riot."

"He's pretty funny, yeah." Greg shut the TV off. "What can we do for you?"

"First of all, you could tell us how you're doing." Andi smiled at both Greg and Kathy. The two shared a look. It was Greg who started to speak.

"We're finally free, so that's something. As for the rest—the doctors told us they have to run more tests on us to make sure we haven't gotten any STDs, and they can't tell us yet what the drugs those assholes have given us over the years have done to our bodies."

"We're so sorry." Andi sat down in one of the chairs next to Kathy's bed, keeping a certain distance so as not to crowd her. "We didn't know what was going on. If we had…."

"We would have gotten you out," George finished.

"We know. It was a lot, and I still can't believe it's finally over." Kathy started kneading her fingers.

"Do you have family we can call? Friends?" George wasn't sure if anybody had thought about getting that information from them. It had all been a whirlwind, and the hospital staff's priority had surely been the victims' well-being.

"No family or friends for me," Greg announced bitterly. "My parents kicked me out for being gay. I'd been living on the streets for almost a year when I was caught."

"I have a mother." Kathy was talking in a monotone, clearly not happy with her memories. "She's an alcoholic. Or was. I don't know. By the rate she was going when I was kidnapped, she could be dead by now. Anyway, I'm pretty sure she didn't even realize I'm gone. One of the nurses said somebody from youth protection is coming over today." Her shoulders started shaking. "I don't want to be taken into some foster home. And I don't want them to separate me and Greg or Mia and Rose. After all we've been through...."

"They won't, Kathy. Isn't that true, Detective Donovan?" Greg looked imploringly at George, begging him with his eyes to say something reassuring. George hesitated only a moment.

"We're going to talk to the representative from youth protection. I'm sure we can work something out. And I don't think they'll let you leave the hospital anytime soon. As you said, there's still tests to run, and this place is also safe."

"You think they'll come after us?" Greg's eyes narrowed.

"To be honest, it's a possibility." Andi reached for Kathy's hand. She didn't flinch away, so he took it to soothe her. "But we don't think they will. What we've seen so far is an organization that calculates with a certain amount of loss. The higher-ups probably don't even know yet that you didn't arrive at your destination. Don't worry. You'll have a guard in front of your door day and night."

Kathy visibly relaxed, as did Greg, although his gaze was still alert. George sat down next to his bed in a silent offer of reassurance. "We do have some questions for you. Do you feel comfortable answering them, or do you need more time?" A part of George hated offering the two time, because with this case, it was the one thing they didn't have, but they were basically traumatized children, even though both Greg and Kathy seemed to be in their late teens.

Greg looked at Kathy, who nodded. "Ask. If anything we can tell you helps you get those assholes, it's worth the pain of reliving this nightmare."

"We can take a break anytime you need it. Just say the word." Andi was still stroking Kathy's hand. The girl was beginning to relax, which strengthened George's conviction about Andi being a decent man and a great cop. After everything Kathy and the others had endured, Andi still managed to gain her trust by simply being calm, even though she probably didn't view men favorably. The only reason he and Andi had decided to visit the two without a female officer present was because of Greg. From the interaction between Kathy and Greg during the previous night, Andi had concluded—and George had agreed—that the two were each other's comfort. When they had talked to Mia and Rose, one of the nurses had been there to reassure the two girls, which had had the desired effect, though they hadn't been able to contribute anything valuable.

George pulled out his cell and set it on record. "This is Detective George Donovan, conducting an interview together with Detective Andrew Hayes about a possible human trafficking ring operating in Charleston. Our witnesses are Greg...." George looked at Greg. "What's your full name?"

"Greg Smith."

George turned to Kathy.

"Kathy Sacks."

"Our witnesses are Greg Smith and Kathy Sacks, both freed in a raid after a tip from Taylor Vance." George shifted in his chair. "Greg, how old are you?"

Greg stared at the ceiling. "I turned seventeen on January the tenth."

George managed to hide his horror by shifting the cell in Kathy's direction. "Kathy, how old are you?"

"I'll be eighteen on August twenty-third."

"Do you remember when you were kidnapped?" George kept his gaze on Kathy. The girl squeezed Andi's hand and then jutted her chin forward in a stubborn move.

"That was three years ago on September the fifth. I was on my way home from a friend's birthday party when a dark van stopped next to me and I was yanked into it."

"Where did you live?" George couldn't believe it.

"I'm from Spartanburg. As I said, my mom's an alcoholic. We lived in one of the poor areas where people tend to keep to themselves." She laughed bitterly. "Not that anybody saw my abduction. It was dark. Nobody was there."

"I'm so sorry." Andi kept gently stroking her hand. "We're going to find you a safe place. I promise."

Kathy looked at the point where their hands were connected. "I'm not so sure if that's going to help," she whispered in a broken tone.

George opened his mouth to tell her that yes, it would most definitely help, and shut it again. This was counseling territory, not his forte. All four victims needed to talk to a pro to help them through this trauma. He settled on, "It's your decision, of course," before he turned to Greg. "When were you taken?"

"I'm not so sure. It was December 2016, but I don't remember the exact date. I was living on the streets, you see, and dates weren't as important as not starving and finding a safe place to sleep."

George didn't know what to say to that, so he asked the next question. "From where were you taken?"

"Actually from here. Charleston. I grew up in Summerville, and when my parents kicked me out for not being the son they wanted to have, I came to Charleston because it was the closest bigger city I could easily reach."

There was a wealth of tragedy and pain in this sentence alone, not to mention all the horrors Greg had endured afterward. That he wasn't broken, that he had managed to keep his fighting spirit, spoke of an inner strength George deeply admired. He had no doubt that if given even half a chance this boy would make his way in life.

"I know this must be painful, but can you tell me what happened after your abduction? We don't need details you're uncomfortable talking about. What we'd love to have are descriptions of people and places, something to help us identify those responsible for your suffering and catch them."

Greg and Kathy shared a look. Kathy's shoulders slumped. "We were drugged most of the time. They gave us sedatives to keep us pliant, and my memory of most of the places is hazy at best." She shrugged. "They looked all kind of the same. Rooms and good beds, I guess because the customers were rich?"

That was something to work with. "What made you think your customers were rich?"

Kathy stared at her hands again, seemingly at a loss for words.

Greg chimed in. "For me it was the way they talked. The clothes they wore. Most of the time the people who used us had masks so we couldn't recognize them. You see, we always knew when something was up when we started getting clear heads. Apparently the customers didn't like playing with drugged-up zombies, so they would sober us up, and after whatever perversion took place, they would pump us full again. The only reason Kathy and I weren't as zonked out as Mia and Rose last night was because they didn't have enough drugs left. They argued about it quite some time before they decided Kathy and I weren't dangerous enough to cancel the transport."

Greg's voice was shaking now. George reached out to him and patted his thigh. "Do you need a break?"

Greg shook his head. "No. I want to get this over with. Go on."

George looked at Andi, who gave a small nod. "From the people who handled you, did anybody ever stand out? Do you think you ever met the boss of the organization?"

"You mean the Lion Man?" Greg's voice was a mixture of fear and hatred.

The Lion Man—Rose and Mia had mentioned him too. A man wearing a lion mask who was sometimes there to oversee things. George hadn't been sure he wasn't an image their fear had conjured up, but if Greg and Kathy knew him as well, perhaps he was real.

"Who is the Lion Man?"

"I think he's the asshole who's responsible for everything we went through. I saw him several times, mostly at orgies, and yesterday when we were prepared for the transport to Charleston. He's disgusting." Greg made a face, and only the slight tremble in his hands betrayed how much he feared the Lion Man. George thought about how to phrase his next question, when Andi beat him to it.

"That man—was he somehow strange?" Andi sounded as if he wasn't sure what exactly he was asking, which was odd. So far George had always seen him confident and in control.

"You mean apart from the fact that he was wearing a freaking lion head as a mask?" Greg asked snidely, overcoming his moment of insecurity quickly.

Andi raised his hands in a placating gesture. "Whoa. Calm down. I meant was there anything about his mannerism, about the way he moved.... Like did you notice a limp or something like that?"

"Now that you mention it." Kathy tapped her lips with her right index finger. "For somebody who clearly wanted to intimidate, he moved kind of—" She struggled for the right word.

"Soft? Without much—I wouldn't say confidence because that he had—emphasis, perhaps?" Greg offered slowly.

"As if he wasn't all that strong?" Andi reminded George of a cougar, ready to pounce.

Greg and Kathy shared another look. They clearly took comfort from each other, just like George and Andi had assumed. "As I said, we were drugged most of the time and frightened, but yeah, he was definitely weaker than the guys watching us, even though he wasn't that much smaller." Greg beat a staccato rhythm on his blanket.

George did his best to neither stare openly nor intervene. Andi was obviously working his strange magic again, and George was equal parts pissed about being left out again and determined to uncover his partner's secret, because this interview had just turned into something from the *X-Files*.

"He sometimes used a walking stick. Like you would see British nobles with on TV?" Kathy offered.

George perked up. This was something they could maybe actually use. "Do you remember what it looked like?"

The girl furrowed her brows. "It was very smooth. A dark brown. With a white horse head on the top. Funny I only remember the horse now. I would have expected him to have a walking stick with a lion…."

George looked at Greg for confirmation. "I don't remember the horse, but the stick was as Kathy said. And he didn't always use it. But yesterday, he had it with him. And the more I think about it, the surer I am his hands were trembling."

George decided it was time to end the interview for this day. They had gotten quite a lot from Greg and Kathy, though he wasn't sure if any of it would be useful. Those kids needed to rest and talk to a counselor. Andi seemed to have come to the same conclusion, because he patted Kathy's hand one last time before he rose from his chair.

"Thank you so much, Kathy, Greg. You've been a great help. If you need anything or if you remember something else you think could be of use for us, please call us." He took two cards from one of his jeans pockets and handed them to Greg and Kathy.

"We will." Greg smiled a bit sadly. "See you."

George and Andi waved at the two before they left the room.

CHAPTER 16
CLOUDS IN THE SKY

THE WAY back to George's car was accompanied by an ominous silence. A silence Andi knew had its roots in the questions he had asked. It was a risk he had taken knowing full well it could backfire spectacularly. Which it now was probably doing. George may think he was able to deal with Andi having a secret "instinct" that helped him solve cases, but theoretically accepting something and having to cope with it in reality were two very different things.

Andi rolled his shoulders in an attempt to loosen up the tight muscles in his nape a bit. He'd been up for too long, without a chance to meditate or otherwise drown out the battery of images from the arthropods. Perhaps his judgment was a bit off. Perhaps it would have been better to keep his questions about the Lion Man to himself, ask them when George wasn't there. Then again, when would he have been able to do that? All he had about the Lion Man was the blurry image he'd gotten from the flea that had jumped from the lion mask to Mia. It was of a man with a blood deficiency, most probably anemia, which made the man unattractive for the flea, hence its jump to Mia, whose blood was—despite the drugs coursing through it—a lot more tempting to the little parasite.

Apart from the lion mask, this deficiency was their only solid lead on the mastermind behind the trafficking ring, and unfortunately, it was a lead they couldn't openly pursue. If there was still a "they" when George was done with his current brooding about the situation. To his own surprise, Andi felt a twinge of disappointment at the thought of not working with George anymore. As much as he had always resented having a partner, being with George hadn't been completely terrible. He was more attentive than the few previous partners he'd had, something Andi appreciated more than he would have thought possible. George also hadn't let himself be deterred by Andi's grumpiness; instead he had tried to cut through it and get to know Andi, which was also new. His previous partners all had known what they would be getting into and had used the fact that he had fulfilled all their worst assumptions about him as an excuse to get out of the partnership as fast as possible. Not that Andi hadn't played into their expectations with that exact outcome in mind. George was also the first to admit he suspected Andi of something, just like the others had done but never said out loud. Talking about his *geschenk* with somebody else, even if it was only in hints, had created the beginnings of a bond Andi would have never dared to hope for. Not being able to tell his partner the truth did put a strain on Andi and their partnership, of course, but so far George being there for him had been strangely comforting. Andi shuddered inwardly. There was no point in getting used to something he would only ever have for a short time and never to its full extent. Even if he let all his other barriers drop, there was always his *geschenk* standing between him and a deep, meaningful relationship, be it with a partner at work or one in life. Andi had thought he'd gotten used to that idea, but the wave of resentment washing through his body told him otherwise. Perhaps it was something one could never truly accept. Which was probably the reason his grandmother had been such a hard, unrelenting woman. When he was younger, Andi had sworn to himself he would never become like her, would never become so bitter he kept everybody at arm's length just out of principle. Working with George reminded him how similar he already was to his grandmother. It wasn't a nice or comforting thought.

They reached the car and got inside. As soon as he had his seat belt on, Andi decided to grab the bull by the horns. There was no use letting the silence between them fester even more until it turned into something that couldn't be healed. If it wasn't too late already.

"You're not happy with me," Andi stated, perhaps a little more bluntly than intended.

George huffed. "What tipped you off?"

This was going worse than Andi had feared. He tried to lighten the mood a little with a small joke. "If you must know—the vein ticking in your right temple is pretty telling, as is your passive-aggressive silence. You really know how to pump the atmosphere with dread."

"Andi, this isn't a joke!"

Apparently his attempt had failed. Suddenly tired of all this shit, Andi let his frustration show in his tone. "Do you see me laughing? I thought we had a truce!"

George slammed his palms against the steering wheel, clearly no less frustrated than Andi. "I thought so too, but what you did in there…. The questions you asked. Any decent lawyer will dismiss them as suggestive. Asking those kids, those drugged-up, traumatized kids, if the lion man appeared somehow weak? No matter how you try to spin this, it sounds an awful lot like you already know who it is. Or as if you have a candidate in mind you're planning to take down. And I was right there with you and didn't put a stop to it!"

Andi scowled. He really hated having his methods questioned when he was definitely on to something. A nasty little voice in the back of his head reminded him that this was one of the reasons detectives usually had a partner—to not become high-handed. He pointedly turned his metaphorical back on the voice and went for a direct assault instead. "First of all, if you're that worried about your career, you should back out right now. I have no use for a lead weight on my ankle. Secondly, if we catch whoever is in charge of that trafficking ring—and that's a big if, as you well know—do you really think the interview we did today will have any weight in the process? Because all we've learned is that the man who is supposedly on top wears a lion mask and moves as if he's exhausted. If that's all the evidence the prosecutor gets to work with, the case will never see a judge and jury, and you know it. So why are you so pissed? You were fine with my—" Andi searched for an appropriate word for his *geschenk*. "—intuition when I managed to get Vance to talk!"

George let out a strangled growl. Andi couldn't tell if he was angry with him, the situation at hand, or the case in general. "You caught me unawares. I thought we were both on the same level of cluelessness, and suddenly I realize it's only me. Again." George sounded even more frustrated than Andi felt, which evoked a strange mixture of kinship and pity in him he wasn't sure what to do with. George went on. "We're supposed to be partners, and I get you can't tell me about your secret, whatever it is, but if you pull shit like that, I don't even feel like a rookie detective with you. I feel completely and utterly excluded from something vital to a case I know we both want to solve at all cost, while at the same time being expected to cover up for you if it leads to something solid— which I know it will because so far that was always the case."

"And that's the second reason I don't want a partner." Andi felt his anger had drained. Now all that was left was a bone-deep tiredness. This had been a bad idea from the start, and he should have stopped Chief

Norris from doing this to him. Now he was here, entangled in a web of brief hope, disappointment on both sides, and a stale taste of the kind of partnership he could never have. All in all, a disaster. Andi vowed to never forget this moment so he would be steeled for future arguments with the chief.

George looked at him sharply. "My trust issues only make it to second rank?" Andi hoped he wasn't mistaken in detecting the hint of amusement in George's words. He allowed the ghost of a smile to flit across his face.

"In case you haven't noticed, my utter dislike for people in general will always be number one."

George chuckled, if only briefly. "Fine. So we've established you have two valid reasons not to want a partner, one of which I just reiterated for you. I'm almost afraid to ask if there's anything good about having me around."

Andi hesitated with his answer for so long that George started to shift nervously in his seat. It wasn't because Andi wanted to make him uncomfortable; he just wasn't sure how much of his thoughts on the matter he should reveal. They were already on thin ice, as their argument just now had proven. George had cooled down a lot faster than Andi would have thought, but Andi had been hurt more by George's anger than he wanted to admit.

Telling George he actually liked having him around would make Andi even more vulnerable at a time when his personal shields should have been up to the maximum. His grandmother's face appeared before his inner eye, the hard lines around her mouth, the cold and unrelenting gaze she had for everybody, even her own family. He saw his own face melting into hers, becoming just like her, never letting anybody in, always pushing people away. Andi shuddered. Ultimately this might be his fate. But not today. Today he would make a conscious effort not to be like her, even if he risked getting hurt.

"To be honest, I like having you around. You bring me tea and bagels. And you're a good detective. Working with you is fun." Andi stared out the window, unable to make eye contact with George. "I'm not going to lie to you. When Chief Norris assigned you to me, all I could think of was how to get rid of you as soon as possible. But you've grown on me. I—I realized having a partner is kind of nice."

To Andi's utter surprise, George checked him with his elbow. "Admit it, you fell for my charming personality."

The teasing tone assured Andi that—at least for the time being—they were good again. "If by personality you mean your willingness to pay for my breakfast, then yeah, I did fall for it."

"Charming as ever!" This time George laughed out loud. He started the car and backed out of the parking space. "I'm sorry I snapped at you. I'm not used to being out of the loop."

"And I'm sorry I didn't tell you beforehand. I'm not used to explaining myself to others. Too long without a partner. I promise I'll try to do better in the future."

"And I promise to be more patient. Deal?" George had stopped at the exit of the parking lot and turned to Andi. The expression in his eyes was sincere enough to let some embers of hope flare in Andi's chest. Perhaps things could work out between them.

"Deal. If it's any consolation to you, all I know about this man is that he's got a blood deficiency. That, and the lion mask."

"Hence the question if he somehow appeared to be weak. I get it."

"Yeah, I wanted confirmation."

"Which you got. What now?"

Andi leaned his head against the seat. "To be honest, I'd love nothing more than to go home and sleep for fifteen hours straight. Before we do that, though, we should check in with the IT department and with Evangeline. Perhaps one of them has something for us."

"Good plan. Let's stop at the Starbucks and get more coffee. My eyelids are heavier than they should be. I think I'm getting old. All-nighters didn't bother me that much when I was younger."

"Amen to that. Starbucks and the precinct. Then back home to get some sleep." Andi was relived to be back on good terms with George. He only hoped it would last.

As IT turned out, Shireen did have information for them. "Do you want the good news first or the bad news?" she asked with her ever-present tablet in hand. "Actually, the good news is kind of the bad news, so limited choice there."

"Just spit it out, Shireen." Andi took another sip of his herbal tea. He had put three tablespoons of honey into it, and the sugar was starting to work its magic, though not fast enough to make him polite. Thankfully, Shireen had known him long enough to just shrug at his grumpiness.

"You're insufferable when you haven't gotten enough sleep." She tapped away on her tablet and the biggest screen on the wall sprang to life. "When we worked on Taylor Vance's phone, we realized he wasn't the only outside contractor to work for that trafficking ring. The next logical step was to search the darknet to see if the suspects made contact there. These days eight out of ten nefarious schemes are set up through the darknet, as you may know. Anyway, we had to go back two years, but there we found an ad, as well as a chat concerning the transportation of 'sensitive' cargo."

Line after line of a conversation about payment for transporting girls and boys across the country appeared on screen. Andi had to fight to keep his tea down. Shireen continued with the false cheer she always showed when something truly disturbed her. "To cut it short, the different parties came to an agreement and, as we know now, started working together. We were able to identify three of the guys you busted the other night as those who made a deal with the unknown person behind the ad. The million-dollar question is, why weren't the ad and chat deleted afterward?" Shireen looked at them expectantly.

Andi shrugged. He wasn't in the mood to guess. George furrowed his brows. "I assume that's what would normally happen?" When Shireen nodded, he went on. "Perhaps they forgot it?"

Andi snorted. "I doubt that. Everything about this organization screams overcautious. They would never knowingly risk exposure like that."

"And we have a winner!" Shireen grinned. "Which brings us to the good news being bad news part I was talking about. Our bad guys are indeed overcautious. They hired the best to get this ad and chat up and running. A guy called 'All-Eye.'" She rolled her eyes to show how unimpressed she was by that name. "The next part is what makes me inclined to believe in some higher powers again. All-Eye died two years ago, the same day he finalized the deal between our charming suspects and the trafficking ring. He was shot when the supermarket where he bought his energy drinks was robbed. We would probably have never found out about his death if the police hadn't searched his apartment. They were looking for clues about next of kin they could inform about his death. When they looked into his laptop, they quickly realized something was very wrong, since the thing started encrypting itself the moment they touched it. So they brought it to the IT people of their precinct, who tried to hack into it. I hate to admit it, but All-Eye was a genius. All they could salvage before the entire hard drive fried itself was confirmation of his identity. Still, we were lucky because he hadn't connected the chat to the virus he used to destroy all the content. That's why it's still out there."

"Why wouldn't those traffickers hire somebody else to take it down?" George asked with furrowed brows.

"A number of reasons. Chances are, they don't even know the ad is still out. I assume the deal with All-Eye was to set the ad and chat up, make the deal happen, and then terminate the site. Since everything else had worked smoothly, perhaps they didn't see the need to check if the site was really down. It would have been in All-Eye's interest as well to delete it, so perhaps they got lazy." She held up one hand with at least one silver ring on each finger when George opened his mouth to say something. "And if they weren't lazy and had seen the site was still up, they may have decided not to take the risk of asking somebody else to take it down. Perhaps they have tried to contact All-Eye about it, and when he didn't answer, they must have realized something was wrong. As I said, All-Eye was a genius and the equivalent of a rock star in the scene. They would have had a hard time finding anybody crazy enough to touch something All-Eye set up. He was known for placing nasty viruses to protect his content. Just leaving the ad up was probably their safest option instead of throwing stones at a potential hornet's nest."

"Can you find them through the ad?" Andi took another sip of his tea. The expression on Shireen's face didn't make him hopeful.

"That's part of the bad news. Even though All-Eye's laptop destroyed itself, the site with the chat is still protected. All communication ran through him, which means any leads to the other party are gone. We'll keep digging, of course, but I'm not overly optimistic. The good news is, they haven't hired anybody new in the last two years as far as we can tell, which could mean they haven't expanded their operation beyond state borders."

It wasn't much of a silver lining, but Andi would take it on a crap day like this. "You think they're not operating countrywide?"

Shireen nodded. "As I said, we keep digging. But the chat shows deals with a limited number of outside contractors, and the routes they've been discussing are all within South Carolina. That trafficking ring is a serious problem, but as far as I can tell it's still local."

"Thank you, Shireen. Keep us posted, will you?" Andi nodded at her, and George briefly touched her shoulder in a silent gesture of appreciation. Shireen nodded.

"Will do. Get those assholes!"

George and Andi left the IT department and headed for the morgue.

EVANGELINE'S WORKPLACE seemed even gloomier than usual, though Andi was willing to chalk it up to him being bone-tired and slightly depressed, thanks to the news from Shireen. If George had similar feelings, he didn't show them openly. He greeted Evangeline with a little less reservation than the first time, which confirmed Andi's suspicion that George was trying to warm her up to him. Smart man. Evangeline turned to Andi.

"You look like crap."

"I love you too," he snapped back, maybe with a little more emphasis than was called for. George visibly flinched. Evangeline just laughed, if a bit sadly.

"Sorry, Andi, I'm just telling it as it is. I'd be a bad physician if I wouldn't point out your bad condition in case you hadn't noticed yourself."

"Evangeline, you cut corpses open, for goodness sake." Andi raised his hands in a defensive gesture.

"Just because the dead are my area of expertise doesn't mean I'm not fit to examine the living, as you well know. Given your sour mood, I have to stress how important it is for you to get some much-needed sleep *ona vave*. We so do not need a repeat of the Harrison case."

Andi sighed. "I know, Evangeline, I know. I'm going home after this, I promise."

"What about the Harrison case?" George chimed in.

"Not relevant to this case. I'll tell you about it later," Andi said. *Or never*, he added in the privacy of his thoughts. That case had come close to breaking him, and he preferred not thinking about it at all. Evangeline shot him a glance before she turned back to George.

"Andi almost collapsed when working that case. As his partner, it's your duty to see to it that he gets enough rest. He tends to overwork himself, which isn't such a good idea at his age anymore."

"I'm not that old, Evangeline," Andi groaned.

George chuckled. "You may not be ancient yet, partner, but we both agreed not long ago that we aren't as young as we used to be. I'll take him home after this, Evangeline."

She nodded, seemingly satisfied with George's assurance. "*Lelei*. Now, I worked on those other two girls while you were busy busting those trafficking assholes."

Andi didn't even bother asking how she knew. Even though she worked down in the morgue, Evangeline had a way of always knowing what was going on.

"What did you find?"

Her eyes narrowed. "A lot of things, none of which make me the least bit happy. Let's just say, if you do get the chance to skin the bastards responsible for all this alive, go for it. I'll cover it up as an inevitable part of arresting them."

"When you're that bloodthirsty, it must be really bad." Andi knew Evangeline was emotionally invested in all the victims on her slab, but it was rare for her to be so vocal about what she wanted done to the culprits. Going from her reaction alone, Andi grew even more determined to get the asshole responsible for all this.

"It's even worse. But enough about me. I found out who your victims are." She opened the first drawer with the second African American girl in it. "This is Tracy Longman, age seventeen. She's a runaway from North Augusta, and we could only figure this out because her school had filed her as a missing person. Apparently her parents couldn't be bothered, since they were too busy getting high on booze and cocaine." Evangeline opened a second drawer, this one containing the Caucasian girl of the trio. "This is Jennifer Stenton, age fifteen. She's from Bishopville, where she disappeared from her foster home. The foster parents are what the nightmare of every foster child is made of and didn't bother looking for her or going to the police since they still received the checks from youth services. It's only thanks to a social worker who insisted on talking to her after her foster parents had warded off any such attempts numerous times that she was finally entered into the missing persons databank. That was a week ago." Evangeline looked like a goddess of revenge, her dark eyes blazing with the fire of righteous fury. Andi couldn't blame her. If anybody had given a damn about those two girls, they might have been found. Or not, as the story of Lilly Cordon showed. But at least there would have been a chance. Andi briefly wondered how many children fell through the social net every year and very firmly shoved that thought to the back of his mind. There was no use pondering it now.

"What else can you tell us about them?" George asked through clenched teeth. He obviously didn't like what Evangeline had told them any more than Andi did, and again Andi felt a strange sense of warmth spreading through his body. Having a partner wasn't as bad as he'd thought. Having a partner who shared his sentiments was even better.

Evangeline lifted a hand as if she wanted to touch Jennifer Stenton's hair but didn't finish the gesture. "They were both strangled, as you already knew. Just like Lilly Cordon, they were drugged up with several tranquilizers, which had started wearing off at the time of death, and they both show signs of sexual assault. There was no sperm I could extract to compare with our databanks, but the signs of repeated rape are obvious." She sighed. "Also, Tracy Longman has been pregnant and given birth no longer than three months ago. I found stretch marks on her abdomen, as well as certain hormones in her bloodwork that would have been gone were it longer ago. As far as I can tell, the child was carried full-term, though I can't say if it survived the birth. It was a natural birth, and it was painful because her entire perineum was ripped open. Somebody tried to stitch her up but did a piss-poor job. Unfortunately for her, that didn't stop her kidnappers from giving her to men."

Andi closed his eyes. Just thinking about what these girls had gone through made his stomach revolt. If his body hadn't been so adamant about keeping the little nourishment it had gotten over the past twenty-four hours, he would have probably thrown up right in the morgue. As it was, he managed to keep it down, but it was a close call. George had his hands balled to fists, the knuckles turning white from the force.

"Do you think the baby's still alive?" He was voicing Andi's biggest fear.

Evangeline shrugged with a hopeless expression. "I hope so. Because why would they go to the trouble of having Tracy carrying full-term just to kill the baby once it was born? They obviously didn't let her keep it, but there's a flourishing black market for desperate couples who don't meet the standards of adopting agencies. I pray those bastards simply saw this as another opportunity to make money and sold the child to somebody who wanted a baby at any cost."

"And if not?" Andi's mouth was operating on autopilot. He didn't want to hear the answer. He didn't want to think about all the other terrible options. Somehow, his brain seemed to not have gotten the memo.

"I don't want to think about 'if not,'" Evangeline said very firmly. "The easiest way to make money with that poor baby is by selling it into adoption. That's what I'm going with; otherwise I won't be able to sleep tonight."

"Is there a way to find the baby via DNA?" George sounded defeated.

"Only if they were treated in a hospital for something serious. I've already added Tracy's DNA profile to our database, and I'm going to make inquiries at the hospitals in South Carolina. I've also alerted youth services, though there's not much they can do at this point. Hopefully, if we have to go across state borders in our search, they will be more of a help. The best way to find the baby would be if you busted that trafficking ring. They have to have information about their victims somewhere."

"Way to put the pressure on, Evangeline." Andi pinched the bridge of his nose. He really needed to sleep.

"See it as additional motivation." Evangeline closed the two drawers with Tracy and Jennifer in them. "I'll send you my detailed reports later and keep you informed about any new developments."

"Thank you, Evangeline. You've been a great help, as always." Andi turned toward the exit. He needed to get out.

"You're welcome. Get some sleep, Andi."

Andi waved. He heard George saying his goodbyes as well, and then they were on their way back to the office.

CHAPTER 17
CUL DE SAC

AFTER A quick stop at their desks, George insisted on driving Andi home. He looked paler with every passing minute, and George was getting seriously worried. He hoped it wasn't his outburst after questioning Greg and Kathy that had contributed to Andi's current state. The eight-minute drive to Stiles Point on James Island was accompanied by the kind of exhausted silence that comes after an all-nighter at work. George felt he was nearing a second wind, but one look at Andi told him it would be plain cruel to try and engage him in a conversation. The man's head was leaning against the window of the passenger side door, his eyes were closed, and now and then he would shudder as if he were cold. George had the nagging feeling he should be doing something and didn't know what it was. It made him nervous and restless, both feelings amped up by his lack of sleep.

The GPS sent him to a palatial-looking house set back from the street by a good hundred feet. George made sure he had the right address, because he couldn't believe this was where Andi lived. He had known James Island was for those with deeper pockets, but he had assumed Andi was renting an apartment, not residing in a gorgeous little villa with blinding white railings on the front porch and a balcony wrapped around the first floor. Even though he was no expert in architecture, George could tell this house was old—not the run-down, shabby old they had seen in the neighborhood where the Cordons lived, but the well-preserved, dignified old that resulted from perfect maintenance over the years. If this house were a wine, it would probably sell at a thousand dollars per bottle, perhaps even more. A cross between a yelp and a snore snapped George's attention back to Andi, who apparently had slid forward when the car slowed down and had narrowly escaped planting face-first into the console. "Easy, cowboy. We're at your house. Only a few more steps and you can fall into your bed."

"Not sure if I can make it to the bedroom. Couch is fine," Andi mumbled while he fumbled for the clip of his seat belt. George managed to contain his eye roll and helped his clearly confused partner out. It was kind of nice, taking care of Andi when he was so helpless. So far the man had shown a degree of independence and self-sufficiency George had found a bit intimidating. Seeing his partner at such a low helped George overcome the last vestiges of resentment he'd still harbored after their visit at the hospital. Having been kept out of the loop had not only hurt his feelings but also his pride, and George was man enough to admit it soothed his ego that Andi was, in this moment, dependent on him.

After he had freed Andi from the evil seat belt, George left the car and went around it to open the door for Andi. His partner all but fell out of the car, clutching at George's arm to keep himself steady. "I think I'm crashing," Andi whispered, leaning a good deal of his weight on George. He was heavier than George would have guessed from his build, though it could be because Andi was more or less dead weight at this point. He somehow managed to get his keys out, and George opened the front door for him.

"Where's your bedroom?"

"Second floor."

George glanced around the beautiful ground floor with the open-living concept—clearly a change made a long time after the house had been built—and the floor-to-ceiling glass doors looking out into a garden big enough to host a broad wooden veranda, a gazebo in the far right corner, a pond roughly six feet in diameter, and lots of greenery that looked like a lot of work to maintain. He didn't have time to ponder the grandeur of Andi's garden, though. His partner was leaning more heavily on him with every passing minute, and if George didn't want to carry Andi upstairs, he had to hurry.

"Come on. It's just a few steps," he coaxed his yawning partner.

Andi cooperated with sluggish movements, and they finally made it to the top, where George saw a hallway with two doors on each side.

"Which one's your bedroom, Andi?"

"Second on the left."

When they reached the door, George supported Andi's entire weight—or so it seemed—on one arm while opening the door with his free hand. They entered the room in a graceless tumble of flailing limbs that almost sent them both to the floor. George managed to get enough forward momentum to place Andi on a comfortable-looking king-size bed with a lavender satin cover. Helping Andi get rid of his shoes and sliding between the sheets only took a minute. With a contented sigh, Andi snatched one of the four huge pillows and buried his head in it.

"I'm getting too old for this shit. Thank you, George."

After that, he was out like a light. George waited for a moment, took a good look at the room even though a little voice inside his head told him to leave and stop snooping around. He silenced the voice by pointing out it couldn't possibly be snooping since Andi wouldn't have found his bed without his help. When the voice insisted it still wasn't right to stare at the three picture frames with photographs of strange-looking beetles in them, George decided it was time to get some sleep himself. On his way out to his car, he couldn't help but notice how exquisite everything in Andi's home seemed to be—the broad leather couch with the two matching love seats was the kind of old only high-quality furniture could ever achieve. A short glimpse into the kitchen—it was practically impossible not to see the kitchen when looking at the couch—showed gleaming steel and glowing marble countertops accentuated by massive wood cabinets with glass doors. George knew there could be—and most probably was—a perfectly innocent explanation as to how Andi could afford such a grand home. Chief Norris wouldn't have sent him to spy on Andi if getting rid of him could have been done through his ownership of the house. Still, the pragmatic cop in him found it highly suspicious. Just like he still found it suspicious how Andi already seemed to know something about the trafficking leader. He had stressed all he knew was that he had some kind of blood deficiency, but Andi could be lying. Hell, he had admitted to lying to George when it came to his "hunches." The question was how much of what Andi told him was the truth, what was a blatant lie, and what lingered in the gray area between the two where the truth could be stretched to a point where it was almost indistinguishable from a lie? And how was George to tell the difference when he'd known his partner for less than a week and Andi was harder to read than even George's mother when she was attending a social function? And it was such a shame too, because the team-oriented cop in him wanted to keep working with Andi. Having a smart, capable partner was something George always enjoyed, since it forced him to be his own best, to push himself to his limits and beyond. Andi sure did that. With a sigh that expressed both his inner conflict and his exhaustion, George closed the door to Andi's house, got into his car, and drove home to get some sleep.

AT SIX the next morning, George's cell woke him from a deep sleep and had him cursing loudly while he blindly reached for the device that wasn't at its usual place on the nightstand. He finally found it on the other side of the bed under a pillow, and if the ringtone hadn't told him it was his brother Danny calling him, he would have simply shut it off and gone back to sleep. As it was, he accepted the call, though his greeting was more rabid wolverine than loving brother.

"What?"

"Good morning to you too, sunshine." George could hear Danny suppressing a chuckle, and it had his hackles rising.

"Don't, Danny. I'm recovering from an all-nighter that turned into an almost forty-eight-hour shift with more insights into the hell that is man's mind than one person should ever have to endure, and I haven't had any coffee yet."

Danny whistled through the phone, causing George to hold his cell at arm's length for a moment. "That's hard, man. Did anything come of it?"

George hesitated. Not because he was pondering how much to tell his brother, because the rules were pretty clear on that and Danny fully understood. The question reminded him of the things he had learned about Andi and of the doubts that had been creeping back into his thoughts.

"We're not sure yet. There's some leads, though nothing solid so far." Which was true for both the case and Andi.

"Why do I get the feeling you're not telling me the whole story?"

"Because I can't reveal details about an ongoing investigation?"

"Har-di-har-har, little brother. If you want to out-sass me, you need more than just one sarcastic comment. Now spill. Does it have to do with a certain partner you've been told to watch?"

George gave up. Without coffee, he stood no chance against Danny, and he didn't really want to. What he wanted was to talk to somebody who could give him advice.

"I did what you told me. I operated on the assumption that he's simply good at his job."

"Aaand?"

"He *is* good at his job. He also has a secret he won't tell me about, but he says he's glad I know he has a secret because now he can use me to cover it up."

Something spluttered on the other end of the line. Apparently, Danny had parted with a mouthful of his daily dose of caffeine. "He's got balls."

"Yeah. Big hairy ones, I can tell you."

"No, don't. I'll take your word for it. Though if he so freely admits to having a secret, how bad can it be?"

George sighed and got out of bed. He felt the need to pace. "My thoughts exactly. He swore it was nothing illegal, and frankly, I would be very surprised if Andi was capable of doing anything unlawful. He's too straightforward for that, even though he's a grumpy asshole most of the time."

"So you believe him?"

"I do and I don't. I'm torn. It's the way he knows things he shouldn't know. When we questioned some witnesses, I felt left out because he was asking about things that sounded like pure speculation. I got angry, and we had a fight. We talked it out, and then later I drove him home because he was so exhausted, and I find out he lives in a little villa in one of the most expensive areas of Charleston."

"And now you suspect there might be dirt on him, and you question your own judgment of him."

"Yes and no. If the house was in any way linked to something illegal, I'm pretty sure Chief Norris would have sunk her claws into Andi already. I'm still convinced he's clean, I just don't know what annoys me more—the fact he's keeping a secret from me or that I want him to trust me enough to reveal it."

This time, Danny's whistle was low enough for George to keep his phone at his ear. "You want to keep him as your partner!"

"I do. And isn't that funny? You know me; I've never been too eager about my partners. I got along and there was a certain companionship, but I never felt the wish to get to know them better."

"But you want to get to know Andi better?"

"Yes. At the same time, I'm supposed to spy on him and we're working on a huge, disgusting case we absolutely have to solve. It's driving me nuts."

"Oh, brother, you do have a talent for ending up in the most interesting situations." Danny made a *tsking* sound.

"I know that, Danny. What I don't know is what I should do. Any suggestions?"

Danny started humming "Singing in the Rain" so terribly off-tune it made George's ears ring. When he was done, his voice sounded entirely too cheerful. "This is a tough one, I give you that. My advice is just buckle up and enjoy the ride. The situation hasn't changed as much as you might think. You've only known this Andi guy for what, a week? Even if he were an ordinary partner, it'd take time to get closer to him. You simply use that time to also decide whether he's a criminal, and to solve a difficult case. Piece of cake, really."

"Thank you so much for nothing. That I would have worked out on my own after some coffee."

"But now you don't have to, because your beloved older brother in his great wisdom has taken this burden from you. You're so welcome, George."

"Tell me again, why did you call?" George wasn't sure if he should laugh or scream.

"Two reasons. One, it's going to be Mom's birthday soon, and I wanted to know if you're on board with giving her a weekend at her favorite spa."

George groaned. "We do that every year, Danny. So yes, I'm on board. Same procedure and everything."

"Gee, forgive me for asking. You could have changed your mind, you know."

"Not really. I'm bad with presents, just like you and Griff, which is why Mom let us off the hook years ago by allowing us to basically give her a repeat present every year."

"You're insufferable without coffee. Well, second, I was a bit worried about you because of the Andi situation, but now we've talked about it and everything's fine, or so I think. Is everything fine?"

"Nothing's fine and you know it, Danny. But you can't do anything to help with this except call me at the butt crack of dawn and remind me why it's a good thing we don't live under the same roof anymore."

"It's my pleasure." Danny snorted, then got serious. "I mean it, George, if you need help, if you need to talk, call me at any time. This is the first time I've seen you so out of sorts, and it makes me a bit nervous. I'd feel better if you gave me regular updates."

"If I promise to do that, will you stop calling me at ungodly hours?"

"That could be negotiated."

George hesitated. "Thank you, Danny. Really. It was good talking to you."

"And it was interesting talking to you." Danny had already left the seriousness of the situation behind. George found he could live with that. His brother's call had helped him relax.

"I'll talk to you soon. Have a good day, Danny."

"You too, George. And catch those bastards!"

"Will do."

George disconnected the call and put the cell on the nightstand. For a brief moment, he considered going back to bed, then decided against it. There were still evil guys to catch, and he wasn't that tired anymore. Coffee, a short workout, then back to work. It sounded like a plan.

AFTER A quick shower, George went out to swing by the Starbucks and get him and Andi breakfast. His partner had texted him that he would walk to the precinct and they would meet there. When George arrived at their desks, Andi was already there, looking slightly better than the day before. The dark circles under his eyes had evened out a bit, and when George placed his usual plain bagel and cup of tea in front of him, he even smiled. It wasn't the kind of smile that lit up a room or made the main characters in romantic stories swoon, but it was definitely more than just a quirk of the lips, and coming from Andi, it was a thousand times better than some stupid lip motion brightening the day of some lovesick fool.

"Thank you, George. You're a lifesaver. And thank you for driving me home yesterday. Without you, I'd have probably ended up sleeping on one of the slabs in the morgue."

"Evangeline would've killed you. And you're welcome. It's what partners do."

Andi's eyes flashed at these words, but not like he was going to lash out. It was almost… tender. George tried not to overthink it. They were both still tired.

"Do we have any new leads?" he asked instead.

Andi shook his head, then took a bite from his bagel. "Unfortunately not. The license numbers on the vans were fake, and the vans were both stolen six months ago in Beaufort." Andi stared at their whiteboard, that showed mainly question marks and dead ends. "I hate to say this, but we don't have anything to go on."

George contemplated the whiteboard as well and had to agree. They had the bodies of the three girls, the testimony of the four victims they had saved, and the less than helpful confessions of Ronald Wallace, Taylor Vance, and the four men they had taken into custody during the raid. They also had Detective Harris, a cop who may or may not be a part of the trafficking organization and Andi's hunch that the person responsible for all this, the one wearing the lion mask, seemed to be somehow sick. That was a lot of dead ends for a case with so many people involved already in contact with the police and/or under arrest.

"You don't have another one of your—insights?"

Andi raised a brow. "Was it hard to find a good word for it?" He grinned, taking the sting out of his words. George picked up on the lighter tone and flipped Andi off.

"Idiot. Insight sounds so much better than nefarious and probably illegal information."

"I told you, it's not illegal. Not really."

George winked. "I know. Any 'ideas'?" He made sure to draw quotation marks in the air. Andi threw a napkin at him.

"Why do I get the feeling you're using my unique talent?"

"Because I do." George shrugged. "The way things are with this case, I'm grabbing at any straw I can reach."

"And now I feel underappreciated," Andi muttered.

"You still haven't answered the question."

"I don't. And before you ask, I still have some options before we have to give up. And one of them is perfectly legal and right in the book of good police work."

"You know the book? That's kind of a surprise."

Andi shrugged. "I read the table of contents. That had to be enough. Anyway, I have an informant, somebody who always has his ear on the ground, so to speak. I'd say we pay him a visit and see what he has to say."

"Wouldn't he have contacted you if there was something major going on? Isn't that what informants usually do?" At least that was how George had operated with his informants. Regular meetings where they told him everything that was going on.

Andi shook his head. "No, Skipper doesn't contact me. If I need something, I go to him. I try not to overtax him. He can be skittish."

"Now I'm curious."

They packed their stuff and headed out to Cortez Street in North Charleston, a drive that took them almost forty minutes instead of the usual twenty due to serious traffic. The house Andi led him to stood a little apart from the others on the street and had a huge garden with four greenhouses in it, each of them fifteen yards long and five wide. The house itself could use a paint job but looked otherwise well-maintained, which surprised George. This wasn't an area where people had time to keep their houses in repair. Even the fence surrounding the property looked solid, although some of the planks didn't match with the rest. Andi stopped at the gate that went up to his waist and was flanked by two wooden poles which were connected by a third at the top and reached for a steel staff. When he pulled on it, a bell hanging from the beam over their heads rang, followed only seconds later by loud, aggressive barking. George took an involuntary step back when a large German Shepherd with an unusually dark coat sprinted around the corner. The dog reached them with a few leaps, put its front paws on top of the gate, and cocked its head to the side while growling lowly. The sound made the hair on George's neck stand up. He'd had his fair share of run-ins with guard dogs, most of them not of the friendly variety, and wasn't keen on adding another unpleasant encounter. Andi, on the other hand, was calmness personified.

"Hey, Indica, good girl. I know, I haven't been here for some time. You're such a good watchdog, girl. Such a good dog!"

The growling stopped. Indica pushed her head forward until her snout was level with Andi's midsection. Her tail started wagging lazily, and Andi slowly reached out so as not to spook her. When she gave no indication that she didn't like what he was doing, Andi started scratching her behind the ears. The wagging became more energetic. "Such a good, good girl. Now, can you tell me if Skipper is home?"

At the mention of Andi's informant, the wagging went up another notch. Before Andi could "question" Indica further, a man stepped out of the house. He was middle-aged, George guessed around forty, about six feet, with some padding around his midsection. His dreadlocks reached down to his waist, and he had deep wrinkles around his eyes and mouth. His skin was only a few shades darker than Andi's, giving him a healthy look. The man whistled, and Indica turned around to bound toward him. This seemed to have been some kind of silent invitation because Andi opened the gate to step through. George followed, still wary of the dog, who was now sitting next to her owner, tongue lolling out.

"Andi, it's been some time." The man didn't sound overly enthusiastic but wasn't outright hostile either. George took that as a win.

"Skipper. You look good." Andi didn't seem fazed by Skipper's cold shoulder. "This is my partner, George Donovan."

Skipper snorted. "Now I know hell has frozen over. You don't do partners, Andi."

"Times change." Andi shrugged. "Can we talk?"

"Can I say no?"

Andi simply raised a brow. Skipper huffed. "Thought so. Come in."

They followed Skipper and Indica inside, where George was immediately assaulted by the very distinctive smell of marijuana. He looked at Andi, who shook his head almost imperceptibly. So Skipper was that kind of informant—one who was, technically, a criminal himself but too small a fish for the police to take him into custody. Skipper didn't offer them a seat, let alone something to drink. He leaned against his kitchen counter, his arms crossed over his chest.

"What do you want to know?"

Andi obviously wasn't deterred by this straightforward approach. His voice was as smooth as always, not showing even a hint of annoyance. George admired his restraint.

"Do you know anything about a human trafficking ring operating here in Charleston? Any rumors?"

Skipper's entire stance sagged when Andi mentioned the trafficking ring. He put one hand on Indica's head and sighed. "Terrible thing. I haven't heard much, only some whispered comments on the quiet. Nobody seems to know anything, and you know how *that* usually plays out."

Andi nodded. "Suddenly everybody knows something."

Skipper shuddered. "It's impossible to say what's true and what's made up. The only facts I'm sure of are that a man who calls himself the Lion is trying to claim the Charleston territory as his base of operations for a human trafficking ring. The pimps aren't happy about it because he apparently doesn't like to share, but they haven't acted against him yet, which means they either don't see him as a real threat or they are too afraid to attack."

"I tend toward option number two. Anything else?"

"No."

George looked between Andi and Skipper. If this were his informant, he would have pressed for more, but he didn't know the nature of Andi's agreement with Skipper, which seemed definitely unusual, so he kept his mouth shut. Andi simply nodded.

"Thank you, Skipper. As always, you've been a great help."

Skipper huffed. "Am I supposed to say you're welcome?"

A twitch that could be interpreted as a smile rushed across Andi's lips. "Not yet. But you can do so after I tell you about the barnacles starting to invade your greenhouse on the very left. They haven't developed far yet, so you still have a chance to get them under control. I would hurry, though. They're a determined bunch."

Skipper paled. "Shit. Thank you, Andi. You find your way out? I've got things to do." With that Skipper left the kitchen, Indica hot on his heels. He was muttering curses under his breath.

"A nice day to you too!" Andi yelled after him. Skipper just waved vaguely in their direction.

"We're done here." Andi led the way outside, closing the door behind them. Once they were back in the car, George looked at him. "Two questions. You probably won't answer the first one, but I simply have to ask. How did you know about those barnacles? Or did you make that up?"

"You're right, I'm not going to answer that. And I never make things up. At least I try. Second question?"

"How do you know Skipper told you everything?"

Andi thought about that for a moment. "I met Skipper about ten years ago. I hadn't been a detective for long, and I arrested him for dealing weed. He was addicted to cocaine and had quit six months before that. The dealing was his way of financing his way back into society. He's the perfect informant because he knows practically everybody through his marijuana dealings, and he also has an in with the shadier types from his addict days. There isn't much he doesn't know about the goings-on in Charleston's criminal underbelly, and nobody views him as a threat. Which is another reason I try not to use him too often. As for why I trust him about the information—or lack thereof—even though it didn't look like it, Skipper and I get along. I help him out sometimes, and I turn a blind eye on his dealing. He appreciates that. I also directed him toward a perfectly legal enterprise with which he makes most of his money these days." This time there was definitely a smile on Andi's face.

"What kind of enterprise? The way you say it, it can't be anything mundane."

Now Andi was grinning. "I told him about the wonderful opportunities in the world of insect cuisine."

George didn't understand. "Can you elaborate?"

"Gladly. Skipper breeds different kinds of bugs—locusts, mealworms, crickets and the likes—for gourmet restaurants all over the US. He's quite famous for the high quality of his merchandise."

"And I'm out." George shivered. "Eating insects isn't for me. The thought alone gives me goose bumps."

"You do realize there's a high chance that you'll have to get used to it? Apart from the fact that there's numerous cultures in which eating insects is the norm, they do have other advantages as well. One pound of beef requires 1,799 gallons of water during production, whereas one pound of insects, like crickets, only requires one gallon of water. Insects also have a high nutritional value because of their mono- and polyunsaturated fatty acids and are rich in trace elements such as copper, iron, and zinc. In light of climate change and a growing world population, insects are likely going to be the food source of the future."

George started the car and tried not to think about food that could crawl off his plate. "That may be the case, but I think I'm going vegan then. Just thinking about eating something with more than four legs makes me shiver."

"It's actually not that bad. Fried crickets are quite tasty, and I like the crunch."

"And here I thought you were picky. What's with the plain bagel every morning?"

"My stomach is delicate in the morning. A plain bagel is all I can keep down. Lunch can also be tricky, but dinner is when my adventurous side awakens." George saw Andi winking at him from the corner of his eye.

"My idea of adventure is ordering the new burger variation at my favorite diner. I normally stick to one dish."

"Sounds like a wild life."

George shrugged. "I prefer my food to be predictable."

"Which isn't wrong. Just boring," Andi teased.

"Believe it or not, I *love* boring. Especially on the job." Boring meant nobody died. George liked that.

"Only our job isn't boring at the moment." Andi sighed. "I really thought Skipper would be more helpful."

"Yeah. We're still stuck. All we have are dead ends and three dead girls. That's not good. Not at all."

"Let's see if Shireen has found something new when we're back at the precinct. If not, I have to take more drastic measures."

"Do you need help?" George couldn't resist offering.

Andi laughed. "Nice try, buddy."

For the rest of the drive, they kept bouncing theories around, but without anything solid to build on, it was more a thought experiment than anything else. When they entered the precinct, Rose stopped them before they could reach their desks.

"Andi, George, Chief Norris wishes to see you. She said you should go to her as soon as you're back."

George saw Andi's shoulders stiffen a little. There definitely wasn't any love lost between him and the chief. He had the sudden urge to touch Andi's shoulder to show his support and was brave enough to actually risk it. He was rewarded with a grateful look from Andi and an open mouth from Rose, who stared at his hand on Andi's shoulder as if it were an alien being. George didn't push his luck, though. Andi was like a cat in many respects, definitely solitary with sudden outbursts of the cuddles but strictly limited and on his terms. That Andi had allowed him to touch his shoulder was already a big win, and George wouldn't risk it by getting cocky.

Side by side they went for the chief's office. George knocked, feeling Andi's reluctance to talk to Norris. The chief asked them inside, and after they had taken a seat, she wasted no time getting to the point.

"Where are we regarding the trafficking case?"

Andi glanced at George, a silent prompt to take over talking. George cleared his throat. "I'm sorry to say we've hit some dead ends today. Neither the vans nor Andi's informant provided any new insights. We were hoping Shireen might have found something on Taylor Vance's phone. If not, I'm afraid there's a chance the case will turn cold."

Norris's eyes narrowed. "Unacceptable, gentlemen. I had a meeting with the mayor today, and Mrs. Manafort was adamant that we break this trafficking ring. At the moment, the press hasn't been involved, and we're trying to keep it that way for as long as possible. But you must solve this case. Human trafficking is a stain on the beautiful city of Charleston which must be eradicated, preferably before the press gets wind of it."

George saw Andi's knuckles going white as he gripped the armrest of his chair. His jaw muscles were bulging, which was George's cue to start talking again. "Believe me, Chief, we see it as a stain as well and we're doing everything in our power, but we can't follow leads that aren't there. Whoever is heading this operation is a paranoid pro who knows how to not create trails."

Chief Norris waved her hand dismissively. "That's not my problem. My problem is keeping the mayor happy, since this is an election year. *Your* job is to hand me those traffickers on a silver platter."

This time, George wasn't fast enough. "We do what we can, and our work would be easier if some newbie chief wouldn't be trying to prove the size of her balls by putting the blame on us even before the case has gone south."

For a moment the office was completely silent. Chief Norris's mouth was opening and closing like she was a fish stranded on the shore. When she finally managed to talk again, her voice was cold enough to create frost patterns on the window. "I'm just pretending I didn't hear that."

Andi shrugged. "Does that mean we can pretend not to have heard your little speech from before?"

George decided now was the time to put his diplomatic talents to use. "How about we *all* pretend we haven't heard anything that has been said so far? Can we perhaps start this conversation anew?"

Chief Norris mulled his words over with narrowed eyes, then slowly nodded. "Fine," she hissed through gritted teeth. "I'm going to pretend this insubordination never happened." She pointed at Andi. "But only this time. Don't start thinking you've got a jester's license with me."

Andi inhaled deeply. "Whatever. Can we go back to discussing the case?"

"Apparently there isn't that much to discuss, if I understood Detective Donovan right." The chief still sounded angry, but she made a conscious effort to tone it down. "Now would be a great time to use that famous 'instinct' of yours. We can't have a human trafficking ring operating in our city!"

"No, we can't. And yes, I'm going to use my 'instinct,' as you so nicely put it, but I would very much appreciate it if you tried to support us instead of putting the screws on. We could operate a lot better if we knew you had our backs."

George rolled his eyes. Andi was right, of course, but his bluntness wouldn't win him any brownie points with the chief. Though George seriously doubted Andi *wanted* to curry favors with his higher-ups. His partner simply wanted to be left alone while solving his cases. "Detective Hayes is right, Chief, even though he was a bit—forward. I think you know we're trying our best, and all we need from you is your support."

Again, the chief was silent for some time, staring at them over her steepled fingers. George knew she was weighing the pros and cons of what had just been said, trying to decide on the best course of action from which she would benefit the most. When she let out her breath on a long sigh, George was sure she had decided in their favor. He would have done the same because the other options were too risky at the moment.

"Let's go with that for the time being." She leaned forward on her desk, her gaze steely. "Make no mistake, though. If this goes south, if you can't solve this case, I'm going to have your badges, one way or another."

Andi opened his mouth, no doubt to make the chief go back on her word immediately, and this time George managed to be faster than his partner. "Crystal clear, Chief. We're going back to work now."

"Yes, do that. And report to me once you find out something new."

"Understood." George grabbed Andi's arm and dragged him out of the office, praying he would keep his mouth shut until they were out of earshot. They made it safely to their desks before Andi inhaled deeply. George put a finger to his lips in silent warning. Andi let go of his lungful of oxygen and hissed instead of shouting. "What a stupid bitch! I bet all she ever cares about is her precious career. It's beyond me how somebody like that could ever become chief."

George knew exactly how such a thing could happen—he was aiming for the same—but he didn't think now was a good time to explain the intricacies of getting ahead in life to his enraged partner. "I know. She's off our backs for now. Let's see if Shireen has found something and then we call it a day. I don't know about you, but I'm still running on reserves, and some downtime and another good night's sleep will surely help us see things more clearly."

For a moment George feared Andi would object. Then his shoulders slumped and a defeated expression appeared on his face. "Okay. Let's do that."

CHAPTER 18
FRUITLESS QUESTIONS

SHIREEN DIDN'T have any new leads, so Andi and George both went home to get some sleep. The next morning, Andi decided to take the next step in his personal escalating scale of drastic measures, which meant going out into the seedier parts of Charleston's nightlife to talk to people Andi usually tried to avoid. Which was perfectly fine, because the pimps and drug dealers did everything in their power not to have to talk to the police—and Andi in particular, he was notorious like that.

"Tell me again why we're knocking on the doors of people who are usually up at night at ten in the morning?" George didn't sound too convinced by Andi's strategy.

"You never did that while you were with narcotics?"

"No. We went hunting at night, when the perps were out and about, committing the crimes for which we wanted to nail them. Catching somebody red-handed and all that." George raised a brow in a badly concealed attempt at telling Andi he was nuts.

"Well, that might be a good idea if we wanted to catch them red-handed. But we're not after their crimes at the moment. We're hunting bigger prey and need those pimps and dealers to give us information that will hopefully help us crack the case. Now's the perfect time for that. They're tired from the night's endeavors, which makes them slower on the uptake, if we're lucky. Also, when they're still in bed, it's easier to catch them."

"I'd love to argue with your logic, but I can't seem to find any arguments against it." George sounded petulant.

"That's because there are none. My logic is as brilliant and undisputable as the sparkling of a diamond."

"And we're reaching ridiculous faster than I'd ever thought possible. You really show me something new every day." George's grumbling was interrupted by the GPS telling him to turn right into a small street where the places of business—bars, restaurants, strip clubs, motels—were so run down it was a wonder there hadn't been any major accidents with collapsing floors or crumbling walls yet. At least none that were reported. For the insects, this area was something akin to heaven.

So many blobs providing blood, rotting wood in the houses giving nourishment and room and warmth for the brood, a space for the colonies, corners where nets could be weaved to catch the blood-drinking predators after the blobs, so tasty when they were full and so keeping, helping the next generation of eight-legged hunters into the world, all the waste the blobs were leaving everywhere, food and places to nest, fueling cycle after cycle of insects, providing the environment for their flourishing, and the blobs always unaware of the kingdoms beneath their feet, all around them, the millions of creatures seeing everything they did, storing the information away for Andi to read it if he wanted or not, and there were two dead bodies on that street, under the bar where the light of the giant letters at the front kept blinking in and out of existence, driving the moths crazy and making the spiders who had taken residence in the crevices between the huge screws fat and lazy.

It took Andi some effort to get his focus back on his human senses, his body still tired from the previous day. He showed George where to park his car, their arrival not yet registered by the blobs, as his inhuman informants assured him. Perfect hunting conditions. Andi went to a strip club called the Moulin Rouge first. The name evoked hopes the establishment itself crushed the moment one entered it, the interior as far from the France of the early 1900s as a hippopotamus was from becoming a ballerina. The front door was closed, as to be expected, but the back door was opened by a grumpy-looking woman with rubber gloves who was clearly cleaning the space, though Andi wasn't sure why she made the effort. The only thing that would improve the Moulin Rouge was if a bomb went off and destroyed the whole place.

"Can we talk to Mr. Poulter, please?" Andi tried for a friendly smile and felt the corners of his mouth not cooperating. He hated people.

"Who's asking?" The woman seemed to share his sentiment.

Already exhausted from the social interaction he so didn't want, and with George holding back for reasons that were beyond Andi—some partner George was—he decided to take the shortcut. He took out his badge. "The police."

She narrowed her eyes, looking at the badge more closely than was strictly necessary. Andi's impatience grew, and she must have sensed the shift in his already foul mood because she took a step back and let them in. "Come in. James is upstairs."

Andi nodded his thanks, and with George in tow he went up the creaking stairs, hoping and praying they wouldn't give under their combined weight.

Pieces of wood splintering, so small it was more like dust, yet enough to eat away at the structure, reducing it bit by bit, someday bringing it down with the help of thousands of tiny mandibles crunching away on the wooden threads until yet another monument of men returned to the ground.

The ominous sounds of the steps prevented any attempt at being sneaky, and Andi wasn't surprised to find James Poulter, proud owner of the Moulin Rouge, standing in one of the doors, eyeing them both with barely veiled disdain. "Hayes. What brings you here?"

Andi raised his hands in a placating gesture. Poulter looked worse than during their last encounter almost a year ago—his dark brown skin was sagging around his cheeks and shoulders, he seemed to have lost weight, more than was healthy for a man of six foot three, and even without the information from the arthropods Andi could tell the man was succumbing to his various addictions in a quickening pace. How he was still able to keep his business running was a small mystery Andi didn't want to solve at the moment.

"I'm not looking for trouble. Just wondering if you heard some interesting rumors lately."

Poulter's brows rose to his receding hairline. "You're asking *me* for information? What makes you think I'll help you after the all the trouble you've caused me?"

Andi shrugged. "Because you're an upstanding citizen who wants to help the law?" He chuckled. "Don't worry, just kidding. I'd never insult you with thinking you're anything else but the human scum I've come to know."

Before Poulter could give an angry answer, George touched Andi's arm and maneuvered himself forward, brushing past Andi in an attempt to avoid contact with the wall. "Uhm, Andi, I'm pretty sure you have to be nice to people if you want them to help you. Please excuse my partner, Mr. Poulter. He doesn't do well in situations requiring social skills."

Poulter stared at George wide-eyed, then barked out a laugh followed by violent coughing. No, James Poulter wouldn't be walking the earth for much longer if he kept on like that. "Don't I know it! And who are you?"

George showed his badge with a quick flick of his wrist. "I'm Detective George Donovan, his partner."

Poulter cocked his head in Andi's direction. "And here I thought you didn't do partners, Hayes. Who did you piss off?"

Andi narrowed his eyes. "None of your business. I do partners now, and his job is to be just nice enough for you to cooperate without me having to threaten you with all kinds of things, of which the abysmal state of your bar is the least concerning."

This time it was Poulter who raised his hands in a placating gesture. "Hey, I never said I wouldn't help you!"

"But you thought about it!"

"Yes, I did, until your charming partner mollified me with his great manners." The sarcasm dripping from every syllable made the corners of Andi's mouth twitch. As bad guys went, Poulter wasn't the worst, almost decent if measured with the very low standards of the company he kept, which was the main reason why Andi had come to him first. He briefly turned to George, giving him a wink. "See, you're already pulling your weight."

George just shrugged, clearly not impressed by Andi's success so far. Andi focused back on Poulter. "Let's get this over with. You look like you could use some sleep."

"I could say the same about you." Poulter rotated his shoulders, which resulted in a crunching sound that made the hair on Andi's nape stand up. "Shoot."

"Have you heard anything about a man calling himself the Lion?"

Andi watched Poulter like a hawk, dipping into the senses of the termites and moths under the loose boards of the ceiling at the same time.

A rush of sweat, a spike in pheromones signaling stress and fear, almost panic, not attractive at all, a warning, stay away, don't come closer, danger, all mixed with the cloying scent of death creeping closer, of organs shutting down and blood so littered with waste it was like a toxic stream not the source of life it was meant to be…

Poulter's eyes widened for a brief moment, his skin turned even paler than it had been before, and he started clenching his fists at his sides. "Only rumors. Nothing concrete." Poulter was desperately trying to get himself under control, which was made more difficult by the drugs coursing through his system. The first beads of sweat started their way down his temples, silently telling Andi more than his words.

"So you have heard of him." Andi waited. Poulter had never been good at hiding things, and experience had told Andi to simply provide an empty, soundless space Poulter would feel the need to fill. Perhaps due to the early hour—at least from Poulter's perspective—the man cracked faster than usual, desperate to make the silence go away.

"He started doing business about two years ago, whoring out kids to rich customers. It was a small enterprise, nothing big, so the other pimps let him be. For the past six months or so, he's been growing, though, stealing customers from the others. Problem is nobody knows anything about him, who he is or where he lives. Never shows himself, always uses subcontractors, doesn't even seem to live here. There were a few who talked openly about getting rid of him, but they all have mysteriously vanished. Now we're all keeping our heads down, waiting for his next move. I personally don't think he wants to take over all of the business, he seems to be focused on the richer clientele, and that's all I need to know when it comes down to it."

Andi managed to keep his frustrated sigh in. What Poulter was telling him matched the information Skipper had given them, and was what Andi had expected, though secretly he had hoped for something more substantial.

"So you really have no idea who it could be?" It was a last effort, fueled by hope more than anything else.

"No. I keep my head down and concentrate on my own business. For the record, though, if I knew who he was, I'd tell you. He's creepy."

"Thank you, James. I guess we're on our way."

Poulter gave a lazy salute, his relief about being off the hook almost palpable in the air. They left the club the same way they had entered, followed by the watchful eyes of the cleaning woman. When they were back in the car, Andi thumped the dashboard in frustration. "Damn!"

George started the engine, glancing at Andi. "Where to next?"

"Straight down this street, turn left at the end." They were silent while George steered the Escalade back onto the street. When he was on his way to where Andi had indicated, he finally spoke. "This Poulter guy wasn't very forthcoming."

"No."

"And he was frightened."

"Yes."

"Do you think he knows more than he let on?"

Andi growled. "Unfortunately, I've been acquainted with him long enough to be fairly sure he's telling the truth."

"And this bullshit about telling you if he knew?"

"The truth." When Andi saw the disbelief in George's eyes he started to explain. "See it from his point of view. The Lion is a nuisance to him, but not a direct threat to his business, since Poulter specializes in people who have no control over their lives left. Plus he knows me and my reputation, has seen me in action. The Lion may not be Poulter's primary concern, but he's an outsider, somebody he doesn't trust, and therefore getting rid of him by telling me what I need to know would be an elegant solution from his point of view. We have already seen how careful the Lion is in everything he does. He's been able to stay under the police's radar for two years, and even now we don't have any clues with which to find him because of the way he has structured his dealings. Using outside contractors is risky but also has its benefits, like no ties back to the client." He let his head rest against the soft leather of the seat. "Let's hope the others on my list have something more to say, though I'm beginning to suspect we won't be that lucky."

George huffed a humorless chuckle and turned into the street Andi had indicated.

As it turned out, Andi's hunch about not being lucky was dead on. After four hours of fruitless questioning, the only thing they knew for sure was that the Lion was a smart son of a bitch and dangerous enough to have even the most brutal of the pimps in Charleston quivering in fear. None of them had been able to provide them with any substantial leads, which meant they were facing the potential of the case going cold. Andi was so preoccupied with thoughts about the case that the battery of sensual input he got from the arthropods in the precinct when George pulled into the parking lot caught him completely by surprise and had him doubling over in his seat.

Bustling like an ant colony before swarming, stress, anger, pheromones flying, the air full of currents carrying and mixing all kinds of scents, making it hard to decipher where the useful ones originated, too many feet running around, the ground trembling in overlapping waves, destabilizing nests and webs and nooks and crannies where the brood was, destroying hiding places, all stirred up like a tornado, insects trying to hide or scuttling around, the soft churning of tiny feet rasping over countless different surfaces, the disorientation, the chaos, keeping the queen safe, hustling the brood away, shouts in the air, adding more currents, more chaos, too much of everything, too much everywhere, no place to hide…

"Whoa, Andi, are you all right?" George's hand on his back was the anchor that brought Andi back to reality. He shook his head, regretting it immediately when a sharp pain needled its way into his brain from behind his eyes.

"I'm fine. Just… just…." He couldn't think of anything to say, his body too busy shutting out the sensory overload and being in pain because of it. He barely registered George leaving the car and coming round to his door. His partner opened the passenger door, released Andi's seat belt, and helped him out when he couldn't seem to get his feet under control. Once he was outside in the fresh air, Andi took a few deep breaths, wrestling his body back under the dominion of his will.

"Something's going on inside."

George kept a hand on Andi's right arm, steadying him with a concerned expression. "One of your hunches?" There was no special emphasis on the word "hunch" this time, only genuine worry for Andi's well-being, and he appreciated it more than he probably should have. They slowly made it inside, where they were greeted by chaos. Chief Norris was barking commands at anybody coming too close to her, while Shireen was standing right next to the chief, wringing her hands nervously and looking as if she was ready to collapse. The chief saw them entering through the door and gestured them to come closer.

"Hayes, Donovan, bad news. Taylor Vance's cell has vanished. My office, now. You as well." She shot Shireen a look of pure venom.

Andi was still digesting the catastrophic fact when George closed the door to the chief's office. His partner appeared calm on the outside, as if they hadn't just lost an important part of their meager evidence after a day of potential leads vanishing into thin air.

"What happened?"

The chief glared at Shireen. "Tell them," she barked, and Shireen flinched.

"I'm sorry, so sorry. I had the cell in my department's safe. I was hoping to perhaps find some more clues on it, so I hadn't sent it back to evidence after the initial sweep was done. I went to get it about twenty minutes ago, to work on it some more, try something with the apps on it, but it was gone. The safe was closed, no signs of anybody having tried to gain access. It's gone."

Shireen's shoulders slumped, her entire demeanor that of somebody who was defeated.

"Have you any idea who could have taken it?" George was still projecting a calmness Andi couldn't find. He was glad his partner was taking over, because he was still too blindsided from the fact that the cell was gone, as well as the still ongoing assault of images coming from the arthropods in the building. Shireen took a shuddering breath, concentrated on George, and ignored the chief, who was silently fuming in her chair. Unhelpful as always. Instead of reassuring her top IT specialist, Norris was making Shireen nervous, and nervous witnesses were useless witnesses.

"No. I mean, it could have been anyone who knows the combination for the safe. It's a simple code, because we don't have the budget to get an iris scanner or even facial recognition. And besides, who's crazy enough to steal something from the heart of the precinct?"

"Somebody who doesn't want us snooping around in the Lion's business." George tapped his index finger against his chin. "Are there any cameras that could have caught our thief?"

Shireen seemed to shrink into the chair George had pulled out for her. "There are, but we were running maintenance today. Checking the wires and plugs, the angles. Whoever did it must have known and chosen a time when everything was down."

"Which makes the whole precinct a suspect. Wonderful." George sighed. "Chief, how do we proceed?"

Chief Norris shot Shireen another death glare before she turned her attention to George. "The case has priority. You keep on digging and I'll assign finding the missing cell to Detectives Merrigold and Vargas. Anything they find, they report to you. Let's hope our thief has made a mistake somewhere."

George looked to Andi, who remembered that he technically was part of their team and should probably give some kind of input, even though he was distracted by all the implications of what had happened. "Fine with me. Can we go now?"

It hadn't been the right thing to say, judging from the sour look on Norris's face, but she dismissed them with a wave of her hand. Shireen tagged along, breathing a sigh of relief once they were outside the office.

"I'm so sorry, guys. I promise you I'll do everything I can to get the cell back."

"It's okay, Shireen, it wasn't your fault. This seems to have been an inside job, and if you weren't working with outdated equipment, this would have never happened, I'm sure of it. I know how meticulous you are about evidence."

It was the right thing to say, Andi could see it in Shireen's eyes. She took his right hand and squeezed it before turning in the direction of the IT department. "Thank you, Andi. This means a lot."

She hurried away, leaving George and Andi with the broken pieces of their case.

"What do we do now?" George let his frustration show now that they were alone.

Andi rubbed his hand over his face, trying to clear his head without much success. They were backed into a corner, and there really was only one way out. "We're going home. I need time to think, and I can't do it here. Too much drama."

George nodded his agreement, and they left the precinct to get some room to think.

CHAPTER 19
THROUGH THE EYES OF BUGS

EVEN THOUGH Andi had anticipated it, he felt empty inside during the ride home. He was still exhausted from their all-nighter the day before. The confrontation with Chief Norris, the greedy hag, hadn't helped at all. He was feeling the pressure building to get results concerning the case, and because of it he was facing the one thing he usually tried to avoid at all cost: opening himself up to the arthropods not only in his close vicinity but all over Charleston.

His gut instinct told him that whoever was running the trafficking ring was at least residing somewhere in the area, even though all the people they had questioned today seemed to think he was an outsider. But even if that was the case, the man still had to keep an eye on everything, especially if he was planning to expand, and with a little luck, he would be able to either find the man or at least pick up on some new leads. The price was high, not only in terms of his own physical and mental health but also when it came to his partnership with George. Andi was almost sure George wouldn't take too kindly to being dragged to several random places in search of a phantom. It bothered Andi in a way he'd never thought possible. In the short span of a week, George had managed to transform himself from the bane of Andi's work to a partner he wanted to keep and get to know better. But a partnership with such a huge secret at its core was doomed to fail, as Andi well knew. Nobody would put up for long with always being left out of the loop, and rightly so. There was no way around it, though. If it were just about Chief Norris and her unreasonable demands, Andi would have felt tempted to let the case go cold just to show her he wasn't some kind of dog she could treat like a flea-ridden stray one moment and like a prized champion the next when it suited her and her ego. Knowing what was at stake, he could no longer take that route, which was a pity. He would have loved to see Chief Norris's face when she realized he wasn't some puppet on a string. A late afternoon and early evening with creeper-crawlers it was.

He and George didn't talk much in the car. George was nice enough to drive him to his house, and he refrained from going over what had happened in the chief's office, which Andi appreciated. He had neither the desire nor the mental capacity to rehash the unpleasant surprise of the cell vanishing. His partner seemed to sense that Andi needed time to digest it all, or he was simply trying to come to terms with it himself. Either way, Andi was glad for the silence. George stopped in front of Andi's driveway, letting him out.

"I'm going to pick you up tomorrow at seven, okay?"

"Thank you, George. I really have to get my own car back home." Andi forced the corners of his mouth upward. Judging from the way George furrowed his brows, he hadn't done a good job.

"Get some sleep, Andi. I'm sure everything will look better tomorrow."

Andi knew things would be a lot worse for him come next morning, but with a little luck, they would at least have some new leads to make up for the loss of the cell.

"Will do. Same goes for you. See you tomorrow." He lifted his hand in farewell, and when George pulled away from the curb, he turned toward the house. It was a good day for what he was planning. The spring sun was drawing out all arthropods, causing them to start building nests, to reproduce and fly about. They were more alert, more receptive than during the winter months, which was both good and bad. Good because he would get more accurate information, bad because the battering of images would send his mind spiraling out of control much faster. Andi went inside the house, changed into his favorite yoga pants and a long-sleeved sweater that clung to his body like a second skin. He took two Advils out of the medicine cabinet, along with a bottle of water from the fridge. He'd need both close by once he had the information he needed. After he was done with his preparations, Andi went to the bathroom to take a piss before he lay down on his bed, his cell on the charger and silenced, the Advils and water bottle on the nightstand. He was just about to close his eyes when he remembered something and got up again to retrieve a bucket from the sink under the kitchen. Now with everything in place, he put his head back on the pillow and closed his eyes. The usual thrumming at the back of his head was already intensifying, due to the lowering of his mental shields. Andi inhaled deeply, exhaled, inhaled again. With every breath, he forced the muscles in his body to relax, preparing himself for what was to come. One last breath, expanding his chest so far his ribs hurt a little, and he let go—

The clicking of tiny legs, the rasping sound of exoskeletons rubbing against each other, the hum of thousands of translucent wings vibrating in the air, the pulsing of convulsions in the earth, telling of animals and people and vehicles going past, the irresistible colors of the spring flowers luring in their pollinators, it all rushed into Andi's mind, burying him under a cacophony of images too alien to really understand. For a moment he was swept away by the flood, desperately trying to regain his footing in the ever-rising tide of what the world would look like if he weren't in the restricting body of a human. Which he was. He was human. He could never forget that or he would get lost and never come back, his body an empty husk while his mind rode forever on the consciousness of millions of arthropods, dying a thousand deaths a second yet still immortal in their vast reproduction cycles. He had to concentrate, had to find what he was looking for before he gave in to temptation, before he decided he had suffered long enough, before he embraced the freedom his geschenk *was offering him. Only it wasn't freedom, just another form of being trapped, like his human body within its own limitations, like working for the chief without being able to show her the power of his right hook, like wanting to get to know George better without having to open up to him. No, the prisons were all the same at heart, they just looked different, some easier to bear than others. No, he was here on a mission, just a temporary guest, not a permanent resident, no matter how fascinating and terrible this prison was. He was looking for a man with anemia, a man most probably in the vicinity of young blood, of drugs and tranquilizers. The images were still bombarding him, still overwhelming him, but now he knew—or remembered?—what he was looking for. What the flea had given him was only vague, but with the additional information about drugs it got easier. So many dealers in this city, so many addicts, so many corpses, some of which would never be found, never be mourned, never get justice, nothing more than a feast for the worms and bugs, and was that really so bad, sustaining life in death? No, he couldn't be derailed, he didn't have much time, couldn't stay here too long, already his thoughts were getting syrupy and slow, while his brain tried to interpret whatever the arthropods had to tell and oh, the stories they knew, about rich feasts and disappointing food sources, and he was already covering almost the entire city and still hadn't found a trace of that combination he was seeking, just a surprisingly high amount of people with blood deficiencies, some of them already dying. His time was running out and yet he still expanded his mind, letting more images in even though he already felt them dragging him to that place of no return where his self would dissolve in arthropods, just like his grandmother's, and he couldn't think of her right now, he had to concentrate or all would have been in vain. He stretched a bit farther, farther than ever before, leaving the city behind and there it was, like a light in a completely darkened room, like the only star in a black night, the picture of a man, so much like the one he'd gotten from the flea, and there were drugs and the distinct aroma of flesh saturated with tranquilizers, and how much flesh it was, and if Andi hadn't been drowning in the logic of insects, he would have been sick from knowing what that meant, a different context for humans, another prison, despicable and yet common, and all the ticks and fleas saw were desirable and undesirable meals and wasn't that much better than realizing what meaning that flesh had? No, he couldn't go there, couldn't give in, he had to nail the location down so he could find the place tomorrow, when he wasn't drowning anymore, when he was Andi again, not a shattered piece of glass, sending its shards in a million directions. He recognized the soil and general shape of the landscape, the huge mansions scattered around, guarded by gigantic trees and wide spreads of dead grass that didn't offer much in terms of nourishment. Berkeley County. Andi took the different pieces of information he was getting from the earth dwellers, the airborne insects, the ones living in the walls of the house and those crawling through the gardens surrounding it to form a picture of where he had to go. Once he was sure he would recognize it without having to dip into the stream of alien experiences again, he started retreating back to his body. It was hard, so hard, to find his way, to weave through all the useless information, to overcome the feeling of being omniscient, because in that moment, he was, and it didn't do him any good, because most of that knowledge was useless without context and context came from dipping deeper and he couldn't do that, he had to come back, had to solve the case to save all those innocent children, had to tell George about the mansion so they could go and have a look and there was his body, looking so delicious and uncomfortable and useless at the same time, his prison, the one he had to actively choose if he didn't want to get lost and why was it important to not get lost? Yes, the children, George, the case, he had to come back, had to detach himself from whatever this different world, his* geschenk *was offering him because if he didn't all would be lost even though he couldn't seem to remember what all was exactly and he knew that was a bad sign and here was his body and he could feel it again, the painful pounding in his head while his brain was trying to do what no human brain should ever have to endure, the heaviness of his limbs, the coldness of his toes and fingers from lying still for so long—had it been long? Time was always so fleeting, nothing solid he could rely on—the queasiness in his stomach, too much saliva in his mouth, oh he knew what that meant, his body was preparing to get rid of everything it didn't need in this moment of profound stress, he had to get to the bucket—*

Andi leaned over the bed and threw up. It was a miracle he managed to direct the contents of his stomach into the bucket with only minimal spillage. When the heaving subsided after what felt like an eternity—his sense of time was still off—he opened the water bottle, swished his mouth, and spit the water into the bucket before he took another long gulp. The two Advils followed. A quick look at the clock confirmed he'd been out for almost five hours, which wasn't good at all. He'd never been gone so long, and every time he opened himself up like this, it got more difficult to return into his own mind. Well, he'd made it back this time, and he had brought valuable information with him. Andi contemplated getting up and emptying the bucket before the Advils kicked in, but when he tried to sit up on his bed, his head spun, and he saw black spots. With a groan he sank back onto the pillow. He didn't like sleeping with the stench of vomit in the room, but it seemed his choice had been taken from him. With some effort, he managed to pull the covers over his body, curling into a ball on his side, the bucket at his back, as if that symbolic gesture could keep the stench from assaulting his nostrils. A bone-deep tiredness overcame Andi, making his thoughts as slow as bluebottles on a cold day. The only thing keeping him awake was the pounding of his head until the Advils finally did their job. Nothing was keeping Andi from going under now, and he succumbed to the temptation of darkness.

THE NEXT morning, Andi was woken by somebody jostling his shoulder and yelling his name. "Andi! Andi! Wake up! Damn, don't make me call an ambulance. Are you all right? Andi!"

George's voice had a frantic quality that made Andi wonder what his problem was. Then his brain finally kicked into gear, the haze lifted from it, and he slowly opened his eyes.

"George. What are you doing here?"

"Thank God you're awake! What am I doing here? It's quarter past seven, and I was supposed to pick you up at seven."

Andi furrowed his brows. "Oh, yeah. Work. Must have forgotten to set the alarm." He rolled his head on the pillow to look at his cell on the nightstand. It looked very peaceful, attached to its charger. "Sorry. I had a difficult night."

"I can see that." George nodded in the direction of the bucket. "And smell it. Are you sick? Do you need to stay in bed?"

The worry almost made Andi smile. Almost, because every movement of his face sent sharp pinpricks of pain into his skull. It wasn't a full-blown migraine he was dealing with, but bad enough that he contemplated staying at home. Only for a moment, though, before he remembered the high number of delicious flesh the ticks had shown him. No, not delicious flesh, poor victims who needed saving, needed him. He slowly sat up on the bed.

"No, I just need a moment. Can you wait downstairs? I want to take a shower. I'll hurry, I promise."

George looked at him doubtfully, but gave in. "Fine, I'll make you some tea. Chamomile?"

"Chamomile would be nice, yes. Thank you."

George muttered something under his breath and left the room. Andi tried not to think about how much he liked seeing George worry about him. Carefully he swung his legs over the edge of the bed and got up. He still felt a bit dizzy, but it was manageable. Scrunching his nose, Andi went first to the window to open it, then he took the bucket to the bathroom and emptied it into the toilet. For a moment, his stomach protested the wave of sour smell hitting his nose and he fought against throwing up again. He used the toilet, took a quick shower that eased some of the pain between his temples, and put on fresh clothes. When he got downstairs, he smelled coffee and the weaker aroma of chamomile tea coming from the kitchen. George had two Starbucks cups on the counter, as well as one of Andi's own teacups.

"I brought your usual from Starbucks, but I think you should drink some chamomile for your stomach. Did you catch something?"

Andi sat down on the counter, warming his hands on the steaming cup. "No, I…." He wasn't sure what to say. He found he didn't want to lie to George but didn't know what to tell him either. "I was thinking about the case. It got late, and I guess I was still affected by lack of sleep. I got sick and was too dizzy to empty the bucket."

George sighed. If he had picked up on Andi's hesitancy, he didn't show it. "You were supposed to rest, not ponder the case. You look horrible."

"Thank you very much." Andi furrowed his brows. "How did you get into the house, by the way?"

"After I tried calling you and it went straight to voicemail, I started worrying. I tried your front door, and it wasn't locked. That's when I decided to go in."

"Ah, I remember silencing my cell. And I probably forgot locking the door."

"You must have been really out of it. I'm sure this is a pretty safe area, Andi, but still, forgetting to lock your front door?" George sounded like a loving father whose patience was sorely tested by his child's antics. Not that Andi knew what a loving father sounded like.

"I'm sorry. I'll try to remember in the future."

"And now you're trying to placate me. I'd tell you where to stick it, but I don't go after defenseless men." George grinned broadly.

"Har, har. Nice joke." Andi took a sip of his chamomile tea. His stomach approved. There were a few minutes of companionable silence while they both drank their beverages. Finally, George reached for the two paper bags which most likely contained his own breakfast and Andi's plain bagel.

"Are you ready to go to the precinct?"

Andi shook his head and immediately regretted it. The pounding in his skull now resembled Scottish bagpipes backed up by at least a hundred war drums. He winced. "We're not going to the precinct. We're going to Berkeley."

"What do we want in Berkeley? That's outside of Charleston, isn't it?"

"Yes, it is."

The following silence wasn't that companionable anymore. It grew more pronounced with each beat of Andi's heart. Finally, George lifted an eyebrow. "You've got a hunch?"

"I've got a hunch." Andi didn't know what else to say.

George's shoulders slumped a tiny bit, and it affected Andi more than it should have. "It's the kind of hunch you can't tell me about, am I right?" When Andi nodded, George rubbed his face with his hand. It was a tired gesture, laced with frustration. "I really don't know what to think right now. I mean, you look like you've been through hell and back, you were sick like a dog, and now you tell me to go to Berkeley. Are you taking mind-enhancing drugs, Andi?"

For a moment, Andi was speechless, not knowing if he should laugh or be offended. He decided on the first. "I already told you I don't do drugs and that my—what did Norris call it?—instinct isn't illegal. The only drugs I took were two Advils to keep the migraine at bay. Can you trust me on this?"

George seemed torn. "I've got to admit this is more difficult than I thought. I want to trust you, hell, I think I already do, but not knowing where you get your information from is hard."

At that moment, Andi was tempted to tell George his secret. Things would be so much easier if George knew what was going on—but no, he couldn't risk it. "I'm sorry, George. I really am. But I can't tell you."

There was a brief flash of anger and hurt on George's features, but he got it under control quickly.

"I understand. I do." He gritted his teeth. "Doesn't make me less angry, though." George grabbed his coffee. "Let's go."

THE DRIVE to Berkeley was accompanied by aggravating silence, and their sparse dialogue was limited to "Can I switch to another radio station?"

"No."

The farther they got, the more space there was between the houses—if one wanted to still call those mansions houses. The driveways reached farther and farther back until the buildings couldn't be seen from the road anymore. Andi felt the familiar images from the evening before pressing against the back of his mind, telling him they were almost there. A quick check on his phone informed him this was the estate of the Castain family, who'd lived in this area for the past two hundred years and was old money. Andi contemplated the best course of action while they drove past the gated entryway. Simply ringing the bell was out of the question without a plausible backup story, which they didn't have. Besides, it certainly wouldn't help the poor victims trapped in the huge building hidden behind several bends in the driveway and a grove of massive old oaks that obstructed the view for anybody who tried to sneak a peek.

"Can you stop at the next possible place?" he asked George, who furrowed his brows but nodded in acknowledgment. He found a turning bay about half a mile farther down the road and stopped there.

"Could you explain to me what's going on here? Why are we stopping in the middle of rich-man's-land?" Apparently, the time it had taken them to get to Berkeley had brought George's anger to a boiling point. Just what Andi needed after the night he'd had.

"We need to check out the estate we passed last. It belongs to the Castain family, and my hunch says we're going to find something there. As you know, I can't back my hunches up by anything solid, which means we have to sneak in there, see what we find, and then call the cavalry."

"You say you can't back up your hunch, but you seem awfully convinced we're going to find something that'll require calling our forces. What is it, Andi? You either know or you don't."

George was getting more aggressive by the minute, and if Andi hadn't seen the frustration about the entire situation shining in his eyes, he would have simply knocked him out, sneaked onto the property, checked it out, and then called it in. As things were, he felt weirdly obligated to placate his partner, and not just because George had made him tea this very morning. This partnership thing was quickly spiraling out of control, and Andi vowed then and there to end it as soon as they busted that trafficking ring.

"Listen to me, George. I know partly what we're going to find in there. And believe me, it's not pretty. But I need visuals before I can call it in because I have to come up with a plausible reason why I want the private estate of a long-established family raided. It's going to be hard enough to explain what we were doing out here, so far from any leads we've gotten until now. So please, work with me on this. We need to get onto the property, check out the house, and then act. Please."

George's shoulders tensed and Andi feared he had lost him. The grim set of his lips wasn't promising either. "Just so we're clear. You want me to follow you onto private property claiming you know we're going to find something there and then fabricate a reason why we were on said property to begin with so we can work with whatever it is you're so sure we're going to get."

"Yes." There wasn't more to say.

"You want me to risk my entire career based on something you can tell me nothing about."

Andi closed his eyes, frustrated. "Yes. Look, if you don't want to do this, fine. I understand. I can see how your precious career is more important to you than solving the case and rescuing potential victims. I know your type, I've seen how you operate, and I'm willing to give you a way out, a chance to have plausible deniability. You can turn around right now, drive back to Charleston where we can split up, you go interviewing some more pimps while I take my own car out here and do what I always do." Andi knew he sounded more aggressive than strictly necessary, but the night he just had was taking its toll on him, leaving his nerves in thin threads easily snapped and his temper building up unchecked. He never wanted a partner to begin with, and no matter how nice George had been the past days, this, *this* here was exactly why having a partner was the worst idea possible for him.

George was grinding his teeth so hard Andi could hear the molars clicking. "Yes, my career is precious to me, Mr. Self-Righteous. There are people in this world who aspire to more than just simple detective, and I'm not ashamed of my ambition. I'm also not willing to risk everything I've worked so hard for because a man I've known for a week claims to have some special insights he can't explain." He sighed, slamming his palm against the steering wheel. "I'm also not going to let my *temporary* partner walk into a potentially dangerous situation without backup. Which leaves us at an impasse. You can't or don't want to tell me more about what is going on and how you know about it, and I'm not going in blind. Not this time. Not when you're so unsure yourself. Give me something to work with."

Andi felt his mental hackles rise. He hated being pressured; he abhorred being blackmailed. George was doing both, adding to the stress of the situation, forcing his hand. George was also right in one point— going in there alone was a bad, bad idea. "I'm sorry about what I said about your career aspirations. That was a low blow." Andi wasn't sure if he really meant it, but he needed to mend some fences and an apology was a good way of doing it. George's features softened a bit, so it might have helped.

"Apology accepted. I'm sorry for implying you don't have enough ambition. Not everybody is wired the same, and you're obviously doing great work where you are."

Andi felt the tension in his own body lessening a smidgeon. "Accepted. As for what I think we're going to find—I hope it's not as bad as the vans, but I fear it's in the same vein."

He was being evasive as fuck and he knew it. Judging from the way George's hands were gripping the wheel, he knew it as well. "How sure are you?"

Andi closed his eyes. "On a scale from one to ten, a solid eight. Time is… difficult for me."

George murmured something Andi was glad he couldn't understand, otherwise he would have surely started another argument. Aloud his partner said, "If we get caught, I'm going to blame it all on you."

"Only fair." Andi wasn't too worried about that. He was used to taking the blame. Had been since he was a child and his father led everything that went wrong in his life back to Andi being an abomination.

George sighed; then he put the car into gear again, turned the blinker on, and drove back onto the street with his face set into a determined mask. "We'll need to find a place to hide the car. Just parking next to the street is probably not the best idea, even if there doesn't seem to be too much traffic here."

Andi felt part of the tension in his body draining. They were far from being happy, functioning partners, but at least the current crisis seemed to be averted, or at least shelved for another time. He drew up a map of the area on his cell in search for a place where they could leave the car. There was a small rest area close by, from where several hiking paths started. It was ideal because nobody would suspect an empty car parking there and they could use one of the paths to get closer to the estate.

Once they had parked the car, they started off in the direction of their destination. The path they followed led them through a small forest of oak trees teeming with insect life. Andi had a harder time than usual shutting the images out, and he stumbled several times. By the fifth time, when he almost fell over a pretty visible root protruding from the ground, George, who had followed him, mumbled something about idiots with their heads in the clouds before he stepped next to him and took his arm to steady him. A wave of gratitude washed over Andi, followed by annoyance about needing help at all, and if that weren't enough, he also felt torn about his decision to not tell George about his *geschenk*.

This emotional roller coaster had to end, the sooner the better. He was getting so far off his center, it wasn't funny anymore, especially not when he had other things to focus on—like ignoring the fact that there was a deer carcass only a few feet to their right, hidden in the underbrush and chewed on by countless maggots and other scavenger insects. Andi hoped the wind wouldn't blow in their direction before they had left it far behind. With George's help, Andi managed to get to the fence surrounding the estate without planting face-first into the soft ground smelling of wet earth and the beginning of a new cycle.

The fence wasn't too impressive, not designed to seriously keep people out. It was more like a statement, a warning to not trespass. Andi and George ignored that implied warning and climbed the six-foot chain link fence with ease. Luckily, the estate had lots of big old trees growing on the premises, which offered them perfect cover. Once they had the main building in their sight, they slowed down even more. A hedge surrounding the kitchen garden offered the ideal place to watch while not being seen.

"Why are we doing this in broad daylight?" George demanded to know in hushed tones. "This would be a lot easier if it were dark."

"I know. I'd prefer darkness as well, but I don't know how long my hunch is going to be valid, and I don't want to risk the lead getting cold," Andi whispered back.

"If we're caught, I hope you have a good explanation as to why we're here. Chief Norris is going to blow a gasket if she has to bail us out."

"That would be a bonus, in my opinion." Andi couldn't stop the words from coming out. So far, his new chief hadn't done anything to endear her to him. As far as he was concerned, she could leave and never come back.

"You do realize her successor might be even worse?" George seemed to be reading Andi's mind.

"Or he or she could be indifferent enough to just leave me alone. We'll never know because we won't be caught. Now shut up. I need to concentrate." Andi got his binoculars from the back pocket of his jeans. They weren't high quality, but perfect for staking out from so close. Unfortunately, all he could see from their point behind the hedge was a part of the west wing, which seemed to be empty, if the linen thrown over the furniture was any indication.

Just dust and millions of mites, living in the linen, the upholstery, everywhere, this place their own exclusively, nobody there to disturb them, to hinder their explosive reproduction.

"Let's move to that shed over there." Andi pointed to his right, where a small wooden structure was huddled between two oak trees that looked a bit younger than the ones at the outer reaches of the estate. They hurried over and found the rickety door open, which allowed them to slip into the small space that was filled with old garden tools and cobwebs. It didn't give the impression of being used frequently, an assumption the spiders living there confirmed. They were less than happy about the two intruders. Andi didn't have time to be impressed by their anger. At the other end of the shed, partly obscured by an old wheelbarrow that was missing the wheel, was a window with a perfect view of the main entrance and the inside of the house. Andi went over there, rubbed at the glass with the hem of his jacket to get some of the dust off, and used the binoculars to look into the house. There was no movement.

Everything was still, anticipation heavy in the air, feasts down in the earth, where it was cool and dank and moldy, the blobs stirring slowly, like termites awakening in the morning after a cold night, sluggish, the scent of drugs wafting around, blood, just hints, but promising, memories of feasts gone by, of bodily fluids everywhere, pheromones clogging everything, fear and hunger and despair and anger and sexual satisfaction. Pain.

"This place seems pretty deserted to me, Andi. We haven't run into any guards, and so far there's been no trace of any cars. Are you sure this is the right place?" George snatched the binoculars from Andi's hands to have a look. Andi shuffled aside to make more room for George at the small window and to keep his partner from seeing the revulsion on his face. They were so at the right place, and Andi was torn between wishing they weren't and relief they had found another lead.

"Absolutely. We'll just have to wait."

George sighed. "We should have brought some food. It's past lunchtime already."

"I'm sorry. I didn't think that far ahead." It was the truth. Andi was getting hungry as well, his stomach reminding him that it had parted with anything remotely nourishing the evening before. A plain bagel was nowhere near enough to make up for what he'd lost to the bucket. It was also getting hotter by the second, turning the enclosed space into a sauna of the unpleasant kind, because getting rid of their clothes simply wasn't an option. He sat down next to the wheelbarrow and leaned his head against the wall. Taking it slow and easy was paramount. They were probably going to need their energy soon, or so he hoped. "Let's take turns keeping an eye on things. You go first."

"Bossy," George muttered under his breath.

"Yeah, sorry, not sorry. I'm going to close my eyes for a bit."

George huffed but didn't try to keep talking to him. After a few minutes, Andi felt his mind slipping into blissful darkness.

CHAPTER 20
PLAUSIBILITY

GEORGE KNEW exactly when Andi fell asleep. There was a little snorting sound, followed by the kind of deep breathing only sleep could produce. George withstood the temptation to wake him up again. It would have served Andi right, for throwing George into the deep end like he had done this morning, but the man looked so wrung out, George couldn't bring himself to be so cruel even though he was still fuming. Instead he used the time he had while staring at the empty house to guess what Andi's big secret was. Perhaps he was some kind of psychic like in the *X-Files* or *X-Factor*. It would explain how he knew about the bodies on the crime scene and why they were on an apparent wild goose chase out in Berkeley County when they should be following solid—albeit cold—leads back in the city. George didn't even know why he went along with Andi's craziness. It definitely wasn't proper police work they were doing. Yet Andi seemed convinced there was something out here. George hated to admit it, but some part of him clung to the hope Andi was performing a miracle and leading them straight to the culprits. Otherwise they would probably be looking at a drawn-out case that was going colder every minute and would eventually be shelved until they would inevitably stumble upon the next bodies. Contrary to what Andi had suggested during their angry spat in the car, George did care a lot about the victims of the crimes he investigated. It was just that he also had a healthy interest in having his good work recognized and rewarded. There was nothing wrong with that as long as he didn't stray from the path and kept things legal and to the book—which he wasn't doing at the moment. George mentally slapped himself. He was such an idiot. And yet here he was, illegally on private property, hoping to find he knew not what. What a mess.

While the wait dragged on and Andi's soft snores filled the small shed, George amused himself with counting the birds flying around on the manicured lawn flanking the driveway to the main entrance. He had just spotted number eighty-four when the familiar hum of car engines drifted toward the shed. The sound was quickly followed by four black limousines, each with tinted windows. George didn't dare look away to not miss any details. He carefully kicked back against Andi's leg to wake him up. A startled groan mingled with the clicking of car doors being opened. Four men in black suits got out of the driver's seats of the four limousines. As if the scene were choreographed, they all went to the back doors on the driver's sides to open them simultaneously. Four men got out, dressed in suits as well and with black masks on their faces. Two of them had graying hair, and the way they moved suggested men in their sixties at least. The other two were obviously younger, their movements more fluid and graceful. They acknowledged each other with nods before they stalked toward the main entrance.

"Showtime." Andi's voice close to his ear should have startled George, but all he felt was reassurance that his partner was here with him.

"What do we do now?"

Andi took the binoculars from him. After a long pause in which he followed the movements of the masked men inside the house, he started to speak. "Now we call the cavalry. Somebody has just brought the victims in."

George snatched back the binoculars while Andi got his cell out to call the precinct. What George saw inside the now lit room made his stomach revolt, and he was glad he hadn't brought food. Two men without masks were marching a group of naked children around the room. The youngest seemed to be about fourteen, the oldest maybe eighteen. The boys and girls looked frightened, especially the younger ones, while the older ones seemed resigned to their fate. The masked men were scrutinizing them like chattel on the market, touching their breasts and genitalia to determine which one they wanted. Through a red haze of pure rage, George heard Andi speaking to the precinct.

"Yes, this is Detective Andi Hayes. I need a SWAT team at the coordinates I'm going to send now. Tell them to come in silent and surround the perimeter. As soon as they're in position, they can reach me on this number. I'll give the signal to strike. There are armed men, likely pros, on the ground, as far as I can see four, plus at least six additional hostile people and eight confirmed hostages. Tell them to hurry."

Andi ended the call. "They're going to be here in thirty."

"I'm not sure I can wait thirty minutes. They're choosing those children like food in a supermarket." George was trembling with rage and horror. How could anybody do such a vile thing? He felt Andi's hand on his shoulder.

"I know this is hard. But it's just the two of us, and if those drivers aren't ex-military, I'm going to hand my letter of resignation to Chief Norris tomorrow."

George chuckled weakly. "Don't go making promises you have no intention of keeping."

"Why don't you let me keep an eye on them and you take my cell and wait for SWAT to call?" Andi gently took the binoculars from George's grasp and directed him to the spot where he'd been sleeping. "It's quite comfortable, I can assure you."

Even though he didn't want to, George sat down with Andi's cell in his hand. He was itching to storm into the house and shoot those sick bastards, but Andi was right. He would likely get himself, his partner, and worst of all, some of the victims killed. As much as it disgusted him, they had to wait.

After what seemed like an eternity, Andi's cell started vibrating in his hand. George accepted the call. "Detective Donovan here."

"Here's Forard. Tell Hayes we're in position."

Instead of playing messenger, George handed the phone to Andi.

"Adam? You in position? Positive. There's four armed men in the house, most likely in the foyer or the room to the left. In the room to the right, there's two unarmed men with four hostages. The other two men are somewhere in the house… I'm guessing still at ground level because the upper floors appear unoccupied as far as I can tell from where we are. There have to be two more men in the back part of the house, probably armed as well."

Andi listened to something Forard said. "Yes." With his free hand, he got his own handgun from the holster under his arm, which was George's cue to do the same.

They moved toward the entrance of the shed. George opened the door for Andi and covered him on their way around it. Andi's voice dropped to a whisper. "We're behind the little shed east of the entrance. Can you see us? Good. Three, two, one. Go!"

It wasn't dark yet, just gloomy enough to make the sudden appearance of several SWAT members in their black gear an intimidating sight. George stayed close to Andi while they fell in line behind the two SWAT members who carried an iron battering ram. From the corner of his eye, George could see more black-clad figures swarming around the house, blocking all escape routes. The door gave in at the second push, a rain of bullets greeting them. It didn't sound like just ordinary handguns either. The men inside were more heavily armed than George would have wished, but then again it made sense considering the nefarious things their employers were doing inside the house. If George had to guess, there were at least two assault rifles aimed at them. What else their opponents might have in store for them they would find out soon enough. One of the SWAT men went down with a yelp. George couldn't see where exactly the man had been wounded because he was busy ducking behind one of the stone pillars flanking the door, but it had to be somewhere on the legs because the whole SWAT team wore body armor. From the corner of his eye he saw two other SWAT members retrieving their colleague, who was able to run in a half limp supported by their arms, which meant the wound couldn't be too bad. George breathed a sigh of relief, focusing back on the large entrance hall and his partner, who was crouching behind the other pillar, trying to get a clear sight. Andi's shoulders were tense, the gun in his hands steady. Another round of bullets whizzed past them, this time doing no harm at all. Then the SWAT team returned fire, aiming high to give them a chance to get inside the house under cover of the hail of bullets. The hall itself didn't offer much cover, and George followed Andi to the right, where the wall made a dip. Several hooks indicated the barely there space was to hang coats, and it was a tight fit for both of them. Had Andi been as bulky as George, it wouldn't have worked. Through the cacophony of whizzing bullets, splintering marble, the distinct *plop* when projectiles from said marble put dents in the walls, the deep voices of men shouting orders as loud as they could just to be heard made it almost impossible for George to hear what Andi was saying. He only realized his partner was trying to communicate because Andi turned his head slightly so he could see his lips moving. George leaned in as far as he dared without becoming a prime target for whoever was trying to kill them.

"They have the higher ground."

Andi sounded upset and resolved at the same time.

"What do we do?" Since George had no clear view of the room from behind Andi, he had to rely on his partner to make a plan. SWAT was still filling the hall with bullets, though without much success as far as George could tell. The only ones who had managed to get inside were he and Andi, and they were too far to the side to do much more than take cover. He couldn't even see their opponents, just knew roughly where they were because of the shouts and the thundering of the various guns.

"Over there is a broom closet that extends to the stairs. The walls are plasterboard, so I should be able to breach them and open fire on the fuckers from there. Give me cover so I can reach the door!"

There were a million things George wanted to scream at Andi from *Are you fucking nuts?* to *How do you know what kind of material the walls are?* and *I really think this is a stupid idea!* But he didn't get the chance to say any of it, because his stubborn partner with the obvious death wish was already getting ready to sprint, and if George didn't want to have to explain to Chief Norris why he lost her top—albeit suspicious— detective during a spontaneous raid in some rich person's house, he had to get his shit together. Andi at least counted to three before he left the cover of their little dip in the wall, and George stepped forward just enough to cover his partner's sprint to the door that was indeed just a few feet from them. Still, he was only able to see it because he left the cover more than Andi had before he came up with his plan. While he was keeping an eye on their opponents on the stairs—who were luckily occupied with SWAT at the front door, which made Andi's plan seem a lot less suicidal than George had initially thought—he wondered what Andi's secret was. The easiest explanation would be that he somehow already knew the building, and if that was the case, George had to admire his acting skills. Or perhaps he'd really gotten a tip, and the source was for some reason so disreputable that Andi didn't want to let George in on it, though George could have put him at ease in this case—when it came to disreputable sources, he doubted anybody could go lower than the detectives at narcotics. Unless Andi was somehow in on it all and was just leading George around. Although their current situation didn't feel like being led around. More like life and death.

The men on the stairs appeared to be running out of ammunition or they had a cunning escape plan up their sleeve, because they started retreating up the stairs. Meanwhile Andi had reached the door and vanished inside the dark hole behind it. While two of the bodyguards were still on the first landing, covering the other two who were sprinting upstairs, a part of the wall directly next to the stairs exploded in a burst of plaster and dust. Andi came out behind the cloud of debris and immediately started shooting at the two men. Since his angle was so weird—to their left and practically beneath them with the handrail on its small columns of stone as cover—they couldn't aim properly while still maintaining fire on the main door. Andi had similar problems but managed to shoot the one nearest to him in the left calf. The man went down with a surprised scream and tumbled down the stairs, which was George's cue to take a risk and leave his cover, opening fire on the second man. Attacked from three sides, the man decided that retreat was his best bet. Before he could reach the second landing, though, a bullet from the front door caught him in the side, felling him instantly. While SWAT swarmed into the hall to take the two wounded men prisoner, George ran across the marble floor to where Andi was aiming his gun upward. The two remaining bodyguards had reached the next floor, barely visible through the many columns of the banister. Since both their colleagues were down, they didn't bother firing again but turned to run. George took a step in the direction of the stairs, the rush of the hunt burning through his veins. Andi held him back.

"No need. There's SWAT people up there, enough to contain them. We need to go into the room where those pigs chose the victims."

Andi led the way toward the arch into the next room. Two of the masked people were still in there, hiding behind a huge chaise lounge. They both were holding their own weapons, handguns, though much smaller than what their bodyguards had used in the entrance hall. The children they had chosen were huddled in a corner, utterly frightened and too close to the two men to not become human shields if things went south. George and Andi took cover behind a pillar. "Charleston PD, you're under arrest. We have your bodyguards in custody, so make this easier for all of us and just give up." Andi's voice sounded a little cracked, probably because of all the dust he must have gotten into his lungs when he had shot his way through the plasterboard. George kept looking at the two men, hoping they wouldn't be stupid. One of them was starting to lower his gun, but the other seemed indecisive. Very carefully, George took aim at the man's head, ready to shoot him should he make one wrong move. In his entire career, George had shot three men so far, always in combat situations like the one in the hall. Until now, he had never had to end someone's life in cold blood, and the responsibility weighed heavy on him. It was his duty to protect his partner, the victims, even the SWAT members outside. And that man surely deserved a bullet to the head for what he had done. George was under no illusion regarding the sins of the men they were trying to arrest at the moment. Still his consciousness reminded him it was a human being he was aiming at, not a mark at the shooting range.

They were caught in a strange triangle, the children in one corner, the two armed men behind the chaise lounge, and George and Andi behind the pillar. The air was ripe with tension, thrumming in the air, drowning out all sounds, crystallizing in his view of the man's head which would sport a hole the moment he made the wrong decision. And it would be George's doing.

A commotion at the other end of the room tore them from their standoff, black-clad SWAT members swarming the room with their weapons at the ready. The man must have realized he had no chance because he let his weapon drop and raised his hands.

The moment SWAT had subdued the two masked men and declared the room clear, George and Andi ran toward the children.

"It's okay, you're safe now. We're with the police, and we're here to get you out. Can you be brave for a few more minutes until we have all the evil men caught? Then we can get you outside."

The children nodded, staring up at George with wide eyes. An older girl, George guessed her age to be sixteen, touched his arm. "There are more of us. Down in the cellar." She quickly withdrew her hand, so fearful of his reaction, George's heart went out to her.

"Thank you. We're going to look for them as soon as possible." He smiled at her, trying to reassure all of them without knowing what to say. What did one say in a situation like this? George hoped somebody had called an ambulance already, preferably with somebody who knew how to deal with traumatized children.

"They're done." Andi got up from his half crouch in front of the children, a determined expression on his face. "I'll go get the others. Can you stay here?"

George felt torn. He wanted to stay and protect the children, yes, but who would be protecting Andi when he went into the cellar alone?

"I'll go with him." Adam Forard appeared next to Andi, his rifle still at the ready. George shook his head inwardly at his own foolishness. Of course Andi wasn't alone in a house swarming with SWAT.

"Yeah, go. See you outside."

Andi nodded at him before he turned toward a door at the other end of the room, left from the one SWAT had entered through. Forard followed closely. The way Andi moved suggested he knew where he was going, another piece to the puzzle of his secret. A piece that seemed to change its shape while George was looking at it, making it so damn hard to find out what was going on. George was more and more inclined to go with the psychic theory. Either that or Andi was an alien stranded on earth. *Or he really is corrupt*, a nagging little voice at the back of his head insisted. A voice he didn't want to listen to but did so nevertheless because he was a cop and it was in his nature to be deeply suspicious no matter what he wished for things to be. After his partner's back had vanished through the door, George turned back to the children, trying to comfort them while he waited for the all-clear to leave the house. In the distance, he could hear an ambulance. Soon these children would get all the care they needed including something to cover them. Unfortunately, there were no blankets or items of clothing he could give them in the vicinity, and he didn't want to leave them alone after all they had been through.

TWO HOURS later, all of the fifteen children they had found were in hospital, the ten men SWAT had arrested on their way to holding cells in the precinct, and forensics had arrived to take the crime scene apart. Adam Forard was coming toward them. Most of the SWAT team were already on their way back to the precinct, and he was ready to go as well.

"That went great." He grinned at Andi. "And let me guess, you two were driving around, discussing your case when you heard a gunshot?"

Andi just shrugged. "Yeah. In this area, a gunshot is worrying, what with all those huge rich-people houses standing around."

"One of these days, Hayes…." Forard shook his head. "This was a major bust. I assume related to your trafficking case?"

"Hopefully. We don't know yet." Andi tried to be vague, but it didn't work on Forard.

"If it walks like a duck and quacks like a duck… I'll eat an entire batch of Rodriguez's chocolate chip cookies if this isn't related." He winked at George, who felt Andi shudder next to him.

"I don't think you should be making jokes about this, Adam. In fact, don't mention those cookies ever again."

Forard threw his head back and laughed. "See you at the precinct." He walked away, waving his hand in the air.

"Do I want to know?" George looked at Andi.

"About the cookies? No. They were terrible, and that's the nicest thing I can say about them. Let's get the car."

George didn't argue. On their walk back to the car, this time on the road, which made it easier, George wondered if Andi hadn't thought about asking somebody to drive them there or if he needed the time to think. Since he was slowly getting to know his partner, he thought it had to be the second. Once they were in the car, Andi leaned his head back, exhaustion clear on his face. George started the engine.

"I think we should go and grab something to eat before we head into the precinct. This looks like another all-nighter, and we both could do with the fuel."

"You're right." Andi hesitated. George waited, knowing that prying would get him nowhere fast. "We also need to talk about the report." It sounded tentative, as if Andi was prodding at an aching tooth, waiting for the pain to set in. George still didn't know what to make of Andi's talent, hunch, instinct, whatever it was. What he did know was they had just saved fifteen children because of it and were hopefully getting closer to busting the entire ring.

"I know. Our stories must be consistent." Perhaps he had sounded a bit harsher than intended because he could see Andi's shoulders slump from the corner of his eye. "I'm sorry, Andi. I didn't mean to be nasty. I'm tired and hungry and pumped with adrenaline, and I still have no idea how you do what you do. I'm trying to be a good partner, and I know at the moment I'm not doing a great job of it."

"It's fine. Honestly, I'm surprised you haven't dragged me to Norris demanding I be suspended as of last year. I'm not trying to be difficult or to shut you out. I'm just so used to being by myself it's a hard habit to shake."

George knew from the hint of desperation in Andi's voice that this was all he would get at this point. Not wanting to aggravate his partner when they had so much work ahead of them, George decided to let it go for the moment. "I understand, Andi. As for our story, I assume what Forard said is your usual explanation?"

"It's the easiest. I've learned it doesn't pay to be creative. Everybody knows cops use the excuse of having heard something suspicious to go onto private property. Nobody thinks too much of it, especially not in an area with so many mansions around. It's usually appreciated."

George couldn't argue with that logic. "Which leaves us with the question why we were out there in the first place."

"And this is where it gets complicated. We had absolutely no reason to be here." Andi sighed as if the weight of the world was on his shoulders.

"We could have gone on a meeting with a possible informant?" George made it sound like a question. This was new territory for him. Until now, he'd played by the rules, if for no other reason than to protect his future career from any skeletons in the closet. For a brief moment he wondered if corrupt cops felt like this all the time—this pressure to make things believable—but then he remembered they hadn't done anything illegal. They just had to find an explanation for the unexplainable.

"Mmm. That could actually work." Andi took out his cell and looked at it. "Yes, yes. We got an anonymous call, asking us to meet at a gas station a mile along the road. The caller never showed up, and after we'd waited for two hours, we were so frustrated we decided to stop at the rest area and go for a little hike to clear our heads. We went farther than planned, then heard the gunshot."

George felt a little proud about his idea. "It also roughly fits the time frame."

"It does. And if anybody asks why we didn't call in immediately, we can say we wanted to investigate first. In an area like this, it could have been a hunter. Especially since we only heard that one shot."

"It'd be a sad day if two detectives of the Charleston PD weren't able to investigate a single shot on their own." George grinned. This was not only plausible, it was airtight. He had a feeling Chief Norris wouldn't look too closely at how they had gotten this breakthrough in their case, so long as the mayor was breathing down her neck, but it paid to be prepared for when she decided to act against Andi.

They made a quick stop at a diner close to the precinct to get some food and then headed to their desks, only to find out all the arrested had lawyered up immediately. The identities of the two men who had presented the victims were still unknown, and the owner of the house, Jake Castain, who was the mayor's PA, was out of town until the next day.

Suddenly, all they could do was write their preliminary reports before heading back home. It was kind of anticlimactic, and they were debating whether they should go home immediately to get some much-needed sleep before facing the victims and culprits the next day. Andi wanted to stay for another half hour just in case something happened, which George could relate to, though not accept. He wanted to go home to his nice, cozy bed. Their discussion was gaining heat when Chief Norris opened the door to her office. "Detective Donovan, a word, please."

George tensed, looked at Andi, who shrugged. There was no escaping this. "I'm coming, Chief." He crossed the bullpen to the chief's office, stepped inside, and closed the door before sitting down in front of her desk. For several minutes, neither of them spoke. George knew this tactic by heart—his mother was a master player—and the chief had yet to master the art of charging the atmosphere with enough intimidation to make her victims break. Lesser men may have given in, but George was carved from different wood. Finally, the chief relented.

"Tell me about the bust."

George gathered his thoughts to give a brief yet accurate statement that left him some wriggling room when he wrote his report. "Detective Hayes and I got a call from an anonymous informant yesterday, asking us to meet at a gas station out in Berkeley County. We agreed and drove there this morning. Two hours after the set time, the informant still hadn't shown himself, so we decided to drive back. We stopped again at a rest station about a mile and a half from the gas station to get some fresh air, since we were both frustrated. As you know, leads were slim in this case, and we thought a little walk would help us focus. We hiked a bit farther than intended, heard a shot, and went to investigate. It could have been a hunter, though we doubted it, because it was early afternoon. We thought it safer to check, and since we were already out there, it didn't seem like a big deal. Then we found the Castain house and registered suspicious movement. Still not sure about what was going on, we watched the house, and shortly after, four limousines arrived. When we saw the children brought in, we called SWAT and here we are."

Chief Norris stayed silent for so long, George started searching his impromptu report for possible holes. He couldn't find any and decided to wait. It didn't take long.

"So you want me to believe you went out to Berkeley County, of all places, to meet a mysterious informant, completely anonymous, of course, and just happened upon an orgy with fifteen kidnapped children?" The sarcasm in Chief Norris's voice was scalding.

George shrugged. "Yes. Life can be funny like that."

"Unlike you." Chief Norris fiddled with a pen on her desk, a nervous habit George had seen several times already. "Detective Donovan, you're aware I've read all of Detective Hayes's reports? They're full of these lucky coincidences, which is one of the reasons for our little arrangement. Do you want to try again?"

George held her gaze, outwardly completely cool, inwardly torn. If he kept up the lie, he would close a door with the chief. Not the last one—she still needed him, and he could always claim he'd still been investigating—but he was getting on her bad side by positioning himself more in Andi's corner than hers. On the other hand, what good did telling her do? He had no clue how Andi had found out about the orgy, and until he did, why rock the boat of his blossoming partnership and endanger a huge case? One that would be a real feather in his cap if they could crack it—and for that, he undoubtedly needed Andi's instinct, whatever it was. Of course, the suspicion of Andi having an unprofessional in with criminals was still on the table, and George wasn't inclined to dismiss it just because the carrot of a potential huge solve was dangled in front of him. He just hadn't any proof one way or another, and telling the chief of his musings would only complicate things if he had to backpedal later. As long as he only gave her the barest hints, he and his career were safest because there was nothing she could pin on him.

"Not really, Chief. All you need to know will be in the reports Detective Hayes and I will write. Was this all? Because Detective Hayes and I were thinking about calling it a night so we can have a fresh start tomorrow. Lots of people to interrogate." This was a bit more forward than he would usually act in a situation like this, but he was itching to get back to Andi.

The chief furrowed her brows, clearly unhappy with him. "Go. I'm looking forward to your report." She waved him out of the office, and George didn't give her a chance to rethink her decision to let him go. He hurried over to their desks, where Andi was waiting for him, already dressed to leave.

"I figured you wanted to get out of here as soon as possible."

"If we hadn't discussed about when to leave instead of just going home, I wouldn't have been summoned," George bit out with a little too much force to still be a joke. Andi was either too tired to notice or very good at ignoring George's anger because he simply handed him his keys and went for the exit. Instead of going to his own car, like he had planned in the morning, Andi went to George's. The automatic gesture struck a chord in George's heart, not hard enough to completely quell the mix of anger, exhaustion, and general indecision in his mind, but it made him relent and simply get in his car without calling Andi's attention to his own ride.

Ten minutes later George pulled up in front of Andi's house, the drive by now familiar. Andi opened the door, turned to him. "Thank you for driving me." He hesitated, some kind of inner debate showing on his face. George waited. "What did she want from you?"

It came out in a low tone, devoid of any emotion. Somehow that made George's anger flare again. "She wanted to know what happened, as is her right as chief. She also hinted at knowing that our cover story is made up." He held up his hand when he saw Andi opening his mouth. "Don't worry. Yes, she's read all your reports, and yes, she is suspicious of all the lucky coincidences you had over the years. That said, she needs us to solve this case, so she won't go digging too deep, and as you said, our explanation is solid. Not much she can do."

"That's not all, though, am I right?" Andi was definitely psychic. George was sure of it.

"Nothing important." George tried to sound dismissive. Andi tensed.

"I need to know, George. I took a risk when I let you tag along. Don't make me regret it." The words hit a little too close to home to not have an impact on George. He felt his anger bubbling to the surface.

"*You* took a risk? Apart from the fact that you had little choice but to take me with you, what about my risk? I lied to the chief to cover your sorry ass, not even knowing *what* I'm covering for. Up until now I've been telling myself as long as we solve the case and rescue all those poor victims, it doesn't matter what you do, but now my career is on the line. The chief paired us so I could have an eye on you, and now I'm not delivering, which makes me look bad." The words came out far sharper than George had intended, and when he saw Andi flinch, he regretted them immediately. It was too late, though. Now a responding anger was glowing in Andi's eyes.

"I'm so sorry your precious career may take a hit. I never wanted a partner to begin with, and whatever deal you have with the chief? Fuck you both! I'm just trying to do my job, helping people. Why can't you leave me alone?" Andi didn't wait for an answer. He pushed the door open, got out with movements made graceless by anger, and slammed the door shut again. George watched him storming toward the entrance of his house. He slammed his own head against the headrest and hit the steering wheel with a slapping sound.

"Fucking damn!"

George opened his seat belt, got out of the car, and followed Andi, who was fumbling with his keys, too agitated to find the right one. George suppressed the urge to touch Andi's shoulder, knowing the gesture wouldn't be welcome at the moment, if ever again.

"Andi, man, I'm sorry. I didn't mean it."

"It sure sounded so." Andi's voice was no longer angry. He sounded lost and sad and lonely and utterly tired. Even more than after their last argument. George knew his partner was running on empty batteries, on sheer determination without any substance to back it up, and yet he had added to his burden.

"Look, I can be a total asshole, I know. Especially when I'm out of my depth. Until now, my life has been a series of meticulously planned steps, each one bringing me closer to my career goals. Now I suddenly find myself doing things that have the potential to destroy what I've been working for so long, and it makes me nervous. When I get nervous, I make bad decisions, as everybody in my family can tell you. I'm sorry."

Andi's shoulders slumped visibly at his words. He finally found the right key and put it in the lock. "I understand. It's just... I...." Andi took a deep breath. "If I tell you, you'll think I'm crazy, and I don't want that. I like having you as a partner. I do. Which is surprising." He turned the key, and the door opened. George waited for Andi to say something else, and when he didn't, George finally dared to touch his elbow.

"You're aware nothing you're going to tell me will even come close to what I've been imagining?"

"I wouldn't be so sure about that," Andi mumbled but didn't shy away from his touch.

"Andi, one of my working theories is you're an alien stranded on earth. I don't think it can get any crazier."

Andi looked at him with furrowed brows. "I have to admit, that's an interesting idea." He sighed, his shoulders slumping even more. He looked so vulnerable George wanted to wrap him in his arms to protect him from all harm. "If I tell you, you have to promise not to freak out."

George could feel it in the air, taste it on his lips. Andi was thinking about telling him. A part of George was ecstatic with joy that his partner would trust him with his biggest secret so soon after they met. Another part was frozen by the weight of responsibility Andi was dropping on him. If he knew, he had to decide whether to help Andi and cover for him or throw him to the wolves. He stared into Andi's tired eyes, not seeing any hope in them, just resignation. How long had he been carrying this burden that he got so close to breaking after a week? Had Andi been so starved for a bit of sympathy and a shred of loyalty—because so far George had offered him nothing more—that his walls were already cracking? It was a strange feeling, seeing a man George had come to perceive as strong and unapproachable so vulnerable. A feeling close to pity, though mixed with respect and admiration, welled in George's chest. It made the question he had even harder to ask.

"Why would you trust me all of a sudden? We don't know each other well, and I just admitted I'm working for the chief." It felt alien, being so open about something shady, baring himself amidst the secrets that were part of his job, not knowing if what he wanted to learn really was worth finding out or if the price, for once, might be too high.

"I don't trust you." The words were like a bucket of ice-cold water. "I don't trust anybody with my secret. The few people who know—my family—they deal with it rather poorly. So I guess I'm going to tell you to assure myself that being secretive and reclusive, shutting others out, is the only way for me." Andi stepped through the door, gesturing for George to follow. "Besides, nobody's going to believe you anyway. My risk of exposure is small." He said it so matter-of-factly, George had to snort even though their topic was so serious. Andi's words confirmed what George had just pondered—his partner *was* lonely, and George was convinced he used his level tone and words to shield himself from a disappointment he didn't want to suffer but thought was inevitable. That he still seemed to nourish at least a tiny spark of hope made George even more determined not to let Andi down. He tried to lighten the mood with a small joke.

"You're saying it as if it's a given I'm going to disappoint you. I think I'm insulted."

Andi led the way to the kitchen, where he opened the fridge to retrieve two bottles of water. "Don't be. That's just how things are." So much for lightening the mood.

"Fine." George opened the bottle Andi handed him and took a sip. He put it on the kitchen counter and looked expectantly at Andi. "Tell me."

Andi froze for a moment. His eyes went wide like the proverbial deer caught in the headlights. Then he let out a shaky breath. His hands trembled, as George could see when he put his own water on the counter next to George's. The words that followed the soft plop of the water bottle making contact with the granite countertop had George freezing.

"I can talk to insects."

CHAPTER 21
LEAPING OFF THE ROCK

ANDI LOOKED at George, waiting for his reaction. The man was just staring at him, still as a statue. Then he slowly narrowed his eyes.

"Excuse me, I just heard you saying you can talk to insects."

"Yes. I can. I do. Well, not really talk, they don't do that. Talk, I mean. I see the world through their eyes, so to speak."

George reached for his bottle, lifted it, put it back down, frowned at it, probably wishing it was something stronger. Andi was glad it wasn't so George's reactions weren't enhanced by alcohol. Liquor made everything worse. "And that's where you get your information?"

So far, the man was taking it quite well. No screaming, no blatant dismissal, or outright disbelief. Andi was feeling a small tendril of hope blooming in his chest, foolish as it may be. "Yes. I've inherited it from my grandmother on my mother's side. Her family calls it the *geschenk*, which is German for *present*, though I see it more as a curse. Anyway, I can access information nobody else can, which is how I solve my cases. There's no place on earth without arthropods."

"And you're expecting me to believe that?" George's tone was still low, lacking the aggressiveness Andi had come to associate with talking about his *geschenk*.

"Well, you just told me you were willing to believe I'm an alien. Isn't it better if I'm from earth?"

George gaped at him, clearly not knowing if he should laugh or scream. He finally settled on a humorless chuckle before his expression turned serious again.

"Is that how you knew about the bodies in the storage unit?" His tone was tentative, as if he was trying to his best to give Andi's claim a chance. Or perhaps he was already contemplating how to convince the chief to get rid of Andi as quickly as possible. It was hard to tell because George's face now resembled more a Kabuki mask than something human.

"Yes, the ants were quite agitated and happy about so much food close to their nest."

George shook his head. "When we looked at the place where Lilly was supposedly kidnapped...?"

"The bees and worms remembered. Time frames can be a bit tricky with insects, they have no concept of time as such, but Lilly was kidnapped a year before, with only one winter in between, which made it easier to verify."

"And the Lion Man being somehow weak?"

"There was a flea on Mia that had jumped from the mask to her. It showed me a bag of undesirable blood because of anemia. That's how I knew."

"When you say it like that, it all makes sense." This time George opened the bottle and took another gulp of water. To Andi, he gave the impression of a detective who was following an impossible lead because he was desperate and had run out of options. There still was no anger, though, and no shouting, so perhaps this would end better than he would have dared to hope. "How did you find out about the orgy?"

"Our leads were drying up in front of our noses, what with the cell being stolen and none of the guys we arrested being directly involved with the organization of the trafficking ring, so I opened myself. I don't like doing it, you've seen what happens, but I felt I had no choice. Usually my *geschenk* is limited to a half-mile radius around me, though I can extend it. I knew I was looking for a person with anemia, probably in the vicinity of drugs, which to certain arthropods have a unique signature. I found the lead to the house in Berkeley and, well, the rest you know."

"But none of the people we arrested seemed to be anemic." George furrowed his brows, latching on to possibly the only logical thing in their discussion, at least from his point of view. How Andi envied him his simple world view where logic led a person to secure conclusions and allowed them to make deductions about the world around them. He had never had that luxury, his world always standing on shaky ground where logic was anchored in the needs of beings whose perception was so different from what the human brain was capable of that trying to align the two was an exercise in futility. Explaining it to somebody who had no idea how to look at the world from a different perspective than the one they were used to was insanely difficult. Andi had no words because words described things humans could grasp. He tried regardless.

"As I said, insects have no concept of time. It could be the person had been there while I was searching, or a few days before. I just knew he'd been there, and when we got close, I could feel the presence of the children. That's why I insisted on staying and scoping the place out even though it looked deserted."

"Okay, let me sum this up. You have a hereditary condition that manifests as a connection to insects which helps you solve your cases and find leads where normal detectives would run into a wall?"

"Yes. It's a bit more complicated, and I resent the term 'condition,' but speaking in cop terms, I'm using arthropods as my informants."

George took another swig from his bottle, shook his head when he placed it back on the counter. "I don't know what to say. This seems more outlandish than my alien theory and yet it's kind of logical. I'm just not sure if I should be freaking out or being amazed."

"I don't have an answer to that, George." Andi felt a little bad for his partner. He could see George struggling with the information, his rational brain trying to process it in a way he could cope with. It was a strange feeling, seeing George like this. Andi had never told anybody about his gift before. His parents had known before he was born, his mother telling his father to prepare him for the possibility, and his father's abysmal reaction was something Andi had grown up with, so he had been used to it. His granny had found out on her own, never judging him for something he had no power over. Her reaction, too, had not been triggered by him coming clean. George was the first person Andi saw working through the realization of what he was, what he could do. It was frightening.

George's throat worked furiously. "I guess it's too much to imply you might need help from a shrink?" Andi could hear from his tone he didn't want to be offensive, which was why he squished the spark of anger igniting in his chest.

"Believe me, if I thought doctors of any variety could help me, I'd already be in treatment."

"This is at the same time better and worse than what I had imagined. You're not an alien, which is good, I guess. And you're not corrupt, which is splendid. I was really worried about that. But you talk to insects." George seemed very hung up on the alien part. "Can you prove it? Because what I've seen so far does fit with what you're claiming, but it would also apply to you being psychic or... or...."

"An alien?" Andi couldn't suppress a smile. It was obvious George didn't want to mention it again.

"Yes. Whatever. So, proof?" George looked at him expectantly. Since things had gone way better than Andi had feared, he decided a little demonstration probably wouldn't hurt.

"Fine." He closed his eyes, more for dramatic effect than out of actual necessity, and let the always present cluster of images and impressions at the back of his mind come to the fore. "If you go outside into the front yard, there's a black widow's net in the Southern Magnolia to the right, at about hip height. She's just eating her partner after copulation. You should be able to see her when you turn on the porchlight."

George gasped. "No way."

"Go out and take a look." There was a moment's hesitation; then George went for the front door. He came back a couple of minutes later, his eyes wide with wonder.

"You were right. There wasn't much left of him, but she was definitely eating another spider."

"Told you. Now, if you go out into the garden, straight to the gazebo, and turn left, you'll see a flower bed with lady ferns. There's a dead mouse full of maggots and crawling with ants."

George went without a word, pulling his flashlight from his belt on his way out, and came back soon after, not bothering to hide the mixture of agitation and awe in his voice. "How do you do it?"

Andi raised a brow while tamping down the input he was getting from the arthropods all around them. "So you believe me?"

"Yes. I mean, there is the—admittedly very small—possibility that you saw the spider when we came into the house and that you found the mouse before you left the house today, but why would you leave a rotting mouse in the garden, and when we arrived, you were too agitated to handle your keys properly. Plus, the spider would have been eaten by now. So I'm almost completely convinced. The rest is just me being a cop, as you probably can relate to. Now tell me how you do it."

"It's not so much a question of how I do it but of how I keep the overflow of information in check." When he saw George's confused expression, Andi went on. "The *geschenk* isn't something I can turn on or off. It's constantly working, and the best I can do is dampen the flood of images I'm getting."

"That's why you look tired so often, isn't it?"

"Yes. It's exhausting to be guarded all the time."

George shook his head. "Man, I can't even imagine. It certainly explains your charming personality. If I were in a state of perpetual information overload, I'd probably kill somebody."

"I have to admit I've entertained that thought more than once. Unfortunately, it's generally frowned upon, so I refrained."

"Your former chief, you said he didn't know?"

"I don't think so. I'm sure he had his theories, just like you. But to him, my perfect case numbers outweighed his need to find out. Renard was a pragmatic man." Andi shrugged, still waiting for George to freak out.

George reached for his water bottle, hesitated, left it where it was, stepped back from the counter, turned around, turned back, then started to pace. Back and forth, back and forth between the kitchen and the opening to the living room. Abruptly he stopped in front of Andi again. "I just don't know what to do or say. Where does this leave us? What am I supposed to do now?"

"I guess you've got to sleep on it. Think it through. As I said, I don't think anybody is going to believe you when you tell them. You can always ask Chief Norris to end our partnership." Andi hated to say those words yet forced them out anyway.

George's mouth opened and closed several times. When he finally spoke, it wasn't what Andi had expected. "What do you want, Andi? You showed great trust in me. This shouldn't be about me. The more I think about it, this is all about you."

"It doesn't matter what I want." Andi couldn't stop bitterness from creeping into his voice. "It never matters what I want. I can't change who or what I am. I can only give you the option of walking away. It's better that way."

George grabbed him so hard by the shoulders, Andi yelped in surprise and a little pain. His body was still sore from the night before and the bust. "And that's what people do, don't they? Walk away from you?" George's voice was soft. If there had been any pity in it or in his dark brown eyes, Andi would have broken his hold and told him to shove it. But there was only understanding in George's expression, a strange kinship Andi couldn't understand. It made him vulnerable, opened up places inside him he'd long ago locked tight. And yet here he was, his dams finally breaking after years of constant strain.

"They do. Always. Being with me is trying at best, stressful almost all the time, and downright unbearable at worst. I do understand that."

"So you push them away before they can hurt you. Smart in terms of self-protection." George sounded almost sad now.

Since he was already having a moment of complete openness, Andi saw no reason to hold back anything. Tomorrow, after a good night's sleep, he would probably regret it. Now, he latched on to the possibility to let some of his pent-up frustrations go. "It's easier. That's all."

A shadow crossed over George's face. "I know all about easy." He hesitated for a moment, averted his gaze only to meet Andi's eyes full-on again, a strange emotion Andi couldn't decipher flickering in them. "And I know about being lonely. With me it's more self-inflicted, I do admit that, what with my career plans and everything, but it's still the same. I don't have anybody either." George tilted his head. "Well, perhaps my brother Daniel, we're close, though he's up north at the moment and we don't talk that often. In my immediate surroundings, I'm pretty lonely as well."

Andi had to smile at George's ramblings. It was almost cute, the way he tried to reassure Andi without lying to him. Andi appreciated those efforts.

"You're not going to report me or wash your hands of me?" Andi raised a brow.

"Are you mad? You said it yourself, nobody would believe me anyway. I also want to nail those trafficking bastards, and you're my best bet to solve this case. I'm not giving up now." George huffed, jutting out his chest a bit.

After a moment of silence in which Andi simply didn't know what to say, George continued, his shoulders slumping slightly. "I'm not going to pretend everything's fine, Andi. I like to think I'm a decent enough human being and a passable cop. Though that doesn't mean I'll suddenly stop pursuing my career goals. I can honestly say I like you and I have sympathy for your... condition or whatever you like to call it. But I'd be lying if I said I'm going to help you solely out of the goodness of my heart. Solving this case will be a nice feather in my cap, and if that means I have to help you tweak the reports a bit, so be it. Your secret is safe with me, and I'm going to tell Chief Norris to leave you alone because you're simply that good. Deal?"

George held out his hand with a waggle of his eyebrows that made Andi wonder how much of his "I'm a good guy with an egoistic streak" speech he had truly meant and which parts were simply to hide the fact that he—maybe, possibly—cared more than he wanted to admit. Andi decided to let it go for the moment, too relieved about George's all-over positive reaction to rock the boat further.

"Deal." He shook hands with George. "Though I do want to point out this was the strangest conversation I've ever had and certainly not because of my *geschenk*."

"Agreed. How about we pretend it never happened?" George winked.

"No can do. I need you to help with my cover. There's no escaping for you now. At least until we've solved this case."

"I knew it!" George grinned broadly. "You're using me." He turned serious. "And you're awfully sure we're going to catch the bad guys."

Andi shrugged. "I wasn't so sure yesterday, but now we have a location, even more witnesses, and four culprits who look rich enough to fear for their reputation and therefor be amenable to a deal. We'll get them."

"Whatever you say, O wise one." George mock bowed. "Now go get some sleep. Knowing why you look horrible doesn't make you any prettier."

"Thank you so much, partner." Andi made a face. "Are you going to pick me up tomorrow?"

"Of course. What kind of partner would I be if I didn't? Besides, your car is still at the precinct. You may want to bring it home one of these days."

"Yeah. One of these days." Andi tried to hide his relief. If George was still willing to pick him up, he couldn't be too freaked out. He only hoped an entire night's time of thinking things through wouldn't change that. A quick glance at the clock told him it was more of half a night's time, since it was already past midnight. George went out the door, and when the taillights of his car left Andi's driveway, he sank onto the couch in the living room, still not sure what to make of this entire day. Fatigue crept up on him, made his legs heavy and his brain sluggish. In a heroic attempt, Andi somehow managed to get upstairs into his bedroom and fell face-first onto his bed.

CHAPTER 22
LIAR, LIAR

GEORGE WAS glad he already knew the way to his own apartment, because he was driving on autopilot, his mind a scrambled mess of *this is impossible*, *at least now it all makes a weird kind of sense*, and *somehow, this is pretty cool*. He was also simultaneously worrying about Andi and his own career, though the worry he had for Andi outdid the one for his personal gains, which was new for George. So far, he had always put his priorities firmly in his own corner. The short explanation Andi had given him about how his—what did he call it?—*geschenk*, worked made George wonder how his partner managed to stay upright most of the time.

Andi had either exaggerated, which George couldn't believe, or he was a much stronger person than George would ever be. Either way, he was determined to solve this case with Andi and have his partner's back. This meant he had to protect Andi from Chief Norris while at the same time staying at least on a neutral footing with the chief, since he didn't know when and if he'd need her in the future. George sighed deeply, parked his car, and went up to his apartment. Normally he liked a good challenge, reveled in it, since it gave him a chance to prove to himself as well as his overachieving family that he was every bit as good as his two brothers. Now, though, there was more on the line than just his personal gain—a high-profile case with many innocent victims, a chief breathing down his neck, and most important of all, a partner who was the self-confident lead in the investigation and at the same time strangely dependent on George to help him. He wasn't yet sure how to balance these opposing situations, not to mention the exhausting mix of prickliness and vulnerability Andi was showing him. George had a suspicion he would have to be the unflappable, steadying presence in this partnership, the mature one, and he had his doubts if he was up to it.

He closed and locked the door before he took a quick shower, doing his best to calm his raging thoughts. What he needed now was rest, not to allow his brain to barrage him with a plethora of conflicting emotions and thoughts. Neither he nor Andi needed that at the moment. Their case had gone from lukewarm to scalding hot again, and they couldn't afford to let themselves be distracted. Calming his mind wasn't as easy as George would have hoped. It took him almost an hour after the shower and a glass of warm milk with honey—always his very last resort when his body refused to take the rest it needed and also a fond childhood memory—to finally drift off to sleep, only to be woken way too early by the beeping of his alarm.

Another shower helped him kick-start his body, though thankfully his brain was still sleeping, which kept him from overthinking his impending meeting with Andi. When he pulled into the driveway in front of Andi's house, he did feel a bit nervous, but not as badly as he had feared. Andi opened the door after the third ring, looking even worse than the day before, if that was possible. The rings under his eyes were definitely black, his cheeks hollowed in as if he hadn't eaten in days, his skin had an ashen tone George associated with the terminally sick, and his clothes were more battered than the ones George had gotten used to.

"Holy shit! I'm pretty sure you shouldn't be up. You look like you're one IV away from pushing up daisies!"

"A good morning to you too, asshole." Andi stepped through the door and closed it. His tone was its usual aggressive self with a dash of extra sharpness George had learned to expect when his partner was tired. He hoped it was a sign Andi had things under control.

All of a sudden, George felt insecure. He knew about the burden Andi carried. Shouldn't he be more supportive? Should he ask questions or just roll with it?

"I can hear you thinking from where I'm standing. If you don't feel up to me, I can walk to the precinct. You don't have to bother with me."

And it was back, the vulnerability that had George itching to pull Andi into his arms and protect him from the world.

"That's not it. I was just contemplating if it's safe for me to ask if you're fine or if there's anything I can do for you. You know, without getting my head bitten off by the cranky praying mantis I've just woken." He winked at Andi, who stared at him openmouthed for a moment before he broke out in hysterical laughter. George let him get it all out before he raised a brow.

"Well, what is it? Do you want to talk, kill me, or just sit in the car while I drive us to the Starbucks?"

Andi wiped his eyes, then got serious. "You know what, I actually want to talk. I've never been able to do this with a partner before, and I find that's something I'd appreciate. You know, despite being cranky to the point of cannibalism and all."

"Talking it is." George nodded in the direction of his car. "Let's get in."

When they both had their seat belts on, George started the car. Andi waited until George was on the street before he started to talk. "I'm utterly exhausted. I think I slept about three hours, tops. There was just too much going on." He leaned his head back with a deep sigh.

"Was it because of me? I might not have been clear enough yesterday. I won't tell on you, and I won't make things difficult for you either. You have my word."

To George's surprise, Andi chuckled. "You know what, that would have been the other thing keeping me from sleeping if not for the silverfish mating in the cellar and kitchen." Andi made a face. "It doesn't happen often, you know, all of them going at it practically at the same time, and of course they had to do it when my defenses were already low. There's nothing like lovesick arthropods to flood my senses to the point where I want to bleach my brain." He shuddered.

"Aren't silverfish unsanitary? I don't want to insult you, but perhaps you need a cleaning service? To help keep a tight ship."

In the silence that followed, George wondered what it would take to get back on Andi's good side. Then his partner chuckled. "Okay, I can see I have my work cut out for me. What do you know about arthropods in general?"

George shrugged, setting the turn signal to get to the Starbucks. "I'm the first to admit it's not much. Butterflies are beautiful and come from very hungry caterpillars...." Andi snorted at the children's book reference, just like George had hoped. "Most of them are pests, and there are a lot of them. Bees give us honey. Wasps sting. Oh, and worms are good for the garden. That's about it. I'm a city rat."

Amusement was clear in Andi's expression when George parked the car in front of the Starbucks, shamelessly putting the blue flashlight he had inside for car chases on the roof to justify his use of public space as a parking lot. They went into the café, the guy behind the counter yelling "The usual?" in their direction, which they confirmed with a nod.

Being a regular had its perks. As they waited, Andi returned to the topic at hand.

"Silverfish like damp, dark places, so cellars, kitchens, and bathrooms are their version of paradise. Lots of food there as well. Anyway, silverfish in your house aren't a reason to be alarmed. *Not* having them in the house should worry you much more. It's usually a sign your home either has an unhealthy climate, often due to renovations where people put in airtight windows, or there's some kind of poison, in most cases asbestos, somewhere. The same goes for spiders, by the way. Yes, they can be annoying, and yes, it's not much fun seeing the floor move when you have to take a leak at night, but it means you're in a healthy environment." Andi shrugged.

George just stared at him. "Please tell me the same doesn't apply to cockroaches!"

"It doesn't. They are truly a sign of lacking hygiene. I'd like to point out, though, that they are one of nature's most ingenious and sturdy designs. Some scientists believe cockroaches would be the only species surviving a nuclear catastrophe."

"Is that supposed to impress me?" George didn't know if he should be horrified or fascinated. His mind decided on a mixture of both, giving him goose bumps all over his body while not stopping his mouth from working.

"Well, given how we react to radiation and how fragile we are, I'd say being impressed is the least you can do."

"They're still gross."

"They are. Gross and sturdy and masterpieces of evolution." Andi sounded too much like he was enjoying George's discomfort. The announcement of their order saved George from confronting his partner. Somehow, Andi managed to beat George to the counter and paid, for the first time since they knew each other, which irritated George a bit. Getting the food was his job!

When they were back in the car, Andi already sipping on his tea, George circled back to the start of their conversation. "You said your defenses were low yesterday. Was that because of our talk, or still an aftermath of what you did to find the estate?"

"A mixture of both, actually, with physical exhaustion because of the bust thrown in for good measure." George felt Andi's eyes on his and risked a quick glance to his partner.

"You can tell me."

Andi closed his eyes. George had to concentrate on the road again. "I told you the *geschenk* can't be switched off."

"Yes. It always works. Like…." George racked his brain for an adequate comparison. The only one he could come up with sounded a bit dramatic. "Like the sun?" He made it sound like a question.

"Yeah, like the sun." Andi chuckled. "That's actually a pretty good picture. The sun shines all the time, but the earth's rotation allows for darkness. Well, my darkness comes through concentration. When I'm at my best, I can suppress the impressions to nothing more than a murmur at the back of my head. A big part of that happens automatically by now, which allows me to function in the world."

"And when your concentration wavers, for whatever reason, it gets harder, which in turn makes it more difficult to focus on blocking, which drains your reserves, which then comes full circle and affects your concentration. Basically, you enter a devil's circle." They had reached the precinct, and George found a parking spot in the shade. "How do you break out of it?"

Andi grabbed the two bags with their breakfast together with his tea. "I sleep a lot. Try to avoid anything that stresses me physically or emotionally."

George groaned. "Exactly what you can't do at the moment! That sucks. Is there anything I can do to help?"

"You already did. You listened. Strangely enough, I feel better now. I can do this." He straightened his shoulders. "Let's get going. There's evil guys to catch."

George followed his partner inside the precinct. He knew, if he really wanted to help Andi, he'd have to up his game. For the time being, he would settle for second best, lend him a sympathetic ear and a shoulder to lean on until he found out how to be the partner Andi needed and deserved.

As it turned out, much to George's dismay, the evil guys were quite elusive. The ten men they had arrested the night before had all called their lawyers and weren't nearly as cooperative as George and Andi had hoped. They also weren't as stupid or easily spooked as the ones they had arrested during the bust with the two vans.

The good news was this meant they were getting higher in the chain of command, closer to the person orchestrating it all. The bad news was it didn't do them a lot of good as long as the arrested kept their mouths shut. The cells they had confiscated from the customers and their goons hadn't offered any leads either. Shireen was sure the organization used burner phones they destroyed the moment a deal was struck, which was very smart and very unfortunate for their investigation. And the customers used this fact as their excuse for not cooperating, claiming they didn't know the person they had struck the deal with. George was inclined to believe them, since it would have been in their interest to get a deal with law enforcement, given the charges they were facing. At least four sick bastards wouldn't see the light of day any time soon, along with their goons and the two pimps. It was a small mercy, for George knew there were ten more waiting for each asshole they put behind bars. The world was a scary place, and at times like these, George felt its weight on his shoulders. Andi was frustrated but put on an indifferent front, mostly to keep other detectives from asking stupid questions during their brief breaks.

The hospital visit with the victims was even harder than the first one with Rose, Mia, Kathy, and Greg. The children told the same story George and Andi already knew and couldn't offer any new insights. Their last hope when they drove back to the precinct in the afternoon was Jake Castain. The mayor's personal assistant had finally returned to the city and had been brought in for questioning. If as a suspect or witness was yet to be determined, though George couldn't imagine Castain not knowing anything about what was going on at his own estate.

Andi was tight-lipped, his answers mostly monosyllabic grunts, the lines around his mouth and eyes so deep they made him look like an old man. George worried about his partner yet had no clue how to make things better for him and if he should even try. When he looked at Andi, he was reminded of a Jenga tower with so many pieces missing already it defied the laws of physics by still standing. It was also clear that the next block pulled out would send the whole thing crashing to the ground, and George didn't want to be the one responsible. He needed Andi to function and didn't know how to ensure it.

When they entered the precinct, Rose was waiting for them, redirecting them from the interrogation room where Jake Castain was waiting to Chief Norris's office. George could feel Andi stiffening next to him. His partner was too tired to give even the illusion of politeness, and George knew he had to take over here. He grabbed Andi's lower arm to gently squeeze it for a moment. "Let me handle this," he mouthed behind Rose's back.

Andi's gaze darkened for a moment before he nodded once. Knowing Andi, this was all the concession George would get. On their way to the office, Rose chattered on and on about how unfortunate it was that Taylor Vance's cell still hadn't been found and how bad Shireen must be feeling and that she'd been thinking about making cake for everybody but there was just so much to do at the moment, what with the obvious breach in security. George was almost relieved when they entered the chief's office, Rose holding the door open while first Andi and then George stepped inside. At least Rose's blabbering had now come to an end. Apart from that, George was sure that if he'd had a decent night's sleep and not just the few measly hours he had managed to get, he wouldn't have felt like a virginal offering for a ferocious dragon, prepared by the dragon's little lackey for easier slaughtering. As it was, the clicking of the closing door sounded like a vault slamming shut in his ear.

"What do you want?" Andi didn't bother with niceties or even sitting down. So much for letting George handle it. He stepped forward and put a placating hand on Andi's back.

"What Detective Hayes meant was what do you need from us, Chief Norris? We were on our way to question Jake Castain."

Norris watched them for a moment with furrowed brows, seemingly not sure whether she should react to Andi's rudeness or just skip over it and concentrate on George. She decided to do the latter.

"I know. Which is why you're here. I'm sure you know Jake Castain is not only a highly respected citizen of Charleston but also the mayor's PA. Mrs. Manafort wasn't happy when she learned of his arrest and wanted to know if there's any base to the accusations made against Mr. Castain."

Out of the corner of his eye, George saw Andi opening his mouth, a dangerous glint in his eyes. He pinched him where his hand still was on Andi's back and started talking quickly to avert the confrontation he saw brewing.

"Well, we did bust an orgy with minors in his family home in the country. I'd say that does warrant at least some questions, don't you think, Chief? Even if he doesn't have anything to do with it—" *Which I highly doubt*, George added in the privacy of his own head. "—he should at least be able to shed some light as to who might use his estate to commit such despicable crimes."

Chief Norris tapped her chin with her left forefinger, thinking. Since Andi was still tense like a wire, George left his hand at his lower back, even though a quick glance from Norris told him the gesture hadn't gone unnoticed.

"I'm sure Mr. Castain will be happy to provide you with all the information you need." Chief Norris stopped her tapping in favor of fiddling with a pen she took from a stack of documents to her right. "Just tread carefully, Detectives. The mayor is quite fond of her PA and was upset about him being treated like a criminal."

"Duly noted." George nodded, in part to hide his expression until he got it back under control. He'd seen enough situations like these to know exactly what was going on. The following year was an election year for the mayor, and George was willing to bet his mother's reputation as a judge that Jake Castain was a generous donor for Deirdre Manafort's campaign. At the moment, the mayor was trying to shield her PA without making it look like she was obstructing justice, using Chief Norris as the go-between. Should they find Castain guilty, George knew with absolute certainty the mayor would drop him like a hot potato, trying to distance herself from him as fast and as far as possible. Until then, Castain enjoyed a certain immunity George and Andi had to consider when questioning him.

"Is there anything else?" George forced himself to sound respectful, even though the chief had just lost several points in his regard. George did understand political pressure. He did *not* tolerate it when innocents where hurt.

The chief hesitated for a moment, her nervous gaze flitting between George and Andi. Finally, she let out a soft sigh. "No, that's it. You can go to your witness now."

The way she put a slight emphasis on the word "witness" was more wishful thinking than anything else, and George conveniently ignored it. He took Andi's arm to drag him out of the office before he could say anything else beside the halfhearted goodbye he'd sent in the chief's direction, not caring what it might look like. Their investigation had taken on a political aspect that required a certain diplomacy George knew Andi didn't possess.

Once they were back on their way to the interrogation rooms and out of earshot, Andi lost what little composure he'd had.

"What a stupid cow," he hissed. "We've literally caught those bastards with their hands down the pants of minors and she has the nerve to ask us to go easy on a possible criminal because he has ties to the mayor?"

"That's politics for you." George shrugged.

"No, not for me. It's for heartless assholes with zero compassion for the victims." Andi was bristling like an alley cat ready to fight over territory.

"I know, Andi. And I'm not saying it's okay. Far from it. But it wouldn't hurt to tread lightly until we know more. The chief and the mayor are in a precarious situation. The chief because she's new, the mayor because it's election next year. Let's try and not antagonize them any more than we have to. Just to make our lives and the investigation easier."

"I hate playing nice with assholes!" Andi's voice was so full of righteous indignation, George had to suppress a smile. His partner was a better man than he wanted people to believe.

CHAPTER 23
CAUGHT

ANDI WAS still seething when they reached the interrogation room that held Jake Castain. His already low opinion of Chief Norris had taken a nosedive into outright detestation. To him, anybody who was willing to protect possible criminals, no matter the reason, was criminal themselves. And when the case involved the most vulnerable members of society? Andi had zero tolerance. The chief was lucky George had been there; otherwise he would have given her a detailed piece of his mind. Andi was the first to admit his diplomacy skills were next to nonexistent, mostly because they required a mixture of empathy and willful blindness he had never cared to develop. That was one of the few good things about the world of arthropods—deceit, hatred, lies, and other very human notions didn't exist there. It was eat or get eaten, but in a straightforward way Andi could appreciate. George stopped, his hand at the door handle. "How do you want to play this? Do you want to take the lead?"

The slight hesitancy in George's voice told Andi his partner wasn't convinced he had enough of a handle on his emotions to do a successful interview. As much as it galled Andi to admit it, George did have a point.

"No, probably not a good idea. Castain moves in circles I rarely enter. This is more your field of expertise." He shrugged. "You know the lingo, the secret handshake. Let him think you're the lead detective and I'm just an observer. If I find anything, I can still chime in."

George nodded. "Fine with me." He took a deep breath. "Let's do this."

They entered the room to find Castain at the table with a cup of coffee, judging from the smell, and a small plate with cheap chocolate cookies he hadn't touched. The man didn't look like the asshole Andi thought him to be. From the info they'd gotten, he knew Castain was thirty-six, but he definitely looked younger, which might have something to do with his slender built and the shaggy brown hair that was artfully tousled on top of his head. He was also pale, with dark shadows under his eyes, though if it was from lack of sleep or something else, Andi couldn't tell. The few silverfish living in the interrogation room weren't very helpful, since for them humans were blobs of uncontrollably moving mass who generated disturbing vibrations on the floor. It seemed they would have to do this the hard way, also known as old-fashioned questioning.

"Good afternoon, Mr. Castain. I'm Detective George Donovan, and this is my partner, Detective Andrew Hayes. Thank you for coming in so quickly to help us with our investigation." George's tone was respectful in a way Andi would have never managed, considering the terrible suspicion they had regarding Jake Castain. It managed to put the man at ease, as his shoulders visibly relaxed and the grim line of his mouth broadened into what would have been a charming smile if Andi hadn't seen a gaping black void where other people carried their soul. He knew he was being dramatic and was glad George was taking the lead, easily slipping into the amiable persona of a well-meaning officer of the law who didn't pose the slightest threat. Andi would have never been able to do that; instead he would have antagonized Castain to the point where the man shut completely down.

"Yes, dreadful business. You can imagine my shock when I was told about what had been going on in my family home." Somehow Castain managed to sound equal parts shocked and annoyed, with just enough dismay thrown in to fool a casual onlooker. Andi was anything but.

"I gather from your words you weren't aware what was going on?" George made it sound dismissive, as if this was just a formality, which had Castain relaxing even further. Andi had to admit, his partner was damn good. It was obvious Castain had recognized and acknowledged him as an equal of sorts from his mannerisms alone, the secret handshake Andi would never know how to do. As annoying as that was, in this case it worked in their favor. A relaxed suspect was a suspect prone to being reckless, and a reckless suspect was easy prey, the simple math of cops and culprits.

"Surely not or I would have reported it immediately. I haven't been to the family home in months, actually. Too much work in the city, what with the election next year and everything. You know how it is." Castain didn't look once at Andi, his entire focus on George, which was just fine for Andi. It gave him more time to read Castain's body language, which told him the man was very carefully upholding an image to distract from something. Though if he was just his normal evasive political self, trying to dodge a potentially damaging situation, or if he was hiding what Andi was almost certain he was doing, he couldn't tell.

"So the family home was sitting empty? Not even somebody there to do maintenance?" George still sounded almost bored, like he was just going through the motions, when in reality this was an important question. Depending on Castain's answer, they would know if he was lying to them.

"It was empty, yes, but of course there were people looking after it. A home so big needs constant care or else the market value plummets." Castain paused a moment. "Especially since I'm planning to sell." He leaned down and lifted a leather man purse onto the table which probably cost more than Andi made in a month. Didn't prevent the thing from being ugly as all hell. "I've brought the emails I exchanged with my realtor. I thought they might be of help." His satisfied tone indicated he thought this was enough to clear him. Andi was sure if Castain could, he would have clapped himself on the back for preempting the police's questions.

George took the binder and quickly leafed through it before handing it to Andi. At first glance, everything seemed in order, the emails dating back as far as December the previous year, talking about formalities such as maintenance, when to set up dates for viewing, and the pricing, which the realtor thought was too high. As alibis went, this wasn't too bad, but certainly not a clean bill either.

"If it's okay with you, Mr. Castain, we'll keep those emails for reference." George still sounded overly polite, with just a hint of thankfulness which made Andi want to gag. Castain, on the other hand, was eating it up.

"Of course. Do keep them, Detective Donovan. And if you need anything else, feel free to call me anytime. I want this solved as quickly as possible."

"Now that you mention it, Mr. Castain, would it be possible for you to give us a list of the people who had access to your house? As you said, it had to be maintained, and of course you didn't have the time to oversee it all the time, I fully understand that. Unfortunately, this is a golden opportunity for criminals to have utilized your home without your knowledge."

Castain nodded gravely. "Sure, Detective Donovan. You're absolutely right. I'll contact the companies who have worked at the house and ask them to send you a list of their employees. I'm sure they do wish to clear their names as quickly as possible."

Andi wanted to make a face but caught himself at the last moment. Castain was in a good mood, no need to antagonize him—yet. George went on with his careful questioning.

"There's one last thing I have to ask of you, Mr. Castain, just to cross all my *T*s, you understand? Being thorough is the heart of every investigation."

Castain's left eyelid started to twitch, but he kept his cool, maintaining his amiable façade. "Whatever I can do to help." His enthusiasm was drying up more quickly than spittle on a hot stove, but Andi couldn't care less. Perhaps, if they were really lucky, Castain would make a mistake out of sheer annoyance.

"I have the pictures and names of the men we arrested at your home, and I'd like to ask you to take a look at them, see if you recognize any of them." George lined the pictures up in front of Castain. The man leaned closer to take a look before he glanced away again, clearly not interested. "I'm afraid I can't help you here, Detective Donovan. I do know two of these men by sight, as I'm sure many people do because they are public figures." He made a dismissing gesture with his right hand. "I can't believe they were involved in something unlawful. I've always perceived them as model citizens."

Just like yourself, Andi thought but kept the sarcastic comment to himself. This interrogation was going nowhere fast, and judging from the tense line of George's shoulders and the smug expression on Castain's face, they both knew it too. George gathered the pictures, his voice still calm and composed as if this were nothing but a friendly chat between like-minded people.

"If you remember anything or perhaps have an idea why your house was used by those criminals, please contact us immediately."

Castain nodded gracefully, a king dismissing his servants. "Anything to help the police."

No mention of the victims, no question how they were doing. The man was ice-cold when it came to the suffering of others, especially those he deemed beneath him. All the more reason for Andi to keep him on top of his suspect list.

"Thank you so much, Mr. Castain. You've been a real help, and we do apologize for the inconvenience. My partner is going to show you out, since the precinct can be a maze for people who aren't used to it. We appreciate your cooperation."

"It's my pleasure." Castain got up, grabbing his ugly man purse tightly with his left hand while offering his right to George. They shook, and then Andi led the man outside. He kept up a brisk walk to avoid talking to Castain. Apparently, he needn't have worried, since the man didn't even try to make conversation. When they stepped outside, Andi nodded at Castain, while at the same time opening his senses wide. Out here were enough insects who could tell him a lot of interesting things about Castain. The man nodded back, not offering his hand as he'd done with George, which showed Andi clearly that he'd been classified as some kind of errand boy, nobody of importance.

He stayed in the shade of the entrance while Castain went to his car, a Tesla, by the looks of it, though Andi didn't know which model. And while Castain walked with the gait of a man convinced he'd gotten away, Andi listened to the mosquitoes dismissing Castain as a source of food because his blood was sick and he carried residues of drugs Andi immediately recognized as the same as on Taylor Vance and the other men they had arrested during their first bust. Andi smiled. Castain was their man. All they had to do was prove it.

Back inside the precinct, George was already waiting for Andi at their desks, the angry line between his eyebrows telling Andi everything he needed to know about George's true feelings toward Castain. George had the binder open in front of him, though his gaze was trained on Andi. "Is Mr. Douchebag gone?"

"Yep. Entered his expensive ride without so much as a 'Have a nice day' and rode off into traffic. May he be stuck in a jam for at least an hour."

George chuckled. "I'm glad to see our estimation of Castain is the same." His voice dropped to a conspiratorial whisper. "Did you get anything else on him?"

Andi didn't know if he should laugh or play along. On one hand George being a bit paranoid about Andi's *geschenk* was a good thing; on the other it smacked a bit too much of teenage drama movie for Andi's liking. Next thing he knew they would be meeting in secret somewhere in the woods where they would then stumble upon some werewolves, or was it vampires? No, Andi was sure he was mixing things up. Were they supposed to become a couple? At some point, probably. If this *were* a teenage drama movie, which it wasn't. This was reality, in all its despicable glory.

He cast a quick glance around, only to find the other cops in the room paying them no attention at all. Most of them were genuinely busy, and those who weren't knew better than to be nosy about his business. Having a bad reputation had its merits. He leaned a bit toward George, just to be on the safe side, before he spoke. "He's our man. The mosquitoes say he's got anemia, which would explain his pale skin and the circles under his eyes, and that he's covered in the stench of the same drugs we found on the guys in the vans. He's the Lion Man."

"Are you sure?" George's gaze said he already believed Andi, but he seemed to need the reassurance.

"Absolutely."

George nodded. "Now for the fun part—how do we prove it? I've looked through those emails and they seem to be real. It's not enough to completely exonerate him, but it casts serious doubts on his involvement. No judge is going to give us a warrant to search his house here in the city if all we've got is that the orgy was taking place at a house he apparently hasn't been to in months. As things are, he's nothing more than a victim himself." George gave the papers an annoyed glance. "Same goes for his medical records. There's no way we can legally access them, and even if we could, saying the mosquitoes told us it's him won't do us any good."

Andi felt a grim smile tugging on his lips. "Welcome to my world. First of all, let's get these emails to Shireen. I bet she can do some digging, and perhaps she can hack his medical records as well. As for catching him red-handed... I'm afraid we'll have to be patient. He's already proven how shrewd he is. I bet he's got contingency plans for every kind of scenario, and he's most certainly going to lie low for the next few weeks." Andi furrowed his brows. Just thinking about all the pain innocent victims would suffer in those weeks made him angry.

"Do we draw him out?" George was closing the binder.

"I'm not sure. I assume the chief's going to keep an eye on us, which means we can't be too obvious."

"But if we don't act and things take too long, the chief's going to breathe down our necks about solving the case."

"A thin line to walk." Andi shuddered. "Let's keep an eye on him and see what CSI finds in his family house. That should take at least two weeks. Perhaps something will pop up. If not, we'll have to get creative."

"How often do you have to 'get creative' with your cases?" George looked curious.

"Depends. A bit of creativity is always involved. The more heavily I have to rely on my *geschenk*, the more free-mindedness is necessary to get the results I need." Andi shrugged nonchalantly. "I always try to throw in as much solid police work as possible to distract from the parts where I'm just winging it. You'd be amazed how easily IA gets derailed by well-researched evidence. Of course, placement in the report is also crucial."

George narrowed his eyes. "You have this down to an art, haven't you?"

"Oooh, yes. And if you're a good boy, I'm going to share my secrets with you."

"I'm not sure if I should be flattered or frightened." The laughter in George's voice was a welcome relief after the stress of interrogating Jake Castain.

"Go with honored. You're the first I'm letting partake in my infinite wisdom." Andi winked, and they both started laughing out loud, drawing surprised glances from the other officers.

THE NEXT two days were spent with following up on all kinds of leads, some to pacify Chief Norris, most of them to solidify their case against Jake Castain. They were baby steps, supporting evidence that would strengthen their case once they got the break they needed to go after Castain directly. The first break happened on the morning of the third day, when Andi found a stack of documents on his desk. Since the children they had saved from Castain's house had been too traumatized to be interrogated in detail, experts from Child Services had taken over and finally provided a list with the full names and ages of all the children, as well as the places where they had been taken. When Andi went over the list, he found five more children had been kidnapped in Spartanburg, just like Lilly Cordon, while the others came from all over

South Carolina, with a maximum of four coming from the same towns. Andi asked George to take a look.

"What do you think? Is this just a coincidence or are we on to something?"

George stared at the five names for a long time. Finally, he pulled up a map of Spartanburg on the PC, comparing the exact places from which the children had been taken. They all came from the same district as Lilly Cordon. George rubbed his forehead with both his thumbs, a habit Andi had already come to associate with George thinking very hard.

"It could still be a coincidence. I mean, it's easier to prey on children from a poor district, and it doesn't get much poorer than Church Street and the surrounding neighborhoods."

"But...." Andi raised a brow.

George sighed. "As Gibbs would say, there's no such thing as coincidence. Especially not in a case like this one."

"Who's Gibbs?" Andi asked.

"Don't tell me you don't know." George couldn't conceal the horror in his voice. Andi grinned broadly, telling George he'd just been played. "Asshole."

"You asked for it. And I think Rule Sixteen is what we should take to heart here."

George furrowed his brows, obviously in an attempt to recall it. "If someone thinks he has the upper hand, break it?"

Impressed, Andi nodded. "Castain and Harris think they have the upper hand, that they're smarter than us."

George mulled this over. "We were thinking about looking into Detective Harris. Perhaps now's the time to dig a little."

"My thoughts exactly." Andi furrowed his brows. "I don't want to alert him in case he tries to cover his tracks, so let's start with his past and only touch his cases once we have solid leads."

"You don't seem to doubt that we'll find something."

Andi didn't dignify this statement with an answer. He simply shot George a look that had him raising his hands defensively. "Whoa, man. I was just trying to manage your expectations!"

"There's nothing to manage, thank you very much. If it walks like a duck and quacks like a duck...."

"Yeah, yeah, then we get the potato dumplings."

Andi couldn't suppress his pleased smile. "You remembered."

"I do listen to you, you know." George winked. "Though sometimes I don't know why."

"Oh, shut up and start digging into his childhood. I'll take his time in the Academy."

George saluted. "Aye, aye, boss."

Andi snorted and flipped George off before he pulled up Detective Clayton Harris's file and started plowing through his past. It quickly became apparent that the man was most definitely not a model citizen, let alone an exemplary cop. His grades at the police academy were mediocre, and how he made it to detective would remain a secret between Harris and the chief who promoted him, though Andi suspected foul play. It certainly wasn't because of the man's shining rap sheet. Tainted as it was, there was no glaring neon sign pointing at any crass wrongdoings on Harris's part. It was more like his entire vita within the force was a muddy gray, certainly nothing worth praising but also not warranting a closer look. Which made Andi suspicious as all hell. Nobody was that prone to illegality without ever tipping over the edge. Andi was tempted to ask Shireen to do some digging into Harris's finances when George let out a whoop of victory.

"Gotcha!"

Andi got up from his own chair and went over to George to look over his shoulder. There was a high school reunion picture on the screen. It read *Palmetto Catholic Academy, Reunion 2010.* George had found it on a Facebook account, using face recognition. It showed Clayton Harris in a rather nice suit, standing next to Jake Castain. Both of them were holding beers, toasting each other. Andi whistled.

"Great job, George. So they went to school together?"

George's hands flew over the keyboard, pulling up the website of Palmetto Catholic Academy. There were no yearbook pictures of past classes available due to privacy measures, but after a few failed attempts, George managed to enter the closed off section for students, parents, and teachers, where he also found an album with pictures of classes dating as far back as the 1960s, when the school was founded. A few clicks later they were looking at the yearbook pictures in the late 1990s and found what they'd been looking for in the section from 1999. Castain and Harris had not only been in the same year but had also participated in the same extracurricular activities. The usual snapshots showed them playing lacrosse, with their arms around each other's shoulders, laughing into the camera, dancing at a party, and sitting on the lawn in front of what Andi assumed to be the school building.

"They sure seem cozy. Though I do wonder how Harris got into that school. From what I've seen so far, he doesn't strike me as the wealthy type." Andi furrowed his brows.

"Me neither, but hacking a school website is pretty much the height of what I can do computer-wise. I think we need Shireen to take a look at Harris's finances. Something's definitely fishy here." George sent an order to the printer in the corner. These pictures were another small brick in the case they were building against Jake Castain and now Detective Harris as well.

"Let's see what Shireen can find before we include IA. These guys can be quite blunt, and I don't want them to alert Castain." Andi knew IA was a necessary evil to keep the police in check—*quis custodiet ipsos custodes* and all that—but they could also be a giant pain in the ass with the tact of a train wreck, something they so didn't need in a case as precarious as the one they were currently dealing with.

"You know we can't not tell them about Harris. We're required to report all suspicions regarding colleagues." George didn't sound overly fond of the idea.

"Well, we could just say we didn't realize *how* important Harris was to the case until we've solved it?" Andi waggled his eyebrows exaggeratedly.

All he got for his antics was a look. "If this is part of your 'infinite wisdom,' I pass. Going toe to toe with IA is so not on my bucket list. Though the two of them going to the same school is hardly damning evidence. This could work. Perhaps. I'm doubting it."

"No risk, no fun." Andi leaned back in his chair when he got the death glare from George. "Fine, let's contact them, play it safe. Perhaps we can convince them to either work with us or leave Harris alone until we're finished with our investigation. Here's to hoping, though. You know how they can be."

George raised one eyebrow. "You're giving in way too fast. Are you still tired? Have they replaced you with a pod person? Where's my stubborn, grumpy partner who doesn't give an inch?"

"Stubborn and grumpy? Surely you're not referring to me. I'm wounded!" Andi put the back of his left hand against his forehead, giving a dramatic sigh.

George stared at him. And a little more when Andi didn't react. Before Andi knew it, they were locked in a staring contest that was surprisingly fun in an alarmingly normal kind of way. So this was what easy camaraderie felt like. Andi prodded the feeling with his inner bony forefinger and found he liked it. He also found that George wouldn't budge. The man seemed intent on not giving an inch and prepared to stay in his chair, pinning Andi with his gaze for the remainder of the day. Andi realized he would have to up his game in the future if he wanted to stand a chance against George, and wasn't that a dangerous thought? George had made it clear this was just a station on his way to greater things, which would leave Andi alone again in the foreseeable future. While exactly this thought had helped Andi in the beginning to put up with George, it now tasted sour on his lips. Loneliness had always been his friend, his safeguard against a world that would destroy him if he let it in. So why was the prospect of reuniting with his trusted companion so bleak all of a sudden?

"Woolgathering won't get you out of this, you know." George's even tone pried Andi from musings that were becoming more depressing by the minute. He shoved thoughts of how nice it was to have a bagel and tea delivered to him every morning firmly to the back of his mind. Now was not the time to get lost in fruitless thinking. Andi was well aware George would win this round eventually, so he decided to spoil the victory for his partner.

"I know. And I'm giving in because you, my cheerful, patient, and kind partner, will be talking to IA. I'm sure somebody with your charm can easily convince them to hold their horses until we're done. Me, on the other hand, I'm so grumpy and stubborn, I can't be trusted with such an important task." Andi tried an innocent smile and knew he had failed horribly when George shook his head.

"You're sneaky, I give you that. Though I do remember being the new guy here. Shouldn't the more senior detective take over this oh so important task?"

"Touché. Though as the senior detective I delegate this task to you as a learning experience. If you want to become chief one day, you need to be able to play nice with all kinds of annoying, irritating, or difficult people."

"You mean like your charming self? I think I'm doing not too bad on that front." George was definitely trying to suppress a smile, which made

Andi strangely happy. While he usually found it extremely tedious to put up with most people, interacting with George felt almost natural.

"You are, and now it's time to put your newfound skills to the test with IA."

"I can't win this, can I?" George threw his arms in the air.

"No, you can't. Though you may take solace from knowing that you won the staring contest. Seriously, man, do you have cats in your ancestry?"

George grinned broadly. "No, just a mother who is a judge, and two older brothers. I may have picked up a few tricks over the years." He reached for the phone on his desk. "So while I'm trying to make nice with IA, what are you going to do?"

"The more questionable part."

At George's raised eyebrow, Andi shrugged. "Castain is a smart asshole. If we want to catch him, we need to start following him around. For that, we need to know where he is at all times."

George whistled. "You want to put a tracker on him?" He furrowed his brows. "Wait a moment. Don't we need the okay from the chief for that? Don't tell me you're going to Chief Norris without me! That's probably the worst idea I've ever heard from you!"

Andi sighed. George really was innocent. He almost regretted tainting him. Almost. "Would you keep it down, please? You should know by now I avoid our darling chief like the plague. Of course I'm not going to ask her to put a tracker on the car of a man she so desperately wishes to be innocent."

It took a few moments for George to catch up. Andi credited him for not freaking out loudly. "You want to go behind her back?" It was more a hiss than actual speech.

"Of course. I do that all the time."

"Are you insane?"

Andi couldn't resist. He waggled his eyebrows. "You're asking me this *now*?"

George went back to his earlier staring mode, and Andi hurried to placate him before he did something stupid—like going to Norris and telling her everything. "Don't clam up, partner. It's for her own good. If she doesn't know about it, she's got plausible deniability, something people in power love. Not that I think she's going to need it, because this case will be closed neatly by her two top detectives. Don't you see the beauty of it? If we get Castain with the help of a tracker, there's nothing she can do about it because we cracked the case. And if, by some miracle, he's *not* our guy, she will never know. Win-win in any case."

"Trackers need to be signed out. Somebody will notice." George seemed to be intent on finding the proverbial fly in the soup.

"Remind me what Shireen does for a living?"

George's eyes narrowed. "This is not the first time you're doing this," he accused. "And I thought you hated other people? For an antisocial grump, your connections within the force are surprisingly good."

"I wouldn't go so far. Shireen likes the thrill of doing something forbidden, that's all." Andi tried his best to sound nonchalant. Nobody needed to know about the favor he'd done Shireen to earn her lifelong gratitude. Nobody but him, her, that abusive rapist she had had for a stepfather, and the ants, worms, and maggots that had made him disappear. And *they* couldn't tell anybody but him.

He wasn't sure if George bought it, but he didn't press the matter further. "I'm going to call IA. You do your illegal thing and don't tell me any more about it."

"Sure thing. I'll also ask Shireen to take a look at Detective Harris's finances."

"Yeah, yeah." George shooed him off with an impatient gesture. Clearly he had accepted his defeat.

Andi went to find Shireen with an unfamiliar lightness in his heart. He couldn't remember when he'd last had such an easygoing conversation with another human being—if ever. George brought out a side in him that terrified, awed, and amazed Andi all at once. He wasn't sure what to make of it. Not at all.

CHAPTER 24
TRACKING A MONSTER

FOR A week they'd been following Jake Castain, and George wondered if the man would ever crack. Putting the tracker on Castain's car had been anticlimactic after the bullets George had sweated when he realized Andi had been perfectly serious about this questionable endeavor. All it took was driving by the city hall around noon, when practically everybody was having their lunch break, stopping in a small side street, slipping out for five minutes, and placing the magnetic tracker on the underside of Castain's Tesla's bumper. They had briefly discussed wiring his cell as well, but since he so far seemed to rely on burner phones for his illegal activities, the risk of getting caught far outweighed the potential benefits of listening in on calls that might or might not incriminate Castain. Plus, any proof they got that way wouldn't be admissible in court because they didn't have a warrant. Fun times.

Then there was Chief Norris, pestering them to get results as if they were magicians who could pull miracles from hats. They both knew they were running out of time, which made Andi even crankier than before and had George so amped up with nervous energy, he'd had to double his running routine. Currently they were waiting for Castain to come out of the city hall from a meeting with the mayor and some committee who wanted to do a fundraiser to place new benches in the various parks in Charleston—and yes, Shireen had hacked Castain's tablet for them, another small favor that George didn't know how they, or more specifically Andi, had earned. Andi and Shireen didn't seem to be close; they certainly didn't spend any time outside work with each other, and yet the hacker had gotten them the tracker and didn't even bat an eyelash when Andi asked her to do an unsanctioned hack into the device of a public figure. George hated mysteries he couldn't solve, but he knew better than to ask Andi for more information. The look on his partner's face when he had carefully hinted at how strange it was for Shireen to be so forthcoming when it could jeopardize her career could have frozen lesser men down to their bones, and George made a hasty retreat while promising himself to let the subject drop for good. At least in front of Andi. What he thought in the privacy of his head was his own business.

"I just wish he would finally crack. Why does he have to be so in control?" Andi moaned into his peppermint tea. Another thing George had learned about his partner was just how little patience Andi possessed. George had known the man would never win any prizes in that regard, but his bitching after only a week sounded as if they'd been following Castain for months. Not that George didn't want to get the bastard ASAP, but he was mentally prepared to stake him out for at least four more weeks—if Norris didn't declare the case cold because they couldn't bring in more evidence. So maybe Andi's impatience was justified.

"He will. He's playing it safe at the moment, but we both know he won't be able to keep it up for long. He has customers to serve. Customers to whom loyalty is a word they have to look up in the dictionary and who will switch dealers without a second thought if he can't deliver." Even though this was a fact working in their favor, it was still depressing. It meant there were others out there who did the same things as Castain and hadn't been caught yet. People they might never get for the hideous crimes they were conducting. Sometimes George wondered why he even bothered trying to make the world a better place. It wasn't as if catching one heartless and soulless criminal was anything but a drop in the ocean, except for the people said criminal had hurt. For them seeing the person punished who had hurt them or their loved ones so badly could make a huge difference on the way to getting their lives back together. And if they stopped in their seemingly endless endeavor, more innocents would get hurt. It was a vicious cycle, and George wasn't at all surprised by the high alcoholism and corruption rates among the force. If you were confronted with the worst of what humanity had to offer on a daily basis, you either got tainted, broken, or so jaded your heart might as well be made of stone.

George shook his head to get rid of his negative thoughts. Stakeouts tended to send him into a philosophical state of mind with a pessimistic view on practically everything. To distract himself, he turned to Andi, who was staring into his tea as if he could see entire worlds in it.

"How are your chitin-clad friends tonight?"

Very slowly, Andi raised his head to look at him. George knew him well enough by now to interpret his gaze. Andi was wondering whether

George was serious or trying to be funny. George lifted his hands in a conciliatory gesture. "Just a question, man. I'm bored and thinking bad thoughts. I need a distraction."

Andi cocked his head. "Bad thoughts?"

"You know, as in, 'Why am I even bothering with all this shit, because even if we catch this particular bad guy, there's ten more waiting in the wings to take over for him.'"

"Oh. *Those* thoughts." Andi played with the rim of his teacup. "Two streets from here there's a house with two corpses under the basement. Well, they're bones by now; they've been there for some time. As far as the larvae and centipedes show me, they're entangled, so my guess is they died together, hopefully giving each other comfort in their last moments."

When he didn't speak on, George furrowed his brows. "If you meant to cheer me up, you failed completely. You just made my point even worse by proving there's, like, a million cases we'll never even know about."

"I didn't mean to cheer you up." Andi shrugged. "You should know by now I'm incapable of it. I'm not even sure what I want to tell you." He put the teacup into the holder between them. "I'm just kind of glad I *can* tell you about them. Strangely enough, it makes me feel better, because I'm no longer the only one who didn't have anything to do with their demise who knows that they're there. I still can't get them out of there or start investigating, but we both are aware of them, and one day there might be a chance to find their murderer."

George pondered those words for a while. On the surface they seemed as gloomy as his own thoughts. When he dove deeper, though, he could see what Andi meant. His partner had to carry so many dead people with him, people nobody knew about, people seemingly nobody missed or cared about. Telling George about them didn't change their fate or the fact that they would probably never be found, but it sure took some of the burden from Andi's shoulders. Knowing he could do such a wonderful thing for another person lifted George's spirits considerably. Besides being able to actually *do* something about it, providing solace seemed like a decent second prize. He opened his mouth to say something along those lines when movement at the entrance of the city hall caught his attention. He nudged Andi.

"I think he's coming out."

"Great. *Finally* some action."

"You're the worst stakeout partner I've ever had." George started the engine.

"I try to avoid them. They're *tedious*." Andi emphasized the last word, reminding George of a whiny teenager who got stuck with too much homework. He watched as Castain threw his man purse onto the passenger seat before getting into the car himself. Since they had the tracker on him, they could keep a generous distance George wouldn't have felt comfortable with otherwise. Just like every evening since they had started their stakeout, Castain drove directly to his townhouse in Grimball Gates, a gated community on Johns Island. It was as exclusive as James Island, where Andi lived, though the neighborhood had a more modern feel compared to the antebellum beauties in Stiles Point. Since it was protected by a security service, following Castain undetected was a little more difficult than usual. Because George had known the stakeout would take longer than just the day Andi seemed to have calculated, he had played with open cards and told the security at the gate—two former Marines, judging from their haircut and the way they held themselves— that they were suspecting illegal activities within the community but didn't want to unduly alarm the residents without solid proof. Which was the truth, though heavily edited. Anyway, the two men had understood immediately and were now letting them through without hesitation.

Castain's house was at a corner, which allowed them to park in the shadow of the house on the other side of the intersection. They had full view of Castain's property without him being able to see them. Through his nightscope, George watched Castain entering through the front door. The lights on the ground floor went on and then off again ten minutes later. Instead, one of the windows on the second floor cast a pale glow onto the pristine lawn.

"I think he's getting ready for bed." George couldn't keep the disappointment from his voice. Only seconds later, the light went out. George sighed. "I guess we call it a night."

He reached for the ignition key, but Andi's hand on his wrist stopped him. "No, wait. Just a little longer. The house isn't settled yet."

George looked at his partner. The little light coming from the nearby streetlamp illuminated just enough for George to see the lines of concentration on Andi's face. Curiosity got the better of George. "What do you see?"

Andi's eyes narrowed, and George was so sure he wouldn't get an answer he actually flinched a little when Andi started speaking. It was in a strange monotone, as if he were reading something off a script only he could see.

"There's mold under the kitchen sink which the silverfish love because it's so wonderfully damp and there's a cockroach running around, a female, heavy with eggs, if Castain isn't careful he's going to have a massive problem soon, there's a few mosquitoes in his bedroom but they're not happy, he's not appetizing, a useless blob of meat, nothing more, and he's moving too much the vibrations he's sending out are disturbing the spiders, he's tromping around, leaving the bedroom, trying to be silent but making it worse because he can't see very well in the dark, he's run into a wall, there's pain in the air, the centipedes can feel it through their legs and it tastes sharp but with a promise of nourishment which excites the ants, there's pheromones everywhere now, his blood is weak but enough of it will do, and he's going down the stairs and to the back, opening the door and the moths fly up and he tramples the grass, shaking the cicadas and now he's going toward the fence...."

"You mean he's trying to escape? How did he find out we are following him?"

Andi flinched as if he'd been slapped in the face. "Man, I'm trying to concentrate here!"

"Sorry. It's just...."

"I know. And he doesn't have to *know* we're following him to suspect it. The way he's done things so far shows how careful he is. Luckily for us, he also seems to be greedy and too impatient to lie low for much longer." Andi started opening the car door. "Also, we should start following him. I don't think he's going to go far, not with his condition, but we need to know what he's planning."

George copied Andi's movements and pulled the balaclava over his face. The area was too well-lit for them to be sneaking around undetected, and the dark fabric provided at least some stealth. They both leaped over the low white fence onto Castain's property, following him into the back garden while taking great pains to stay in the shadows. This was the part of the chase George usually enjoyed the most, when the prey was finally moving and adrenaline swamped his entire system. Under normal circumstances and with every other partner, he would be the one taking the lead, letting his inner predator come to the fore. In this case, he followed his partner, who didn't have to see or hear their suspect to know where he was—an advantage they needed if they wanted to come close enough to listen in on any possible calls or secret meetings. They moved silently across the lawn, using the rhododendron as cover. When they neared the far end of the property, where the whitewashed brick wall shielded the garden from curious glances from passersby on the street, George watched as Castain grabbed some kind of ornamental fruit or flower—it was hard to see in the weak light from the street lamp and with the smaller light from the porch creating more shadows than illuminating the scene—and pulled it out. A hollow space appeared, into which Castain shoved something small, most likely a piece of paper. Then he put the fruit/flower back into place, spun around, and stalked back to his porch without a backward glance. George and Andi remained hidden in the shadows, waiting for the porch light to go out. It felt like an eternity, the blasted thing probably being on some kind of timer. Finally, there was a flicker and the shadows that had been cut out from the dark like the paper figures done by some giant child became one with the night again. Only the much softer edges from the streetlamp remained, helping them to see where they were going.

Andi cocked his head to the side, listening to his arthropod informants again. After a few moments, he moved forward, George trailing behind him. At the brick wall, Andi didn't hesitate to remove the flower—now that he was close enough, George could identify it clearly—and pulled out a folded piece of paper. He unrolled it, and George whipped out his phone to take a picture, their bodies shielding the flash from the house. Putting the paper back inside the hollow space and sneaking back to their car only took a few minutes.

Once inside, George pulled up the picture on his phone to stare at the combination of numbers and letters on the piece of paper. It was definitely some kind of code. Andi got his own phone out of his pocket.

"Can you send me the picture? So we both have it?"

George hit a few buttons. "Of course. It's always better to have things backed up. Are you going to send this to Shireen?"

"Already on it." Andi stared at the screen for a few heartbeats. "Now for the next question. Are we going to wait to see who's picking up the instructions?" He didn't sound too enthusiastic about it, and George had to suppress a smile, though he had to admit he wasn't looking forward to spending the night in his car either. Strictly speaking, they had the information they needed, and this stakeout also wasn't sanctioned, but on the other hand it could be vital to have as much additional evidence as possible should this case go before a judge. As to *how* they would enter said evidence without having plausible reason to even be at this place— that was a question for another day, preferably after a good night's sleep and with at least one cup of coffee in his system. And yes, he was already thinking of Andi and him as a unit, which didn't bother George as much as he would have thought.

"We're already here. Might as well see what's going to happen."

Andi groaned. "I knew you'd say that. Fine. I take the first shift and you try to get some sleep."

He grabbed the binoculars, then hesitated. "After you've parked the car someplace else. We can't see shit from here."

"Have I mentioned how much I love doing stakeouts with you?" George gave the sarcasm in his tone free range, having learned by now how much Andi liked it.

"Not yet, but I do appreciate the sentiment. Now move the car." Andi's tone was bone-dry, and it was too dark for George to see the little twitching of Andi's mouth he was sure was taking place.

"As His Highness pleases." The rumbling of the engine almost drowned out the snort he got.

CHAPTER 25
DIGGING DEEPER

WAITING FOR somebody to pick up the paper Castain had hidden in his wall had proven to be an exercise in futility. Nobody had shown, so the dawning of the sun forced Andi and George to abandon their post and return to the precinct. Now Andi was valiantly trying to wake up with nothing but the help of some herbal tea and sheer willpower. George, on the other hand, looked almost chipper, though if it was from the caffeine in his second triple espresso mocha or if he had simply reached those hyper lands beyond exhaustion was anybody's guess. Anyway, Andi had never felt deeper regret about not doing caffeine than on this particular morning. Luckily for them the chief wasn't in her office, sparing them the scalding gazes she had started shooting them in the wake of their continued failure of not getting any further with the trafficking case. As far as Andi was concerned, he could live with the silent treatment, since it was so much easier to ignore than outright yelling. George didn't like it as much, preferring a more direct confrontation over "pussyfooting around" as he called it.

They had sent the picture of the code to Shireen before she arrived in the precinct and were now waiting for her call while trying to look productive without having to move too much. He was now paying for his nightly foray into the minds of the arthropods in Castain's house with a humming headache that was gearing up to becoming a full-fledged migraine if he didn't watch it. An hour of meditation sounded perfect right now and was—just like real sleep—simply not in the cards. Andi sighed. The beeping of his cell ended his contemplation of how much he pitied himself. It was a text from Shireen, with a date four days from now, plus a time and GPS coordinates she had already translated for them into a spot in the Goose Creek area, not too far from St. James Street, where they had found the bodies of the three girls. Andi sent her a quick thank-you, which she ignored, as usual. Then he forwarded the info to George's cell, not wanting to distract his partner from whatever fascinating thing he was seeing on his PC. His leg was bouncing in a rapid staccato, making Andi nauseous from just watching it.

Without taking his eyes off the screen, George pulled out his cell, swiped it with his thumb, punched in his PIN—no fancy pattern drawing for him—and then read the text. He turned around to face Andi. Slowly, a predatory smile appeared on his lips. "We're going to get those bastards."

Andi mirrored that smile, even though it increased the hammering between his temples. "We will." The surge of adrenaline in his system was only hampered by the way his skull tried to burst at the seams. George furrowed his brows.

"Are you all right, Andi? You don't look so good."

Andi's first reaction was to shrug the concern off, but then he thought better of it. George *knew* and would understand. This was a such a novel feeling, Andi wasn't sure if he could get used to it anytime soon. Probably when George went on to greener pastures, which was just Andi's luck.

"I'm getting a migraine. Last night was—trying."

George's eyes rounded, and he hissed a curse under his breath. "Why didn't you tell me sooner? I would have dropped you off at home and found an excuse. Come on, let's get you out of here." He got up, put on his jacket, grabbed his car keys, and reached for Andi's hand to help him up. The gesture was so sweet, it tore at something Andi didn't want to examine too closely. At least not while his heartbeat tried to kill him with how loud it resonated within his skull, bumping his brain around as if it were a basketball. He let himself be led out of the station, too busy basking in George's genuine concern to acknowledge all the curious stares they were getting. This felt nice. For the first time since his gran had died, somebody was concerned about his well-being. Somebody who knew about his weirdness and the problems it caused.

George maneuvered him into the car, even went so far as to close his seat belt for him, then hurried around to the driver's side. After a ten-minute drive, they reached his house, where George half-carried him inside, helped him get out of his clothes until he was only in his T-shirt and boxers, and tucked him into bed, after he had given him an ibuprofen to deal with the sharper edges of the pain. Before he left, George brought him a washcloth dipped in cold water to put over his eyes, as well as a bowl filled with ice cubes—he must have found those in the freezer, though Andi couldn't remember when he'd made them—so he could suck ice chips and freeze the washcloth anew when it got too warm.

"Thank you," Andi managed to croak when George placed a water bottle with another ibuprofen next to the bowl.

"You're very welcome. I'll go back to the precinct now, but I'll come by later to see if you need anything else. Do you think you might be hungry later?"

Andi honestly didn't know. Usually his migraines had him mostly incapacitated for at least twelve hours, though it seemed they had caught this one in time to prevent the worst, which could mean he'd be able to have a light dinner. Perhaps. Probably.

"Soup, maybe?"

George smiled as if Andi was his star pupil and had just gotten the answer to a complicated problem right. "I'll be back tonight with some soup. You go and sleep now. We'll have to make battle plans later."

For a highly charged moment, Andi had the feeling George was on the verge of leaning down and pressing a kiss to his forehead, but his partner spared them both the awkward moment, even though a part of Andi kind of wanted this intimate gesture, which he associated with the greatest care. George waved and left the room, leaving Andi to his cold washcloth and foggy mind.

When George came back, Andi was—to his own amazement—awake and able to string two thoughts together in his head, which was a first after a night like the one before. George took charge of the situation like he had in the morning, sending Andi to have a shower while he heated the soup he had gotten from a deli close to the precinct. Andi had no problem getting bossed around when a dinner he didn't have to do anything about was his reward. Freshly showered, he sat down at the kitchen counter just in time to see George pouring the soup into two bowls, which he then carried over to the counter.

"I hope chicken soup with noodles is okay," George remarked and handed Andi a spoon.

"It's food, it's warm, it's light, I didn't have to prepare it. The hallmarks of a perfect meal." Andi showed George a happy smile before he dug in. The soup was good, the flavors bursting on his tongue with just enough of a hint of pepper to have the sting Andi liked.

"This is good. You can come over and bring food more often."

George grinned. "I'm so glad you approve." He turned serious. "How are you feeling? You look slightly better, though still a little mangled."

"Your way with words is amazing. I'm freshly showered." Andi managed a wink.

"And you pull the drowned rat look off like a pro."

"Ass." Andi took another spoonful of soup, reveling in their easy banter.

"Takes one to know one," George muttered, suppressing a chuckle, which resulted in some soup spilling on the counter. Remorseless, George kept on eating, ignoring the little sea of broth with a lonely piece of noodle half floating, half stuck to the counter surface like a dead worm after a stormy night. Andi had not gotten to where he was today by being fussy, so he followed George's example, concentrating on battling his hunger. After a few minutes filled with nothing but blessed silence and some images from the silverfish—*something warm and wet, spilled but out of reach, blocked by the big blobs causing all the tremors in the ground*—Andi decided it was time to talk shop.

"According to Shireen, we have four days until that ominous meeting." It had taken Shireen some time to figure out the date and place of said meeting since the information on the piece of paper had been in a more complicated code than what they had found on Vance's cell, which was still missing, thank you very much. Merrigold and Vargas hadn't found the slightest clue as to who could have taken it. They were seriously entertaining the idea of it being just some kind of prank, though Andi was convinced somebody at the precinct was trying to sabotage their investigations. Because of his suspicions, he had asked Shireen to keep the decoding of the piece of paper from Castain's garden as quiet as possible. Apparently Castain had used the Greek acrophony system to code the date, time, and place of whatever he was planning next, and as soon as Shireen had realized that she had been able to do the rest of the work in her own little office, which she rarely used because it was so small. All they could hope for now was that the mole inside the precinct wasn't smart and alert enough to realize Shireen had done the most important part of the work away from her usual place and that he or she wouldn't get another chance to keep sabotaging them. Since the theft of Vance's phone, things had been suspiciously calm with no tampering whatsoever, but then again everything they had found since then had been straightforward and hard to manipulate. The victims were all in hospital, the perps in custody and silent. The evidence they had found was only circumstantial and therefor more or less useless at the moment.

"Yep." George gulped the last spoonful of soup down, then put his spoon in the bowl, causing a slight clicking the silverfish interpreted as something akin to a jumbo jet starting. Andi did his best to block them out. George steepled his fingers above the bowl, staring at Andi as if he were searching for the answer to everything. Andi couldn't resist.

"It's forty-two."

"Huh?"

"The answer you're looking for."

George's eyes narrowed. "Nice try, Mr. Nerdy Nerd. But I do happen to know my classics. And no, forty-two is *not* the answer I'm looking for, though I'm willing to put it in the report we have to write for Chief Norris. Perhaps it can fool her into thinking we did any actual police work."

Andi furrowed his brows. "We did a ton of actual police work. Just the unorthodox kind."

"I know. I'm just nervous we'll see that fucker go free on a technicality." The real worry in George's tone kept Andi from giving him a snarky answer. Instead, he reached over the kitchen counter to briefly touch George's hand. It wasn't an overly intimate gesture, simply one cop reassuring his cop partner, but to Andi, who had deprived himself for years of any contact, physical or otherwise, from other people, it was a great step. And George, being the great human being he was, knew that and picked up on the enormity of the moment. He smiled at Andi, nodding at him in silent understanding. "This is all new for me. I'm not used to being in such a state of ambiguity when it comes to a case. Knowing for sure yet not being able to prove most of what I know—it's unnerving. I don't know how you can stand it."

Andi shrugged. The answer to that was a lot more pragmatic than he would have liked. "I have no choice. You get used to it."

George furrowed his brows, not liking it one bit. Andi started talking again. "Our problem is that we know Castain is our man, and hopefully, he will serve himself on a silver platter in four days. What we now need is enough circumstantial evidence—evidence we can get through old-fashioned police work—to deflect from how we were able to bust him when officially we'd been told to leave him alone."

"You make it sound like that's going to be easy."

"It won't be. But we do have other avenues we can walk to get back to Castain, Detective Harris being one of them. It's like one of those labyrinths for kids, where they have to draw the way to the treasure in the middle. We already know what the treasure is, and where it's hiding, so to speak. Which means all we have to do is follow the strings back to sources we can use in our report."

"Ways," George said absentmindedly.

"What?"

"In a labyrinth, you look for ways, not strings. You have to stay true to your metaphors if you want them to work." He winked.

Andi couldn't suppress the full belly laughter that was forcing its way out of him. "I could have been referring to Ariadne, you know."

"Which would make the strings more plausible, I grant you that," George conceded with a small smile. "Though your starting out with a children's labyrinth made that quite the leap, don't you think?"

Andi held his hands up in defeat. "Fine, fine. My bad. No mixing of metaphors when working with you. I'll keep that in mind. Now back to our current problem. We have four days to find dirt on Harris and perhaps some other connections to Castain. Since we don't want to spook him, we have to be very careful not to stir up too much dust, though we do need something substantial. A fine line to walk."

"But we can do it." George sounded determined.

"We can definitely do it. All we have to do is steer clear of Chief Norris and keep our investigation close to our chests."

George sighed. "Easy-peasy."

"Yes. Easy-peasy."

They both stared into their empty soup bowls.

CHAPTER 26
LEASHED AND MUZZLED

EASY-PEASY ENDED the moment they entered the precinct. Chief Norris beckoned them into her office with a sharp gesture of her head, her eyes hard as flint. George had a sinking feeling in his stomach, and as soon as they were seated in front of the chief, his worst fears came to life. Norris didn't bother with any niceties; she went straight for the jugular, and George was sure he could detect a hint of morbid satisfaction in her tone.

"It has come to my attention that you're still bothering Mr. Castain. He has made a complaint about you two harassing him about the unfortunate incident at his house." She glared at them. "I thought I was clear when I told you to leave the man alone. The mayor wants his involvement kept on the down-low because he's obviously just as much a victim in this as those poor children. You still following him around makes me look as if I can't control my own force on top of making it seem as if he's involved, which reflects badly on the mayor once the press gets wind of this whole mess."

She was still standing behind her desk, looking outraged at their insubordination and at the same time strangely pleased to be able to yell at them. George felt Andi tensing next to him and managed to put a hand on his partner's lower back to keep him from saying something they both would regret later. In situations like these, it was always wise to keep one's mouth shut and wait for the person in power to calm down. Unfortunately, Norris didn't seem to be in the mood to calm down. George suspected it was because she finally had something she could pin on Andi, a chance she had been waiting for since she took over as chief.

"I simply can't let this kind of blatant disregard for your superiors go unpunished. I'm assigning the case to Detectives Merrigold and Vargas, since they are already familiar with it because of the stolen cell. You will hand them everything you've found so far, and then you're going to take a week of unpaid leave to cool your heads and think about your stance on authority. If your chief gives you a direct order, you have to follow not ignore it. Is that understood?" She obviously didn't expect an answer from them because she went on without taking a breath. "Once you are back at work, I will be watching you both more closely, assuming the way you handled this case isn't a first. You're dismissed." She made a shooing motion with her hands, clearly not interested in anything they might have to say. George got up, keeping a close eye on Andi, fearing his partner would explode any minute now, but the man seemed eerily calm. He simply nodded in Norris's direction, something that made her eyes flash in anger, before he left the office, George trailing behind him.

Outside Merrigold and Vargas were already waiting, embarrassment written all over their faces. Norris must have planned this whole scenario down to the last detail, eager to get them off the case. Andi still remained calm, as if nothing out of the ordinary had happened, which freaked George more than anything else. He watched as his partner gave their colleagues all the files they had been working on, only noting that he had kept the one about Harris to himself when Merrigold and Vargas left and Andi shoved the binder into his backpack. Without saying a word, he then led the way to Shireen, who greeted them with a pitying look on her face. News traveled fast in the precinct, and everybody seemed to know already.

"I'm so sorry, guys. All your hard work…."

"It's fine, Shireen. Do you have my tablet?" Andi sounded almost as if none of this had anything to do with him. Shireen looked surprised for a moment; then she nodded hastily.

"Of course. It's all done. Ready for full use again," she announced, perhaps a little too loudly, but there was nobody with them in the IT department, the other staff having fled when Andi and George approached. Andi put the tablet into his backpack as well.

"Thank you, Shireen. I guess we'll see you next week." Andi turned for the door. George waved at Shireen, still not sure what to make of his partner's strange behavior. He followed Andi outside to the car and didn't protest when Andi sat down on the passenger side. Once George had taken his seat behind the wheel and they were back out in traffic, Andi broke his Zen-like silence.

"What a stupid, arrogant, selfish, clueless bitch!"

That was more like Andi, and George sighed in relief. "Yeah to all of it."

Andi tapped a sharp rhythm on the dashboard. "The nerve of her!"

"I would be more interested in how Castain found out we were following him. I could have sworn he didn't detect us." George was deeply frustrated by this unexpected turn of events. They had been *this* close to solving the damn case and getting Castain. Now with a week's unpaid leave, the meeting from the paper would happen without them. Not to mention what a blow this was to his career aspirations. Reprimands from higher-ups never looked good on a CV.

"And I'm pretty sure he didn't." Andi sounded very matter-of-fact. George shot him a glance before concentrating on traffic again.

"You heard her. He complained to somebody who then told her."

"Exactly. Did Castain strike you as somebody who would be satisfied complaining to some low-level cop when he could air his feelings with the chief herself?"

George froze. Now that he thought about it... "You think he didn't complain?"

"I think that whoever stole Vance's phone saw another chance to keep us from investigating. A golden one at that. It also cements my theory that it has to be somebody who knows the precinct and the people in there very well. I bet there's not even written proof for the complaint. Whoever ratted us out knew the chief dislikes me enough to latch on to anything that makes me look bad. The way I see it, both we and the chief have been played." Andi paused. "Unless the chief is the mole, but I doubt it. As much as I dislike her and the fact that she's breathing the same air as me in the precinct, she hasn't been here long enough to be a useful mole."

George couldn't say anything against this logic. It all made sense, and he was still too enraged about losing the case to think straight and try to find the holes in Andi's reasoning. So he went with what he could control at the moment.

"Where are we going?"

"My place, if it's okay for you. We have lots of thinking to do, and that I do best in a familiar environment."

"Where you know the insects?" George asked.

Andi nodded. "It's always stressful to adapt to a new building, and with all the adrenaline pumping in my veins at the moment, I wouldn't be of any use."

"I understand. Your house it is."

They made a detour to the deli and bought enough food to last them for at least two days. George made vague plans to drop by at his apartment sometime later that day, but it was clear Andi wasn't going to let go of this case. George wasn't too sure about endangering his career even further, the thought like a constant needling in the back of his head. Leaving Andi alone wasn't an option, though. They might not have been willing partners when all this started, but George felt obligated to solve this case, even if it meant going against every self-preserving instinct he had. Knowing Andi wouldn't stop working no matter what George decided to do was another incentive to stay with his partner. If Andi decided to do something stupid, George would be there to maybe prevent it or at least protect him.

At Andi's house, they rearranged the furniture in the living room to make the table there their workplace. Andi pinned a map of South Carolina on the wall and put the file about Harris and the tablet he'd gotten from Shireen on the table. Then he went and got his laptop, which had been sitting on the kitchen counter.

"Didn't know you had two devices." George eyed the laptop.

"I don't. This tablet is going to give us access to all the police files we need, hopefully without alerting anybody to our snooping."

George felt his mouth gaping open. "Do I want to know why Shireen would give you one of her toys?"

Andi shook his head. "No, you don't. And before you keep asking, I'm also not telling you." He showed a grim smile. "Just be glad we have it and leave the rest to me. Ignorance is bliss."

"I'm beginning to see that. At least when working with you." George took the tablet and powered it up. "Password?"

Andi leaned over and typed it in, a combination of numbers and letters George couldn't make heads or tails of.

"Thank you." George hesitated. He needed to say it. At least once, just so he could tell himself he had tried. "You really want to go through with this? Even though we're on unpaid leave? You know the chief is just waiting for us to make a mistake."

They locked gazes for a long time, Andi's eyes so full of different emotions, George was almost sorry he had asked. The stress in his partner's expression cut him deeply. When Andi finally spoke, it sounded pained.

"If you don't want to do this I understand. Well, not really, but I think I can relate to you not wanting to endanger all your plans for the future even more than you've already done. Me, I can't turn my back on this case. It's part of who I am, I'm afraid. As for the chief—you know what I think of her."

Andi looked so vulnerable, so lonely, and George realized something he would have never thought possible—Andi needed him. He'd been alone for too long, had carried the burden of his *geschenk* for too long, had kept everybody and everyone at bay for too long. He needed somebody in his corner, somebody who had his back. George knew without a doubt that he could be that somebody. No, that he *needed* to be that somebody. The realization settled deep in his bones, seemed to hum in his blood. Knowing full well what a nosedive his career could take when he stood by the words he was going to say, George went on regardless. "I'm with you, Andi. I'm going to have your back, I swear."

The way Andi's eyes widened only strengthened George's resolve. He would and could do this. And hadn't he read somewhere that the really great careers never developed in a straight line?

"Now, where do you want to start?"

THREE DAYS of not going home to his apartment, eating takeout all the time, and taking naps on Andi's couch later, they were finally starting to see a pattern. An ugly pattern, granted, but a pattern they could work with. The map of South Carolina had been replaced with city maps where the poorest districts were full of pins with differently colored heads, those heads enhancing the aforementioned ugly pattern. A pin with a red head for a detective who had an unproportionally high number of abduction or missing person cases in his or her district and blue pins for all the persons—mostly children and young adults—who had not been found and whose cases were considered cold. Pins with green heads represented missing persons whose cases had landed on the desks of other detectives, and pins with yellow heads—those were so rare George wanted to scream in frustration—showed cases where the missing person had been found. In all the bigger cities of South Carolina, there were clusters of blue pins around one or sometimes two red ones. Their search for incriminating connections between Harris and Castain had led them to the discovery of ties Harris had to a detective or police officer in every city where children had been kidnapped. Some of those ties were obvious—snapshots on Facebook, pictures from seminars Harris had attended—others they found when they realized what was going on and started doing backward searches as well. In every city and town where children vanished, they found somebody they could trace back to Harris. It was both a frightening and shocking web of corrupt members of the police who obviously had no qualms about preying on the weak and defenseless. Seeing how those men and women abused their power and ignored the oath they had taken made George sick.

Without Shireen they weren't able to hack the accounts of the cops in question, but George had no doubt whatsoever what they would find once they got the chance to do so.

"I still can't identify Harris's contact here in Charleston. It has to be somebody in our precinct, because how else would Castain and Harris manage to sabotage us? But the cases of missing children are so spread out, I can't find a single person with a cluster. Damn it all to hell!"

Andi was frustrated and George could relate. The evidence before them was clear and damning and still only circumstantial. Charleston was also the only city where there was no clear cluster of blue pins around a red one. They didn't have a red one here, and knowing there had to be and that they weren't able to identify the person was annoying as all hell.

"Do you think we should tell Merrigold and Vargas?" The words tasted bitter on George's tongue, but he had to put the idea out there. Andi shook his head.

"No, they're not the sharpest tools in the drawer, which could be one reason the chief chose them to take over from us. And giving them the information now means we're admitting to having worked the case despite being on leave. I don't know about you, but I have no intention of giving the chief even more ammunition against us."

George sighed. "No, that wouldn't be smart. Are we going to that meeting?"

The question was rhetorical; of course they would be going to the meeting. After everything they had found out so far, they couldn't afford not to go.

"Yes, we are. And we need to have all our evidence lined up perfectly because depending on what we find, shit's going to hit the fan big-time. I'm not entirely sure about the legalities when we report something we have stumbled upon during our leave, but if this turns out to be as big a bust as my gut is telling me, then we need enough evidence to justify warrants for all those detectives and officers. IA is going to have a field day."

George rubbed his face with his palm. "I'm still not sure about not contacting at least them now. Sure, they said they would wait to not endanger our case, but technically it isn't our case anymore...."

"Let them wait. It's only one more day. After tomorrow evening, we either have the case solved or are permanently off it. Then Merrigold and Vargas can worry about it."

Andi may sound nonchalant, but George could hear the tension in his voice. They had to find something tomorrow. *They had to*. It wasn't just their careers on the line, it was also the lives of countless children and youths who would keep vanishing without a trace if they didn't catch the assholes responsible for it all. George stared at the maps on the wall, at the pins representing a person who was missing, some of them probably, surely already dead.

"Let's put our files into some kind of order. Then we need some sleep."

Andi nodded his agreement, and they went to work.

CHAPTER 27
TIGHTENING THE WEB

SLEEP HAD been evasive for both of them, and while Andi did a long round of yoga to center himself, George called his brother Danny to get some distraction. The call had been short because Danny was on a case as well and George hadn't wanted to relay all that had happened, especially the part with the unpaid leave, but hearing his brother's voice and doing some light bantering had helped soothe his nerves quite a bit.

Now they were getting ready to hide close to the spot written down on Castain's secret paper in the wall. Andi had even gone so far as to officially declare the whole thing as following the tip of an anonymous informant, of which he seemed to have quite a few. George could admire the simple beauty of that move. Should nothing come of tonight, they could write it off as faulty information. Should they succeed, they had a credible reason to have been there, which made the explaining a lot easier than having to come up with excuses afterward.

The unpaid leave and them officially being withdrawn from the case made things a little more complicated, but since they were not suspended, they could say the tip had not been specific. Imagine their surprise when it turned out to be related to their former case. George just hoped whatever they would find tonight would be grave enough to distract people, especially lawyers, from looking too closely. Or so damning there would be no question as to the culpability of the people they were hopefully going to arrest. Plus, the equipment they "borrowed" with the help of Shireen would be officially accounted for, which made things a bit more legit, because someone had known they were taking it. Well, someone would know about the other day because Shireen had taken the equipment to them and "forgotten" to forward the paperwork. It was almost above board. Close to it. Definitely not as shady as putting a tracker on Castain's car without official permission.

George hoped they were getting lucky, because if not, they would have to step on the toes of a hell of a lot of other precincts to perhaps crack the case open—if they still had a job then.

Andi was holstering his weapon with a determined gleam in his eyes. He was looking better than four days ago, when George had feared he would collapse before he could get him into bed. The lines of exhaustion permanently etched around his eyes were still there, though a little less prominent than when George had first met him. He felt himself hoping it had something to do with Andi having him as a partner, not because he was vain, but because he really wanted to help this man who seemed not to have had somebody in his corner for far too long. He also had no problem admitting that he liked Andi's dark, witty humor and pitch-black sarcasm. In fact, Andi was the first partner George could see himself with for longer than his usual one or two years.

"Hey, stop dreaming and get moving! We have to be in position well before the meeting is supposed to happen."

Politeness wasn't part of Andi's vocab. George would have been surprised if the man knew how to spell the word. He holstered his own weapon and grabbed the car keys. The thrill of the hunt was slowly building in his veins, adrenaline flooding every cell in his body, making him overly aware of his surroundings. Even though George knew this was simple chemistry, a trait that had kept their ancestors alive in a hostile world, and not a special gift like Andi's *geschenk*, he still wondered if this feeling came anywhere close to what Andi was experiencing on a daily basis. Even if not, it still gave George an insight as to what Andi's world looked like. Imagining being wired like this all the time, with no chance to turn it off—George shuddered. He was sure it'd take a stronger man than him to deal with such circumstances.

"I'm coming. Let's get those bastards behind bars."

"Or six feet under."

Since George was almost a hundred percent sure Andi was joking, he refrained from acknowledging those words. Why look for trouble when he was pretty sure trouble would find him soon anyway?

They got into the car and drove to Goose Creek, bypassing the empty parking lot where the meeting was supposed to go down. They had scouted the area the day before and had found the perfect spot to hide their car. Across from the parking lot was an abandoned factory building with shattered windows and crumbling brick walls. All the streetlights on that side of the road were dead, bathing the parking lot in a pattern of shadows of various depth. No doubt the sparse lighting was the reason this place had been picked as a meeting spot, but in this case, it worked in their favor as well. George parked in the deep shadow of an open gate and got his nightscope and the directional microphone out, *official* courtesy of Shireen. Both had a black finish so as not to accidentally betray their user's position through a reflection. He handed the microphone to Andi, who rolled down the window and adjusted it to the right direction. George did a quick sweep of the area with his nightscope, finding everything clear. Now for the hard part—the waiting.

They hadn't spoken during the ride here, both of them too preoccupied with what was hopefully the break in the case they needed so badly. Even though they weren't talking, sitting together in the car felt intimate in a different way than being with a lover. For one, there was a more violent undercurrent in the air, making the hair on his nape stand up. Stakeouts had a similar feel, but with the added tension of being on the hunt, George felt primal. As if the two of them were a pack out to get the prey. Of course this, too, was an easily explained phenomenon, the psychological dynamics painfully obvious and the reason why team building adventures worked so well. And still George couldn't suppress a feeling that with Andi, it was different. The connection felt deeper, rawer, as if it wasn't just the hunt binding them together. Perhaps it was because he had already taken care of Andi twice when he was defenseless or because he knew he could count on him to cover bases George wouldn't even realize were there without him. He glanced over at Andi, who was either as deep in thought as he had been or ready to fall asleep. George was willing to bet on the second. His partner didn't get enough rest.

"Everything okay?" He looked out of the window again, not wanting Andi to think he was worried—which he wasn't.

"Yeah. I was just… checking in with my other informants."

George snorted. "Nice euphemism. Is this going to be our thing? Finding ways to paraphrase the fact you're talking to insects?"

Without turning his body, Andi hit him square in the chest. "Nothing will ever beat your awkward hand gesturing in combination with that squint as if you're trying to get a shit done and nothing's coming out."

George placed a hand on his chest, waving the nightscope with the other. "I'm wounded! There's nothing awkward about the way I move. I'm grace personified."

Andi just snorted, giving him an eye roll worthy of every teenager in the whole world. "You're about as graceful as a penguin on land." He stroked George's arm as if he wanted to console him. George knew better and was prepared for the barb that followed. "But you make up for it by being really funny, even though often involuntary. That's why I've decided to keep you."

"I'm not sure if I should feel honored or insulted. I think I'll go for both. Penguin, my ass."

Andi opened his mouth to give a retort, when they both heard the rumbling of an approaching vehicle. All of a sudden, the outbreak of playful nervousness was gone, replaced by laser-sharp focus.

"They're a bit early." Andi was fiddling with the microphone.

"There's two parties meeting. In my experience, one is always early, the other late. Kind of a law, I think."

"And you're full of shit tonight. When the two of us meet, we're both late."

"Yet I'm usually early late while you're *always* late late."

Andi muttered something George couldn't understand.

A beat-up black van had pulled into the parking lot, giving the weeds there a taste of what times had been like before the area had gone down. The van did a circle around the entire parking lot, apparently not sure which spot to take—too many choices, George assumed—before it settled on one next to a broken streetlamp with a bent stem that made it look a little drunk. Or as if a giant had played a game of Mikado and forgotten the last straw. Nothing else happened, nobody came out of the van, and the minutes ticked by agonizingly slowly. George glanced at Andi, whose gaze was glued to the van.

"Can you pick anything up?"

"There's six people in the back. Drugged, but it's wearing off."

George suppressed a growl. "They're getting them ready for the customers. Sons of bitches."

A second van pulled into the parking lot. It was also black, though it looked a little newer and better maintained. It drove straight toward the other one and stopped a few feet away. The lights of the first van flashed in a sequence—two short, one long, one short—which was answered by another sequence—one long, one short, two long, one short—before the driver's doors on both vans opened almost simultaneously. The passenger side doors followed, each van vomiting three men in total. George kept watching them while Andi relayed their conversation, which he was getting through the earbuds from the directional microphone, in a hushed tone.

"They're exchanging greetings, seems like another code to me, now they're talking about the cargo"—his tone became angry when he said that—"the asshole from the second van wants confirmation that there's really two eleven-year-olds in there"—George's hand was itching for his gun, but they had to stay strong, had to get them all—"bastard from the first van says yes, they're ready to do the exchange."

George watched in helpless fury as the backs of both vans were opened and six minors, two of them indeed looking awfully young, were half dragged, half carried from one to the other. Both groups of men returned to their respective vehicles, closing the doors so loudly the sound echoed over the empty parking lot. The first van left, turning right onto the street, the second one going left. George started the car and followed the second van with the headlights off, keeping as much distance as he dared. Unfortunately, arthropods were unable to distinguish between cars, which meant they had to do this the old-fashioned way. While George focused on not losing their prey, Andi radioed the first van in, requesting them to take the driver and his companions in for whatever traffic violation the officers could come up with, claiming he and George had been out to get groceries and recognized the van as one from a crime scene, thus maintaining the story of them still keeping a low profile, as ordered by the chief.

Then Andi focused on the van as well. "I wonder where they're going. Castain is surely not dumb enough to use his own mansion a second time."

"We'll see." George was too busy watching both the van and traffic—which was very light, but still, driving without your lights on when it was dark outside was dangerous—to engage in any guessing games. Luckily for them, the van steered clear of all the main streets, navigating through the labyrinth of narrow back streets where the chance of meeting another car or some sort of law enforcement was close to zero. After about forty-five minutes of seemingly aimless driving, the van entered Mount Pleasant, a suburb of Charleston where mostly upper middle-class families resided. The driver still did his best to avoid well-lit areas, which was a lot more difficult here where money kept everything running than in Goose Creek, where any financial prowess had left long ago. They finally stopped at the very fringes of the suburb where the houses were farther apart than closer to the center and more than two-thirds were dark.

"Holiday homes. Gotta give it to Castain, he's smart." Andi sounded as if he'd bitten into a lemon.

"Makes sense. This is a rich area; the houses look nice and spacious. Wanna bet the owners of this house don't know it's being used while they're away?"

"I don't do bets. Now let's see what's going on."

George steered their car behind the house across from the one where the van was parked, hiding it in the shadows created by a huge carport. They slipped out silently, donning their black balaclavas to hide their faces. While George wanted to call the cavalry, namely Adam Forard, who Andi had discreetly asked to take this night's shift and who had complied without asking any questions, Andi was hesitant.

"I want to make sure Castain is there. We need to catch him, you know this."

"Yes, we do, but there are terrified minors in that van, and we don't know how many are already inside the house. I don't want to add to their trauma because we put catching that asshole above their needs. That's what everybody else has done all their lives."

Andi looked pained, and George immediately regretted his words. "I'm sorry. I know you want to help them. It's just...." He trailed off. There were too many emotions warring inside his chest, anger and worry being the most dominant ones. Putting the chaos in his mind into words would have taken a more eloquent man than he was. Andi put his hand on George's arm for a moment.

"I know. I understand. We're not waiting until something bad happens to them." He pulled out his phone and started texting. When he was done, he put the phone back into his back pocket. "I've sent Forard the address and told him to get moving, but silently. They'll be here in less than fifteen minutes, waiting for the go from us."

George sighed in relief. "Thank you. I feel better now."

Andi nodded. "The time of the call doesn't really matter anymore, because we do have proof something foul is going on here. I was just overly cautious."

Those two sentences drove home how precarious the path was Andi was walking with practically every single one of his cases. If the call for backup was sent too early, a good defense attorney would be able to poke holes into an otherwise airtight case, letting a criminal who should be behind bars walk free. If it came too late, innocents might suffer. So the timing of everything he did had to be impeccable and absolutely logical. Because telling IA or the state prosecutor that Andi had acted on information gained through creatures whose brains were so small they could find room on the head of a pin would not go down well. Especially when Andi shouldn't have been on the case in the first place.

"I'm sorry. You've been doing this a lot longer than me. I should trust you more."

Andi smiled. "Perhaps. But it's good you're not. I need a partner who can think quickly and who has no problem calling me out on my actions. Now let's see what's going on."

They slowly crept toward the house, using the shadows created by trees and bushes to hide from the two guards that were patrolling the vicinity, although a bit lax, probably lulled by the remoteness of the location and the absolute lack of any traffic. If a car came up, they would immediately know it. The only reason they hadn't picked up on George's car was because the sounds of their arrival had been masked by those of the van with the cargo.

They managed to reach the back door without incident while the guards were busy having a smoke in the front yard. Clearly, they weren't pros.

George picked the lock to gain them entry, and they slipped inside quietly. The house was not nearly as grand as the Castain mansion in Berkeley County, but big enough for whoever hosted this "party" not to use all the space, which meant George and Andi could move through the dark parts of the ground floor without any trouble. It seemed the action would be concentrated on the second floor where the bedrooms were located, or so George presumed. There was no need to light the entire house, risking exposure. After checking the door to the cellar, which was closed, and the one to the pantry, which was open but revealed nothing of interest except a fondness of the owners of the house for spaghetti and premium vodka, they got close to the main entrance, where they hid in a broom closet that looked roomier from the outside. Once inside, they barely fit in without tumbling anything over, but through a crack in the solid wood of the door George could see the main entrance. The children had been brought inside as soon as the van had arrived, and now two rich-looking older men and one woman whose age George couldn't guess because of the heavy makeup she was wearing were standing in the hall *lined* with white marble tiles, drinking champagne from crystal flutes, apparently waiting for somebody or something. Three men in dark suits were positioned along the wall, and the way each of them was focusing on one of the "guests" made it clear they were bodyguards.

Then the front door opened, and George's adrenaline spiked while his inner predator started panting. A man in a lion mask stepped through, leaning heavily on a walking stick but refusing the help from the goon at his side. The gesture with which he shooed the helpful man away was all George needed to recognize him, though his stature also gave a clue.

Castain had just entered the house.

CHAPTER 28
END OF A HUNT

ANDI COULDN'T see anything with George blocking the door, but his ears worked just fine, and the information barraging him from the various arthropods in the house helped him get a picture that was almost as good as seeing through the crack George had his face pressed on. Granted, it had a psychedelic quality, a bit like those 3D patterns that turned into pictures once the eyes adjusted, only in Andi's case it was his entire brain adjusting, ignoring the confines of his body altogether. Moving while his other sight was fully turned on was not advisable, as he had learned the hard way early on in his life, but here, in the relative safety of the closet, with his partner shielding him, it was a good way of gathering all the intel they might need later for when SWAT was ready to go in.

Entering the house had been a calculated risk. They could have just waited outside for Forard to arrive and let him handle the raid. It would have been safer for them, though not for the poor kids trapped inside the house. Even though Andi could pinpoint exactly where they were because the roaches and the pill bugs were going crazy from the pheromones their fear was producing, him and George being inside the house meant they could potentially stop any of the suspects from going upstairs. Not that he really thought they would try once SWAT came at them, but people in a panic tended to overreact, and there was no hostage more perfect than a child. He also sensed three adults with the children who would pose enough of a problem without some bodyguard with a pressing wish to escape waving his gun around.

At the moment the children were upstairs in twos, most probably in the different bedrooms. Houses like this tended to have four to six bedrooms, and Andi could sense eight kids, which made a surplus of two for the disgusting scum waiting in the hall. Or Castain wanted two for himself, which was entirely possible. He wouldn't be the first dealer who used his own merchandise.

The front door opened again, and George stiffened like a tiger ready to pounce. It could only mean Castain had entered the building. The errant pictures of a few mosquitoes from outside confirmed that an undesirable lump of flesh had just passed by, which caused Andi to start typing on his cell again.

How far out are you?

Forard's answer was quick. *We're already getting in position. Where R U?*

Inside. Three bodyguards, armed. Four civilians, and at least three more people on the second floor, possibly armed. Eight hostages on second floor.

While the dots indicating that Forard was answering started dancing, Andi concentrated on the entrance hall again. He could hear muffled voices and laughter, Castain's smooth voice saying something affirmative. Andi wanted to puke.

We have the house surrounded. Coming in from all sides. Can U give us cover?

On the ground floor. We try to take out the bodyguards and contain the civilians. Be quick upstairs. Children there. On your count.

Roger.

Andi tapped George's shoulder lightly, waited for his partner to turn around. When he had George's attention, he showed him the texts. George nodded, inclining his head toward the door. Andi shook his own, gestured to the cell, indicating that they were waiting for Forard to give the command.

The dots started dancing again. *Coming in NOW.*

Andi reached for his gun the same moment he heard glass shatter somewhere above. George slammed the closet door open, his own gun already drawn.

"Police! Freeze!"

Screaming erupted, and Andi hurried to get to his partner's side, using the door as flimsy coverage while trying to get a picture of what was going on. Castain and his three "guests" were already on the ground, covering their heads. Apparently the shouted order from George and one of the SWAT members had taken the direct route to their muscles without giving the brain a chance to interfere. Then again, they *were* civilians, even if their tastes were dark enough to make upstanding citizens gag.

Luckily for them there was a difference between hardened criminals and people rich enough to not give a damn about the law.

One of the men was screaming something about police brutality while SWAT was pouring in through the front door, as well as the windows on the ground floor.

Castain was sprawled on the ground, his lion mask lying next to him, staring into nothing with empty eyes. The man who had brought so much suffering and terror to innocent kids remained silent, seemingly unperturbed by what was the end of his life as he'd known it. Andi didn't have time to ponder whether Castain had another ace up his sleeve, was really that indifferent, or simply couldn't believe that he'd been caught. In the end, it wouldn't matter. They finally had him.

The three bodyguards had their weapons drawn as well, pointing them around wildly. From the way they handled themselves, Andi could see they were pros, so he waited for them to realize they were outnumbered and drop their weapons. He really didn't want a repeat of the shootout at Castain's mansion. When the first one finally did, the others followed suit, slowly putting their guns on the ground, then lifting their hands in the air. Wise choice. SWAT descended on them like a swarm of angry wasps, cuffing the seven people. George had his gun still trained on them, reading them their Miranda rights.

"You have the right to remain silent. You...."

Andi blocked him out, stretched his other sense to see how it had gone upstairs. The insects were in an uproar, *too many heavy boots disturbing the ground, too much screaming stirring the air, and oohh, blood on the ground, food for the roaches and the pill bugs, if only the stomping would stop and the lights would go out so they could come forward to collect their bounty.* Before Andi could determine who was injured, Forard spoke into his headpiece. "All clear. Report what's going on upstairs, Spencer?"

He listened for a moment before he turned to Andi. "Everything good. One of the men tried to run and tripped. He's got a head wound. They have all the kids and are bringing them down now. Ambulance should be on the way."

Andi nodded. "Thank you, Forard. It's been a pleasure, as always."

Forard grinned broadly, slapped Andi on the shoulder. "It's a pleasure working with *you*, Hayes. All those successful raids look mighty good on my team's resume. It's always worth the wait with you."

They shared a look that expressed everything they couldn't and wouldn't say out loud for various reasons.

Their intimate moment was disturbed by somebody contacting Forard through the headpiece and by George, who stepped closer to Andi while holstering his weapon.

"Well, this was a bit anticlimactic." He grinned.

"Be glad our SWAT team is one of the best. I don't know about you, but I'm always grateful if I don't have to use my weapon. The paperwork if you hit somebody is a nightmare. And with us being *on leave* at the moment, it would be hell."

George started laughing a little harder than the joke merited, a clear sign of the adrenaline coursing through his veins. He was still pumped up and ready to go, as the mosquitoes attested, yet Andi felt safe in his presence, knowing George was looking out for him. It was a strange feeling to get used to, an alien thing inside of him and he didn't yet know how stable and trustworthy it was. He yearned for it to be as solid as George's build, while fearing at the same time it might only be as fragile as a piece of glass and—worst of all—temporary.

Oblivious to Andi's musings, George checked his watch. "Almost two o'clock. Let's get to the precinct. The night's not over yet."

Andi groaned. Of course it wasn't. They still had to be there for the booking of their perps, which could take a while, and then they would have to explain how and why they were at the precinct when they were on leave. Most probably the chief would come in immediately, trying to find a way to somehow spin this against them, and then going home would simply not be worth the trouble, which meant another all-nighter ripping holes into his psychic barriers, inviting another migraine in. He felt George's hand on his back, his partner's voice smooth and soothing.

"We book those assholes, then I drive you home so you can rest. I'll write the report and deal with the chief, and you come back in when you're good and ready. I'll tell everybody those migraines of yours are chronic and triggered by stress. No arguing with that." He smiled softly at Andi, leading him outside with one hand at the small of his back. The heat gathering there helped, keeping the fatigue at bay.

It seemed that alien feeling was more like a rock than a piece of glass.

CHAPTER 29
TRAPPING THE RATS

GEORGE DROVE Andi home as soon as it was possible without raising too many eyebrows. He could tell how exhausted Andi was by the glassiness of his eyes and his jerky movements when he tried to zip up his jacket. George furrowed his brows. Being cold was another sign of fatigue, and Andi couldn't afford to burn his body's reserves like that. He needed some fuel to keep his defenses up. Since George had absolutely no desire to hold Andi's head while he was puking his soul out, as was entirely possible when a migraine hit him full-on, he tried to get his partner home as fast as traffic laws would allow. Dragging Andi inside the house and up to his bedroom was by now almost routine, as well as stripping him down to his underwear and T-shirt, tucking him in, and bringing him a bottle of water and two ibuprofen in case he felt the headache he surely had turning into a migraine.

Andi was already asleep when George placed the pills on his bedside table. Even in sleep his partner's facial expression was tense, as if the sensory overload from his connection with the arthropods was following him into his dreams.

Another thing he would have to ask Andi about. The more George found out about Andi, the more questions he had, but for now he would let his partner rest and write the report about how they caught Castain red-handed.

BACK AT the precinct—and fueled with a ginormous amount of caffeine—George actually managed to get about a third of his report done before Chief Norris called him into her office. She had come in while he had brought Andi home, and it seemed she was ready to take him on now. Since Castain and his three detestable guests had made it clear they wouldn't say a word without their lawyers present, they needed to wait until said lawyers could make it into the precinct. Meanwhile CSI was tearing the house where everything had happened apart, as well as Castain's residence here in Charleston. Getting a rushed warrant had been a piece of cake as soon as the judge heard that they had caught the suspects red-handed. George hoped they would find enough evidence to truly nail the fucker down in a way not even his expensive lawyers and family money could get him out.

Norris's call came shortly before lunch, sounding more like a bark than a friendly invitation for one half of the detective team that had just solved a major case. He followed her ungracious summons nevertheless, because she was his boss and all that. After closing the door, she motioned for him to sit down on one of the chairs in front of her desk. For several minutes she simply stared at him without saying a word. George didn't flinch, didn't avert his gaze, didn't give any indication that her silence was doing anything to him. He just gave her time to gather her thoughts, secure in the knowledge that he had the upper hand.

"So, you solved the case." She sounded as if she couldn't decide whether that was a good thing or not.

"Yes, we did."

"And it really was Castain. Just like Detective Hayes predicted."

"Yes."

Chief Norris glared at him. "I'm sure both your reports are going to be thorough, especially concerning the fact that the case was no longer yours and you were on *unpaid* leave when you just happened to stumble upon your main suspect committing yet another crime." Her voice was dripping sarcasm with an undertone of annoyance and a very small dose of respect. Though said respect was barely detectable under the general layer of animosity that seemed to now include him as well. What was the saying? *If you don't have enemies, you've lived like a coward.* Having Norris pitched against him was not ideal, but George found he could live with it. She went on, her tone going from bark to vicious hiss in a nanosecond. "But would you care to explain to me how he managed to crack a case that was going cold so fast you could get frostbite just from watching?"

"He?" George raised a brow, not really insulted but wanting her to realize he knew what she was doing—trying to verbally separate him from Andi to maybe still get him on her side, despite being so hostile and for whatever good she thought it would do her.

"Don't play games, Detective Donovan. We both know you're too new in this city to have contributed a lot to the solving of this case. Now stop playing dumb with me and tell me how he's so damn successful!" Her tone made it entirely clear she was done being diplomatic and ready to launch into full-on war.

George rubbed his face. The answers he'd been working on in his mind were lining up perfectly, forming a stringent, logical summary to be laid at Norris's desk. "I think his success is a combination of truly admirable instincts and a net of informants one can only be jealous of." George was particularly proud of this phrase—telling the truth without actually *saying* anything. "Detective Hayes is also very good at putting together even the smallest hints to form the greater picture."

Norris's eyes turned into slits, her voice tinged with suspicion. "You almost sound like a groupie, Detective Donovan. Did he brainwash you?"

George was almost sure this was a joke, so he allowed himself a small smile, crossing his fingers that what he would say next was Andi's wish as well. "I don't know about that, but I certainly managed to brainwash him. We'd like to remain partners, Detective Hayes and me. If that's okay with you, Chief."

Norris looked absolutely shocked, which gave George no small amount of pleasure. He was pretty sure that when picturing his work with Andi, she never thought this kind of outcome a possibility.

"You want to stay partners with Detective Hayes." She sounded incredulous, tasting the words like some new dish she'd never had before and wasn't sure she liked. "And Detective Hayes is okay with it? I remember him being pretty clear about not wanting a partner ever again after this case was done."

"I changed his mind. We work well together, and I think he likes me bringing him breakfast every morning."

Chief Norris shot him a strange glance. The ire from just moments before had gone down a few notches, was now replaced with a certain resignation, as she had obviously realized she had no chance of winning here. They had solved a huge case that would gain her a lot of prestige, after all. And she was the type to be swayed by something like that. It didn't mean they were friends now, God forbid, and it certainly didn't mean she would leave Andi alone; George knew this for sure. He also knew he wanted to be there to protect his partner from her as long as he would stay in Charleston.

"Are you trying to be funny with me, Detective Donovan?"

"I wouldn't dream of it, Chief."

She didn't seem convinced, but after a moment she apparently decided to let it drop. "I guess there's not much I can do. You have my approval. Now leave. I do expect your report by tomorrow. Both your reports."

George nodded and got up, ready to leave the chief's office. When he reached the door, she called him again. "Detective Donovan?"

"Yes?"

"Good work. I'm proud of you and Detective Hayes. The entire city is."

With this reluctant and meager praise ringing in his head, George marched back to his own desk.

An hour later he was on his way to Andi's house, to check on his partner and hopefully pick him up for the interrogation of Castain and the other suspects. When he parked in the driveway, he thought he detected movement through the window next to the door, which sent a spike of satisfaction through his veins. If Andi was up, he couldn't be in too bad shape. It also meant his own call to take his partner home to rest had been the right decision. George left his car, unconsciously patting for the keys to Andi's house he had taken with him. There was no need for that, though, because the door opened before he reached the porch.

Andi looked a lot better than when George had tucked him into bed, the ever-present dark circles under his eyes a lot less glaring, his skin color almost as one would expect of a human being. Even his lips twisted briefly into something akin to a smile.

"Hi, Andi, ready to go to the precinct with me?"

"Yes." Andi motioned for George to come into the house. "Just let me get my jacket and shoes. Do you want something to drink? You look exhausted."

"A water would be fine, thanks. And yes, I am exhausted. The adrenaline and caffeine are starting to wear off, but we need to nail those assholes, especially Castain. We can't give them more time than they already had to come up with possible excuses."

"No, we can't do that." Andi went into the kitchen to get the water for George. When he came back and handed it to him, his gaze was serious. "Thank you for bringing me home. I needed the rest."

Andi being so open with him did strange things to George's heart, things he didn't want to examine too closely. He took the water bottle.

"That's what good partners are for. We look out for each other." He unscrewed the cap to take a long, refreshing swig. "Speaking of which, the chief summoned me while you were at home."

A dark expression flitted over Andi's face. No, he definitely wasn't a fan of the woman. "What did she want?"

"Well, she did congratulate us, especially you, on solving the case. She wasn't all roses and champagne, but I guess that's to be expected when you find out that not only the detective you want to get rid of was right from the start but also that a pillar of the community and close acquaintance of the mayor is behind one of the most abhorrent crimes in the city's history."

Andi raised a brow. "Do these monster sentences come naturally to you, or do you prepare them at night in your bed?"

"It's a talent." George shrugged, trying his best to appear modest. Andi shoved him out the door, so he probably hadn't been too successful.

After Andi closed the door, they went to George's car. Once they were inside and their seat belts on, Andi turned to him. "What else did she want? Asking for my head on a silver platter?"

"Something like that. I assured her your methods are perfectly legal and that a huge part of your success is based on your extensive network of informants."

Silence hung in the car until George reached the street. Then Andi spoke. "I'm not sure if I should applaud your genius phrasing or sock you for it."

"I'd say applause and awe are the appropriate reactions, partner. I didn't lie to her."

"No, you didn't. You didn't tell her anything either. Fine, it's genius." Andi sounded grumpy, as if admitting such a thing was against his very nature. For all George knew, this was the first time his partner had to do it. Since they were already talking sensitive topics, he decided to bite the bullet.

"I also asked her to make us permanent partners."

This time the silence stretched until they were almost at the precinct. When Andi finally opened his mouth, George realized he was actually afraid of his reaction.

"You'd really want to be burdened with somebody like me?"

It wasn't what George had expected, so it took him a moment to react. "Are you kidding me? Working with you may not be as easy as with another partner, I admit that, but the things I can learn from you? The cases we might be able to crack because of your *geschenk*? That's worth a lot of trouble. Besides—" He winked when he felt Andi's stare at his face. "—you've kind of grown on me. Who needs a constantly perky partner? Plus, you're low maintenance. Plain bagels and herbal tea are cheap."

"I'm so glad there's so many pros to working with me," Andi snapped, reaching for the passenger door handle to open it.

George killed the engine and got ready to exit the car as well. "Don't forget your sarcasm. I love it."

"Fuck you."

"No, let's fuck with Jake Castain. Together."

Andi closed the door with a little more force than strictly necessary. A predatory smile appeared on his lips.

"Yeah. Let's do some fucking over." He hesitated. "Together."

JAKE CASTAIN'S lawyer was the picture of snobby elitist. If there existed a blueprint for slimy, arrogant white men with way more money than conscience, Henry Anthony Thornton III was it. George guessed him to be in his late thirties, he was a partner in his daddy's law firm, and judging from his perfectly cut suit, the expensive leather shoes, and the Porsche Cayenne parked outside the precinct when they had entered, he wasn't shy about charging high fees to maintain his luxurious lifestyle. The light brown leather of his exquisite briefcase glowed softly under the harsh lights of the interrogation room, just like his gelled blondish hair. Since they had no reason to play nice anymore, George gladly let Andi take the lead, just to see his partner's disdain for humans in general and for this vermin in particular in action. Jake Castain's lips were pressed into a tight line, his entire stance rigid. He'd lost part of his patronizing aura and seemed to be intent on not letting a single sound escape from his mouth. Thornton on the other hand looked down his long nose at

Andi with all the arrogance that often came with money and privilege. George inwardly crossed his ankles to enjoy the show. He was a bit miffed because he'd forgotten to bring popcorn.

"Detective Hayes, I presume?"

Andi smiled broadly, like a shark before it crushed an unsuspecting seal between its jaws. "Yes. This is my partner, Detective Donovan. We were the ones to arrest your client."

"A highly suspicious and unlawful arrest, as you well know. I was told you were on unpaid leave and no longer involved with the case when it happened. I demand my client be released immediately and all charges dropped. If this happens quickly enough, we may refrain from pressing charges against the two of you. We will insist on a suspension, though, for at least two months. Unpaid of course." Thornton leaned back in his chair, seeming satisfied with the threats he had just dealt. Andi turned to George.

"Did you hear that, Detective Donovan? Mr. Thornton wants us suspended. I'm quivering in fear."

"Yeah, me too. I'm this close to pissing myself." George made sure to let his Boston accent come fully through. Thornton furrowed his brows. He did seem to be familiar with the concept of sarcasm, though he obviously didn't like it when it was directed at him.

"This is no joke, Detectives. If you don't cooperate, you'll be lucky to get a job flipping burgers in this city by the end of the week."

George was sitting with his chair slightly behind Andi, just enough to have a prime view of his partner's shoulders tensing. Andi's voice turned low, menacing, like the growl from a guard dog just before it attacked. Thornton and Castain both leaned back instinctively. A warm feeling of satisfaction built in George's belly, seeing those two predators taken down a few notches.

"If I were you, I'd be a lot more concerned about the charges against my client. And about what we're going to find about *you* when we start digging into all the files Mr. Castain has stored in his house."

If George hadn't watched Thornton very closely, he probably wouldn't have caught the tic in his left eyelid when Andi mentioned Castain's files. CSI had found dozens of them behind a fake wall in Castain's cellar, together with two additional lion masks like the one he'd had on him when they had arrested him. So Thornton had known what

Castain was up to, had perhaps even participated in his sick "parties." What an asshole. Andi kept on going.

"We have evidence, tons of it. Not only circumstantial evidence, but we also caught Mr. Castain in a house which doesn't belong to him, attending a party where minors and drugs played a major role. In the face of so much very damning evidence, the question as to why we were there to arrest him will be nothing but a footnote, and you know it. Thanks to a lot of good old-fashioned police work we did when we were still on the case, we have also connected him to at least ten corrupt cops who aided him in getting minors for his trafficking ring. As we speak, IA is tearing those cops' lives apart, no doubt finding all kinds of incriminating evidence." Andi turned his full attention on Castain. "No matter how good you think your lawyer is, Mr. Castain, the only thing that's going to help you now is a full confession. You may even be able to get a deal with the DA if you give your full cooperation in finding every last asshole involved in this. But I have to warn you, that deal will only be available for a short period, and if somebody else decides to talk first… well, then you're screwed. I'm not going to tell you about the things they do to pedophiles in prison. You're going to find out soon enough. And if you don't crack, I'm sure your lawyer will."

With that, Andi got up and turned to leave the room. George followed suit, not saying a word until they were outside. Once the door had closed behind them to let Castain and Thornton steep in their own juices—quite literally since it was hot as hell in the interrogation room—George made sure nobody was listening in on them. "The lawyer?"

"He's taken the same drugs as the rest of them, quite recently too." Andi shrugged. "Makes sense for him to know about it. Castain was nothing but methodical in all this, so of course he has prepared insurance in case things go south. And what's better than having a lawyer who has almost as much to lose as yourself when you go down? Even if Thornton had nothing to do with the trafficking, which I doubt, he still uses the same source for drugs as Castain, and you can bet Castain has proof of that. I'm pretty sure, though, Thornton is going to drop him like a hot potato unless Castain has some additional leverage aside from Thornton being his customer. The question is which rat will leave the sinking ship first?"

"An interesting question. Though I doubt Castain has a lot on Thornton." George started walking toward the small common room on the interrogation floor where a vending machine was located. "People like Thornton tend to keep their dirty secrets close to their chests. I'd bet my career on him having more than just his penchant for underage sex partners or drugs, but the chances of anybody but him knowing about them is almost zero."

"It doesn't matter. He's going to go down with Castain. Have you seen the tic in his eye? We're going to find something on him, I'm sure of it."

"Then we better see to it that he can't leave the country."

They exchanged a long look of deep satisfaction. The hunt was almost over. The prey was down. All they had to do now was wait for it to succumb.

CHAPTER 30
LOOSE ENDS

IT DIDN'T take long until both Castain and Thornton broke down. In Andi's experience men who prayed on the weak, especially minors, were utter cowards more often than not, only feeling strong when their superiority wasn't questioned. Castain was a conniving bastard with contingency plans for almost every scenario, which was the reason he'd been so successful, but once all those plans fell through, he cracked, and after that the DA had problems making him *stop* talking. Thornton, too, struck a deal with the DA, after which getting the remaining customers and helpers for the trafficking ring was a bit like shooting fish in a barrel. News that Castain had been arrested had been kept secret, so nobody tried to run. The list of people who had used Castain's services was shockingly long, and some of those names caused major ripples not only in the higher society of Charleston but also in the entire state.

The only person they hadn't been able to get their hands on was Detective Harris, who somehow had gotten wind of what was happening during the three days after they had arrested Castain. He was nowhere to be found, and CSI had just started working through his many accounts, trying to entangle the vast net of aiders he had built seemingly over many years. Unlike Castain, Harris hadn't kept any files in his house or he'd been smart enough to destroy everything before he went underground. Which meant they still didn't know who the mole in the Charleston PD was, something that galled Andi. He wanted the person responsible for sabotaging them behind bars, not to mention how difficult it was for him to enter the precinct every day knowing somebody in there was an enemy. The chances of finding Harris were slim, but they had a chance to catch the mole once all the detective's accounts had been combed through. He sighed. This was the part of cases he hated the most—waiting for the last knots to unravel, which could take weeks.

"Andi, you ready to go home?" George was grabbing his keys, obviously wanting to leave the precinct for the day. It was already past six, and there wasn't much they could get done this evening that couldn't wait till tomorrow. Andi switched his PC off.

"Coming." He followed George through the door and into the car. George driving him was now a fixture Andi wasn't unhappy about. They didn't talk much during the short drive to Andi's house, each of them lost in their thoughts. It was a companionable silence Andi had learned to relish in the days since the arrest of Castain. George always seemed to know when Andi needed room and never filled a good silence with useless chatter.

When George pulled up in front of the house, Andi was relaxed, but the images bombarding him from inside his home made him jerk back in his seat so violently, he hit the back of his skull on the headrest.

Hints of blood, already coagulating, still sweet, promising nourishment, pain, sharp in the air, intruders, not meant to be here, upsetting everything with their heavy footsteps, chair scraping over the floorboards, sending shock waves throughout the second floor, the silverfish hiding in their nooks and crannies, the huge blue bottle stirring in the corner where it had rested, woken by the blood and the alluring scent of sweat, tinged with fear, fear was always good, it promised a meal, a place to lay the eggs, the spider in its web on the ceiling waiting, the air in waves from the wings of the blue bottle, prey, hunger, INTRUDERS, food, nourishment—

"Andi? Andi! Are you all right? What's going on?" George's worried voice disconnected Andi from the maelstrom of sensory overload that was coming from his kitchen, threatening to drown him because he had let his guard down. Andi was not ashamed to cling to George's arm, anything to center him after having been sucked into a different world and then yanked from it again. He took deep, calming breaths, and once his heartbeat was back to normal, he grabbed his cell, dialing Forard's number. The SWAT leader answered after the second ring.

"Hayes. What is it?"

"Forard. You're on speaker. Donovan is with me."

"Shoot."

"Two intruders in my home, possible hostage situation, though I'm not entirely sure. We're going in now."

"Be there in ten."

"Come in silent. Key to the back door is under the first step to the gazebo. Hurry."

"Copy." The line clicked and went dead. George lifted a brow. "Trouble?"

"I'm not sure. There's drying blood, and the insects are going crazy because of all the adrenaline in the air." He closed his eyes, this time diving into the stream on purpose to get more specific information. "*There's a gun, recently fired, not here, somewhere else, gunpowder flaring up when the male moves, female on chair, fear, pain, all so sweet, blood, both are healthy, delicious, heartbeat too quick, adrenaline—*"

"Okay, snap out of it. You're becoming too incomprehensible for my liking." George had his gun already out, one hand on the door to open it. "If there's somebody waiting in there, we can't stay out here much longer without them getting suspicious. Since Forard is on his way, I'd say we go inside and see who it is."

Andi nodded. "Be careful. I-I'm distracted. This is my home; there shouldn't be so much upheaval."

"Can you do this? If you're not sure, stay outside. I've got this." Instead of getting Andi's hackles up, George's worry ignited a warm feeling in his chest.

"I'm not going to let you go in there alone. I can manage. I just need a moment to adjust."

"Fine. I'll take the lead."

They left the car with their weapons held behind their backs. Whoever was inside the house must have heard the car approaching but was not leaving their spot in the kitchen, which meant they could get to the door unseen. Still, hiding their guns was a somehow automatic reaction. George took the keys he still had out and opened the door. Since there was no use in being silent, he did so as if nothing were amiss, trying to fool the people hiding inside.

"Man, I'm beat. I can't wait to have that beer you promised me." George started walking quickly in the direction of the kitchen. From the door, they could already see the edge of the cooking island, and the intruders were directly behind it, just out of sight. Andi followed, concentrating to shut out the arthropods, since they were more a distraction than an actual help at this point. When they rounded the corner, George stopped so abruptly, Andi almost smacked into his back.

"Harris." It was more a hiss than anything else, and somehow, Andi wasn't surprised. He peered around George's shoulder and saw Harris standing behind a chair. Rose was tied to it with her hands behind her back, drying blood on her chin and a ghastly looking cut in her lower lip. Harris was holding a gun to her temple, an angry gleam in his eyes.

"Drop the weapons, Detectives. Or do you want me to blow her brains out here in your kitchen, Hayes?"

Andi had stepped next to George, and they exchanged a short glance. George made an almost imperceptible nod, affirming Andi's own assessment of the situation. Even though they might be able to overwhelm Harris, the risk for Rose's life was too great. One hand in the air, they both put their weapons down. Harris jerked his head in the direction of the fridge. "Kick them over there."

They complied, and when both weapons hit the base of the fridge, some of the tension seemed to drain from Harris's shoulders.

"Detective Harris, we've been looking for you." George sounded almost bored, as if Harris wasn't a rogue detective who could kill them all with a few well-placed shots.

"I know that." Harris practically spat the words out, making Rose flinch. She had been very quiet the whole time and didn't seem overly relieved to see George and Andi.

"Well, now that you're here, perhaps you could answer some questions for us?" Andi had to admire George's cockiness. He wasn't sure poking the already angry detective was a good idea, but then again, backup was already on the way and they had to stall him somehow.

"What questions could you still have? You've already ruined my entire business!"

"Your business?" There was a hint of disbelief in George's tone, echoing Andi's thoughts. "This was Castain's enterprise from beginning to end. He confessed to it."

"Ha! That spineless uppity asshole! Of course he did. What kind of deal did you offer him?"

"None of your business," Andi snapped. Harris's eyes narrowed.

"Well, whatever he told you, it was a lie. That weakling could have never pulled off something as big as this."

"We do admit we were surprised by how vast his net of connections was." George cocked his head, clearly trying to get Harris to keep on talking.

"His net? *His* net? This was all my doing! I was the one who made contact with every single cop out there, talked them into helping me. All Castain did was provide money and locations, giving my business a face."

"A mask, you mean. Wearing a lion mask—a bit over the top, if you ask me." Andi had to admire George's interrogation skills. Harris was either not aware what was happening or he didn't care, which meant he thought he had the upper hand. Rose was still suspiciously silent, not making eye contact with either Andi or George, which made Andi's gut instinct scream at him.

Harris scoffed. "Showy idiot. But it helped build a narrative, and these days, if you want to successfully sell something, you need a strong narrative. Those rich freaks loved the whole mystery thing, and as long as the money was flowing, I couldn't care less how he was doing it."

"Sounds plausible." George hummed. "But if you were the boss, why did you allow Castain to keep doing business here in Charleston when we were already breathing down your necks? You don't strike me as being the reckless type."

A vein in Harris's left temple started ticking. George had obviously hit a nerve. "Son of a bitch was getting cocky. Thought he knew better, when he was simply just his arrogant self. I told him his status wouldn't protect him, but no, he said he had everything lined up to establish Charleston as our base of operations and couldn't wait to go through with it. Fucking idiot."

"So he ignored you." Andi knew he sounded smug and did nothing to hide it. Harris turned to him with fury in his eyes.

"You! You had to ruin it all! And after we managed to evade you for the past two years!"

"You've been evading me?"

"Please! Everybody knows about Charleston PD's golden boy! You're the reason I befriended charming Rose here, so I had somebody who would keep an eye on you and see to it that you didn't get any cases related to my business."

Rose flinched when Harris patted her head with his free hand, the gun still trained on her temple. Andi stared at her wide-eyed. "You're the mole!"

"Yes, she was my little mole, making sure Charleston PD was blissfully unaware of what I was doing."

George whistled. "That's the reason we couldn't find a corrupt cop here."

"It was safer to keep the abductions to a minimum in this area. I couldn't risk *him*"—Harris glared at Andi—"to get wind of anything. The few cases that reached a level where you could have been involved, Rose redirected to other detectives, keeping you in the dark."

"And then Ronald Wallace murdered Lilly Cordon." George barked a laugh. "Your perfect system worked against you."

Harris uttered a colorful curse, pressing the muzzle of his weapon into Rose's temple until she whimpered. Given what Harris had just revealed about her, Andi didn't feel that much sympathy. "It would have worked if it weren't for him!"

Andi didn't feel that much sympathy with Harris either.

"You told Rose to sabotage us." George made another attempt at keeping Harris talking. The man was clearly getting ready for something, the feeling of violence in the room notching up with every second. Andi didn't even need the input from the insects to sense it.

"I did. She had to be careful, though, because I couldn't afford to make you even more suspicious. Her telling the chief about a complaint from Castain was actually pretty ingenious."

"There never was a complaint, right?"

Harris's gaze turned to Andi. "No. Rose thought it would be better that way. Didn't do us any good, though." Harris gripped his weapon harder. "Anyway, I'm done here. I just wanted to get my revenge before I take my flight to Cuba." He took the gun away from Rose's temple and aimed it straight at George. "I had planned to kill you and her"—Harris nodded at Andi and Rose—"but getting your partner as well is a nice bonus." He pulled the trigger.

A bang so loud it sent tsunamis of sonic through the house, the moths flying up in a panic, the silverfish quivering under the floorboards, a heavy thud when two bodies hit the floor, the impact sending up dust, stirring the air even more, whirling pheromones and the scent of blood, now fresh, appetizing, more shocks, boots, huge blobs, shouting, the finest of sawdust raining down on the brood under the planks, the walls transporting the waves through the entire house, uproar, the spider finally catching the blue bottle, flying around in a panic because of all the commotion, another thud, a high-pitched scream, the scent of gunpowder in the air, sharp and repulsive, no nourishment, deadly, poison, the blobs moving around more, shouting, a wail outside, flashing lights, rattling of wheels on the planks, metal clanking, stomping around, around, around—then—silence.

CHAPTER 31
ENDINGS AND BEGINNINGS

GEORGE WATCHED over Andi, who was sleeping peacefully in the hospital bed, due to the drugs they had pumped into his partner to keep the pain at bay. George was still reeling from what had happened. One moment Harris had been spouting in almost classical villain style, the next he had his gun trained on George and pulled the trigger. At the same moment, Andi had slammed into him, catching the bullet meant to end George's existence with his upper arm. Thankfully it was just a flesh wound, a clean through and through, and Andi would be released as soon as he woke up. George hoped that would take some time, the entire night if he had anything to say about it, because Andi definitely needed the rest. Sighing, George stretched his legs and tried to find a more comfortable position in the chair next to Andi's bed. There wasn't a single scratch on him except for some bruises forming at his left side where he crashed to the ground when Andi shoved him. Nothing big and certainly nothing that would keep him from staying with his partner and guarding his sleep.

TWO DAYS later they were back in the precinct, Andi with his arm in a sling and an almost healthy skin color, thanks to George staying with him at his house and seeing to it that he got enough rest. Forard and his men had come into the kitchen the moment Harris pulled the trigger and had managed to catch him alive. Now he was sitting in a cell waiting for his trial to begin. Since he had given away all his bargaining chips by confessing his deeds to Andi and George, there was no deal in sight for him, and George had heard rumors that the DA was going for a lifelong sentence. Everybody in the precinct was still shocked by the fact that Rose—sweet, cake-baking Rose—had been the mole. Apparently she had met Harris during a seminar about drug dealing and he had picked up on how fed up she was with her job, her income, her entire life situation, and had used it to get her on his side. She, too, was awaiting trial, though her full cooperation with IA had earned her some brownie points. Speaking of IA, they had not only a field day with the corrupt cops but more like a field month, more and more of them falling with every new file from Castain CSI worked through and every bank account of Harris they discovered. They even managed to find Tracy Longman's daughter, Melody, who had been adopted by Sybil and Thomas Wickersham, a very nice couple from Colorado who had thought they were adopting through a legitimate, though highly specialized, agency. They were both in their late forties, which made it practically impossible to adopt a child through official channels. Since they couldn't find any family of Tracy Longman willing and able to take the baby in, Child Services was more than happy to leave little Melody with the Wickershams, thus giving her a much better start in life than her unfortunate mother ever could have. All in all, the case was unraveling nicely, which meant commendations—grumpily given by Chief Norris—for both Andi and George.

As for George, Andi wasn't sure what to think of his now steady partnership with the man. When he had met him, all he'd been thinking about was how to get rid of him. Now that George knew his secret, hadn't run screaming, and was unbelievably supportive and caring, Andi found he liked the idea of working with him on a permanent basis. Or at least until George went on to another city to further his career. Andi had no illusions about George's ambition, and he wondered if attaching himself to George and his help even more than he already was, was worth the trouble of having to get used to doing things alone again when his partner left. He also knew it was too late contemplating these things, because he had already started relying on George more than he should. It simply felt too good not having to shoulder his *geschenk* alone, even if it was for a finite number of days. And he did save the man out of pure instinct, so there was that.

Andi decided to see the time with George as a reprieve from becoming like his *oma*. Even though he resented the very thought, he knew deep down that was where his life was headed. With the baggage he was carrying, it was kind of inevitable. The human psyche wasn't built to be the host for more than one consciousness, let alone millions, and the best he could hope for was turning into a grumpy old man nobody wanted anything to do with. They'd probably find his body weeks after he'd died, being a victim to the arthropods even in death.

A hand on his shoulder pried Andi from his dark musings. Since there was only one person suicidal enough to dare touch him, he didn't have to guess who it was.

"George."

Andi turned to look into his partner's grinning face. "I've handed our final reports in. We're free to go, and Chief Norris graced us with a free day tomorrow so we can 'relax' some." He lifted his index fingers when he said 'relax.' They both knew relaxation wasn't something a cop came by easily.

"So what do you suggest we do?"

George's grin broadened. "We should celebrate. I mean, look how many bad guys we caught in this case. Many of whom had been masquerading as upstanding citizens and pillars of society."

"You think that's a cause to celebrate?" Andi lifted a brow. "If you think closely about it, it's a reason to cry into your beer. The predators are everywhere, and many of them we'll never even suspect."

"Dude, don't remind me. Let's bask in the fact that we've gotten a nice portion of them. Besides—" George winked. "—a beer's a beer. You can cry into yours while I celebrate our victory."

"Like a partner effort—covering all bases." It was a weak joke, Andi knew it. But he wanted to steer the topic away from the dark thoughts lurking at the back of his mind, as well as show George that he did know how to be a normal human being. An adjusted human being. Perhaps being human was enough in the beginning. George, being the tolerant man he was, slapped him lightly on the shoulder that was not injured.

"A joke. How delightful. Did I tell you how much I like your dark humor?" His partner kept the tone light, obviously picking up on Andi's wish to leave the depressing zone.

"I didn't even know I had humor. And I think if you asked anybody, they'd have you committed."

"Wrongly so. Come on, partner. Let's go to this nice Italian restaurant I found on TripAdvisor. My treat." When Andi didn't react, George furrowed his brows. "If you don't like Italian, we can go someplace else. You've been in Charleston longer. I'm sure you know some good places to eat."

Andi shook his head, fighting a wave of mixed emotions he was determined not to examine right now or possibly ever. He managed to keep his voice steady. "I usually celebrate the end of a case by starting to work on a new one. Going out instead feels—odd."

"Good odd or bad odd?" George sounded completely serious, for which Andi was grateful.

"Good odd, I think."

"I guess we'll have to go to that restaurant and actually eat there to see if it is indeed a good kind of odd." George grinned. "We can treat this as an experiment." He took a quick look around the floor, where the usual bustling activity was taking place. Nobody spared them a glance. "And if the restaurant's kitchen isn't above all suspicion, you'll know immediately and we can go somewhere else." He winked.

Andi couldn't help it. He felt the corners of his mouth going up into a smile. The flash of pure satisfaction in George's eyes when he saw it was worth the unfamiliar pull on his facial muscles.

XENIA MELZER grew up and still lives in rural Bavaria, where not much of anything happens—an escaped cow or some lost tourists now and then, but nothing truly mysterious or even scandalous. For that reason, trying her hand at some mystery of her own seemed like a good idea. Xenia has also recently discovered that she's demisexual with a dash of asexuality thrown into the mix, which has opened her eyes to a lot of things and given Andi and George, the two main characters in the Andi Hayes Mystery series, their own special spin. A certain fascination with insects of all kinds has provided her with the real detectives for the story. Xenia loves NCIS, snuggling with either her husband or her horse—the children don't keep still long enough—and crocheting, the latter a newly discovered hobby.

COMING SOON

Eruca

An Andi Hayes Murder Mystery

By Xenia Melzer

When Detective George Donovan and his eccentric partner, Detective Andi Hayes, need a break from their gruesome job, a hike seems like just the thing.

Unfortunately, the job catches up with them.

Despite the fact that they find three dead men in a lake, the promising clues soon dry up. George and Andi turn once more to Andi's "gift"—but this time things aren't so easy.

Andi's mysterious talents are growing stronger, making it harder to block out the barrage of information and taking a toll on his physical and mental health. The cryptic clues his informants offer are even more bizarre than the case itself. And the more they discover about the victims, the more uncomfortable the investigation becomes.

Torn between catching a killer and serving justice, between George's career and Andi's sanity, the detectives have their work cut out for them if they're going to solve these murders.

CASTO

GODS OF WAR

XENIA MELZER

Gods of War: Book One

All is fair in love and war. Renaldo has lived happily by that proverb his entire life. But he has finally met his match, and he's about to discover how unfair love and war can be.

When demigod and warlord Lord Renaldo takes a beautiful stranger captive during an ambush, he is delighted to have found a distraction that will keep him entertained during the upcoming siege. Little does he know, Casto is keeping more than just one secret from him. Slowly, Renaldo gets sucked into a turbulent roller-coaster relationship with his mysterious prisoner, one that begins with hatred and soon spirals into a whirlwind of conflicting emotions. And when it seems that things can get no worse, an old enemy stirs right in the heart of his home.

Determined to keep Casto by his side, Renaldo has to find a balance between the capricious young man and his own destiny as a ruler and god to his people.

www.dsppublications.com

LOVE
AND THE
STUBBORN
GODS OF WAR: BOOK II

XENIA MELZER

Gods of War: Book Two

All is fair in love and war. By now, Renaldo has found out the hard way how utterly stupid this statement is once you've met your match. And Casto won't give an inch in their ongoing war for love.

After a tumultuous start to their relationship, Renaldo and Casto seem to have finally reached calmer waters. But just when Renaldo starts getting comfortable and thinks he can relax, things get out of hand again. His old enemy, the Good Mother, is dangerously close to defeating the divine brothers by reaching out to what is most dear to him. Casto still clinging to his stubborn pride is all the plotters need to drive him and Renaldo apart. Burdened by the secrets of his past, Casto fights with everything he's got not only to save his life, but also to secure his future happiness. Facing the destruction of everything they have built together, Renaldo and Casto must choose between pride and love.

www.dsppublications.com

For more
great fiction
from

DSP PUBLICATIONS

visit us online.

WWW.DSPPUBLICATIONS.COM